AT THE CRIME SCENE

Terry sucked in a breath. "Crap. The cameras are here." He moved away to make sure that the uniformed cops were strict about keeping the TV camera crews and reporters behind the barricades. He detailed four more to shield the body from being seen on the sidewalk.

He heard Rose say suddenly, "Terry! See that flash?"

He turned and saw a bright white glitter atop an abandoned five-story warehouse on the next block.

Rose shouted, gun drawn, "Gun! On the roof! Everybody down!" and she pointed toward the warehouse roof. Terry shouted too and the crowd squealed in unison and the people scattered abruptly, the cops and the news crews taking shelter behind their trucks and squad cars.

"Get somebody over there now!" he yelled to one of the uniforms.

He crouched beside Rose. "Good call. Good eyes."

"Shooter might still be up there," she spat heatedly....

WILLIAM P. WOOD

PRESSURE POINT

LEISURE BOOKS　　　　　NEW YORK CITY

LEISURE BOOKS ®

November 2004

Published by

Dorchester Publishing Co., Inc.
200 Madison Avenue
New York, NY 10016

ISBN 0-8439-5467-1

The name "Leisure Books" and the stylized "L" with design are
trademarks of Dorchester Publishing Co., Inc.

Printed in the United States of America.

Visit us on the web at www.dorchesterpub.com.

PRESSURE POINT

"A million deaths are a statistic. A single death is a tragedy."

—Joseph Stalin

"You will only see a tiger when he wants you to see him."

—Nepalese folk saying

Prologue

"I don't like losing," Leah Fisher said. "I'm a very bad loser, Dennis."

Dennis Cooper sat back in his office chair. He let a false smile brighten his face. "We didn't lose. The world knows he's guilty."

Leah shook her head. Her long wheat-blond hair was tied loosely. She wore a gray sweatsuit because she was going to work out after she put in her hours on a Saturday at the office. He'd somehow forgotten her diligence. He somehow thought he'd be alone for what he had to do. No witnesses, Dennis thought somberly. Not for this kind of call.

"We lost, Dennis," she said, arms folded. "So what do we do now?"

He stood up and came close to her. "We go on to the next one. Then the one after that. We've got a big caseload. We've got Valdez, Stiles, and Watts, all death penalty trials, starting in the next couple of months and a hell of a lot to do before then."

"I hate the idea that that bastard won."

"Good." He smiled falsely again. "Stay competitive. That's why I wanted you with me on Major Crimes." The smiled dropped. "But when it's over, you move on. We did our best."

"I am a very bad loser," she said slowly. "No joke."

"I don't like it any more than you do." He glanced at his crowded desk. "Go work out, Leah. Just be ready to hit the ground running on Monday."

"What about you?"

"Office personnel stuff for a little while, then I'm going home too." He moved her toward his office door. "Go on. Burn some calories."

She hesitated, thinking it over, then nodded. "All right. I lost two Folsom Prison gang cases I should've won a couple of years ago. I think about them almost every day. What's your gimmick, Denny? You go on and it doesn't seem to get to you."

He wondered how and when he ever became such a convincing deceiver outside of a courtroom. Maybe that explained the divorce after ten years and one son he rarely spoke to. *But I never lied in court,* he thought. *I always told the judge or the jury what the truth was and how they could see it like I did.*

"I'm gaming the system like everyone around here," he said. "You remember every loss and every victim. You just have to keep working."

Leah thought for a moment, reckoning the truth of how she had chosen to spend her days. "I may come in tomorrow and do some work on Valdez."

"Good. Go on. Relax for a while. You did a good

job." As he closed the door while she walked out, he called to her, "Sore loser." She grinned back at him. He wanted her to stay, but that was impossible if he was going to go through with it. He had to take the weight of it, not she. Secrets again, he thought bitterly. Like this whole case.

He tried working. He tried to eat part of the sandwich he'd brought, then stopped, letting it grow stale on his desk. The office was very quiet on a Saturday afternoon, the smell in the air of summer rain coming by evening. He tried not to look at or think of the telephone. But it always seemed to be waiting for him to make the call.

His head hurt and he held his forehead.

There is no other way, he thought.

There is no other justice.

Dennis Cooper had been a deputy district attorney for twenty-two years. He was respected and a good man at parties and played well at office baseball games or in the league against the judges and defense attorneys, and men and women liked him. But no one really knew what he thought about his cases. *Until this one, I didn't even know myself,* he thought. *I didn't know what I was willing to do.*

He got up and looked out his fourth-floor window at the downtown Sacramento buildings nestled among thick green trees, across to the silent, white, and cold county courthouse.

I'm going to do it, he realized.

He looked at the telephone and sat down.

He was still astonished that this case was less than two weeks old and it had changed his life, like it changed so many others, the cops and the witnesses, everyone, drawn in by its inexorable, terrible tidal pull. By its damning secrets, he thought.

Dennis fumbled reaching for the pad with the telephone number he would call soon.

There is a moment in every case when a prosecutor sees the police reports and evidence, the law and the witnesses as a coherent whole. This is what he must tell a jury if he is to show them the truth of the case and the hope of justice.

This one didn't seem different from all the others, Dennis thought. Not at the beginning.

Chapter One

Shortly after seven P.M. on Tuesday, August 5, Mrs. Constantina Basilaskos hurried off her bus at Thirty-third Avenue in Oak Park, a neighborhood in California's capital, taking the bus stairs so quickly that the varicose veins on her left leg began to painfully throb. She didn't notice. Nor did she notice the people she brushed past when she got to the sidewalk and started walking north briskly. She had been complaining all day, like everyone else in Sacramento, that the heat, which officially topped ninety-six degrees at one P.M. that day and had persisted for the previous three days, made every step leaden and even talking a miserable chore. It was a tropical heat, unusual for Sacramento because of its thick humidity. She no longer noticed the heat or humidity as she walked, her black-strapped, dull-metal-bound purse clutched tightly under one thick arm. Every few steps she squeezed her arm just to feel the purse

5

again, to make certain she held it so securely in her grip she couldn't accidentally let it go.

Overhead the brutal, lingering sun was pale yellow. The small older homes and stores on Thirty-third Avenue had burst open, people clustered on the sidewalk, talking sharply as they leaned against low steel railings or sat on plastic chairs. It was a loud, hot early August evening. The air was stagnant, acrid with fried oil and exhaust fumes.

Mrs. Basilaskos didn't notice anything except the reassuring weight and shape of her purse. She blinked rapidly, her mind working as she walked more quickly. She nodded gloatingly to herself.

Wait until Angelo sees, she thought. *He'll jump out of bed and dance around the whole place and the doctor can go to hell.*

She was two blocks from her home when the shots blasted out.

Detective Terry Nye swore and dabbed at a stubborn spot of soy sauce on his silver and red tie. He went on talking to his partner across the small Formica-topped table.

"Like I was saying . . ." He paused and swore again. "Somebody explain the physics of this thing to me. I got chicken and sprouts and a little soy on my fucking chopsticks, so how does the damn soy sauce manage to jump on the one place on the one thing I got on today? Rosie? Want to try that one?"

His partner, Detective Rose Tafoya, shook her head and grinned. She slowly chewed on a spring roll. "Finish about the lox you stole. I cannot believe you stole food from a religious service."

Both Rose and Terry were sweating because department policy said no matter how hot it got you had to wear your suit coat when the public could see you. But, as Terry sourly noted during the course of the last few days, Rose liked the stubborn, heavy heat. Until she was sixteen she had lived just outside Manila and she seemed to carry its thickly humid weather and boiling street energy with her across the world in her new country.

"Look, it wasn't during the service, schmuck," Terry went on. "It was the reception. I was thirteen. I must've gone to a bar mitzvah every weekend the whole year. Everybody was getting bar mitzvahed. Except me. The folks never agreed on whether I was going to be a good Catholic or I don't know. Just Jewish."

"So you got jealous and swiped the lox."

"No." Terry hurriedly shoved another mouthful at his face and chewed happily because he'd beaten his dinner's assault on his wardrobe. "This was an Orthodox service, hours and hours. Larry Carnow, I think. So we finally get to the reception and these plates of food and I'm thirteen, I got an appetite every five and a half seconds, and I start shoving as much lox wrapped in napkins into my pockets as I can."

Rose waved for more tea. She had liked hot tea since she was a kid because it made her sweat. Today the white-walled, plastic-chaired Chinese-Vietnamese diner was crowded. "Give it up, Terry. You nailed the most expensive item on the buffet. Petty theft."

Terry ignored her. "So Rabbi Dolgen spots me. He comes over and says, 'If you're going to walk out with so much salmon, you better have enough bread to go with it.' And now everybody's watching the rabbi, big bearded guy with thick old glasses, break off big old pieces of challah and shove them into my coat pocket, into my hands. He thought it was kind of funny. Got a big laugh from the audience."

"You never forgot."

Terry shook his head. "Six, seven years ago I run into Dolgen again. Residential 459 at his house in Carmichael. He's a little, shriveled guy now. All scared and he's been crying because the pukes took his plaques, silver, menorah. I try to cheer him up. Tell him, 'Hey, Rabbi, you remember the kid long time ago who tried to start his own deli with your lox after a bar mitzvah? That's me."

"He feel any better?"

"He stares at me. He shakes his head. Big deal for me and he didn't remember it at all." Terry grunted and sipped the sweating glass of ice water. "That ever happen to you? Something really important and the other party's given it a complete blank?"

Rose nodded. She was almost as tall as Terry. At thirty she was nearly twenty years younger and athletic, her black hair clipped straight and short. She was attentive to her wardrobe, how she looked. After a tough day, Rose somehow managed to be fresh, alert, ready to keep going for another shift without batting an eye. These were troublesome differences, Terry admitted. Rose favored dark matched skirts, and blouses carried her gun easily. Terry got by with poplin in the summer and something heavier in the winter. After being a cop in Sacramento for twenty-six years he still felt a little awkward with his gun on. He felt much more exposed without it.

It was sometimes hard to find topics of conversation with Rose, even on the job, that had common points of reference. But he worked at it. He'd been divorced three times. He'd had so many partners since he became a cop that he did not, at this late stage in his police career, feel much like breaking in any more after Rose. They were still, after nearly eight months, in the shakedown phase, working out sharp edges and things that got on each other's nerves. It was important to find out what could be talked about over meals, in the car, across the desk, and even more important what had to be avoided so nobody's hackles went up. Politics were off-limits because Terry didn't know five cops who cared about national politics very much and city bickering was a spectator sport unless it touched on pensions or benefits or the image of the department. Sports were fine to talk about, but he didn't share Rose's enthusiasm for soccer because of her eight-year-old daughter, so they generally stayed with basketball and baseball. Basketball meant the follies and fortunes of the Kings mostly. Kids, discussed sparingly, were fine. His former wives and her kid and husband and dopey in-laws generally were all right too. Police department or Sacramento County Sheriff's Department gossip was a close second to war stories. War stories, the glorious and the inglorious, were the best of all. Put any two cops together, from any city anywhere in the United States or probably the world, and within ten minutes, tops, they'd be swapping war stories.

Terry liked Rose's still-not-quite blunted passion and dynamism for the job. So Terry had privately vowed that this partner and he'd be successful. Like the long, long boozeless days now, you had to take it one step after another and keep at it.

Rose worked away on her noodles and pork and her damn beige blouse and jacket were still spotless, as always. "Yeah. Best one I got was a liquor store deal. Guy had a wicked sawed-off, half blew the victim's left arm off. This's about 1100 block on Madison Avenue off Arden."

"Used to be a housewife named Shirley who ran a cardboard dungeon out of her place up around there when I was in Vice. Husband said he wondered where all her extra spending money was coming from."

"Okay, so I pop this bastard for the liquor store and the owner's arm and I've been on the job all of maybe seven, eight months and, Terry, swear to God, I was going to make this guy eat a half block of sidewalk."

"Did you?"

"He didn't get booked in exactly the same condition as he got popped. No trial, he pleads, doesn't pass go, into the joint. Jesus. I forget his name now." Rose's eyes widened slightly. She still had a hint of an accent, a different cadence from most cops. "So this bastard's got to remember me, right? Same as you, six, seven years later, I'm working midtown patrol."

Terry winced. "Douche bag city."

"On good days. So I roll out to a corner liquor store. I'm second car there, my partner and I go in and I recognize this same bastard, looking a lot worse for wear after seven years. I go, 'Hey, asshole, remember me? Remember what happened last time

10

we met after you shotgunned a poor fucker trying to pay his taxes?' "

"Let me guess. He says he meant to write, come visit, but he was too busy with the job, the wife."

Rose chuckled. "He looks at me, he's cuffed. He stares and I think I've got the bastard scared and then he goes, 'Fuck, man, you say I capped somebody?' I nod and I want to do an encore of our first date. The bastard rolls his eyes, 'Fuck, man, you want me to remember you off some guy I busted a cap on, you got to give me more. I got a lot of data on my spreadsheet and you don't stand out.' "

"Data on his spreadsheet? Oh, sweet Jesus." Terry laughed. "Just a day in the life for these guys. Nothing special."

Rose went to work on her snow peas and shrimp. "Okay, what about the guy's leg you found in the locker at the Greyhound bus station downtown? Everybody says I got to ask you about it."

Terry didn't get a chance to answer. He glanced up and knew Rose's pager had silently gone off too. They both checked and read the same message. Terry sighed. "When my kids were little, I got in the habit of eating anything, steak, meat loaf, corn on the cob, in under five minutes. You got to with kids. I was still in practice I'd finish more meals."

They both stood. Rose said, "Your turn?"

"Screw you. I bought lunch day before yesterday."

"I got to keep swinging, Ter." She grinned. "You forget stuff, old man."

As they headed for the door, Terry didn't think that was his problem at all. He didn't forget anything. He remembered quite clearly, for example, that Rabbi Dolgen died only several months after his apartment was broken into and burglarized. And where his lifetime of mementos and sacred objects had gone, no one knew.

For an unaccountable reason, Terry desperately wished he was at that long-ago bar mitzvah and he could have warned Rabbi Dolgen what lay ahead.

Rose drove the four miles to the address they had been given. Terry knew the drill so well he could sleepwalk through its choreography. Roll up, slow down to get past the crowd in the street, spilling over from the sidewalk, get the uniforms to open the wooden barricades to let you through, stop, get out. On a summer night like this when it's hot, put the coat back on, clip the badge to the upper pocket so it's plainly visible. Make sure the area is secure.

Find out who's been killed. Pin down by name and number how much the population of the state's capital had been diminished this time.

Without the feeble air-conditioning in the diner, the early evening was like a clinging sweaty hand gripping his head. He and Rose walked from the car to the center of activity. The doughty black and white city CSU, Crime Scene Unit, was already there, along with five squad cars. Their massed stark black and white striping, and flashing blue and red lights made Terry still warily hopeful they could stop whatever violence and chaos had leaped into this neighborhood instead of just cleaning up the mess. This was always the most discouraging part, when the storm had moved on and only the shattered landscape remained.

He and Rose had exchanged complaints on the drive over and they didn't stop until they got to the body on the sidewalk. Terry said to a sallow, ginger-mustached crime scene tech who was methodically taking pictures, "What's cooking?"

"Purse snatch, looks like."

Terry surveyed the body and its bright cape of blood. "She didn't want to give it up."

The tech shrugged. "Just got here, Detective. Working our way through it."

Terry glanced up because the tech, like him and Rose, was talking in a raised voice just to be heard. The crowd pressing against the barricades was a mix of adults and kids, all shapes and sizes, all stripped down to the barest clothing against the heat. Fanning themselves, laughing, or pointing. A knot of kids bouncing to hip-hop from a boom box on the sidewalk. Oak Park had had more than its share of bodies and shootings over the years. It was just starting to pull away from that heritage of decline and anarchy.

"Got an ID?" Terry said loudly.

The tech shook his head. "Purse snatch, Detective," he said as if talking to an idiot.

Terry's temper flared and he turned to the closest uniform. "Get these bastards to keep it down," he ordered sharply. The cop darted to the sidewalk barricade.

Rose said, "I'll start checking for witnesses." A woman in the crowd flapped her hands at Rose.

"Good luck," Terry said, taking out the small pad he used for notes. He swept a sour gaze, tinged deep down with despair, at the boisterous crowd and its obvious pleasure at this diversion on a hot night. "Just another day in the life," he said, looking down at the gray-haired, stout woman in a lightweight yellow dress, her white, purple-veined legs crossed where she had fallen on her back, as if relaxing on the sidewalk to muse about the dying day.

Rose tapped his arm. "I got a neighbor. I got the victim's name."

Chapter Two

"When I heard the sirens and the noise, I had this awful feeling it was Connie."

"That's Constantina Basilaskos?" Rose asked. She was having trouble, Terry could see, keeping a straight face and making notes.

"That's right," said the skinny black woman in red stretch pants and a striped sailor shirt. "We been neighbors for almost twelve years and we always run into each other when I take Lucien for a walk at night. Connie and Angelo, that's her husband, they're just coming up the street from the bus. We all live up the street. I'm at 165 Thirty-third Avenue. They got the little two-story with the porch at 169."

"Where's her husband now?"

"At home. He's in bed, he's sick." She made a small face. She had been making this scrunched-up face every few seconds and it was very funny. She was about forty and weighed ninety pounds and her hair was dull gold and she had fuzz on her chin. She cradled an aged and fat dachshund in her arms, on its back. It stared up at her with wet, patient eyes. It seemed to be following her words with intense interest and understanding.

They were out of the fading sun in the shade of the CSU. The woman, Lynnette Vincent, wouldn't look at the sidewalk where the body lay.

"What's wrong with Mr. Basilaskos?" Terry asked.

"His bowels," she said with another small face. "Diverticulitis. Too many peanuts. They rush him to the hospital three days ago."

"You said you'd meet them coming from the bus stop? Where were they coming from?" Rose asked

"They own a diner, a Greek diner, downtown some place. Near the capitol. I don't recall the address, we're not friends, just really good neighbors. I never been there." She absentmindedly stroked Lucien's nearly hairless belly. "Poor, poor Connie. Poor, poor Angelo. What's he going to do? Who's going to tell him?"

Terry abruptly found himself having the same trouble as Rose. He wanted to laugh, one of those tickled, erupting laughs that can go on and on, because standing in the heat with this woman and her dog, and the way she held it like a baby and it had those big brown eyes like it was listening, was hilarious. He frowned instead. That's where twenty-six years of training and experience paid off. You could frown when you really wanted to bust a gut.

"Do Mrs. Basilaskos and her husband have any family living with them?"

16

"They've got three boys, all grown. They all live, I want to say Louisiana or Alabama or somewhere like that."

"Anybody else?"

"They lived alone. They've got friends, lots of people who come over for these parties and keep everybody on the block awake." She stopped. "Oh, damn. Oh, damn whoever did it."

Rose nodded. "Would you mind giving a full statement to that officer there?" She pointed at a uniform helping the crime scene techs identify points of interest around the body with small numbered markers. One by a shoe that had come off Mrs. Basilaskos, one by a shell casing, one by a blood spatter near her head. Another tech gently pulled small plastic bags over her hands, as if helping her put on formal gloves.

"Of course. I'll help any way I can."

Terry jotted a note. "Was there anything unusual about Mrs. Basilaskos coming home tonight?"

"No, just like always. Except she was by herself because Angelo's sick."

"So she's been running the diner without him the last couple of days?"

"I suppose so. I don't know." She drooped slightly. "I guess I didn't know them well at all. After all these years."

Rose gently patted her thin arm. "We'd appreciate your statement." She pointed over at the uniform again.

The woman nodded wanly. "Can I take Lucien for his walk first? With all of this, he hasn't had his walk and he really must need it." She cooed at the wet-eyed little dog. "You've been so good."

Terry's face scrunched like hers and he tried to maintain his stern frown. "Yeah, sure. You take Lucien for his walk first."

As soon as she had turned and walked away, Rose giggled helplessly and Terry shook his head, the pressure of holding the laughter in almost painful. What was really funny about this moment? Anything at all? He didn't know. It just seemed horribly funny that a fat old lady minding her own business on her way home, within sight of her house, got shot and her purse stolen. It was a punch line to some very complicated gag that otherwise didn't make much sense. Like a lot of things he saw lately.

"Oh, man," Rose gasped.

"Oh, man is right." Terry sucked in a breath. "Crap. The cameras are here." He moved away to make sure that the uniform cops were strict about keeping the TV camera crews and reporters behind the barricades. He detailed four more to shield the body from being seen from the sidewalk.

He heard Rose say suddenly, "Terry! See that flash?"

He turned and saw a bright white glitter atop an abandoned five-story warehouse on the next block.

Rose shouted, gun drawn, "Gun! On the roof! Everybody down!" and she pointed toward the warehouse roof. Terry shouted too and the crowd squealed in unison and the people scattered abruptly, the cops and the news crews taking shelter behind their trucks and squad cars.

"Get somebody over there now!" he yelled to one of the uniforms.

He crouched beside Rose. "Good call. Good eyes."

"Shooter might still be up there," she spat heatedly.

He didn't want to be reminded that his own vision was steadily getting worse. Next year or the year after that and he wouldn't pass the eye test. The slide into retirement would be irreversible.

His radio hissed. "Nye," he said. "What's going on?"

"We don't got nothing," said the uniform on the warehouse roof. "It's clear."

"Anybody been there?"

"Can't tell. Door lock's been busted for a long time. There are marks all around here, bottles, cans, looks like shit too, but that could be bums or kids. No sign of any weapons."

"Okay. Check around and then come on back."

Rose stood up and gave everyone the all-clear. "I saw a reflection, Ter. From a gun sight. Someone was scoping us out."

Terry nodded. "Maybe you saw some asshole with binoculars. I wouldn't put it past somebody to want to get a real good look at all the fun we're having."

"Bastards," she muttered, holstering her gun.

He and Rose went back to Mrs. Basilaskos and her busy crime scene attendants. When she was alive, she'd never had so many people fussing over her with such attention and dedication. The crime lab and coroner's crews had arrived and joined the half dozen men and women tending to the remains.

"This is an unexpected honor. Welcome to the slumber party, Doc," Terry said genially to the balding, stoop-shouldered, middle-aged man in a white sport shirt, brown pants, cobalt-colored tie. His glasses were half down his fleshy nose. He had sunk awkwardly to his haunches, tentatively touching the dead woman as he examined her.

"Detective Nye," he said without looking up. "Little did I realize when I took the chance to get out and grab some fresh air that I'd run into you."

"Rosie, this is Dr. Fabiani. Best forensic pathologist in the state. You need a medical opinion in court to back up a shooting, he's your guy."

Rose crouched down too and put out her hand. "Rose Tafoya. Terry's partner."

Dr. Fabiani didn't shake hands. "Detective Nye is being sarcastic. We had a case together some years ago. He claimed he fired into the asphalt and it ricocheted, striking the suspect in a domestic dispute and causing significant internal injuries."

Terry's voice tightened. "Doc here testified that there was no way the bullet could've been a ricochet. No asphalt particles. Trajectory all wrong."

Terry's anger was rising. He avoided the arrogant and dismissive Fabiani, whose testimony in that trial had nearly cost him his job and might have put him on trial for perjury except that the jury decided a maimed wife beater was not a bad solution, no matter what the truth of the matter might really be. Terry never expected to see the forensic pathologist come out to a crime scene. Bodies came to him. He stayed indoors, where it was cool and the light coldly artificial. Like a fucking vampire.

Rose caught the signs of Terry's anger and coolly changed direction. "So what's your take, Dr. Fabiani? What hit this lady?"

"Two shots. Two close-by entrance wounds." He drew his fingers down from just below her chin to her throat where a puckered hole was barely visible in the great welter of blood that congealed around it and on the sidewalk. His finger continued down to the scoop of the light yellow dress just above her doughy breasts where another hole appeared, also drowned in blood.

Terry had his hands on his hips. "You got a guess what kind of weapon?"

"Shall we roll her over a bit?"

He wore thin latex gloves, two pairs on each hand. He reached into the metal kit beside him and passed gloves to Terry and Rose. Then they carefully lifted Mrs. Basilaskos by the shoulders. Her head sank forward. The exiting bullets had carried plum-sized chunks of bone and flesh.

What hit Terry suddenly was not the dead weight of the woman, but the stench of blood. He'd already told Rose about his first homicide scene. Two old alcoholics, sharing an apartment on Sixty-fifth Street, had been working a homemade still making raw vodka. For some reason, one of them became belligerent and paranoid when his roommate wouldn't pick up his scattered clothes and dirty plates. So the quietly enraged old alky got a .44 he'd stashed under his bed and shot his roommate twice in the chest, just at the heart. The large slugs basically blew out the victim's back, along with whatever had been in their furious path. Terry had been on the job for four months when he joined the other cops picking up the pieces in that filthy, overstuffed apartment, stinking of unwashed clothes, rotting potatoes and grapes. But what stuck in his mind, and what came back every time he'd been at the scene of a stabbing or shooting or even a vehicular homicide, was the over-powering, cloying smell of blood that rode over even the most powerful odors like the ones in that apart-ment. The quarts of it that pumped out and sur-rounded the body, uniquely perfuming a crime scene.

"I'd say a nine millimeter," Terry offered.

"Good guess." Dr. Fabiani nodded.

"It ain't a guess. We got one shell." He pointed at the spent casing on the sidewalk beside a marker. "The mope shot her twice with a nine millimeter."

If the killer had been on the warehouse roof after shooting Mrs. Basilaskos, he had preferred close-up work earlier.

Rose said, "No stipple. No crud on her I can see." A gun fired close to a body left bits of gunpowder and other debris on clothing or embedded in the skin in a characteristic star-shaped pattern. Like a meteor impact into the earth that sprayed vivid evidence of its passage.

"No GSR," Dr. Fabiani said, meaning gunshot residue. "Nothing visible without a closer look. So she was shot from a distance of anywhere from five feet to infinity. I'll see what in the way of gunpowder or other residue turns up on her clothing."

They lowered her down again. Terry motioned for the coroner's crew to gather her up. The body had been examined and the area photographed. The sooner she was no longer a possible gruesome object of curiosity, the better. The crowd was showing no sign of dispersing after the brief false alarm earlier. The TV reporters were mingling and doing interviews.

"How soon can you get us something?" Rose asked the pathologist.

"For Detective Nye, I'll make this one a priority."

"Thanks," Terry said with a scowl. He looked at Mrs. Basilaskos's hands, wrapped in their hygienic bags. "You're going to check her fingernails? There's something under the nails."

"I can guarantee you," Dr. Fabiani said, pushing his glasses up slowly, "this lady won't have an inch on her I haven't examined. But it's going to be quite a feat if she got something off the shooter since she was dead on her way to the sidewalk."

Terry grinned crookedly. "Well, Doc, maybe she put up a fight and he shot her after. It can happen." He didn't need to add that a lot of things happened in ways that were amazing, grotesque, even incredible. Like a bullet bouncing off the hard asphalt and pristinely boring its way through a rampaging, meth-freaked guy who had been punching his wife senseless.

Rose and Terry made sure the uniforms were canvassing the crowd and people in the closest houses for anyone who might have seen or heard the incident. It was a little after half past eight. There were witnesses to locate quickly, while everything was fresh and vivid. People who had been on the sidewalk, perhaps in the street. They would help open or close avenues of the investigation. Then the slower, more laborious process of rooting out witnesses who did not want to come forward took place. This one was just getting started.

The sweat had dripped down the back of his neck and made his shirt stick to his back. His gun in its holster hung heavy and uncomfortable against his body.

Rose asked, "Walk or ride?"

"Exercise'll do us good," Terry said. "I just want to get to the husband before he sees something on the damn tube."

"I'm hoping it isn't him. I'm not up for a husband-wife thing tonight."

"The worst," Terry agreed from absolute personal and professional conviction.

They started walking up Thirty-third Avenue toward a row of one- and two-story older homes, people staring and talking on the small lawns or pointing out open windows.

Chapter Three

"You're a liar! You are a stinking liar! Why are you lying about her?" yelled Angelo Basilaskos as he tried to grab Rose's jacket sleeve. She had won the imaginary coin toss on the way to the stolid white-painted old house and she had just told Mr. Basilaskos that his wife, of thirty-one years, was lying dead outside in the fading summer evening.

"I'm sorry, sir, believe me," Rose said, gently keeping the much shorter, wiry man from actually touching her. Terry had a hand on Mr. Basilaskos's shoulders and he guided the struggling, cursing little man to the sofa. Angelo was in his blue pajama bottoms and a damp, limp T-shirt. He'd been in bed when Terry, Rose, and two uniforms they'd brought along came in and he got the news. Terry knew there was no best way of doing this repulsive chore. The only kindness was to get it out quickly, bluntly, and then deal with whatever the victim's nearest and

25

dearest did next. Some were stunned into bewildered, horrified immobility. Others exploded in crying jags. Still others assumed the cop was somehow to blame, or if he was not, the cop made a convenient target for the malign indignity that must, apparently, rule the universe.

Angelo Basilaskos fell into the latter category, trying to strike out at Rose. She happened to be nearest.

The four-room house was furnished cleanly, the sofa and chairs still looking showroom bright under clear plastic covers. There were framed photographs of sons and their wives, and a much younger Constantina and Angelo Basilaskos standing in front of gray cathedrals, sunny antique ruins, looking out over the vastness of some ocean from the railing of some cruise ship. Terry surmised they'd liked to travel a lot of years ago. On one wall was a teakwood rank of shelves with a collection of miniature liquor bottles, rum, ouzo, scotch, and bourbon, memorializing their travels. For an instant Terry thought longingly of popping one of the little bottles, like a carefree snack. But one, he knew, would lead to another and then another and soon he might have drunk his way around the world.

He sat down on a crinkling plastic-covered upholstered chair across from Angelo. Rose sat beside the little man, maybe five-three, brown, hairy arms, a small potbelly. He had thick, graying eyebrows.

"We don't know who did it, Mr. Basilaskos," Rose said sympathetically. It was the answer to the one question, once he got past swearing at the cops, that Angelo repeated.

"We need your help," Terry said.

"You'll find out. You find who did this to her," Angelo Basilaskos said, shaking his head. "You will do that?"

"We're going to try," Rose answered.

"You must do it." He pointed a shaking finger and began weeping, head down. "You must do that, you sons of bitches." But because he had a thick accent and he was crying, this came out "somsabisshes."

"Is there somebody who can come stay with you? A neighbor? Family?"

"Yeah, sure. I got lot of friends. I call my brother in Red Bluff, he get everybody, I have everybody here for her. For her. Who did this? What happened? Who did this to her when she's doing nothing, just coming home." He groaned and doubled over.

"Are you sick?" Terry asked.

"Who's your doctor?" Rose added.

Angelo Basilaskos waved a hand. He gave the name and number and Rose asked one of the uniforms to call immediately. The color had left the little man's face and he wasn't looking good at all. Rose glanced at Terry. Go on? Wait until they found out what the doctor recommended? Terry nodded slightly.

"We'll make this as quick as we can," Rose said. "Had you spoken to your wife today?"

"Before she left for the diner. Five. We always left at five. I got this trouble so I been in bed this week, so she goes out alone." He put his head in his hands. "They kill her when I'm not there, so it's two of us, maybe two of us they leave alone?"

"You have somebody specific?" Rose asked.

"Yeah, yeah, every fucking son of a bitch out there who does this every day to people minding their own business and the son of a bitch cops don't stop it."

Terry ignored the diatribe. It was familiar. It was almost as familiar as its twin, the effusive compliments. *Like we can change much of anything most of the time,* he thought. "What Detective Tafoya means, did your wife or you have enemies? People, names you could give us? It would be very helpful."

"Enemies? Who has enemies? We run the Korinthou, we run our diner for twenty years, same place, same customers, they come in same time, eat the same things, we all friends. We name it after the street where I'm born in Patras, you know, like San Francisco, big harbor, ships."

"Where's the diner?" Rose asked.

"Tenth and J, 1037 J Street. Twenty years breakfast, lunch, no dinner. We get people from offices, very loyal customers. I can tell you who comes in, what day, what time. All friends, they love her. They love Constantina."

"You have some names?" Rose glanced at her notes.

"Sure, sure. I don't know where they live. There's Joe, Mr. Volovak, Mr. Doyle, Mrs. Paxinou," and he went on for a minute, his breath rasping.

Terry nodded. "How about employees?"

"One. Constantina and me, we do all the work, but we got one dishwasher, cleanup."

Rose said, "Name? Address?"

"Jerry Karamandrachos, because I know his father. He lives on Arroyo Boulevard in Citrus Heights. He's okay, you got to keep an eye on him, he does the work." He doubled over, rocking slightly.

Terry raised an eye to Rose. "We're almost finished, Mr. Basilaskos. Would you mind if we took a look around at the diner now? You have a key we could use to get in?"

The little man waved to a bunch of keys on top of the large-screen TV. One of the uniforms handed it to Terry.

"Does your wife usually have a handbag or purse with her? She didn't have any identification on her when we arrived."

"She's always got this bag." He shaped his hands in the air a foot apart. "Black with gold metal around it. She's got everything in there, her wallet, money, stuff for her so she looks nice, her set of keys, all kinds of things. I tell her, it weighs a ton, you don't need to carry everything like that. But she never listens."

"Did you or your wife carry much cash from the diner?" Rose asked.

"Are you crazy? Every night, we close up at six, maybe, we make deposit at the Wells Fargo Bank on Capital Mall, the big bank. We got three hundred maybe, sometimes five, we put it in."

"So your wife would have made the deposit and then gotten on the bus to come home tonight?"

"Sure, sure. What, you think somebody thinks she's got money, they kill her for money she works hard for?" he yelled.

Terry said soothingly, "Look, we don't know what

happened. We'll take a look at your regulars and people who've worked for you."

"Who did this, I kill them myself," he swore, sitting back, his skin visibly blanched.

"Let us handle everything," Terry said. "How about we get you back to bed until the doc calls back?"

He motioned and the uniforms, two younger heavyset men, had no trouble supporting Angelo Basilaskos, heading him toward the bedroom at the end of a short hallway.

Rose stayed beside him. "How come if you stop serving at lunch, you don't close until six, Mr. Basilaskos?"

"You ever been in the business? You know how long it takes, get things ready for the next day, clean up, take care of things? We got kakavia soup, fish soup, takes time to get ready, tyropita, keftedes." He started speaking fast, as if running down. "Mousaka, souvlaki, spanakopita, ham, eggs, coffee."

He went completely limp, hanging in the grip of the uniforms, one of whom shouted to Terry. They lowered the little man to the bright orange carpet, his mouth wide open.

"He ain't breathing," Terry said. "How about you doing the honors?" He pointed at the youngest uniformed cop.

But Rose instantly knelt down first and started working on the little man. The younger cop took off his uniform hat, and crouched over Angelo Basilaskos, nervously waiting for someone to tell him when to step in. Rose sat back, breathing hard, pushing her hair back. Terry made an emergency call for paramedics.

Ten minutes later, Angelo Basilaskos was strapped onto a gurney and hauled downstairs for the siren-screaming rush to Sutter General, the closest emergency center. Terry and Rose left too.

Terry drove this time, heading back to Interstate 5 to downtown Sacramento. The sun was nearly gone; it was nearly nine, the thick weight of the hot evening all around them. Everyone seemed to be out on the sidewalk in Oak Park, lights everywhere had come on, and the streets had a fevered, tense excitement. He got onto the freeway on-ramp, accelerated into the thick traffic.

"Do the math," Rose said. She looked at her notes. She didn't seem to notice Angelo Basilaskos's collapse.

"You do the math. I'm driving."

"Five hundred bucks a day times five, because they're only open weekdays, right?"

"Right. That location, no point in staying open weekends," Terry agreed. Both he and Rose had noticed the significance of the diner's address, and it made Terry less edgy because he didn't have to go point by point with his partner.

"Okay, so every week it's like twenty-five hundred, times four is ten grand. Times fifty-two . . ." She paused, working a pocket calculator. "Makes a gross of sixty-two thousand. Give or take."

"You think they have any other money coming in? Like some after-hours deal between lunchtime and that run to Wells Fargo?"

"I didn't see anything. Just a couple of hardworking old people."

Terry changed lanes, speeded, honked rather than using the lights or siren, swung back into a lane, horns following him. "That'd be nice. That'd mean she got capped by somebody at random or some upstanding citizen just got out of county jail and wanted a big plate of mousaka."

"Damn. I'm hungry again. Talking about all that food." Rose started to look for some place they could grab something quick. Terry had called ahead for a squad car to meet them at the Korinthou Diner.

It was, both he and Rose had recognized, only a few blocks from the diner to the Sacramento County Jail, a ten-story high gray block that looked very much like any office tower nearby except that its windows were slits and the rooftop covered with link fence and razor wire. The streets and sidewalks were filled from morning until night around the county jail and the nearby Sacramento County Courthouse, another almost featureless white bulk beached not far from the sprawling Southern Pacific railyard, with the men and women he and Rose spent their days trying to take off the streets.

It was no great leap of imagination, Terry knew, and knew Rose knew too, for someone to get out of the county jail or leave a courtroom and end up at the Korinthou Diner.

Where only one old woman had been at work that day.

Chapter Four

They got inside the Korinthou Diner, nestled between vintage office buildings from the 1950s or older, surrounded by a used record store, very downmarket clothing and shoe stores, competing with an Indian restaurant on the same block, the massive Cathedral of the Blessed Sacrament rising across the street along with the creamy white dome of the state capitol just beyond. The streets were almost empty because everything was closed, but Terry heard the crack of breaking glass in an alley close by, a bottle smashed when it was empty.

"Daytime," Rose said as they did a quick tour through the diner to make sure there were no lurking surprises, "you have people coming in and out of the stores, the offices. You also get the foot traffic from the jail, the parolees from Folsom getting dropped off at the Greyhound station and strolling over here kind of pissed off."

Sacramento was the closest transit point for Folsom State Prison and nearby jails, including Sacramento County. A constant stream of former prisoners flowed through the downtown.

"Yeah. Somebody wanted to follow Mrs. B out of here, who's going to spot them?" Terry finished. "You want the front?"

"I'll do the kitchen and find the paperwork."

Terry left the two uniforms just outside the front door. He heard Rose rummaging around in the pots and trays of utensils. The offensive chores would come shortly, a check through the garbage. Terry called for the CSU to come out and meet them.

The Korinthou had ten booths and a counter for eight, aluminum-stamped trim, white and black tile floors. Inside it was heavy with the lingering smells of oil, onion, cooked tomato, fried batter. The kitchen was behind two flimsy brown-painted doors. Terry poked around the counter, the cash register, the booths. He didn't see anything very unusual. There were restrooms for men and women. He did a slow walk through both. They smelled sharply of disinfectant and the cracked tile floor glistened cleanly. In fact, everything gleamed in the diner. Like the apartment with its plastic-covered furniture. The Basilaskoses were neat, they apparently liked things in good order.

He caught up with Rose in a small alcove off the kitchen. There were two rusted file cabinets and a scored little wooden desk in the alcove. On the walls were more family photos of the Basilaskos clan, the distant sons at a Little League game.

"I didn't see any H and S violations," Terry said, meaning the Health and Safety Code. "I'm thinking you could get a meal here and figure you weren't going to lose it after a couple of hours."

Rose nodded. She'd opened the cabinets and was poking through the overstuffed files. "These folks are neat freaks, but their bookkeeping stinks. They just crammed papers into files." She held up a torn, bloated file folder with flimsy paper exploding from it. Like Terry, she wore latex gloves. "See? This is employee junk."

"Different names?"

"Three, four, five." Rose flipped through the file. "Maybe they got a family friend's kid working now, but they've been through half dozen employees in the last year maybe."

"The hours are crappy."

"Maybe. There're a hell of a lot of names."

Terry sighed. The more names they found in the diner's employment records, the more interviews they would have to conduct. The purse-snatch shooting of Constantina Basilaskos could easily be a random event. She was merely a target of opportunity. But Terry wondered about that. She was on her way home sometime after six. Had it taken her that much time to get from the diner to the bus stop? Had she stopped some place first? They'd have to retrace her route. Rose had already done a cursory check with the Sacramento Regional Transit Authority and found out that the bus carrying Mrs. Basilaskos was right on time. At about seven when she got to her stop, there must have been several people getting off the bus, and more on the sidewalk. If she was the victim of a random crime, Mrs. Basilaskos was an extraordinarily unlucky woman. Like the guy who gets hit by lightning in his own driveway.

He also didn't think that Oak Park, which had a history of shootings and drive-bys and was still, even with its improving crime profile, one of the busier patrol sectors, indulged much in daytime robbery-homicides.

On the other hand, it was still very early in terms of gathering evidence. There could just as easily be links they didn't see yet. Maybe an employee. Maybe one of the regulars.

"Hey," Terry said, helping Rose with the first look at the paperwork, "wouldn't it be swell if this wrapped up tonight? I mean, a nice easy one for a change?"

"Dream on, Ter. We haven't had a nice easy one all month. Nobody's copping to anything. We're doing grunt work on every case."

"For Christ's sake, shut up," Terry said in mock anger. "You'll jinx this one."

"Think about it. Victim gets nailed because she sells somebody a bad gyro."

"They don't do gyros. It ain't on the menu."

"See? Greek diner that doesn't sell gyros, something's really wrong. This's going to turn out to be a bad lunch hit."

Terry chuckled. The other file cabinet was locked. He jiggled the keys Angelo Basilaskos had given them and tried one after the other until he opened the file cabinet. He grunted, bending over to pull out the lower drawers. He frowned. "What's this look like?"

He held up a plain brown paper bag, neatly folded closed. On it was the word *Kelso* in black pen and a date. "Day after tomorrow," Terry said. He peered into the file drawer. "Three more, different names, looks like. Couple days apart."

Rose paused. "Open it."

Very carefully Terry peeled the folded bag open. He sighed again. "Cash. Twenties." He didn't want to handle anything more than necessary at this point. "Maybe a hundred, little more."

"Tips? Money they didn't want to report?"

"Who knows? I just know my dear sainted mother never made up little lunch bags of cash and stuck them in a locked file cabinet."

Rose pointed at a barely visible door frame at the rear of the alcove. "You got a key for that one?"

Terry squeezed by her and went through the same tedious routine with the keys. He opened the door finally. He took out his tiny but powerful flashlight when he couldn't find a light switch after running his hand inside the wall.

"Shit," he said sourly.

Rose stood behind him in the narrow space. A sloping room about five feet deep and five feet high appeared in Terry's flashlight. Sweat rolled down his neck. There were, he thought, ten or twelve boxes of brand-name cigarettes in the little space. He broke open one box. It was filled with cartons of cigarettes.

"No stamps on them," Rose said. "They're not here legally."

"Bootleg," Terry said. "Little side enterprise when the lunch crowd don't turn out, I guess."

He snapped off the flashlight. No United States authority had stamped, taxed, and sent these cigarettes on their way. They were strictly under the counter. It was disappointing to discover this side enterprise.

"Okay," Rose said, stepping out of the alcove, "at least we know the Basilaskoses could have been dealing with people they shouldn't. Kind of people who get mad, hold grudges if you don't pay on time or skim."

"They must've been holding a lot of smokes back if she got nailed because of them." It didn't sound right, but the damage was done, Terry admitted. His dead victim was not an innocent. Her death might even be connected with the boxes of contraband cigarettes or the odd little paper bags of money.

Still, it was her death that concerned him and even if he couldn't work up outrage or sorrow, he could set the record straight. No matter what—and he genuinely hoped neither he nor Rose would find anything more than low-level graft—Mrs. Constantina Basilaskos, mother of three, probably a grandmother by now, wife of Angelo, hardworking co-owner of a diner that served the hungry and provided a clean and pleasant place for people to come back to day after day, didn't deserve to be shot down on the city sidewalk for the handbag she had carried for years.

Terry called Sutter General as Rose worked down the file drawers. The CSU rolled up outside, more uniforms and crime scene techs came in, the chattering convivial and reassuringly familiar.

Terry said to Rose, "The old guy's in ICU. Major heart attack."

"What's his status?"

"I wouldn't make bets the regulars are going to get their fish soup tomorrow."

"Too bad." She cocked her head at Terry. "When we get out of here, I definitely want to get something juicy and with some onions on it." They hadn't found any place suitable on the way over.

"Give it another half hour, let the other guys grab stuff, we hit the road," Terry said. He was getting hungry again too. And if he thought about the work that must done and the break in thirty minutes, he wouldn't think about the diner, the dirty secrets it held, the two old people whose lives had careened from order to chaos in the space of a still relatively early evening.

But the timetable changed abruptly when Rose got the call that the uniforms back at the scene had located an eyewitness. He had seen the shooting death of Constantinta Basilaskos.

Leaving the chore of gathering the files, whatever physical evidence could be tagged, bagged and photographed, to the techs, Terry and Rose headed back to the shooting scene.

"Ter," she said hesitantly, then belligerently, "I don't care if you think I'm paranoid but I get a feeling we're being tailed."

He glanced around the nearby freeway lanes and in his rearview mirror. "Who? What do you see?"

"I don't see anything," she said. "It's a feeling. I just have a feeling."

"Christ. Don't get spooked on me. I had a partner when I was new, Shaeffer. Big lummox and he started thinking Internal Affairs was eyeballing him after every call we got."

"Were they?"

"Who knows with those assholes? Shaeffer got so shaky he quit after a year."

"I'm not shaky," she said, looking out her window at the speeding cars around them. "Forget it."

"Who the hell would want to follow us?"

"Right," Rose said. "It's nothing. But ten bucks says this one goes crappy like all the others this month, Ter. Eyewitness or not."

Terry liked the fact that his new partner was a sport. It always made the day feel better if you could bet on time of death, likely suspect, or whether the victim's tattoos were amateur or professional.

"I'm feeling lucky tonight," Terry said. "You're on."

He didn't add that if the case was resolved speedily, neither he nor Rose would have to expose any more of the lives that Constantina and Angelo Basilaskos had led.

Everybody deserved a secret or two.

Everybody had a lot more.

Everybody, he thought.

Chapter Five

The witness was named Harry Standhope. He prowled restlessly in the cluttered living room of the light blue house three doors down on the other side of Thirty-third Avenue from where Constantina Basilaskos had been shot. The TV was blaring loudly until Rose politely asked Harry's sullen girlfriend, Kaneesha, to turn it down. She glared at Harry and lowered the volume. Every few minutes she left the room, her slender black arms crossed angrily, to soothe a wailing child in one of the back rooms of the small house.

A uniformed cop stood beside the front door. There were two more outside. The neighbors had expressed varying opinions about why the police were back to see Harry and Kaneesha. From their nods and shaking heads as he and Rose had knocked on the door earlier, Terry surmised that SPD had made more than one courtesy call on the young couple.

"So you don't live here, Harry?" Rose asked. She and Terry had carefully found small open spots on the ragged chairs. The floor was dangerous, a minefield of toys, food cartons, clothes.

"I come over. I live in Rancho Cordova." It was a nearby neighborhood. Harry was twenty-three, in a gaudy sleeveless T-shirt that was so brightly colored it made Terry's eyes hurt. They had early on established that Harry arrived from Jamaica, the island, and not the New York address, ten years earlier. He had thick arms and a pointed face and his dense beard and dreadlocks gave him a startling, satyrlike appearance. "We were going to the Kings over at Arco." He meant the home game of the Sacramento Kings at Arco Arena in north Sacramento.

"How come you didn't make the game?"

"That old lady got blown away, man. In front of me almost. I ain't going to a basketball game after that, no matter what she"—he jerked his head toward the back room where the child's cries had stilled—"says we got to do."

"The kid yours?"

"I pay for her food," Harry said.

"So, okay." Terry shifted carefully because there was something wet and ugly wrapped in a small towel beside him on the chair and it might roll closer. "You and your girlfriend are on the way out the door when you saw the old lady get shot?"

"*I* didn't see anything." Kaneesha reappeared and stood like an angry sentinel near the open window, the city's street noises drifting in, while Harry paced. "I didn't hear anything. I'm with my little girl and this dumb fool comes in and goes, 'I just seen a

42

lady get shot outside' and I go, 'You better keep your fool mouth shut.'"

They started bickering again. Harry's muscled arms bunched. Rose got between him and Kaneesha. Nobody liked domestics, Terry thought, even when they didn't go so out of control like the one that had almost gotten him pilloried.

"Hey, settle down," Rose said. She was good. She had a reputation for hotheadedness, but Terry was impressed with the way Rose could let the pressure out of a rising, nasty situation. "Harry, we're grateful you came forward."

Harry scowled at Kaneesha. She scowled back.

"So, let's walk through what you saw."

Harry laid it out simply and vividly. He had come by around four-thirty to help Kaneesha settle the year-old down, arrange for a neighbor to watch the kid while they went to the basketball game and maybe didn't get back until late. He went outside because he was going to the small market on the corner to pick up extra baby food.

"It's about seven," he said. "This old white lady is in front of me. Coming up the block."

"How far?" Terry asked, jotting notes.

"Me to the door there." He pointed to a closet about fifteen feet away. "She's walking pretty fast."

"She have a purse or handbag?"

"Yeah, black one, stuck here." He pressed his right arm against his body. "Like that, like she won the lottery."

"What happened then?" Rose asked, leaning forward. Terry tensed because the wet thing was looking as if it might start moving.

William P. Wood

"This guy, white guy, comes from some place, goes right up to her. Boom. Boom. Grabs her purse." Harry shook his head and swore, low.

"Fool," Kaneesha muttered. She stomped to the kitchen and they heard glassware clattering.

"What'd the white guy look like?" Terry asked.

"Couldn't see much, could I? He's got his back to me. But he's about your height." He pointed at Rose. "Kind of big guy." He pointed at Terry.

"Older?" Rose volunteered unkindly.

"Yeah. Older too. He's got on this funny striped coat deal you see old white guys wearing."

"Seersucker sport coat, I bet," Terry said, assuming that Rose would not recall the somewhat out-of-date summer-wear fashion. "So, let me get this straight, Harry. A white man, older," he muttered, "comes up to this woman, who's got her purse held tight, and he shoots her twice? Did he say anything? Did she say anything?"

"I didn't hear anything, man. It was so fast, there wasn't time for anything much."

"How about, 'Give me your handbag'? Something like that?"

Harry stopped pacing, bit his lip. "He just shot that old lady down, man. Just like that and he grabs her purse and this car comes up and he gets in and they're gone, just like that."

Rose squinted at Terry. The tale was more or less credible until that last detail. The idea of a reasonably dressed white man gunning down the owner of a Greek diner on a busy street and then having an accomplice drive a getaway car strained things a whole lot.

44

"What kind of car was it?" Rose asked

"Big. Four-door. Light, maybe brown, beige, something like that. I didn't catch much, I was running over to see what I could do for that lady." He seemed shocked and perplexed by the brutality and incongruities of the sudden crime.

"Get a license maybe? What kind of plates even?"

"I think California. Nothing else."

"Anybody else nearby? Somebody else help you?"

Harry shook his head, the dreadlocks trembling. "Naw, man. They all scattered. I'm all alone for a minute maybe. Just me and this old lady bleeding away. There wasn't nothing I could do."

Terry peered at him. "I don't see any blood on you, Harry."

Kaneesha barked a laugh. "Well, you ain't seen his other shirt, the one he was wearing so's we could watch the big fucking deal Kings. There's plenty of blood on that."

"Where's the shirt?" Rose asked.

"Washed. Twice," Kaneesha said. "I ain't having no bloody damn shirt in this house, not with my baby here."

Rose politely asked for the shirt anyway. Kaneesha brought it out and Rose called for one of the uniforms to bag it. Two washings would have severely compromised any evidentiary value, but Forensics could pull something perhaps. At least corroborate Harry's story that he had been close enough to come in contact with the victim.

Terry just barely avoided the wet thing when it rolled toward him. He hopped from the chair. Outside he could hear the sporadic laughter and shouts, the die-hard spectators still drawn to the crime scene after several hours.

"Harry, I got to ask this," Terry said, knowing Rose well enough that she was ready for whatever happened next, "so, I'm just going to ask it. It's not personal. Did you shoot the old lady for her purse?"

It was Kaneesha's hoot of derisive laughter that caught Rose off guard, not Harry's angry spray of expletives. She clapped her hands. "I told you, fool. I said you'd get it. I said they'd blame you. Didn't I say it?"

Terry put his hands up, his face stony. "Hey, hey, both of you, keep it down. Just answer me, Harry, and I'll be happy."

Harry stared at Terry, then Rose. "I did not hurt that old lady. I did not shoot her. Man. Man. I am a naturalized citizen, man. You can't send me back to Treasure Beach."

"I don't want to send you back. Where's Treasure Beach?"

"The asshole of the world, where I came from. Bad enough around this dumb place all the black folk they make fun of how I talk, call me Bob Marley, say I should sing reggae all the time. I'm just trying to be a good citizen, right? I support my daughter. I tell the police what happened when something bad happens and I saw it. Man." He regarded Rose and Terry with undisguised bitterness.

Not missing a beat, Rose asked, "You got a gun, Harry?"

"No, I do not own a gun, have a gun, use a gun; I don't even know how to use a gun."

46

Rose nodded. "Can we take a quick look around?"

Terry was enjoying Rose's sense of timing more and more. Harry would certainly want to underscore his innocence and say yes.

"Look any place you want."

Rose got up. Kaneesha was in her face, finger wagging. "Oh no. This is my house, not his. I pay the rent, not this fool. So, no."

"We can get a warrant. It's a lot faster and easier and we got to do it anyway, it's standard," Rose said calmly. "So, how about it?"

Harry radiated coldness toward Kaneesha and Terry felt it returned with compound interest.

Kaneesha heard her daughter start to cry again. "All right, go ahead. This fool's messed us up anyway. Just stay away from my baby." She was gone again.

Terry exchanged a quick nod with Rose. Rose would stay and keep Harry company, just in case there was a weapon or Harry tried to run. Besides, merely chatting, even if it was unnatural and strained, was more likely to ensure Harry's long-term cooperation than if they left him with the stolid-looking uniform by the door.

Terry didn't dawdle as he did a search of the bathroom, the bedroom, the three bursting closets. Kaneesha ignored him and tended to her child.

He didn't find any guns. Nor did he find any bullets or any indication of a gun. In the larger closet, just down the short hallway from the living room, behind a sour mass of unwashed jeans and shirts and one or two items he didn't want to dwell on, he pulled out a negligently sealed plastic bag. He opened it, already fairly certain what the dark green, dried vegetable matter was. He sniffed. He clinically hefted the bag. Possibly 150 grams or maybe a little over a quarter pound of marijuana. He closed the bag and slipped it back where he found it. He ran his hand farther back in the clothes and retrieved another, tightly sealed bag. One in use, one in reserve. He put the second bag back where he found it. He stopped in to see Kaneesha, who had the baby over one shoulder and was softly singing. The anger had dissolved from her face. She looked small, young, and yet completely maternal. "Sorry for the trouble," he said. "What's her name?"

"Amanda." The voice was very soft.

Terry went back to the living room. Rose and Harry were standing out the window, peering at the street garishly lit up by lights the CSU techs had rigged. They were relaxed, like old buddies. "Everything's square," he said to Rose. Then to Harry, "You think you could come down to the police department tomorrow so we can try to do a picture of this guy?"

"Yeah, sure. I didn't see his face, did I? I saw what he's wearing, what he did, and the car he got into."

"Appreciate it."

Rose tapped her lip. "You see what kind of gun? Small, big, revolver, automatic?"

"It was a gun, man. He shot twice and he took the old lady's purse."

Harry had gone, Terry and Rose both saw, as far

as he would that night. Tomorrow was another day and he was hooked into the investigation. It would take effort on his part to wriggle free. Most witnesses who had to be ferreted out exerted themselves at the outset to be relieved of the burdens of what they'd seen or heard or knew. After that, in Terry's experience, most people resigned themselves to being caught up in the inexorable coils of the system. Harry at least had stepped forward.

On the sidewalk, Rose glanced at the empty marked space where Constantina Basilaskos had fallen, the techs still checking, and the search for more witnesses continuing. The TV crews had left and the night belonged to the cops, the dwindling spectators, and the bugs darting and maddened by the streetlights and new harsher lights brought in by the cops.

"Okay," Rose announced, "we grab something to eat like right now. I'm hungry like I was when I was carrying my kid."

"Fine by me," Terry agreed as they went to their car. "First thing after that, I want to check in and let Bernasconi know what's happening on this one." He meant Lieutenant Vance Bernasconi, the head of Robbery-Homicide for the Sacramento Police Department.

"We don't know what's happening."

"Listen to the voice of real experience, little miss," Terry said, sliding into the driver's seat. "We know that this one stinks. It is stinking rotten and all wrong. We know that right now for a certain fact."

* * *

The aged stone block that housed the Sacramento Police Department had rust-streaked grillwork barring the windows on all three floors and chips in the early twentieth-century granite. It sat on a tree-shaded street and it was connected to the county jail about a block from the 1964-era county courthouse. The Sobriety Testing Station where drunks were brought in by every law enforcement agency from the California Highway Patrol to the state police nestled against the back of the old building. It did not look very different at almost eleven in the evening from the way it did at eleven in the morning. There were six hundred uniformed police officers and twenty-five detectives in the department and cars revved and drove in and out of the parking lot until early morning when things slowed. A stream of uniformed cops singly or in pairs came in and out of the faux-colonnaded entrance. Sometimes the cops had civilians with them and some of the civilians were in handcuffs. If anything, the warm evening's obscuring shadows lent the continuous parade and the old, always busy building a quality of vigor and purpose. You couldn't see the chips or the cracks or the places where the city scraped graffiti off so crudely that the stone was rubbed white.

Terry and Rose had hit a late night deli, provisioned themselves with turkey and roast beef on rye with horseradish mustard to go and coffee. They ate as they went up to the robbery-homicide section on the second floor.

Three other detectives hollered as they walked by. A Hispanic woman sat slumped in a chair, weeping into a paper towel and blowing her nose. The fluorescents overhead, several flickering because the city never replaced light fixtures with even a spark of illumination left in them, cast a white, cold glare over the shift and the mustard-green walls. The scratched wooden door to Lieutenant Bernasconi's office was open, meaning he didn't mind his detectives strolling in.

"Don't sit down," he said when they went in. He never raised his eyes from the stacks of printouts and papers all over his desk.

"What's up?" Rose asked between bites.

"Yeah, how come you're still here?"

He looked up. Bernasconi was in his mid-forties, a former college wrestler slowly going to fat but still solid. He had brown hair and wore half glasses. On the cluttered table behind him were pictures of his wife and three girls. "How come *you* two are hanging around?"

Terry grinned. "Oh, we went on double OT about two hours ago." Double overtime meant considerably more extra pay.

"Why is that?"

"Purse snatch turned into a stone-cold homicide."

"I need coffee," Bernasconi said, getting up. They followed him to the gurgling coffeemaker just outside his office. He blew out a weary breath and poured a thick black substance into his personal cup. "Anybody join me?"

Rose shook her head. Terry said, "Gives me the d.t.'s."

Bernasconi sipped and blew a breath out again.

51

"We've got a million Starbucks in this city, probably we've got a hundred right around the corner. Why am I drinking this?"

"Tradition," Terry said.

They went back to his office. "You didn't say why you're working so late," Rose prodded.

Bernasconi surveyed the pile of papers with distaste. "Deputy Chief Mayer's got a directive. Every section's got to show a clearance rate improvement of six percent this month. That's Auto. That's Fugitive Warrants. That's Burg. And that's us. I'm trying to make our clearances come out."

"Murder's down, I thought. Life's beautiful," Terry protested.

Bernasconi grimly drank more coffee. "We've had sixty-seven homicides this year. Compared to last year, that's a fourteen percent drop. Compared to the last two years it's an eight percent drop."

"Hooray for our side."

"And compared to the previous eight years." He picked up a piece of paper. "It's a 67.4 percent drop. You would think that earns us some points, wouldn't you?"

Rose nodded. "You'd think."

Bernasconi sat down wearily, closed his eyes for a moment, and hunted around for an errant aspirin bottle. "But the *deputy chief,* which means the *chief,* which means the *mayor,* doesn't like the sound of those stats changing in the other direction. Even if we're still clearing more murders than we ever did. So the *deputy chief* chugs down here and personally lays it out for me. So that's why I'm here way, way past my bedtime and seeing my girls and my wife

52

and why I'll probably still be here tomorrow when you two have had a good night's sleep and come to work all bright-eyed and ready to save the city. Got to keep everybody around here and over in the legislature safe and happy so they can keep busy cranking out all those great laws we have to enforce."

Terry grimaced. "You have my sympathy."

"You want to hear about the purse snatch?" Rose asked gingerly. "Ter thinks it's funny."

"We got a problem," Terry said seriously. He told Bernasconi the outline of the investigation quickly and economically. Bernasconi found his aspirin, took three with the powerful coffee, and got up to put the cup back on top of a file cabinet.

"We getting any more witnesses?"

"Maybe. So far we haven't turned up anybody except Standhope who'll lay out the action. I'm optimistic. Maybe we'll get a better ID on the shooter or the car."

"If we don't," Bernasconi said, "where are you going next?"

Rose said, "Go through the Basilaskos' employee stuff. Check with the regulars. Check to see who the visitors were at county jail today, who got out. Who Folsom dumped off downtown to catch a bus."

Bernasconi got up and snatched his cup off the cabinet. "Goddamn, I need another shot to get through this."

They went out with him again. Terry said, "But it's the shooter and the car that sticks in my way. It just doesn't work. I'll go with the angry employee, maybe the mob or whoever peddled the cigarettes, I'll go with some puke from county jail or state prison or some local dipstick. But I can't get past a white guy in a fucking seersucker and a getaway car."

Rose nodded. "So Harry's jiving."

Bernasconi shook his head. "Why? He's not a reluctant eyewitness. What does he get out of fabricating a story?"

"Beats me right now," Terry admitted. "Like I told Rosie, all I know right this minute is that this one's not sitting right."

"Victim's got something valuable in her purse. Shooter knows she does," Rose said.

"So maybe old Angelo's giving us the bum's rush. There's more cash coming out of the diner at the end of the day than he tells us. Maybe the victim doesn't deposit it like he told us. Maybe they've a bank account in the cookie jar too."

"We just don't know," Rose agreed.

Bernasconi groaned. "I do not need to hear that we've got another open homicide and we may not close it."

"We'll close it," Terry said. "Detective Tafoya's going to pay me ten of her very-hard-earned city paycheck bucks if we don't."

"Oh, good. Incentive." Bernasconi started working on numbers from the papers arrayed around him. "What's next?"

Terry glanced at Rose. "If he's better tomorrow, we go and see what Angelo's got to say about the cigarettes and the brown bags in his office. Tonight—" he began and Rose cut him off.

"What tonight? We're done."

"Let's go to Citrus Heights, see the Karamandrachos kid, and close that out, okay? Won't take long. Unless the kid's added a lot of years and a lot of weight and likes to wear seersuckers."

"He can keep until tomorrow," Rose protested. "My husband's already thinking bad things about me tonight being out so late with you."

Bernasconi waved at them dismissively. "Go make up your minds and let me try to make your sorry careers look good for this report."

They started out the door and Terry stuck his head back in. "Guess who caught this one for the coroner."

"Who?"

"Fabulous Fabiani. The Sacramento Police Officers' Association's best friend."

Bernasconi snorted. "Now I know Rose's going to win your bet. I'm going to have one big hole in our weekly stats."

"Never happen. This one's going to clear as easy as they come." Terry grinned. His pessimism about the case was for his partner only at this stage. He went out and found Rose talking to a rangy, nearly bald, western-looking detective jarringly named Felderstein.

"So I got the new SUV, and I got the boat-towing package. Sweet deal," Felderstein said with nearly erotic delight.

"You don't have a boat."

"I might get one."

"Where you going to sail a boat? When are you going to sail a boat?"

"Who said sail? I get a motorboat. I go fishing. I drive to Folsom Lake, go out on the American River.

I could use a boat. We got water everywhere around here."

"You don't go fishing. When have you ever been fishing?"

"When I want to, when I want to sit in my own boat, I got to have a tow package or it'll cost a lot more to put one on."

Rose got out of her chair when she saw Terry. "Bottom line, Felderstein, you don't have a boat, you just paid five grand more for a tow package you do not need."

"It looks sweet," Felderstein repeated with the same ecstasy.

"So did my first wife," Terry said. "And she didn't cost five grand."

"That's not what I heard," Felderstein's partner, McGivery, popped in.

"Yeah, yeah," Terry said, not unkindly, "she had you down as one of the regulars who got a discount on account of he only stayed long enough to open his pants."

Felderstein laughed and McGivery turned a little red, not because he was embarrassed but because he couldn't think of anything fast to say back to Terry. Terry grinned. McGivery had been pegged for some time as the slow learner in Homicide. It was always easy to at least get a base hit from anything he pitched.

Terry worked on Rose as they walked down the cracked broad staircase to the first floor, uniforms passing them on the way up, energetic with early shift exuberance.

"My husband's mad, Ter," Rose said.

"One less thing to do tomorrow. It'll make Bernasconi feel better, the wheels are rolling, our clearance's just around the corner."

They both wanted to help Vance Bernasconi. He had their loyalty because he was not one of the few favored by the distant deputy chiefs and the chief locked away on the third floor's carpet row. He wasn't preening for promotion or notoriety. He looked out for his detectives.

Rose held up her hands in surrender. "One hour. That's it."

Terry nodded contentedly. "Young Jerry's probably sound asleep, maybe he hasn't even heard he doesn't have to be at work first thing in the morning."

Unspoken, maybe even unconsidered, underlying Rose's comment, Terry thought briefly and unhappily, was the truth of the matter. Rose had a husband to get mad at her, a child who would miss her, waiting for her at home. He had no one now.

"They heard," Rose said when she and Terry got to the Karamandrachos house, a neat brick box, in a line of identical brick boxes, with identical screened porches and the same boiling cloud of insects around their street and porch lights. There were half a dozen cars parked in the driveway and the living room was filled with older men and women, hastily dressed, all loudly and angrily talking, a harried couple of women moving among them, handing out glasses of liquor and iced tea.

The elder Karamandrachos hauled his plainly reluctant son into the kitchen. The people pressed Terry and Rose about finding whoever shot Constantina and sent Angelo to the hospital. Several burly men offered rewards and offered to accompany the two detectives on an armed sweep of the neighborhood around the Basilaskos home. Terry thanked them courteously and asked Jerry's parents if they could talk to Jerry alone for just a few minutes.

"Alone?" asked the elder Karamandrachos suspiciously. His wife shook her head. "Not alone. Jerry's our son. Has he done something else?"

"No, we just need more information, that's all," Terry said. He exchanged a covert nod with Rose, who immediately said, "And if you wouldn't mind, could I talk to you both, get some information? It would be very helpful to us in tracking down whoever shot Mrs. Basilaskos. You were good friends."

"We were friends," the elder Karamandrachos agreed heavily. "We're going to the hospital in a few minutes to keep a vigil for Angelo." His round, sad eyes grew moist. "I pledge to hire the best lawyer in California to find this filth guilty and make sure they are killed."

Rose was already taking Jerry's agitated parents aside. "Well, of course, in California, we've got district attorneys who prosecute cases like this and when we catch whoever shot Mrs. Basilaskos, with your help, they can make sure the killer is convicted. And executed." That ought to make them feel better.

Terry and Jerry Karamandrachos threaded their way past irate friends of the victim and her ailing husband. Terry closed the door to Jerry's bedroom. He was nineteen, dark-haired, dressed in jeans and a white T-shirt. Serpentine tattoos wound up one arm.

"You know who shot her?" Terry started right in.

"I didn't."

"Who did?"

"I don't know. I think it was a pretty good idea. Old bitch never paid me, made me work all the time, swears at me. She kicked me once."

Terry looked around the room. It was papered with posters of tennis players and slightly out of date rock singers, as if Jerry just inhabited the room someone else had decorated. "You tell your mother and father how Mrs. Basilaskos treated you?"

"Like they'd give a rat's fucking ass. Angelo and my dad have all these friends from Greece, they drive up to Vancouver every couple weeks, supposed to be to see my second cousins. Bet they go up there to get laid."

Terry thought trips into Canada might explain the illegal cigarettes. The trips could also be familial, just as the Karamandrachoses claimed. "So I'd be correct in figuring you didn't like Mrs. Basilaskos. How about her husband?"

"They're the same." Jerry Karamandrachos nervously, truculently eyed Terry. "Nobody works for them. They're so fucking cheap everybody quits and they hire some other stupid bum."

"So how come you're at the diner doing your morning chores?"

"I'm a fucking slave. They don't pay me," he said bitterly. "That's the deal with them." He jerked his head toward the murmuring, outraged gathering beyond the door.

Terry realized his earlier optimism about the Basilaskos' secrets was mistaken. There were certainly tax and California employment regulation violations here. Which meant, to start with, that he and Rose would have to run through the Wells Fargo Bank account to see how much had gone into it and whether the receipts from the diner matched. It was becoming clear that the entire financial history of Constantina and Angelo Basilaskos would have to be reviewed. Credit cards, telephone, payments on appliances or furniture, tax records. Somewhere there might be a reason for the shooting.

He felt sorry for this kid. He felt sorry for Constantina Basilaskos too. What she deserved was an avenger, like some of the men outside were volunteering to be. What she would get, sadly, was her life laid bare, the avarice and pettiness that, compared to what had befallen her, was profoundly unfair. It was not justice. It was the way things were.

Terry made a few notes. "So what'd your mother mean, had you done something else?"

Jerry Karamandrachos stiffened. "I'm on probation. Another year and a half. Felony vandalism and I got to do the probation working for my dad's best buddy, Angelo Basilaskos."

A nice arrangement, Terry thought. Free, dedicated if not contented labor for the diner. A probation taken care of for the family's sake and the kid's record. And the Basilaskoses would know they had the upper hand, always. Jerry couldn't say or do anything or he'd get his probation violated.

"What's the probation for?"

"I got bombed, shit-faced with some buds, and we trashed our school. Trashed it," Jerry Karamandrachos said, for the first time with a look of delight on his face.

"The Basilaskoses, they have people who didn't like them?"

"Anybody who ever worked for them or ate that shitty food."

"Any specific people?"

Jerry Karamandrachos thought and then rattled off several names and addresses. Terry carefully wrote them down. Interesting folks, the Basilaskoses. They had friends willing to turn vigilante for them and other people who despised them.

Terry went over a few more points, when the diner opened, how many customers came in, to verify the kind of business Angelo claimed, and it did sound more or less in the ballpark. He had Jerry give him the day's itinerary, where he had been, whom he had seen or who might have seen him. After work today, Jerry Karamandrachos got together with a girl he'd known for about four months, Patty Russo, who was a waitress at Dawson's in the Hyatt Regency three blocks away. They'd met on errands for their respective establishments. He didn't get home until nine. He could have a very straightforward, very impregnable alibi.

Finally he said, "Okay, thanks, Jerry. You've been helpful."

"Shit. I didn't mean to be."

Terry nodded wryly. "Whose room?"

Jerry Karamandrachos was surprised for an instant that Terry had read the posters and athletic trophies so accurately. "My brother Gus. He's in the navy."

"You got a year and a half to go on your probation. What're you going to do then?"

"Join the navy," Jerry Karamandrachos spat. "Get the hell away from here."

"I could've guessed," Terry said. Heading to the living room, Terry let the kid push by him toward the kitchen. That was the ultimate club the Basilaskoses held over their bonded servant, the threat that if his probation was violated he would never be able to join the navy.

Except for the fact that the shooter was a much older man, Terry would have given Jerry Karamandrachos's motive for harming the victim a great deal of credence. It would have made this case very simple.

He sensed his ten dollars was sailing, inexorably, toward Rose's wallet.

As he reached that sobering, irritating conclusion, he heard the mixed loud wailing from several women in the living room. The Karamandrachoses cradled each other.

"What's going on?" he asked Rose in alarm.

"Angelo died thirty minutes ago."

Terry let his breath out. "That's pretty good shooting. Two slugs, two dead."

Chapter Six

Terry did not like the weather report he heard on TV and then read in the paper for Wednesday, August 6. The summer heat had parked itself in the form of high pressure over most of the West Coast. The humidity would continue. It would be another day of spiking temperatures in the mid-nineties and the air, to add the final touch of perfection, was in the unhealthy range for those, according to the meteorologists, in "sensitive categories." Terry thought that encompassed anybody who had to breathe the damn stuff.

He took another shower. He'd taken three showers in the last twenty-four hours. Then he left for work. He did two things before he got downtown to SPD and resumed the hunt for Constantina Basilaskos's killer. He stopped in at the Cathedral of the Blessed Sacrament, the Gothic angels and carvings and stony saints ringing the outer front of the sandstone-colored cathedral strange companions to the office buildings around it. The usual assortment of mumblers and crusty-eyed early morning street people waited for unwary passersby or shambled to the priests when they came out to open the doors. Terry came here often in the morning. He sat for maybe fifteen minutes. It was always cool and dark, the altar always lit. He didn't pray. He wasn't even quite sure why he made this detour now. But he felt better afterward. He wondered, sometimes, as he sat in the cool stony dimness with the altar alight before him, what it would have been like to drink here. Nice, probably. Maybe it wouldn't have been so bad all those years to drink quietly in a church instead of a succession of bars around town.

He glanced around this morning. He recognized the half dozen regulars. Old gents with shabby clothes, Hispanic women. The guy in a dark three-piece who Terry figured was someone at the capitol or the legislature with a lot of guilt.

And today, he spotted two new faces. One ahead of him in a pew, a young man in a yellow wind-breaker. Behind him, another man in his forties maybe, in a business suit without the tie, like he'd just slipped it off to look more casual.

Terry thought he was getting as spooked as Rosie last night. Shooters or sightseers on rooftops. Unseen cars trailing them. Now a couple of tails on him when he came to sit in the cathedral? *Maybe a drink's what I need to shape me up,* a seductive little voice nudged inside his head.

Angry at his own imagination, he abruptly got up and walked out. There was no one following him or

Rose. *Because, you shmuck,* he swore at himself, *no one gives a shit where one old cop goes or what he does.*

He liked being a cop in the capital. He'd had the run of burglars and thieves and assaults like every other cop everywhere, but he'd also busted a state senator for urinating on a Monterey cypress on the capitol grounds one night. He'd helped out on the dignitary protection detail for two presidents when they visited Sacramento. He'd just missed, in fact, being on the detail that helped the Secret Service guard Gerald Ford when he came to town and Squeaky Fromme tried to shoot him. Her gun jammed.

He wondered whether it was the long nights and long days, the increasing volume his job took up in his life that squeezed out his wives and his two kids, a son and daughter now grown and living in Nevada and Arizona. He rarely saw either of them. Cards on birthdays. Calls on Christmas. The rest of the time, silence. He was supposed to be a grandfather in seven months when his daughter Ella had her first baby. He assumed he'd get a call when it happened.

He looked up J Street. He must have passed the Korinthou Diner a thousand times over the years and never eaten there or thought about it. Now it was an integral part of his most intense efforts. Like so many places around Sacramento, stores, even vacant lots where he had memories of crimes and people as vivid as any time he spent with his family.

He headed over to Carl's Jr. in the Downtown Mall under the milky, hot morning sky. He ate breakfast there, like he tried to most mornings. It was fast, anonymous.

He was pleased to feel eager, as he went through cornflakes and coffee and orange-flavored juice, to get at what happened to Constantina Basilaskos. Terry paid jauntily when he was finished. Anything was possible, even on this miserable day when everyone else looked wilted and irritable.

He and Rose were going to clear this one.

The bastard in his seersucker sport coat didn't have a chance.

Everybody in Robbery-Homicide pretended they didn't see Bernasconi and Deputy Chief Arnold Mayer conversing with some animation in his office.

Rose had gotten in a little before Terry. She was working the phones and her not very recent desktop, the limited computer technology available to detectives.

"What's going on?" Terry asked, sitting down, the case files on his desk on other matters rebuking him for his inattention to them.

"He showed up a little while ago. Went straight in."

"That doesn't look good."

"No," Rose said, low. She nodded to someone on the phone and scribbled on a pad.

Terry saw that there were eight phone messages since he had left last night, one from Fabulous Fabiani. He called the pathologist and made an appointment to come over in thirty minutes.

"Take a look." Rose shoved rap sheets at him across their conjoined desks. "Harry Standhope and Jerry Karamandrachos."

Terry ran down the printout entries with a practiced eye. Standhope was being very civic-minded.

He had left one of the messages. He could come in at ten to do his duty with the police artist. Terry called quickly and set it up. Standhope was, as he said, a naturalized citizen from the sovereign nation of Jamaica. He had two arrests in the last five years, one for disturbing the peace, one for misdemeanor possession of a controlled substance.

Rose was off the phone. Terry pointed to Harry Standhope's rap. "First bust is for a rumpus with his girlfriend. Second's marijuana. Harry's not on probation." That was worth a sigh of relief. When the case went to court—and Terry was keeping his optimism firmly in place about that—Harry Standhope's credibility, based on his prior record, would be critically important. He had to be believable to the trial jury. Terry told Rose about the stash he had left in place the night before.

Rose nodded. "Good call. No point in burning him on that."

Rose had worked Narcotics and knew the delicate compromises that sometimes had to be made. She added, "How you going to let the DA know, the time comes to put Harry to work?"

Terry shrugged. "I'll whisper in Harry's ear, he should go to the DA, come clean on his own. DA'll have a lot more confidence in him."

Rose slid two paper-clipped pages to him. "Your half of the Korinthou employees for the last two years. There've been ten. The kid was right. Nobody wanted to work for them. I been on the phone to Tax and Consumer Affairs, see what the Basilaskoses declared and what kind of complaints might've been made against them for unfair labor practices."

"You are a hot dog, Tafoya. Take it as a friendly warning."

Terry was half serious. There were side effects if one partner was obviously and certifiably churning out more paper than the other. The other partner, through no fault of his own, could appear lazy. Terry had been tagged as a hot dog himself in the past and forcibly but quietly told to cool his ardor for casework. His response had been to agree absolutely, buy as many rounds of drinks as it took to damp down the situation, and go back to working like he always had, prudently slipping some of his efforts to his partner. It made everyone happy.

Rose waved it aside. "Look at the Karamandrachos kid's rap. He's clean except for a traffic beef and the felony vandalism."

As Terry went down the brief printout, Rose said, "Hey. Here comes Mr. Rogers."

Terry, along with the six other detectives and assorted clericals in Robbery-Homicide, at that moment watched Deputy Chief Mayer shake hands with Bernasconi and leave his office, tugging closer the lapels of his dark blue suit coat as if it were nippy today rather than hot. He was called Mr. Rogers because, although a generally well regarded and decent commanding officer, he was not an imposing figure even if he had a fairly spacious office on the third floor looking out at the enormous new federal courthouse. He had a sallow, round face and sloping shoulders and mousy gray hair. He also had been seriously wounded during an auto supply store burglary as a patrol cop eighteen years earlier.

Bernasconi stood in his office doorway, pensive,

until the deputy chief was into the elevator to whisk him upstairs. He glanced out at the detectives. "Terry. Rose. Come in. Then McGivery and Felderstein."

Rose raised her eyebrows and they both went into his office.

"What's doing at the high command?" Terry asked lightly.

Bernasconi folded his arms. "Deputy Chief Mayer wanted to make a personal visit to what he referred to as our 'troubled' division. He's very concerned our 'troubled' division will screw up the report he's sending to the chief, who then sends it to the mayor and City Council at the end of the week on this year's crime stats to date. The trend lines need to continue in the right direction, was the way he put it."

"We're troubled?" Rose asked.

"He's taking a very personal interest in our success, he said. He doesn't want bad clearances to turn into a problem."

"Like what?"

Bernasconi shook his head and sat down. "He said there would be consequences."

"Oh," Terry noted unhappily. "What do you want us to do?"

Bernasconi spread out his matrix of cases being handled by the pairs of detectives he supervised. "You two have five cases open. Three more came in last night and I've assigned them around so you can wrap up what you've got. Give me the ones that you can close up now."

Rose and Terry alternated reciting the investigations they were handling and the likeliest to be completed. Two grocery store holdups with fatal shootings, a carjacking in which the driver was dragged to death when thrown out, an arson at a mattress warehouse with a burned transient, and a baby bludgeoned to death by his mother with an old-fashioned lead window weight.

"And the purse snatch, right?"

"That's turned into a double homicide," Terry said gently. "The victim's husband died of a heart attack last night. Hearing about what happened did it. Whoever shot her is good for him too."

Bernasconi frowned. "So how close are you?"

"Well"—Rose gave Terry a quick acknowledging nod—"we started last night with a random shooting. That isn't looking good at all. Shooter accosts the victim, lets her have it, and he's got a car to drive him away."

"So we're talking about two pukes?"

Terry nodded. "Yeah. And the car makes a puke from county jail or state prison unlikely. Impossible. What we end up with right now are old employees who we'll run down today, many as we can. Somebody who knew how the diner was run, somebody close to the Basilaskoses." He told Bernasconi about Jerry Karamandrachos's complaints.

Rose said, "Ter and I haven't brainstormed this one, but I'm thinking the kid for this. He knows the diner, knows the victims and hates their guts, and he could've set up something."

Bernasconi, Terry noted, caught the implication instantly. "Set up a murder? Set up a robbery?"

"Provided information to the shooter and the driver."

"What were they after?"

Terry shrugged. "We got to go through the stuff from the diner and the financials for these people. There's got to be some money angle here."

"Find it soon," Bernasconi said. "I don't want to be a 'troubled' division and I do not want consequences coming down on us. We won't like them."

They turned to leave. There wasn't a sense of desperation in Bernasconi's comments; he was not prone to flattery or being intimidated. But Terry and Rose knew what he was saying very directly: Clear some cases. *Clear this one quickly*.

Terry paused at the door. "Does the name Kelso ring any bells?" he asked Bernasconi.

"Kelso?"

"Name on one of the paper bags of cash we found last night at the diner. It bothers me."

Rose added, "We got a couple of other bags and names. Anfuso, Carrillo, Keck."

Bernasconi brightened and found a dog-eared telephone directory from a short stack of notebooks behind his desk. It was a listing of city employees by department.

He flipped the pages. "How about Michael Kelso, Building Department, Inspection Division?"

"That's where I heard it," Terry chortled. "He came through court one morning about a year ago when I was waiting to testify on a case. DA dismissed a couple-count indictment for bribery."

Bernasconi flipped more pages in the city employee directory. "Albert Schultz, Fire. Paul Carrillo, Health Department. Alonzo Keck, Sanitation." He beamed, pleased with his impromptu contribution to the investigation. "Well, you better go take a look

71

at these four esteemed public servants. I think you've got a much better chance finding a white man in a seersucker with a getaway car and driver there."

They passed Felderstein and McGivery about to go in, looking as if they'd been summoned to see the principal. Terry couldn't resist pimping Felderstein. "You shouldn't've been spending the money, Nick. Tough times, you got to have every buck you can lay your hands on."

Rose said mournfully, "Tow package on an SUV doesn't buy any groceries."

Felderstein and McGivery exchanged brief worried glances and closed the door.

Terry said, "That felt good. Okay, let's see what the uniforms dug up."

He and Rose reviewed the reports compiled by the CSU techs and the uniformed officers. Four additional witnesses had seen parts of the incident. One described the man in the seersucker who jumped into a car that roared up as being about forty years old, which perked Terry up given Harry Standhope's and Rose's characterization of the shooter as being as old as him. The witnesses filled in the shooter's clothing: gray slacks and loafers, a dark blue or black tie. Mrs. Moselle Washington also saw the unmistakable Harry Standhope rush to the victim's aid, bending over her, even ripping his own shirt off to try to stanch the gush of blood from her neck. That was swell, Terry and Rose agreed. Harry the Good Samaritan would be a vital witness. The car too was more clearly identified as probably a Crown Victoria or similar large four-door. It was brown. It was clean, late model. It definitely had California plates, but no one had gotten any numbers. There was only one other person in it, the driver. No witness could say anything more concrete than that it appeared, in the shocking suddenness of events and the glare of the sun, that the driver was a man.

Terry said, "So we got to work the houses around the scene. There's got to be a better witness."

"Harry's the best so far," Rose agreed. "See the six statements, people who were on the bus with Constantina? She was excited. She's holding that goddamn black handbag like it's going to blow up."

"Harry's good on that. None of these six observant citizens saw anything else. Nobody on the sidewalk or in the street saw the thing go down."

Rose let her phone ring until the voice message rolled over. "That's what bothers me, Ter. All last night. The more I thought about it. That's why I think the Karamandrachos kid's good for something in this."

"No. But I see where you're going." He looked at his watch and the white-faced, fly-specked old clock hanging over the watercooler. "Standhope's coming in at ten. You want to take a jaunt to see Fabiani first, find out what rabbits he's pulled out of the hat?"

"Let's go," Rose said. "But you got it too? The thing that really sticks out here?"

"Like a one-finger salute. Suppose we got crooked building or fire inspectors getting paid off. They get stiffed, they get mad, they decide to nail Mrs. B because she's holding out. What, I don't know because

73

the brown bags were all ready to hand out. Sake of argument, dirty city public employees are shooting people they're squeezing."

Now Terry's phone was ringing, but he let it go too. "Or how about we got something worth bucks we don't know about yet, the Karamandrachos kid or some former employee or some regular does, and they either sell it or get the word out and the bad guys nail Mrs. B while she's carrying whatever the hell it is?"

"Right, right," Rose said enthusiastically. "A setup means you pick some place nice and quiet to take the handbag from her. That's why it's a setup. You've got places all the way from the diner to the bus, couple of miles."

"So how come," Terry finished up, "if this is a setup by someone, we've got this Wild West shoot-out on a city street? Who cares if you've got a getaway car? Look at the risks. A cop comes along. There's a traffic tie-up. Cal Trans's got the next street all ripped up and you're backed up to Sutterville Road. So why's the shooter playing cowboy on Thirty-third Avenue?"

Rose grinned. "Maybe it is city employees. Maybe that's how they think you do it."

"I'm sticking my neck way out here, but you can't get on the city payroll if you're that fucking stupid."

"You are way out on that one."

They went to Sacramento's necropolis, the coroner's office.

It would have been just as easy to talk to Dr. Fabiani on the phone. Or he could have faxed his report. But he'd gotten under Terry's skin yesterday and it seemed appropriate to return the favor.

The Sacramento County Coroner was a twenty-four-hour operation. The graveyard shift was as busy as any other, perhaps to live up to its unfortunate name. Bodies were brought to the steel crypt in the basement from accidents all over the county, hospitals and nursing homes, suicides and homicides. Bodies were wrestled from wrecked cars, railroad and Metro Rail tracks, sloughs and the American or Sacramento Rivers, from attics and bedrooms and under homes. Rose told him about the memorable time, as a rookie, when she had gone into the American River near Garden Highway to help heft a three-hundred-pound male body back to where it could be winched up. Sometimes bodies came from bathtubs or on boats along the rivers, hanging from ceiling fixtures or rafters, even from cars and motor homes with the motors still blindly running. Terry disliked the grim cold gray-blue labyrinth intensely. But like every cop, homicide in particular, periodic visits were a necessity. He and Rose passed through the steel crypt crowded with bodies, the eerie snap and blue light of a bug zapper competing with several small radios on long white tables, coroner's assistants munching on jelly beans.

With distaste, Terry saw a crew of assistant coroners measuring, photographing, weighing, and then wrapping two bodies in plastic and sliding them into refrigerated shelves. It unpleasantly reminded him of fish sticks in the freezer at home.

"I love what you've done with the place," Terry

said when he and Rose went into Fabiani's small office off the main floor.

"This is an occasion. Twice in less than twenty-four hours, Detective Nye."

Rose wrinkled her nose at the vague but distinctly disconcerting smells. "You've got the autopsy results on Constantina Basilaskos?"

"Even better. I have both Mr. and Mrs. Basilaskos. Knowing that Detective Nye was involved and anxious, I bumped Mr. Basilaskos to the head of the line when he came in late last evening."

"I didn't think you ever slept," Terry said.

"Would you like to see them?"

"Is there anything to see?" Terry asked, sensing Fabiani was needling him.

"A trained observer like you will glean a lot of vital information, I'm sure. Come with me."

Rose shrugged and grimaced and they ended up in front of a bank of stainless steel refrigerator vaults. Fabiani found the two he wanted and slid open the contents. The bodies, separated by their metal trolleys and shiny in plastic wrap, barely looked human.

"Let's begin with Mrs. Constantina Basilaskos."

"Let's," Terry said.

"Age sixty-two, female, sixty-seven inches—"

Terry interrupted because he was feeling annoyed and sickish in the unnaturally chilled room and he didn't like seeing his two victims in their present peculiar condition. It was somehow more disorienting than the violent way Constantina had died.

"What's the damage, Doc?" he demanded. Rose peered thoughtfully at Angelo.

"Constantina Basilaskos died from massive tissue

and blood loss from wounds to the upper thoracic area and spinal cord. She was dead before she fell. There was no sign of gunshot residue, so her assailant or assailants were some distance away when she was shot, at least five feet, I'd say. This is basically what we knew last evening."

"Yeah."

"The wounds are consistent with a nine-millimeter bullet. I understand you found nine-millimeter shell casings? I retrieved a single nine-millimeter bullet, deformed a great deal, from this victim."

"So tell me something we don't know," Terry said impatiently. One of the radios had started putting out "Twilight Time."

"We move to victim number two, Angelo Basilaskos. I'll skip his statistics. Mr. Basilaskos suffered from diabetes and kidney stones. He had an attack of acute diverticulitis three days prior to his death, which involved a trip to our marvelous emergency room because he had lost approximately a quart and a half of blood."

"How the hell did he do that?"

Fabiani grinned and slid the trays back, closing the doors. "Apparently during defecation. The effect of this blood loss and the subsequent shock of his wife's death contributed in my opinion to his fatal coronary incident. He had a ninety percent blockage of one coronary artery and a fifty percent blockage of another."

"So the news of his wife getting shot killed him? You can say that?"

"He might have had a heart attack if the teakettle went off unexpectedly but yes, this got him first."

Terry nodded appreciatively. That was good news. The medical evidence would allow the DA to charge whoever killed Constantina with Angelo too. It had a satisfying symmetry to it. It was fair.

Fabiani relished his meticulous and swiftly made reports. Then Rose said, "That isn't Angelo Basilaskos."

"Yes, it is," Dr. Fabiani said testily. "I supervised the encapsulement myself."

Terry was intrigued. "Simple to find out. Let's roll the old boy out again."

"That isn't necessary," Fabiani protested, but Rose and Terry had already slid the metal tray and its plastic contents out once more. Terry studied the unfamiliar flat, white, toothless face. "You showed us the wrong body, Doc."

Fabiani pushed him aside and stared. He sputtered. "The numbers match." He hastily examined a clipboard hanging nearby. "This *is* Angelo Basilaskos. Deceased August fifth at 2245 hours."

Terry patted Rose on the shoulder. "We know Angelo Basilaskos. That ain't Angelo Basilaskos. You mixed your stiffs up. You better be more careful with your work, Doc. First time in your life you might make a mistake."

Fabiani spun to face Terry. "I'll be prepared to give impeccably accurate testimony at the trial *if* you ever arrest the killer."

Terry let that go by because he felt the trip had been more than worthwhile. "Send the paperwork soon as you figure out who you got bunking beside Mrs. B."

Fabulous Fabiani was not about to let the detectives leave on that note. He snapped, "You better see

Forensics, Detective Nye. I found something underneath Constantina Basilaskos's fingernails."

"What is it?" Rose asked, intrigued.

"Plastic."

"It's plastic, garden-variety plastic," said the skinny, chirpy criminalist next door in the crime lab. "I did some microscopic examination, ran a polymer test, and it's plastic okay." He held up the small clear evidence bottle, sealed, that appeared to contain four or five tiny greenish fragments.

"That's all?" Terry asked disappointedly. "Anything special at all?"

"Nope. Just plastic. Like a trash bag. That's what I think it is."

Rose nodded. "This lady worked in a diner. Probably had a lot of plastic trash bags around."

"Can you match it if we get you more?"

The skinny criminalist shook his head quickly. "Probably not. Plastic is pretty generic. Best I'd be able to give you is what I've got here." He shook the bottle slightly. "Green color. Polymers match generally."

"Okay," Terry said. "We better get out of here, make sure everything's all set for Harry."

The criminalist tapped his forehead and held out several typed SPD form reports. "I did your blood test right away. Shirt's got a big old bloodstain partly removed by chlorine bleach and detergent."

"Standhope's shirt," Terry said, taking the reports. "Just what he told us and our witnesses said."

"And right this minute," the young criminalist said excitedly, "I'm doing your shell casing and the bullet. You want me to start the paperwork for an atomic plasma deal?" He seemed to relish the idea of taking the bullet and subjecting it to a stream of high-speed particle bombardment, which could reveal the specific atomic structure of the elements and isolate the bullet almost as starkly as a fingerprint. The only problem with the very sophisticated test was that the FBI performed it, there were forms to fill out, and it could take some time to get the results.

"We'll see," Terry said. "With any luck we won't need it."

The young criminalist shrugged and Terry read that the kid didn't think he was much fun.

Rose nodded and she examined her own fingernails, which were cut short and well tended, unlike Terry's because he absentmindedly chewed them occasionally. "How do you get plastic from a trash bag under your nails?"

The criminalist moved his head around to show he didn't have the slightest idea.

Terry had never considered the mechanics of the process until that moment. He brightened, looking to his partner. "How about you try to scrape a trash bag open with your fingers?"

"Yeah? Why would she do that?"

"Really good garbage," Terry answered. "Come on, let's get out of here."

Chapter Seven

Harry Standhope was punctual and Terry and Rose greeted him and got him settled in with the police composite artist.

"I didn't sleep too good, man," Harry said, sitting down on a lime-green plastic chair. "Thinking about it again all night."

"You're lucky you don't see something like that every day." Terry thought, despite his unusual appearance, that Harry would present well to a jury. He spoke directly. He didn't equivocate. DAs like witnesses who can answer simply and sound certain.

"Did you remember anything else while you were waiting for the sun to come up?" Rose asked.

"Little bit. Maybe some of his face. He's losing his hair."

"Come again?" Terry asked.

"I saw the back of his head. He's got a big bald spot there, shiny bald spot."

Rose said, "Sounds kind of like a tonsure."

"A what?" Terry demanded. Rose liked to do crosswords in the *San Francisco Chronicle* or whatever was lying around. She was always coming up with nutty words or phrases.

"Tonsure's a shaved round spot on the top of a monk's head. You know, a monk? Used to be something they did. I don't know if that changed."

"Yeah, thanks for the breaking news," Terry said. To Harry, "Okay, we really appreciate you taking the time to come down. This's going to be a big help." He didn't add that, at the moment, Harry was their best witness to both the crime and the suspect's appearance.

"I try to get it right," Harry said. "I got the morning off."

Last night they'd established that he was a carpet installer for a small outfit on Del Paso Boulevard.

"Kaneesha any better about this?" Terry asked.

"She won't let me in today. She's mad." He grinned ruefully.

"Sorry, man."

Harry Standhope folded his big hands as the composite artist readied the computerized jigsaw pieces of human face, eyes of all shapes and sizes, chins, noses, facial hair, mouths big and small, that he would display until Harry made a selection. Piece by puzzle piece they would layer up a suspect's face and create a final picture. SPD would make a wide media distribution, local TV and include the Bay Area stations too, the newspapers. Terry was confident somebody would identify this man if Harry could just summon up enough detail.

Terry and Rose went out to their desks. "Tonsure," Terry said disgustedly.

"Can I help it if I had a good education and you didn't?" Rose replied.

They worked out an order to the investigation since the lists of people to interview were increasing. Already they had witnesses to follow up with, the names of former employees who had worked for the Basilaskoses, Jerry Karamandrachos's names of people who might be hostile to the dead couple, Angelo's partial collection of regulars at the Korinthou, the Karamandrachos clan itself, and other friends of Constantina and Angelo, and the newly exposed city officials who might shed light on why their names were carefully affixed to brown papers bags of twenty-dollar bills.

"We got a resource problem," Rose said, when she looked at the scope of the task.

"So what's new? We ain't getting McGivery or Felderstein or anybody else to lend a hand." Terry frowned. "What feels good to you?"

"I like getting rid of stuff." Rose yawned. "I didn't sleep so great. When I did get home, when I did start to get some sleep." She grabbed her notebook, stuck her handcuffs in their holster on her belt under her tasteful jacket at the back. "Walt and I did the same dance again. I'm gone too much. Too much time on the job."

"Major family problem?"

"I don't sleep." Rose sighed.

This troubled Terry. His own breakups began in exactly this fashion. "Take my advice, Rosie," he said, "I ask for you to spend too much time, tell me to go to hell."

"I don't do it for you, Ter," Rose said a little sharply. "Egomaniac."

Terry stood up. *Let it go.* It was a raw nerve. "Very funny. So you're saying you'd like to take the time this morning to check out the Karamandrachos kid's alibi?"

"You said we'd close it out last night, right? That's how come we stayed out, I got home late."

They walked out into the heat and the noise from too many cars, trucks, and buses on the city's busy downtown main streets. The cries and taunts floated down from inmates playing basketball on the county jail's fifth floor overlooking the street.

"I call them best I can, Rose. I ain't perfect, appearances notwithstanding."

"Notwithstanding? You are on me for *tonsure* and you're trying to sound like a damn lawyer."

"Christ, you're right. Been around the bastards so much I talk like them."

They went to see Patty Russo, Jerry Karamandrachos's girlfriend and purported alibi.

It took a little while to track her down at Dawson's, the fashionable restaurant on the main floor of the Hyatt Regency where she worked as a waitress. The Hyatt had its own valet parking, but Rose didn't want to pay and then wait and wait for the department to reimburse her, so they had a hard time finding parking on the street, which really meant a space she could put the unmarked police car without worrying about it getting clipped or otherwise damaged.

Because if something hit or scraped the car, she and Terry would have to account for it in excruciating detail on several department accident forms.

Patty Russo was twenty, brunette, and she smiled automatically. She was carrying plates of English bangers and fried eggs to a table of jabbering dark-suited men and one jabbering woman Terry took to be either in a financial profession or an attorney.

Terry and Rose, with the permission of the elegantly-business-suited woman who asked if they wanted a table for two, guided Patty Russo to one side so they weren't in the middle of the important people gobbling working breakfasts.

"I'm very busy this morning," she said pleasantly. "Two other girls called in sick."

"This'll be quick and painless," Rose said, equally pleasant. "Do you know Jerry Karamandrachos?"

"Yes, I do. I do."

"When did you last see him?"

"Oh. Can I ask why?"

"You can. Be a big help if you'd give me an answer first."

Terry smiled, avuncular and calming. Rose was a little grating for some reason. "Look, we can see you're swamped here. We just need a few things and we're on our way."

Patty Russo smiled again. "I saw him yesterday. Last night."

"About what time?" Rose made notes and regarded her levelly.

"I got off work at four. We were supposed to get together when he was off work at five-thirty. That's not what happened."

85

"No? What changed your plans?" Rose asked.

"Jerry called me around, no, just before four. He said his boss was letting him go home early. So we arranged to meet at Capital Park at five. We had dinner, we went to my apartment over on N Street. He left around eight, maybe nine."

"Anything unusual about his getting off work like that?"

Patty Russo smiled for an instant. She noticed the business-suited woman gamely trying to keep two remaining waitresses moving briskly and seat people coming in. "I really better get back to work."

Terry blocked her. "How often had Jerry gotten off work early?"

"Never. I was very surprised. His boss usually kept him right up to the last minute and sometimes later. He didn't like his boss."

"That would be Mr. or Mrs. Basilaskos?" Terry asked.

"Mrs. He didn't say much about the husband. I think she pretty much ran the diner. She ran Jerry ragged anyway."

Rose glanced up. "Jerry didn't like her?"

"No. Not much."

"Meaning he disliked her? Hated her? Could you be more specific?" Rose pushed.

"He really disliked her."

Terry nodded. "You talk to Jerry since last night?"

"I talked to him this morning. He told me what had happened."

Rose nodded as if this confirmed a sinister fact. "Did you both agree on a story to tell us?"

"No. He's making plans now."

"To do what?" Terry asked.

"He's moving in with me. We'd been thinking about it for a while and it seems right suddenly."

"Great," Rose said, clearly unsatisfied. "Did he say anything about why he was getting off early? Why Mrs. Basilaskos was doing something so out of character?"

Patty Russo shook her head. "He thought it was about her husband. She was very excited. He assumed there was some medical problem."

She smiled engagingly and said she had to go, navigating her way by four tables calling for her. Rose closed her notepad and sourly looked around. "Well, we know it wasn't Angelo. He didn't mention it last night."

"Coulda been him and he didn't get a chance to tell us." Terry thanked the hostess on their way through the darkly paneled entrance where more jabbering and arrogant diners had lined up.

"She's going to alibi the kid," Rose said, when they were on the sidewalk again.

"So that's why the attitude in there?" Terry asked his partner with curiosity.

"Yuppies." Rose glanced back irritatedly. "Yuppies," she repeated.

"I know what you mean," Terry said, grasping all in the one word. "Jesus, this stinks." He squinted into the blue sky scattering hot sunlight around the sharp corners of the office buildings, glaring off the capitol's dull metal dome across the street, making the shadows of the panting people stumbling down the sidewalk look twenty feet long.

Terry suggested that Rose could best work

through her envy, frustration, or whatever base emotion had gripped her in the last twenty minutes if they smoked one of the city employees who would be missing a paper bag of money this month.

"Let's give somebody a hard time," Rose agreed. Maybe it would compensate for the bad times at home. Terry really liked the way she got into the spirit of these things.

It took several calls from the car, checking a map, and then more calls to pinpoint where Deputy City Building Inspector Michael Kelso was that morning. Rose gunned the car through several red lights, hitting the siren, and screeched up to a former car dealership in the process of renovation just above Sixteenth Street, near the sprawling Convention Center Complex where something always seemed to be under construction and cement trucks and scaffolding blocking street lanes slowed traffic to a crawl. Terry didn't begrudge or chastise her about her driving even if it was an unnecessary display. It seemed to make her feel better.

They bought sweaty cold cans of soda from a cart and tromped into the dusty, empty auto showroom.

Michael Kelso was on the second floor pounding on the walls with a rubber-tipped hammer. Terry did the honors and laid out who they were and why they had come to find him in particular in this unkind and unforgiving heat.

Kelso opened his eyes very wide and stopped pounding.

Terry spotted Rose's confusion that Michael

Kelso was a short, broad Asian about thirty-five years old. "It's like the old joke," Terry murmured. "His name used to be Sheinbaum but he changed it to Gottlieb."

"I don't know what you're talking about," Kelso said. "Money? A diner? I don't know what you're talking about."

"You ever been to the Korinthou Diner, Mr. Kelso?" Terry asked, wearing his most bored, disbelieving expression.

"I don't know. I don't keep a logbook of where I eat. Maybe I was there sometime."

"Big tipper?" Rose offered.

"I beg your pardon?"

"She means, did you leave a big tip or somehow make such an impression so that the diner's owners would want to set aside some extra walking-around money for you?"

"I don't know what you're talking about," he said, sweating heavily, fingering the hammer. He had one pair of thick glasses on and another dangling around his neck by a black cord. He was in a blue short-sleeved shirt and a yellow tie.

Terry knew Rose knew that they had a twitching contact just by connecting him to the Korinthou. He pressed in swiftly. "Okay, bud. Let's take it the hard way. If you've ever inspected the Korinthou Diner, we'll find out. If you've ever set foot in the place, we're going to find out and then we'll be talking to your supervisor downtown."

Kelso blinked and wiped his upper lip. In the street, truck drivers and construction workers were shouting at each other in Spanish. "I really don't know what you're talking about," he said again.

Rose strolled around the large, empty, still-to-be renovated office space, pausing at a sooty fireplace left over from the building's earliest incarnation as a nineteenth-century corn baron's home. "Detective Nye's right, Mr. Kelso. We will find out. If we don't find out from your records, I bet Schultz, Carrillo, and Keck can fill us in."

"Have you talked to any of them yet?" Kelso gurgled.

Terry nodded. "They've been very cooperative."

Rose instinctively ducked and reached for her gun, at the same time Terry reached for his, as Kelso threw the hammer violently at the wall to their right.

"Don't move!" Rose shouted, snapping into a firing stance.

Kelso's short arms shot into the air and he stood, shivering with anger and fear. "Those bastards!" he said. "Stupid cowards."

Terry let out a tense breath and put his gun away slowly. "Easy does it, bud. Why don't you sit down on that cement bag and tell us what's going on?"

Rose roughly maneuvered Kelso to a stack of cement bags four high. Kelso lowered his head and wiped his glasses on his shirt, then slipped on the pair around his neck. "You all right?" Rose asked, breathing a little hard.

He nodded. "I am not a criminal. I am not a greedy man. I don't think like that."

"Who does?" Terry said sympathetically.

"We play poker together, Paul, Alonzo, Al. I bet it was Alonzo who couldn't shut up, wasn't it?"

Terry nodded noncommittally. "What can I tell you?"

Kelso coughed nervously. "So we play cards for about a year, once a week, we alternate houses. So one Thursday night, Paul looked around the table and he said, 'I just realized we've got everything you need to make a living in Sacramento sitting right here tonight.' It was a joke, that's all."

"Meaning what?" Rose asked.

"Well, Paul's in the Health Department, Alonzo's in Sanitation, Al's in the Fire Department, and I'm with Building Inspections."

"It dawns on you four that you've got businessmen in a box, if you want," Terry finished and Kelso nodded. Rose crossed her arms. She seemed to look down on the sweating, timorous deputy building inspector from a great height.

"Not immediately, we didn't put it together like that," Kelso forced out. "But Paul kept after it and it sounded so simple and we only had to find overlapping businesses, places we all could plausibly be assigned to check."

"Why's that?" Rose asked calmly.

"None of us could take advantage of the others, we'd all know exactly where we were asking for contributions and the amounts."

"And the shakedown was born," Terry said. "How much? How many places we talking about?"

"Twenty to thirty. We added and dropped businesses if they were really having a hard time coming up with it."

"Nice," Rose said.

Kelso straightened stiffly. "It wasn't much for any

one business. Our going rate was one hundred a month. For the four of us that came to four hundred dollars. A business that couldn't afford four hundred dollars a month probably wasn't going to make it anyway," he said defensively.

"And you and the gang were working the Korinthou Diner?" Rose asked, uncrossing her arms. "Those two old people who came in at the crack of dawn every day slipping it to you guys so you wouldn't write them up?"

"It wasn't like that," Kelso protested, rising off the cement bag, quivering with misplaced indignation. "There weren't any fire or health violations. There certainly weren't any structural problems. We weren't letting public safety violations go uncorrected."

"Big of you," Terry said harshly. "Everybody paid up for the insurance, right? You get your goddamn hundred bucks first of the month and the Basilaskoses figured you guys wouldn't haul them in front of your agencies. Bet immigrants like them were big fans of yours. Scared of government clowns."

Rose moved very close to Kelso. "That why you shot Constantina Basilaskos yesterday? She going to turn you in? She wouldn't pay anymore?"

Kelso shook his head so sharply his glasses came off and would have gone sailing except they were tethered around his neck. "I didn't shoot anybody! I'm not a criminal!"

"You and one of your poker-playing buddies shot that old lady yesterday and we've got a witness who saw you," Terry said levelly. "We get a look at Anfuso, Carrillo, and Keck, it's over. You got a little window here, bud. You tell us what happened now and we can help you with the DA."

Rose nodded slowly. "Later, you're on your own. No deals. We got the death penalty in this state. People stacking up on death row. Pretty soon we'll be giving you guys the needle like you're on a conveyor belt."

Kelso wailed once, head down. "Believe me! I didn't shoot anybody. I've got three kids. None of us hurt anybody. It was just extra money."

Terry looked helplessly at Rose. "Okay, it seems a shame too. I think you just got led in too far. That's what I think. Stand up."

"What for?"

Rose had her handcuffs out, taking the man's shaking arm, cuffing him efficiently. "You're under arrest, sir. Right now it's for extortion. Later that could turn into two murders. Both murder one, that means you got a needle for sure in your future."

They took Kelso by an arm and hustled him downstairs as Terry recited the Miranda warning. Kelso started talking quickly, his voice squeaking up from fright. "I can prove where I was, I can tell you everything, all the businesses we've been dealing with, because I did not kill anybody, I could not kill anybody, and Paul and Al will say the same thing and Alonzo—" He suddenly stopped talking as they got to the glass door of the auto showroom. Rose had called for backup and two very nearby units roared up, lights and sirens heralding them, as she and Terry, with Kelso between them, stepped to the sidewalk. Uniforms jumped out and surrounded them.

Kelso said slowly to Terry, "I was so rattled I forgot Alonzo's on vacation in Yellowstone until the tenth. That's why we didn't pick up this month's payment on the first, we all agreed it was fairer to wait until he was back."

Head pushed down, Kelso was crammed into the back of a patrol car. "You lied," he scolded Terry and Rose. "You haven't talked to any of them."

"What can I say?" Terry shrugged. "When you're right, you're right."

"Think of it as an oversight," Rose added. "We'll see two of your little buddies today. And somebody's going to Yellowstone. For sure."

The uniforms took the necessary information to get Kelso booked and processed and sped off, lights and sirens once again making heads up and down the street—construction and office workers, bike messengers—turn in fear, relief, or curiosity. Terry thought for a moment he could tell Rose about his unsettling experience at the cathedral, but decided against it. He didn't want to let her know her sense of danger or being watched had apparently gotten under his skin.

They went to get lunch and track down the remaining recipients of Constantina's brown bag specials. Rose suggested they find Jerry Karamandrachos's parents to see if there was any link between the contraband cigarettes and the monthly payoffs. It was possible that the city officials were working the cigarettes too.

Rose said, "Could be this is a done deal. Maybe you get that ten bucks after all, Ter."

Terry had been on so many promising arrests and trails of evidence that blew away like dust. All he said was, "Let's hope one of these assholes has a bald spot. Or like you say, a *tonsure*."

Chapter Eight

It was close to four in the afternoon when Terry and Rose drove back to Citrus Heights and ended up at the Brendel and Sons Funeral Home on Auburn Boulevard. Terry was tired, his feet hot and sore, and his current transitory pleasure was that they had managed to get across the six lanes of Greenback Boulevard, a main thoroughfare in north Sacramento, before much rush-hour traffic clogged it.

Earlier, after a hurried lunch, snatched at a counter up the street from where Kelso was arrested, they had tracked down and located the other three city employees. Doing so had required bringing in the Sacramento County Sheriff because Carrillo and Anfuso were outside the city. Neither Terry nor Rose had ever had trouble with the sheriff's detectives who worked Homicide, but it was rankling anyway because now they owed favors to detectives in another agency.

"Top it off, no pun, neither of these bastards has a bald spot," Terry swore. "They're both so goddamn bald they should've sprung for decent rugs."

"No sense of personal appearance," Rose agreed.

To get at Alonzo Keck they had spoken with both the Arizona State Police in Phoenix and the Yellowstone Park rangers directly. The paperwork to bring Mr. Keck back to California was hastily put together and faxed. Unfortunately, Keck fit no part of Harry Standhope's description or that of any of the other witnesses to the shooting.

He was a short, fat, black man.

The partial success and partial failure of the day's effort caused Terry and Rose to deteriorate into arguing about the best route back downtown to the police department after rush hour started, and this quickly evolved into a heated discussion about the merits of the Kings, who were on a winning streak and headed, said all the sportswriters, for the play-offs. They were playing again that night after winning the game Harry Standhope and Kaneesha had been scheduled to attend. This discussion broadened to soccer, in which Rose vainly tried to interest Terry, even when she graphically described her daughter's obliteration of another team of equally aggressive little girls the previous Saturday. "We keep this up," Rose said with pleasure, "we're going to the championship. It's down in Riverside this year."

"Hold me back."

"Okay, Riverside's a pit. But didn't your kids play anything you got really involved in?"

"Both of my kids inherited their old man's belief that the best sports are spectator sports."

"Best thing to keep the family together, sports everybody's playing," and she stopped, realizing that was the wrong thing to say to Terry. "I mean, other things are good too."

"Forget it," he said. But it did bother him because it was true. Someday he wanted to tell Rose that when things went wrong in your family, you second-guessed yourself afterward all the time. Every day.

When they got to the Brendel and Sons Funeral Home, redbrick fronted and green-and-white trimmed with great green awnings, they had settled their arguments on how to get back to the police department without fighting too much traffic and how wrong, truly and profoundly wrong it was for someone to write a gossipy, destructive biography of DiMaggio.

They found their way to a large chapellike room where a dozen men and women, including the elder Karamandrachos, spoke in hushed tones. It was a room scented with lilac. It looked, Terry thought, like the auto showroom where they'd found Kelso except it was plushly carpeted in soft blue. The air-conditioning was as bone-chilling as the coroner's office.

Mr. Karamandrachos was not pleased to see them.

"You must leave!" he said loudly. "This is a terrible time. We are making plans to bury our friends. Why are you disturbing us, why aren't you looking for their killers?"

The other people all nodded and balefully eyed Terry and Rose.

"We need to talk for just a second," Terry said to Mr. Karamandrachos. "You and your wife."

"You should be investigating this crime!"

"We are, sir," Rose said.

Not pacified very much, Mr. and Mrs. Karamandrachos went with Terry and Rose to the adjacent room. Rose closed the doors. There were ranks of folding metal chairs set out and a closed, white-lily-draped casket in front, a large smiling color photograph of a white-haired woman on a stand beside it.

Terry chewed his lip for a moment. He was not indifferent to death so much as accustomed to it in more natural surroundings, like Constantina Basilaskos last night. Funerals and the paraphernalia that went with them disturbed him greatly. When his younger brother David died of bad cocaine, after all the anguish and terror for years leading up to the horror and the inescapable feeling he had of letting David down, it was the funeral preparation that he couldn't shake off more than anything.

It was death packaged and cleaned up that scared him. It was the unspoken denial of what lay behind the flowers, the carefully chosen casket, the orchestrated service.

Being a homicide cop only prepared you to face death on its terms: shocking, unexpected, violent, chaotic.

But being a cop didn't prepare you for how most people and society treated death. It was the strong bond that linked them all, Terry thought, Rose and Fabulous Fabiani and Bernasconi, everyone they worked with. They knew what was real behind the stage show of funerals.

And every case carried with it the potential to be cleared, for some justice, however inadequate, to be done. Terry had no idea what potential lay in funerals. At this point in his life and career, he had no conviction about what came after the end.

"Ter?" Rose asked.

"Yeah?"

"I was just telling the Karamandrachoses we need their help with a problem we found last night."

"Right," Terry said, cursing himself for drifting away and leaving Rose without his full attention. "This is kind of difficult, but it may have a great deal to do with what happened to Mrs. Basilaskos."

"Yes?" Mr. Karamandrachos demanded imperiously.

"We found a secret room at the Korinthou Diner," Terry went on. "It was filled with illegal cigarettes. No duties or taxes had been paid for them."

"This must be explained in the bookkeeping," Mrs. Karamandrachos said, glancing at her husband. "Connie and Angelo never cheated anybody. They paid their taxes, state, United States. They never cheated."

Mr. Karamandrachos rose. "Yes. We have to finish the funeral plans. We want the service at St. Demetrios, the big church in Stockton. There is much to do. We must go."

"We know about your trips with Angelo to Vancouver every month," Rose said, not moving from her chair. "I bet we're going to find that the illegal cigarettes came from Canada. We can check where they were manufactured."

"We have cousins in Vancouver," Mrs. Karamandrachos snapped. "Of course we go to see them."

"You didn't go, did you?" Terry asked Mrs. Karamandrachos. "Just your husband, Angelo, and some buddies? Every couple months?"

"Of course I went," she said quickly. Terry saw the same spark of deceit between her and her husband that Rose did.

"This is nothing for us, nothing for this crime," Mr. Karamandrachos said sharply. "Why are you bothering with cigarettes when Connie was shot on the street, on her own street?"

Rose took that one easily. "The unusual nature of this shooting makes us think that the illegal cigarettes could've played a part somehow. It wasn't a random shooting. It wasn't a plain purse snatch. So we will have to devote our time and resources to tracking down this lead, sir."

Terry saw Mr. Karamandrachos sweep a fierce, incredulous gaze over him and Rose. His wife frowned.

"Listen," Mr. Karamandrachos said sharply, "the boys are coming this evening, flying in with their families. Connie and Angelo's boys. We're trying to make this easier for them, take the pain. We can't waste time, you understand?"

"Save us some time. What about the cigarettes?" Terry said.

Mr. Karamandrachos swore, caught himself, patted his wife's shoulder. "It's nothing. Okay? I give it

101

to you. Connie and Angelo work hard all their lives here, they try to make the diner big success, but they only make a little money. Enough to hang on, but not a lot." His face drew together in fury. "Then these bloodsuckers, leeches, fucking leeches come around and they tell Angelo, you pay us or we'll close your business. Close the Korinthou. So these are important Sacramento people, yes? Officials who can write a little order, stick it on your front door, and you can't open, your customers stay away, they're scared your food is poison."

Terry remained impassive but Rose's face softened slightly. Mrs. Karamandrachos said in bewilderment, "I didn't know. Poor Connie. Angelo. They should've told us, we'd do something."

"I did something," Mr. Karamandrachos said firmly. "I said, I will get you things you can sell for extra money, enough so you don't have to worry. So we go to Canada, we bring back cigarettes, and Connie sells them. It's not very much. So we were going to figure out how to stop these fucking leeches but it's too late. They get away with making Connie and Angelo criminals. Just to save their business." A heavy tear dropped down his face, then another. He patted his wife again. "So I helped. I'd do it again. I wish I could get those bastards myself."

Rose said, "We arrested them this afternoon. What you just said will be extremely valuable when the case goes to court."

"But I broke the law."

Terry put his notepad away. "Yeah, well, laws sometimes get broken. We'll work with the DA, Mr. Karamandrachos. I think it'll come out okay."

The older man nodded and helped his wife to her feet.

"So we finish the plans for burying them with dignity. In the big church. With Father Paras."

They all went back to the other room where it looked like staff from the funeral home were mingling, offering words and business cards.

"Mr. Karamandrachos," Rose asked quietly, "do you have any idea why Mrs. Basilaskos would've closed the diner early yesterday?"

He shook his head. "Close early? Never. She worked when she had pneumonia, Angelo didn't take time off. I thought Jerry might see how decent people work hard, might learn from it. But he didn't."

Terry knew that every human being and everything every human did was like a ray of light shot through a prism with an infinite number of facets. Where you stood, how you looked at the light bursting from the prism determined what you saw. No one quite saw the same thing. No person was ever seen the same way by two observers.

Jerry Karamandrachos chafed at being at home. So the Basilaskoses were domineering overseers. His parents knew two hardworking friends and were willing to bend the law when there seemed no other way to prevent their friends from being bled by city officials abusing their power.

"Fact is, she did let Jerry go early yesterday," Terry said. He spotted one of the funeral directors working his way toward them.

"She called me," Mrs. Karamandrachos said. "I didn't know she closed early. She called me around

103

four, four-thirty." She frowned trying to remember, appalled, as most people were that she had been oblivious to some life-and-death fact.

"You didn't tell me," Mr. Karamandrachos said reprovingly.

"Why did she call you?" Terry went on, keeping track of the funeral director so he wouldn't overhear them.

Mrs. Karamandrachos was perplexed. "Connie was very excited. Oh, I haven't heard her so excited in such a long time. She must have had so much on her mind she didn't tell me."

"What was so exciting?"

Mrs. Karamandrachos guiltily held her hands up. "I guess I didn't believe her. I didn't believe she could have such luck. She said she was going to make more calls after me, talk to people who knew about such things. Jewelers."

Her husband stared at her. The funeral director glided up to them, his face solemn.

Terry wanted an answer. "What did she call you about, Mrs. Karamandrachos?"

"She said she'd found a diamond. A big diamond."

Chapter Nine

"A diamond? That certainly changes things," Bernasconi said, licking his raspberry shaved ice. "That's a motive for sure."

"Mrs. B finds a hot rock, she sticks it in her purse, and the guy who lost it goes after her," Terry said. He was working slowly on a lime-flavored shaved ice. Bernasconi had sprung for shaved ices from a coffee shop and they walked back to the police department on the shady side of the street, dodging kids with basketballs and old people shambling along.

"One question," Rose said, chewing her strawberry ice in three brutal bites. "How do you lose a diamond in a diner?"

"You mean like overtipping?" Terry chuckled.

"Yeah. Who're we looking for now?"

Bernasconi wiped his mouth with a paper napkin, balled it up, and tossed it into a garbage basket on the street corner. "Let's start with the diamond trade, see who works around town. Check and see if anybody's lost a gem or two recently in a burg or a robbery."

"Guy goes to lunch. Guy mislays his diamond. Guy and his bud trail Mrs. B home, nail her, and take off?" Terry shook his head and laughed. "Not possible."

"Why?" Bernasconi asked. They were near the building, and it looked gray, sluggish, and uninviting just before seven P.M. with uniforms drifting in and out. A flock of pigeons, startled by a noise or movement, wheeled into the air just ahead of Bernasconi.

Rose answered because she and Terry had been going over and over the diamond revelation since Mrs. Karamandrachos unveiled it.

"The Korinthou Diner closes around three. They do lunch, nothing after that. Usually the Basilas-koses and the Karamandrachos kid would clean up, start making stuff for the next morning."

"Okay," Bernasconi said. "So our guy and his friend who drove the car had a late lunch and stayed around."

"Nope," Terry said firmly. "We got it nailed down that Mrs. B closed early yesterday, sent the Karaman-drachos kid home at four, so she didn't do any cleaning much. We didn't see anything made up for the next day either. She spent the time until she got the bus making phone calls, checking on diamond prices. We'll get the phone records tomorrow and see exactly where she called."

"Okay, then let's start with the people who knew she had a diamond."

Terry crumpled his soggy paper shaved ice wrap. An Amtrak passenger train heading to Chicago hooted at the Southern Pacific station two blocks away. "Van, we're back where we started right after this went down. So the guy finds out he's lost his diamond, so he traces it back to the diner, he waits for her, he gets his bud to drive. Why the hell do they shoot her in the middle of Thirty-third Avenue? Where everybody and his neighbor can see?"

Rose added, "She's on the bus from downtown until her stop in Oak Park. How's either the shooter or the driver keeping an eye on her? Follow the bus? Maybe they knew where she lived and were just waiting for her."

Bernasconi nodded. "You've got to start some place. Recent robberies and burglaries involving jewelry. Who the victim called to find out how much her windfall was worth."

Rose twisted her neck around, uncomfortable in her blouse. "We can go down the customers yesterday, see if anybody makes a guy in a seersucker. We could get lucky and we get a description of the other guy with the shooter."

Terry said, "Right. We also better let the DA know about Groucho, Harpo, Chico, and Zeppo."

"Zeppo?" Bernasconi said in surprise. "I thought there were only three Marx brothers."

"There were five," Rose said, grinning. "I bet Terry first day we were partnered he didn't know all five."

107

"She lost," Terry said. "*Nobody* ever remembers Gummo."

"I didn't remember Zeppo." Bernasconi sighed, as if it signaled another burden in his life like his scrutiny by the deputy chief. "Okay. Make sure the DA's aware we've got four gentlemen in custody and they might be good for a double homicide."

It wasn't hard to track down Deputy District Attorney Dennis Cooper, Major Crimes bureau chief. "He's doing jury selection on Nagy," Terry explained to Rose. "McGivery's crazy Hungarian? Shot his wife in the family van in Goethe Park, rolled her into a nice snug carpet, and lit her up. Ten months ago McGivery's bitching about trying to scrape her soot off his pants. Now it's finally going to trial."

"Yeah? So?" Rose said. "Court's been out for hours."

"You haven't had Cooper working one of your cases. He's just starting his day."

Cooper's office was on the top floor, the fourth, of the squat bunkerlike John Price Sacramento County District Attorney's Building at 901 G Street downtown, just across the corner from the county courthouse where the fruits of his labor, and that of the other deputy district attorneys for Sacramento County, were laid before judge and jury for disposition. It was an unadorned glass and beige-colored building named after the longest-serving district attorney in Sacramento County history. When John

Price left office in the late 1970s there were about seventy deputy DAs. There were now nearly 140. That was progress of some sort.

Cooper was not the only DDA working into the evening, but he was the most senior. He was a tall, broad, dark-haired man in his fifties who seemed to frown even as he smiled. He was in his shirtsleeves, rolled irregularly, marking pages from three stacks of accordion files.

Handing him pages, hovering at his shoulder, was one of the most stunning young women Terry had seen in a while. She looked fresh and alert after what must have been a very full, tiring day. She wore a blue suit with carefully placed gold jewelry. She smelled faintly of old-fashioned lemon verbena.

"My two favorite detectives," Cooper said with mild pleasure when Terry and Rose knocked on the open door frame. "You've got either very good news or very bad news at this hour."

"Kind of both," Terry said. He couldn't take his eyes off the young woman, but forced himself. Rose, on the other hand, had gone stiffly formal and cold. She was wary around professional women like this one, a little intimidated and resentful she felt that way. She tried to cover by pretending to look past her through the partly open venetian blinds of Cooper's window onto the mostly empty streets and sidewalks around the courthouse, the only signs of life coming from the nearby cluster of bail bondsmen's offices.

Cooper noticed their glances. "You haven't met Leah Fisher. She's just up from the ranks into Major Crimes to work with me."

The blond young woman, eyes set wide above a high-cheekboned face with a mouth posed in slight irritation, put out her hand. Terry shook it. Rose shook it. Cooper watched, a little amused.

"Leah's a buzz saw in court, so I'm putting you both on notice. She's from Stanford Law. Do you have any idea what kind of hard-core attorney comes out of that bastion of liberalism and goes to work as an underpaid and overworked prosecutor in this county of crime and corruption?"

"I'll stay on my toes," Terry said bashfully.

Leah smiled. "Dennis's told me a lot about the detectives around Sacramento. You are definitely on the good list."

"Oh. Thanks."

Rose smiled back thinly. "What about me?"

Leah sucked air in, glanced at Cooper. "Can I tell her?"

Cooper frowned grimly. "Might as well."

"One of the good ones. Actually, we had a case or two together when you were in Narcotics."

"I'd've remembered," Rose said so grimly that everyone laughed. She managed a smile.

"They folded up when the CIs all went south." She said it flatly, without recrimination. It was an occupational expectation in narcotics cases that the human element failed frequently.

"Damn," Rose said fiercely. "I knew there was another reason I hate my confidential informants. They kept us from working cases together."

Terry sensed Rose's increasing annoyance. She and Leah did not mesh well at all. He was relieved when in the next instant the young DDA said, "Dennis." Leah held another file out to him. "We've got a lot to do for tomorrow."

"Too true. So, what's your news, Detectives?" He smiled, taking the file, opening it, and laying pages in front of him like dealing cards in poker. He got up and brought a large cardboard box from near a bookcase and laid it carefully on the leather sofa.

Rose took the lead, probably to demonstrate her knowledge of the investigation, and explained the shooting of Constantina Basilaskos, the death of Angelo Basilaskos, and the link to the four city officials now languishing overnight in county jail until their arraignment the following day on conspiracy and extortion charges.

"We thought you'd like to make sure whoever's handling the bail reduction requests these guys will make at their arraignment knows about the Basilaskos murders," Terry said, mostly looking at Leah.

Cooper made a quick note beside his telephone. "I'll call the deputy handling the in-custody arraignment calendar at the jail first thing in the morning." There were four courtrooms in the county jail building, one dedicated to arraigning people arrested within forty-eight hours of the charges against them and setting the new cases for further proceedings. He glanced at them. "Thanks for the heads-up. I'm assuming that was your good news."

Rose said, "We're running down the leads. We got a good one a little while ago."

"But at the moment, except for the four jokers, you don't have anything for me?"

"That's it. But it's looking good," Terry said. "I got a feeling it's looking good."

"He's got ten bucks on it looking good," Rose said.

Cooper sat down, running his hand through his hair. Terry noticed the paper plates with the remnants of Indian curry, the empty soda cans, and the shot glass. Only the whiskey bottle he knew Cooper kept stowed in his desk, left-hand side, third drawer down, brought out for the toughest ones and the ones that were not going to be won, was missing. *Put it away when he heard us coming,* Terry thought. It would be in keeping with Cooper's sense of propriety and his sensitivity to Terry's alcohol appetite. It was a nice courtesy.

He wondered if Cooper and Fisher shared dinner and drinks too.

"Well, I'll look forward to handling this one," Cooper said, yawning abruptly, rubbing his eyes.

"As soon as you have somebody in custody," Leah said. She seemed irritable again, annoyed the flow of the Nagy case preparation had been interrupted.

"How's Nagy going?" Terry couldn't resist asking. McGivery had been such a pain about the problems of figuring out what the barely English speaking Nagy was babbling when interviewed and the forensic evidence that had to be laboriously worked from the burned van that it would be nice to have some scrap to needle him about when they got back to the police department. Besides, it was an excuse to look at this very interesting new DDA for a little longer.

Cooper laughed shortly. "Could be better. Right, Leah? Our prime piece of physical evidence, a burnt car door, has apparently been misplaced by Evidence. I just got word today that two percipient witnesses decided this would be a good time to take a vacation to Barbados, so I'll have to drag them back. I've got one peremptory left and the defense has three, so he'll get to shape the jury probably. But, fine, fine. The trial's going fine."

Terry nodded with mock sympathy. "But you always got McGivery as a witness."

Leah barely smiled. "He must be interesting for you to work with."

Cooper waved them out with another laugh. "Now all you're giving me is bad news. Go get me some killers."

"Wow," Rose said sarcastically outside.

"A wow for sure," Terry agreed, without sarcasm.

"You think she's really tough?" Rose was definitely down on Ms. Fisher.

"Listen, I been there three times. I know the look. That one'd break your chops and not even chip a fingernail."

"I think it's an act. Maybe she's sleeping her way up."

"Any way you can, Rosie. Just like everybody else."

"Man, you are a cynic about women."

Terry shook his head, a finger pointing at her. "I resent that one, Rosie. A man of experience like me is a skeptic. A cynic just don't give a damn anymore."

They worked for another two hours, staying away from Bernasconi, who was closeted in his office for the second straight day, the division's stats still not aligning as he needed them to do.

Then Terry and Rose ended up at the Back Door, a raucous bar in Old Sacramento, off an alley across from the more sedate and venerable Firehouse Restaurant. Old Sacramento at night was like stepping back into the nineteenth century, the restored old Gold Rush–era buildings making it easy to imagine that prospectors were roaming the streets looking for a little liquor and excitement. The place was smoky and filled with loud music and from which, recently, two new patrons who thought karaoke would liven nights up had been forcibly ejected by the older patrons who were mostly cops.

Rose bet on liar's dice for drinks. Terry made the rounds, slapping a few backs, picking up the news of the day from different detectives from his agency, the sheriff, and a couple of state cops. Everyone treated the state police guys with a little disdain. They wore unstylish brown uniforms on duty and the rap on them was that they mostly rode horses around the capitol for tourists, guarded the special elevators for the governor and legislators, and wrote lousy reports. Terry collected the swizzle sticks from his glasses of mineral water just like it was the good and bad old days when he kept track of his drinks by the lengthening line of red plastic swizzle sticks on the bar. A guy should never, he thought, jettison all of his habits.

Hernandez, another homicide detective in the sheriff's department Terry and Rose sometimes worked with when their cases crossed into the county, was sprawled back in a booth, boneless, talking at the top of his voice. "So this asshole beats her up, then he tries to throw her out of the car, right? They're heading down Marconi Avenue at like forty, fifty miles an hour, scaring the crap out of everybody. Only she don't go out of the car, right? She's all tangled up in the fucking seat belt and she just kind of hangs out and he's whapping her with this Glock and he's letting her have a couple pops."

Terry grimaced. Like hearing about a hoop shot that just missed. Frustration—and he could imagine the irate puke's utter frustration in that situation—was always hard to deal with.

"How's he take care of things?" Terry asked.

Hernandez leaned back, head lolling, called for another Wild Turkey neat. "He didn't, my man. He pops her a total. Total, right? Total of six times. Torso. Neck. Face even. And she's not going out of the car completely and she's just dangling out into Marconi Avenue now. So now he figures, this asshole, that he'll shake her out, so he speeds up and he's doing sixty down Marconi, like about Sunrise Boulevard, bat out of hell, cars going every place, civilians getting out of the way. He takes out two bike messengers. And he's still got his victim hanging by the fucking seat belt."

The audience of detectives chuckled appreciatively at the recital and the suspect's awful bad luck. Terry glanced over and Rose had just cleared up the pot for that game of dice. He was worried when she brushed aside any intention of letting her husband know she'd be late. He didn't feel quite comfortable enough to ball her out about it, so he just kept quiet.

"So?" Terry demanded.

"So he leans over and he pushes, he kicks, he's doing everything to get this broad out of the car. All he does is drag her from Sunrise down to Fair Oaks Boulevard. That's where we catch him because he bangs into a cab, this Pakistani's gotten all turned around and he's going the wrong way."

Terry laughed. Rose strolled over looking smug and satisfied.

"We roll up, I'm first out of the car, my partner's right behind me," Hernandez said, trying to sit up, but having too much trouble. "So I go to this asshole, and he's all bloody, he's like banged into the steering wheel or something when he took out the cab. I go up to him and I do a traffic cop. I go, 'Sir, do you know how fast you were traveling on this street? Do you know the posted speed limit on the public streets in the county of Sacramento?' "

"You jackass," Terry joked and everyone leaned forward expectantly, waiting for the punch line.

Hernandez finished his petty traffic cop performance. " 'Sir, I'm going to have to cite you for speeding and unlawfully discarding.' I stop, like I'm just seeing this woman, she's like been peeled from head to belly button where she's dragged down the street, just a damn raw tomato, like I'm seeing her for the first time. This *asshole*"—Hernandez's face hardened—"he's like looking at me like *I'm* nuts, *I'm* the crazy fuck. So I go, 'Sir, it's an infraction in Sacramento County to throw things from your car. I'm going to make you go back and clean this up.' I point all the way back up Marconi."

Terry nodded and Rose grinned.

"So the asshole, he's all bloody and now he's all pissed at me, he says, 'But she was *wearing* her seat belt! Don't *that count* for something?' "

Hernandez fell back laughing and the music grew louder, the place more convivial, and someone shouted, "Hey, Nye. Tell the one about the locker at the Greyhound station and the guy's head."

"It was a leg," Terry swore and Rose tapped him.

"Lot to do tomorrow." So she was thinking about the home front. Terry felt better.

So waving aside the loud entreaties to tell his story, because he was prized for recounting frolics on the job, Terry held up a hand. "Got to go. Catch me next show. You're a great audience."

"What's so important?" someone shouted and Hernandez smirked at him.

"Nye can't go the distance when I'm laying it out," Hernandez said.

Terry drew himself up. "Come on, partner," he said to Rose. "These motherfuckers are beyond hope. We've got thirty-two jewelers in and around our lovely city alone to commune with in the morning."

"Right," Rose said contemptuously to the rowdy detectives. "Some of us have work to do."

They were trailed by obscenities as they left the bar.

"Beat you to work, Ter," Rose said, jingling her car keys.

"Never happen," he said. "I'm setting my alarm for six A.M."

"I'm on your tail, old man," and she headed for her car.

That didn't bother him. He just wanted it all to come out right for her because he saw so clearly why it hadn't for him.

117

Chapter Ten

The next day, Thursday August 7, Terry and Rose started their labors by making stops at jewelers in and near the Downtown Mall, then working their way closer to the Korinthou Diner. They quickly grew tired of display cases of glittering diamonds and gold watches, and salesmen and saleswomen who had led safe and secure lives lately. No one had any gems missing and none had any otherwise unaccounted for.

Rose said, "I am so glad my husband doesn't know where I am today. Do you have any idea what grief I'd get if he knew I was in and out of jewelry stores all day and he was waiting for the bill for whatever I bought?"

"I got a faint notion," Terry said with the grimness borne of his own actual experience. Rose's husband, he knew, was a naturalized citizen from Cebu City in the Philippines. He was very cheap. Rose

118

smacked him sometimes when he tried to take money from her purse so she wouldn't spend it.

They had finished with jeweler number ten down the street from Macy's, and they headed toward J Street. There were no flashes of recognition when Rose showed people in the stores the computerized sketch of the shooter, based on Harry Standhope's description and embellished with additional details from other witnesses.

"Face it," Terry admitted, "that picture don't look much better than Mr. Potato Head anyway."

They spent most of the day going down J, doubling back to hit places like Macy's that also sold jewelry, over to nearby shopping centers, then to pawnshops clustered mostly downtown, stopping to eat at a Thai place Terry liked on Twelfth Street. The tangy cilantro and coconut milk sauce on his shrimp was about the high point of the day. Both Terry and Rose were pleased with a fair-sized story in the *Sacramento Bee* on page one of the metro section: FOUR CITY WORKERS ARRESTED IN KICKBACK SCAM. No mention, fortunately, of the Korinthou particularly or the shooting of Constantina Basilaskos. That connection was for the DA only.

And, counting all of the blessings of the day, the weather had broken. The fierce sun and heat gave way to a humid padding of gray clouds. Rain was coming, the summer rain that turned Sacramento's streets shiny black and steamy and made the ranks of trees that shaded and colored the old heart of the city stark sentinels in the shimmering haze.

But they were getting nowhere and Terry and Rose both wanted to save Bernasconi from the unspoken penalty hanging over his head if they didn't close this case fast.

It would make their lives easier too. Lots of good reasons to do their jobs that day.

After four in the afternoon, they changed focus and gathered up the records of the Basilaskoses at Wells Fargo Bank. They turned these over to the forensic accountant maintained by the SPD. He would sort through the transactions, the flow of money in and out of the savings, checking, and Kehoe accounts, and if he found anything unusual he could explain it in court. He had stacks of credit card receipts from the Basilaskos home too, showing that Constantina and Angelo had MasterCard, Macy's, and a very expired gas card for some long-gone automobile they must have once owned. The forensic accountant would explain it first to the detectives, of course.

They also took custody of the Basilaskos' telephone records, both the house and diner. They pored through these records until nearly eight. Rose happily checked off three jewelers they had visited that afternoon.

"Maybe they just forgot," Terry offered.

"*Right*. Old lady calls you and says she's found a diamond, no setting, got to be a decent size to get so worked up. How much is it worth, please?"

"No, no, she just said she's got a family heirloom, got to get rid of it, how much could she get for it?"

"Screw your skepticism," Rose said. "You believe anything."

It appeared that Constantina Basilaskos had called

six jewelers, including two not far from the diner downtown, on the afternoon of her death. She had then called the Karamandrachos home.

"She. didn't call Angelo," Rose said, flipping through the telephone number printouts. "How come?"

Terry shrugged. "Maybe she wanted to surprise him, flash it at him."

Rose snorted. "I think she was holding out. I think she wanted to find out how much, and then see you later, Angelo."

"Yeah, definitely," Terry said, tossing his pages down and pulling another handful toward himself. "I see Constantina on a beach getting oiled up by two, three beach boys. I see that. I do."

"Not a beach," Rose protested. "She wanted to get out. Little apartment of her own some place."

"She wanted to surprise him. She wanted to come home, he's in bed feeling like crap, and she wanted to wave it around and say, here we go. No more five A.M. to six P.M. cooking and cleaning up for us." Terry squinted at the numbers swimming in front of him. "Trust me. That's the way it was supposed to go."

On Friday August 8, the air thick and the clouds black enough to promise thunder and the crackle of lightning around the tallest office buildings in the capital, they returned to Grebetski Gems, Best Buy Diamonds, and Corsair Jewelry, all huddled near the popular draw of the Downtown Mall. Terry and Rose took turns prodding the same salespeople they had seen the day before.

"Now I remember," one willowy woman in a gray and green blouse and skirt said. "I did get a call around five. A woman said she had a stone, a diamond to sell. She wanted to know prices."

"What did you tell her?" Rose asked.

"What could I tell her? I said I had to see the gem. This annoyed her. She sounded very excited. She said the diamond was about the size of her thumb. What good does that do me?"

"How so?" Terry said with interest.

"Well, look at my thumbs." She held them up. "I have no idea how big hers might be."

"What was the outcome of this conversation?" Rose asked.

"I said she'd have to come in and bring the gem with her and we'd be delighted to give her an estimate."

"What did she say?"

"She'd think about it."

"Did anything strike you about the call, besides that she was excited?"

"People come in, they call, they all think they've got a very valuable stone, but so much depends on the quality, the cut, the color. Sometimes all they've got is a zircon."

Terry nodded, chewing his lip. "You tell her that possibility?"

The woman frowned and cleared her throat. "That's when she hung up on me."

"She say anything else at all? Her name, if she would come in, show the diamond to you?"

The woman shook her head. "I got the impression she didn't want to hear anything negative. She just said I was wrong, she had a diamond and she was rich."

"Thanks," Rose said. "A diamond about the size of my thumb." She held her right hand up. "What's that going to go for? In the ballpark?"

The woman sighed because she obviously had not made her point about the variables. She rolled her eyes. "Oh well, just a wild guess, you could try anywhere from fifty to seventy-five, perhaps a hundred thousand."

"Dollars?"

"Yes. Of course dollars."

"So she was right thinking she'd be rich," Terry said.

"If you consider a hundred thousand dollars rich." The willowy woman sniffed and turned to a man and woman both dressed impressively, who might actually purchase a gem or two.

"I don't know about rich," Rose said when they were outside. "I'd say an okay night on the town maybe. Counting a sitter and parking."

"Don't stretch it," Terry warned, wagging his finger.

Rose sighed loudly. "I found a diamond at work, you wouldn't find me taking a bus home."

By the end of the day they had established at least who Constantina Basilaskos had spoken to about her windfall. Since she had never identified herself to any of the diamond merchants, their possible involvement vanished. Nor did the calls to the Karamandrachos home indicate anything other than a woman who was bursting with what seemed to be magical, incredible good fortune that had to be shared with an old friend.

"So it's back to the diner, the gourmets who came in Wednesday morning for breakfast and for lunch," Rose said.

"Maybe the regulars spotted our guy and his pal."

Which, both Terry and Rose recognized, left wide open the question of how the killer and whoever was with him knew that Constantina Basilaskos had a valuable diamond in her purse when she left the diner. It seemed to stretch credulity to think she had displayed the gem to eaters bent over plates of feta cheese pie.

The list of diners on Wednesday was elastic: It grew by a name or two whenever they spoke to a witness. By midevening, with a break for Chinese eaten at their desks, they had a list of sixteen names.

"We knock off at ten," Terry said. "Nobody's going to want to answer questions after that."

Rose held up her notes. "We are hot, Ter. We are getting some place. I'm covered at home, so let's keep going."

"It was me, the phone rings, I'd answer it and say, 'I hope you're satisfied, buster. My wife's got a bad heart and she was sleeping and you just scared her into a heart attack and she's turning blue and I got to call 911.'"

Rose nodded, dialing another number. "We are hot," she repeated, her sometime gambler's intensity asserting itself, the sense that a streak of brilliant luck was starting.

Okay, Terry admitted to himself, it was a chance

to clear a very dramatic case and make Bernasconi's stats shape up, perhaps prevent another visit from Deputy Chief Mr. Rogers or worse, a command performance on the third floor in the chief's office or before the august and fearsome city council itself.

He glanced at his own notes. The witnesses had been segregated as to the times they came and went from the Korinthou on Wednesday. While not eliminating it entirely, Terry and Rose agreed the likelihood was that Constantina Basilaskos made her find sometime after noon. She didn't tell Jerry Karamandrachos to go home early until shortly before four. She didn't start making her calls to jewelers until he was gone. That left a window, at least as a working premise, of about three and a half hours.

Several people did remember seeing a man in a seersucker sport coat. He came in around one. He sat in a booth near the front of the diner. He ordered a sandwich of some sort and he drank iced tea. He visited the men's room. He came back and drank more iced tea. He did not seem to be a remarkable individual because when it came time to specifically describe him, words like *average, medium, quiet, blend into a crowd* recurred time after time.

Terry frustratedly asked one woman, a first timer at the diner, "What about this guy made you notice him at all?"

"It was that sport coat. Those blue and white stripes. It looked so eye-catching."

Terry hung up. "It's his fucking coat. They all saw what he was wearing. He faded into the scenery."

Rose looked up. "So where's the other guy? Where's the driver?"

Terry frowned. "Nobody saw him talking to anyone else. Came in alone. Sat alone. Ate alone. Left alone."

"So where's the driver come in?"

"Outside in the car?" Terry held his hand up. "Just kidding."

"We're missing something. We got one guy in the place the whole time. How about he calls a buddy when he leaves?"

"Okay, for fun, let's try that," Terry allowed. "The seersucker follows her on foot. Driver follows and they catch up with Mrs. B together."

"How'd they know where she lived?"

"They found out," Terry said, looking at his watch. "How should I know? The guy in the diner gets hold of a buddy and they tail her."

Rose was on the phone with another witness, so she hit the mute button for a second. "Then they blow her away in the middle of the sidewalk? That still doesn't work."

Terry sat back, rubbing his eyes. He wanted to go home, shower, maybe have a glass of ice water with a lot of ice, and then take half a dozen aspirins and go to bed. He nostalgically thought of the surefire cop cure for an aching back, one of the many occupational hazards. You threw down a good-sized tumbler of Wild Turkey and chased it with six maximum-strength aspirins. You could swing from the rafters all day after that.

Now all he could manage was the chaser.

Rose said, "I'm going to put you on speaker so my partner, Detective Nye, can hear you. Would you repeat that, please?"

Terry hunched forward. A woman's voice boomed out, making the other detectives look up, like surprised gazelle at a waterhole when a lion appeared, "I certainly remember the man. Mr. Hickcock, he said his name was. We had a conversation. I know I was imposing on him because he quite clearly wanted to be alone." The paradox was that while her voice was electronically very loud, it was in fact soft, almost apologetic.

"What did you talk about, Mrs. Rutherford?" Rose asked.

"Subjects of interest to me in my particular situation, which was similar, I thought, to his own."

"What situation would that be?" Terry asked. He raised his eyebrows to Rose.

"I must be somewhat stubborn now, I'm sorry. I'll be glad to tell you everything about my conversation, my observations. But I must insist we do it in person."

"You're out of town, Mrs. Rutherford," Rose said. "We can take down your information and arrange an interview in person later. Tonight—"

But Mrs. Rutherford softly cut Rose off. "I don't think we can, Detective Tafoya. I'm going into the hospital for major surgery the day after tomorrow."

"Well, I still think we could at least take down what you can tell us now." Rose tried again and again, but was softly but implacably interrupted.

"No. I want to see someone in person. I'm dying."

So it came to pass that after losing another coin toss to Rose, Terry found himself on an United Airlines red-eye leaving Sacramento International Airport,

127

which really wasn't because it had no direct flights anywhere outside of the United States, at one in the morning with stops in Denver, Tulsa, and his destination, Kansas City, and then continuing on into the night. He cursed. He ranted. Rose was unmoved. Rose had a husband, a family.

"I can get the first plane out in the morning, you bastard," Terry swore, standing over Rose, the other detectives grinning. "Why go in the middle of the goddamn night?"

"So what if she kicks tonight?"

"You're all bastards," Terry said to the detectives. To Rose: "Payback's coming, partner."

She gave a delighted, gloating chuckle.

That was how he found himself frantically making reservations, finding out that, oddly enough, this flight was not full, tossing a few items into a small bag, and getting to the airport and lifting off into the thick, lightning-shattered night.

He touched down in Kansas City at four A.M. after bouncing and thumping around in the turbulent stormy air, eyes glued to his lids, aching for some balm, preferably anything eighty-proof, got a car, and drove the sixty-two miles to the city of Blanton, which was very dark and very quiet, and only the traffic lights changing from green to red indicated it was inhabited at all.

Mrs. Barbara Rutherford said she would be awake. She did not sleep anymore.

So it was that Terry was in her modestly but tastefully furnished living room, sipping weak tea, on a couch across from the chair in which the middle-aged woman sat swaddled in a green terry-cloth robe, a turban of green cloth wrapped and pinned to her head. She had lively gray eyes and a hectic, sad expression.

"You must think I'm a selfish, terrible person," she said.

"I don't. Really," Terry said, moving slowly because he was so tired he was afraid he'd spill the tea or just topple off the couch, taking out his notepad.

"Dying people are always selfish, Detective Nye. It's our last grasp at life, imposing on others." She seemed fairly pleased. Her husband had died a year earlier. They had no children.

"Let's talk about this guy who said his name was Hickcock," Terry began, sitting forward, setting the teacup on a small teak table. "What time did you see him?"

"Oh, I should say two or so. As I told you on the phone, I was in Sacramento sightseeing. I'd been to Seattle and before that Los Angeles. My last sightseeing. So I went just where I pleased. I saw the state capitol and Old Sacramento, which was charming, and the Railroad Museum and Sutter's Fort, and then I was tired and I happened to have ended up near city hall more or less and, well, there was this quaint Greek diner, so I just went in."

Terry jotted things down mechanically. Outside, through the chintz curtains on the front window, it was starting to show signs that there was a sun some place, orange and violet piping at the horizon.

"Where was this guy and what was he doing?"

"He was sitting alone, in a booth near the front. I had the impression he was killing time."

"Why's that?"

129

"He had four empty iced tea glasses in front of him."

"Can you describe him?"

She shut her eyes and swayed a little. "He was forty-three or so. About five feet ten. Fleshy around the cheeks and the chin. A broad nose. Thinning brown hair. He had blue eyes. That was a little surprising. He was not athletic. I don't think he kept in shape at all. He had big, soft hands. He had a gold wedding ring on."

"That's very thorough. What was he doing, sitting alone in the booth?"

Mrs. Rutherford nodded. "He was reading. I noticed when I sat down in the booth just behind him, I passed him."

"Reading?"

"*The Imitation of Christ*," she began and Terry interrupted her this time.

"Thomas a Kempis. I remember from parochial school. I went to St. Francis and Jesuit High School." He grinned lopsidedly. "I didn't get along with that book when I was a kid."

"I'm not particularly religious." Mrs. Rutherford sat forward and clasped her thin, very white hands together.

Alabaster, like a statue, Terry thought.

"Mostly Easter and Christmas was when my husband and I went to Good Shepherd, the Presbyterian church a few blocks over."

Terry smiled but through his fatigue and the fact that he was powerfully afraid he'd yawn in this woman's face, he was puzzling through the increasingly strange customs of the man who would, in a few hours from when Mrs. Rutherford saw him, brutally shoot down Constantina Basilaskos. A man, moreover, who somehow had knowledge that she was carrying a valuable diamond.

A man who sat waiting and drinking glass after glass of iced tea in the Korinthou and reading a medieval monk's devotional work in the middle of the afternoon.

"You see people with paperbacks over lunch," Terry said thoughtfully. "You just don't see so many reading Thomas a Kempis."

This pleased Mrs. Rutherford. She unsteadily got to her feet and braced herself against the chair back. "Exactly, Detective Nye. I felt drawn to Mr. Hickcock because he had a very reassuring presence, solid and secure. So as bold as brass I sat down opposite him in the booth."

"Bet that caught him by surprise."

"It did." She smiled gleefully. "I introduced myself. I said I was a tourist and I couldn't help noticing that he was reading such a deep book."

Terry sipped his weak tea, hoping to get a little lift from it. It was merely sour, though. "What did he do?"

"For what seemed the longest time he pretended I wasn't there. So I persisted. That's when he mumbled that his name was Hickcock and he was from out of town too."

"This might be a strange question, but did he look like he was armed?"

"It isn't strange," she said quietly. "When he moved in the booth, his coat opened a little and I saw a gun at his waist."

"What kind of gun?"

"I'm not very good at that, I'm sorry."

"Weren't you worried? Didn't you mention it to someone?"

Mrs. Rutherford touched a framed photo portrait of her husband. "Why should I be afraid? Now? Who would I tell? For all I knew, he was a policeman."

Terry's blood went cold for an instant, because that thought had immediately come into his mind. Who carried guns in Sacramento? Cops and crooks. Most crooks did not dress in somewhat outdated seersuckers or sip tea or read Thomas a Kempis.

Nor did many cops for that matter. At least in his experience.

Please, he prayed to the loathed and feared lords of the third floor of the Sacramento Police Department, *do not let this involve cops.*

"What did you and Mr. Hickcock talk about?"

"He didn't want to talk. He had a gentle voice, but he was very, very tense and he kept glancing around to see who was in the diner. I thought there was something wrong with him too. Maybe he was ill."

"Why?"

"He was sweating very heavily. He kept having to mop his cheeks and his hands just to hold the book."

"Hot day. Everybody was sweating."

She shook her head. "This was very different. Have you ever been so afraid you sweated, Detective? I have been that afraid very recently. Mr. Hickcock was sweating like that, great big drops so he looked shiny and wet. But he was trying very hard to appear calm and collected."

"Did he talk to anyone in the diner? Acknowledge anybody?"

"No. I think he may have said one or two words to the old woman who took his order, but that was all."

"So what did the two of you talk about?" Terry asked, very intrigued.

"I apologized for imposing, but I think he could see I was unwell, so he didn't get angry. He said he was just trying to have a little peace and quiet on his lunch hour."

"Did he say where he worked?" Terry asked quickly.

"No. But it would have to be some place nearby, wouldn't it? For his lunch hour?"

Maybe he was a lawyer, Terry thought hopefully. Maybe someone from city hall or the capitol. Maybe even one of the esteemed senators or Assembly members hanging around town during the legislative recess. Anything at all but a cop.

"Did he say anything else to the old woman who was cooking that day?"

Mrs. Rutherford slipped back into her chair wearily. She shook her head. "He didn't. I can't imagine why he shot her as you say. He stared out the window every so often while I chattered about the city, what I'd seen. What I'd never have the time to see." She paused. "He nodded a little. Then he started reading to me."

"What'd he read?"

"Would you hand me that copy of *The Imitation of Christ*? I bought it when I got home. I'm taking it to the hospital with me tomorrow."

Terry gave her the slim dark book and she thoughtfully flipped its pages. "Here it is. Mr. Hickcock said he was sorry I was feeling so poorly. Then he said he always found strength in this," and she read in a clear, soft voice, " 'Also if thou in every chance standest not in outward appearance nor with the fleshly eye turnest to things seen or heard but anon in every cause thou enterest with Moses to ask counsel of our Lord, thou shalt hear ofttimes God's answer and thou shalt come again instructed in things present and that are to come.' "

Terry sat back. "Did he explain that to you? How it fit for you or him?"

"We talked a little about Sacramento, how big California is and how strange to an outsider. He said I should do what Thomas a Kempis advised. 'So thou oughtest to fly into the secret place of thine heart beseeching inwardly the help of God.' He repeated that. He said he did that every day."

She was silent, closing the book. Terry turned and saw that the sun had started to rise coolly above a line of trees across the street, and that cars were appearing on the road. Blanton, Kansas was waking up.

"Did he ever say anything about a diamond or who he was waiting for?"

She shook her head and touched the cloth wrapped around it. "Not a word. I got up and he was still sitting there, pretending to read but always keeping an eye on the diner. Always mopping his hands and his cheeks. I left after I had a very delicious lamb dish." She nodded slightly. "It's always very strange when you realize that may be the last time you'll taste or see something."

Terry stood. "You've been very helpful. I'm sorry."

"I'm sorry too. You were kind to come all this way."

"It's my job." He paused. "Things could still turn out, couldn't they? They don't operate unless there's a chance."

"No, Detective Nye. There is no chance, but I appreciate your thoughtfulness." She rose, hand out, a dry, cold, already nearly lifeless hand. "The surgery is for the pain that is supposed to come very soon. They're going to cut some nerves so I won't feel it."

Terry started to drive back to the airport in Kansas City, but about twenty miles out from Blanton he felt overwhelmed by fatigue and a nauseating sense of despair. The kind he'd felt when there were victims you couldn't help at all, when there wasn't even the mercy of a surgery to sever nerves that made the pain unholy.

Or when your brother dies and there is no answer from God about things present or that are coming at you. Which was a problem, he realized, he'd had with old Thomas a Kempis even all those years ago when the sisters insisted on grace and mercy.

He found a motel along the highway, registered just as the sun was up, got into the cool, stale, clean room, and called Rose, leaving a message for her at the office about what Mrs. Rutherford had said. He told Rose he'd be on a flight later that morning.

He undressed, washed his face, turned down the covers on the hard, cold bed. He heard cars coming and going on the highway outside, a throb of life and daily existence. He lay awake for a while, eyes staring up. Then he sat up and found a Gideon Bible in the telephone table beside the bed. He read for a few minutes, thought more, and lay back.

He didn't sleep very well.

His United flight landed at Sacramento International Airport at 11:25 A.M. on Saturday, August 9. It was still overcast, a moderate breeze clipping along. He had tried Rose's pager and cell several times without success.

Coming into the terminal, about to head for his car and drive downtown, Terry was surprised and pleased to see Rose standing there, waiting for him.

"At least I ain't in Kansas anymore," Terry snapped. "Is this supposed to make me feel really lousy, you got to sleep in your own bed, you got your husband and kid to bring you coffee, some eggs and toast in bed? I just went through four cups of that airline coffee, Rosie. You're messing with a wired, dangerous man."

They walked briskly, Rose shaking her head, quite pleased with herself.

"You better be wired enough to hit the ground right now, Ter."

"How come?"

"Constantina Basilaskos's Macy's card and Master-Card are in action as of late yesterday afternoon. Somebody's buying stuff with them."

"Praise the Lord."

They pushed their way through the milling, oblivious mob of air travelers swirling in and around the terminal entrance, a chorus of cabs and shuttle buses and car horns making it hard to hear.

"Say again," Terry shouted to Rose.

"You won't like it. ID on one buy with the MasterCard at five-thirty yesterday, a minimart in North Highlands."

"Don't tell me." Terry kept walking.

"Yeah. It sounds like Harry Standhope. Our guy."

Chapter Eleven

They waited in their unmarked car two doors down from the light blue house on Thirty-third Avenue where they'd interviewed Harry and Kaneesha on Tuesday. Rose was running communications, keeping up with the patrol cars they'd gotten to sit on the building. A few fat drops of rain splattered on the windshield. Terry glanced into the dark sky. Rain. Perfect. It was about twelve-thirty.

"They both in there?" Terry asked again. "For sure?"

Rose nodded, radio in her hand. "Harry showed up around ten. Kaneesha came out around eleven, got some milk, the papers at the store on the corner."

Terry sighed. "I am so disillusioned. Harry seemed all right under all that hair."

"Action on the Macy's card and MasterCard have Harry buying food and a couple of big-ticket items like a crib, chairs at Macy's. Kaneesha's been using the MasterCard for baby stuff too."

"Just your average unmarried parents buying the kid supplies with a credit card stolen from a woman who got shot."

"Wonder what tale he's been telling when he uses the cards." Rose grinned. "It's not like he could pass for a member of the Basilaskos family."

"Maybe he's putting out that it's a very strange story, like Clinton and all those half brothers and sisters coming out of the woodwork when he was president."

Rose chuckled, froze. "Here's Kaneesha."

Terry stared out the slightly-rain-obscured windshield. Dressed in a blue poncho, holding Amanda, Kaneesha came out of the house and strode purposefully up the sidewalk toward the little market on the corner. She had apparently forgotten to buy something on her earlier trip.

"You sure you want to let her go?" Rose asked again.

"We stick to Harry, he goes, he stays. Miller and Lapsley can keep an eye on her."

Rose relayed their decision to the other team of detectives working on the joint surveillance with them. The radio crackled acknowledgment.

Terry sucked harder on his eighth or ninth mint. Rose blithely, and Terry thought, recklessly, continued to drink a paper cup of coffee. Long years of sitting in cars waiting for suspects to move had taught Terry that mints were a much safer bet. No telling when a suspect was going to take off and if you been drinking coffee, you couldn't afford to leave the car. It didn't seem to bother Rose, though.

"Old lady's out Saturday afternoon, here comes Daddy to run his errands." Rose pointed as Harry Standhope, a gray army surplus raincoat hanging open around him, darted from the house, around it to the driveway and a yellow VW Beetle. The car coughed to life and Harry made a sudden U-turn and headed up Thirty-third Avenue toward the stores along Broadway.

Terry had started their car already and smoothly pulled in behind Harry about three car lengths. The rain was still mainly long-spaced fat drops splashing on the windshield so it was not hard to see the bright little car ahead of them.

"We got Charles and Balch behind us?" Terry asked.

"I'll make sure," Rose said, talking to the radio and confirming that they had a second team to make stops after Harry moved on. She and Terry would stick to Harry and either hope to see something themselves or get word from the backup teams that Harry or Kaneesha was using the murdered woman's credit cards.

Terry had called Harry's boss at the carpet installation outfit an hour earlier as they drove to the stakeout. "You see that motherfucker, you tell him he's fired!" the man shouted. "Quit? He can't quit, I got three jobs today and they're his goddamn jobs. He calls me Saturday and quits and leaves me with three jobs? Screw him! He's fired."

Terry had turned to Rose and said wryly, "See

what the financial security of a couple of credit cards gets you? Harry just blew off a good job with a great future."

Now, tailing the yellow VW, Terry and Rose hoped Harry would make use of one of Basilaskos's credit cards. It would be a tight arrest and a great club to hold over Harry. He had, plainly, been less than truthful with them.

"Bets on where he goes first?" Rose asked.

"Not me. This puke could go nuts and spring for a Lexus."

Rose chuckled. "He's only using the cards for relatively small stuff, Ter. Come on. I bet he goes for a six-pack of Cobra."

But Harry Standhope circled a block on Broadway just down the street from the bulk of the Department of Motor Vehicles headquarters building, miraculously found a parking space, and dashed out. Terry pointed at the red and white letters on the broad storefront he'd run into: GEMS BOUGHT AND SOLD.

"You lose," Terry said to Rose. "He ain't messing with credit cards today. He's got the diamond."

In the course of the next two and a half hours, Harry Standhope continued driving downtown. He made stops father down on Broadway, cut over to midtown, and went into two more down-market jewelers around Alhambra Boulevard.

"He's comparing prices," Rose said.

"He sure ain't buying anything," Terry agreed. The other detective team, Charles and Balch, had gone into each of the jewelry stores Harry visited after he left. He was indeed only inquiring about diamond prices. Like Constantina Basilaskos he described a bright gem, about the size of his thumbnail.

Kaneesha, according to the detective team watching her, had returned to her house long ago and was still inside. She had paid cash for the food and paper towels she bought at the corner store.

"Here he goes again," Rose warned.

"I can see," Terry said.

Harry stood outside the jewelry store's garish neon and glass entrance. He looked around, clearly thinking. He belted the surplus raincoat and then screeched his double-parked VW heading south, away from downtown.

"Now where?" Rose asked crossly.

"Now I'll bet you," Terry said, as they turned south, heading back toward Thirty-third Avenue, turning right onto Fifth Avenue, passing the ascending streets pointed at the minimalls of check-cashing and rental furniture stores nearby. "He's heading to some spots he knows, right? Why's he doing that?"

"Why's he doing that?" Rose repeated.

"Because he didn't show anybody any goods. He did the same thing Mrs. B did, he talked about the diamond. He shows it, people might get suspicious, so now he's got some idea what it's worth, he's going some place he knows. Where he can put his feet up."

Rose nodded. Harry's yellow VW was shiny in the sluggishly falling rain, the other traffic glistening too. Close to the I-5 on-ramp, Harry pulled up in front of the Golden Day Pawnshop. It was in a squalid neighborhood of broken windows and scattered garbage and people moving slowly or simply standing, even in the rain, as if they had nowhere to go.

"He gets top dollar here, for sure," Terry cracked. "You want to grab him after this one?"

"He's got that rock and he shows it, we're taking him. Give SO a holler and let them know what's going on," Terry said, indicating Rose should alert the sheriff's department, which was always referred to as the sheriff's office for some reason.

Terry parked carefully as Rose radioed the sheriff's department there might be activity on their territory, depending on where Harry went next. Fifteen minutes later, Harry came out of the pawnshop. He rubbed his chin and glanced suspiciously around him, taking in the men leaning against buildings or standing on the corner. Harry got into his VW and headed north briefly, then turned left and left again onto the freeway, this time going back downtown.

Terry felt the tension rise. Rose felt it too. The paper side of a homicide investigation could be dry or stimulating when a fact or piece of information locked almost magnetically to another fact and a coherent picture started to reveal itself. But the paper side never touched the minutes or seconds on the street when the investigation was physically in motion, like it was now on a slightly rainy Saturday afternoon, tailing a witness who had just turned into a suspect to some part of a brutal murder. This was the hunt. This was the quarry running ahead, unaware he was the quarry.

Something would happen soon. Fighting, a chase, even shooting.

Terry thought for an instant of the woman last night, where she was and what awaited her with certainty. He did not know what awaited him in the next few minutes. He had never known all these years on the job whether the outcome of a chase like this was a safe, simple arrest or a bullet.

Maybe that's why I'm in church these days in the morning, he thought. *Insurance.*

"Ter," Rose said crisply, "Charles says Harry flashed the rock at the last stop. Pawnshop dealer said it was worth maybe a grand or two, right now."

"Harry's going for a better deal."

"What do you want to do?"

Terry glanced quickly around him. The traffic was relatively heavy on the northbound freeway, cars packed in the lanes. "Okay, he stops, we get him on the way out."

Rose passed the plan along. They would have backup when Harry came out of his next stop.

The rain spattered more quickly on the windshield.

Harry chose another pawnshop, more upscale, on J Street, down from a newspaper and cigar store on one side and a shoe repair shop. It was the sort of business that traded with people who pawned expensive cameras or family silverware for ready cash.

Harry double-parked and went through the revolving glass door. Terry checked the time. It was three thirty-five. Terry parked and he and Rose got out casually, taking up positions on either side of the door. Rose was on a portable radio. She was cool but coiled, ready for whatever was going to happen. Two patrol cars had moved in up the block.

Terry breathed through his nose slowly, trying to stay calm. Rose shifted from one foot to the other with excitement, both of them staying just out of sight of anyone in the store. They could see Harry off to the right talking with a man in a shapeless three-piece black suit. Harry reached into his pants pocket and took out a small dark pouch. Terry cursed because Harry's back blocked what the man in the suit did with the small pouch.

Rose mouthed an obscenity in Tagalog and then in English, stretching out each syllable. Now Terry knew she was worked up. She'd only lapsed into Tagalog twice since they'd partnered.

The pantomime inside the store concluded. Harry took the pouch back, put it in his pocket, and turned to the door.

"He's coming," Rose whispered into the radio.

She and Terry then moved swiftly as Harry walked out, each of them grabbing an arm, pushing him relentlessly forward to the ground.

"Hands behind your head," Terry ordered, his gun drawn. In the corner of his eye he saw the pedestrians freezing, turning, cars passing slowing or even honking. The two patrol cars roared up, lights and sirens going wildly, the uniforms jumping out, guns drawn, as Rose slipped handcuffs onto Harry and he was jerked to his feet.

"What are you doing, man?" Harry tried to say with fierce indignation and failed. "I'm just out, I'm not doing anything."

Terry nodded. The uniforms were keeping Harry in place and curious people away. Terry noticed that only he hadn't dressed for the occasion and the rain falling on him spotted his suit, while it dripped off Rose, the other cops and even Harry in raincoats.

"Harry," Terry said, "you got anything in your pockets that's going to stick me or cut me or make me mad?"

"I got nothing, man," Harry sputtered angrily in another attempt at oppressed innocence.

Terry's hands went into the army surplus raincoat's pockets, Harry's shirt, and his pants with quick, sure moves, the result of a cop's years of pat-downs of all sorts of people wearing all sorts of clothes in all sorts of places. Junkies and drunks were the worst to pat down since they often lost control of basic bodily functions at inopportune moments from Terry's perspective.

Terry caught something out of the corner of his eye across the street. Two guys head to head for an instant, watching Harry's arrest. Then even before he could register more than the fact that they were both in plain olive raincoats, trim, they split up, vanishing into the rapid movement of people on the sidewalk.

"Hey!" Terry said to Rose.

"What's up?" She gripped Harry tighter.

"Forget it," Terry said. "Thought I saw something." But there was nothing. There had been nothing. *I'm just getting old and I see stuff*, he thought.

Harry squirmed, protested loudly, Rose cautioned him to shut up, and Terry pulled up the small cloth pouch. Harry fell silent.

Terry opened it and peered inside.

"Yeah?" Rose demanded impatiently, holding one of Harry's handcuffed arms.

"Son of a bitch," Terry marveled. He grinned at Rose. "The rock really is the size of your thumbnail."

They brought Harry to the police department, shaking off a little rain. The place smelled, as usual on a wet day, of damp clothes and the musty residue rising up like a mist from decades of cops and criminals cloistered too closely between its walls.

They parked Harry in an interview room, identical to two others. The dull green paint had been done over so many times that it had a thickness all its own and cracks in it looked more like veins. Harry was handcuffed to a bolt on the metal table, which was in turn bolted to the floor. The light was pale, high overhead, and protected by wire mesh.

Bernasconi stared in through the one-way mirror in the small room attached to the interview room. Terry and Rose stood beside him.

"How do you want to play it?" Terry asked him.

"Your call," Bernasconi said. "Let's find out the truth this time. You've got a good witness for the shooter." He pointed at Terry. "Now we need to know what really happened on the street."

"Okay," Rose said, still pumped up from the rush of the arrest.

Bernasconi looked at Harry, who turned and squirmed every few seconds in his chained position. "Well, see if you can get us any closer to wrapping this one up. I've got an appointment at nine-thirty Monday with Mr. Rogers upstairs."

Terry winced. "We officially a 'troubled' division now?"

"Let's just say I'd really like to have something to give the deputy chief when I walk through his door."

Terry and Rose stood on either side of Harry. This forced him to turn his head constantly and increased his anxiety.

"Where's Kaneesha?" Harry asked again.

"Being processed," Rose said. "We got her dead on using stolen credit cards. You too."

"Oh, man. This is my fault." Harry moaned and lowered his head. "I give everything up, you can let her go? She didn't do anything, she didn't. This is my deal."

Terry feigned looking to Rose in consultation. "Well, listen, Harry. We can't make any promises, you understand? We can go to the DA and tell him how cooperative you've been."

"Better late," Rose agreed.

"DA'll take what you tell us. That'll determine what happens to Kaneesha. So it's up to you."

Harry sat back as far as he could, his head going back as he let out a great sigh. He had been Mirandized and refused an attorney. It was up to him.

"Okay," he said finally, bringing his head forward, staring from Terry to Rose and back again. "You promise I tell you everything, you make sure the DA skates her off this?"

"Scout's honor," Terry said, three fingers raised. "So let's start at the point the shooter's out of the car. We okay so far on that? No strikeouts or corrections?"

Harry nodded. Outside the door someone started

shouting, there was a scuffling burst of noise, then quiet. The rain softly hitting the building. The murmur from the homicide section and the waiting room attached to it drifted in.

"Yeah, all the same, just like I told you. I did hear something first. He says something to the old lady like, 'You got my stuff' or 'You took something of mine' and then he just shot her, just like I said."

"Okay. Now I bet we need to make a couple of changes, right?" Rose asked.

"Right." He sighed again. He stroked his beard with his free hand. "This white guy, he kind of stands there for a second, like he's going, I can't believe I did that. Then he reaches for the purse, she still got it under her arm. Blood now, blood going all over the place."

Terry wrote, Rose nodded sympathetically.

"Me, I'm like scared shitless." Harry laughed very nervously. "This white guy, he still got his gun, and I figure he can just turn and see me and start shooting, but I was so scared I couldn't move. Very strange feeling. I got high so good I couldn't move one or two times, but I was not high on that sidewalk."

"So he grabs the purse," Terry prompted.

"No, no, man. He don't get the purse. Just then, like in the movies or TV, this big old car shows up, drives right up, and some other white guy, he starts shouting from the car."

"What's he shouting?" Rose asked gently. Do not startle a witness when he's reciting. Do nothing to break his flow of words or impede his admissions by some distracting note yourself. It was interrogation and interview technique taught but really always only perfected on the job through much practice and many mistakes.

Harry's face screwed up as he tried to imitate what he'd heard. "*Get in! Get in! Jerry! Get in!*"

"Jerry? The guy in the car called the shooter Jerry?" Terry asked.

"Sounded like."

"What did Jerry do?"

"He kind of froze. He's all freaked. He looks around, he sees me, and I go, oh, shit. I am dead. He got that gun. But then he kind of runs to the car, the car door's open, he gets in, they go out of there real fast."

Harry swallowed hard.

Terry moved to a chair in front of him and sat down. "Anything you want to add about what Jerry looked like?"

"White guy. Blue tie. That's it. I told you the truth the first time. Only . . ." Harry paused. "He ran funny."

"Funny?" Rose sat down too, everybody pals.

"You know, clumsy, funny. This white guy ain't going to do no marathon or sprint at the Olympics."

Terry thought suddenly: *I don't think he kept in shape at all,* Mrs. Rutherford had said. Sure he didn't, and he'd just spent a couple of hours sitting on his fat ass drinking iced tea.

"Anything else about the car? The driver?"

Harry shook his head and went back to nervously stroking his beard. "Just like I said the first time."

Terry grinned faintly. "Now we get to the interesting part. So what's your next move?"

Harry shifted. "The car goes down the street, I'm

like all alone. Nobody's out. So I go see what I can do for this old lady. That's it. You think I just leave her like that?"

"You tell us," Terry said.

Harry hunched forward, rattling his handcuffs. "I get down, I see she's got these big bloody holes, man. Big, you know? I take off my shirt, I wasn't thinking, I'm going to stop the bleeding." He paused, glancing at both of them in extreme embarrassment. "But like I realized she was dead. You got to be dead, you shot like that. I see the purse, so I wrap it up in my shirt, wrap it completely, and I get out of there."

"Where'd you go?" Rose asked.

"Home. I say, 'Kaneesha, you got to hide this quick.' I give her the whole bloody thing, man. She take the shirt and she stick it in the washer and she take the purse and she hide it in the baby's crib, under the covers at the end."

Terry blew a raspberry. "So call me a jackass. I didn't even look at the crib."

"Kaneesha figured nobody's going to hassle a baby, even if someone come in and you two"—he grinned—"didn't come for a long time."

"Okay." Terry stood up, unlocking Harry's handcuffs from the bolt. "Let's go get the goods, Harry."

On their way through the homicide section, they passed Kaneesha, the blue poncho and little Amanda in her lap as she sat being processed by Felderstein. She looked at Harry and she said distinctly, "Fool."

"After you left that night," Harry said, "I move the stuff in here." They were in the small closet where Terry had retrieved and returned Harry's marijuana.

151

Rose smirked at him. Terry shot her a hard, warning glare.

They had been joined by a tech, who actually went through the same pile of clothes and located the purse, handling it carefully and bagging it for processing.

"So what do we have here?" Terry asked the tech.

The middle-aged man in glasses with brown frames gingerly opened the blood-spotted black purse. Using long tweezers he extracted several items.

Harry stared at each one. "Except for the credit cards and that mother of a diamond, there didn't look like anything in there."

"Maybe," Rose said. "What's that?" she asked the tech, who now bagged each item separately.

"Woman's wallet, red leatherette. Keys, yellow metal. Miscellaneous papers. And some folded green trash bag."

"Be real careful with that," Terry said. "Fabiani found some green plastic under Mrs. B's fingernails, right?" Rose nodded.

The tech went on. "Here's something. Untitled CD in a jewel box." He held it up. "Clear plastic all around, no writing or lettering of any kind."

"No music neither," Harry snorted. "I tried that in my player and Kaneesha's. Nothing. Who carry a CD with no music on it?"

"I wonder," Terry said, puzzled. "Where was the diamond, Harry?"

Harry, hands cuffed in front of him, just pointed up. "In the purse in that little bag, just like you got."

"Just so we're real clear now." Terry came close

to Harry, close enough to smell the acrid grass, his fear sweat. "This is it? This is exactly all that was in the woman's purse?"

"I swear."

"Then we'll see what we can do for Kaneesha. Because she's got a kid too," Rose said.

They took Harry downstairs, outside into the rain, which had become a drizzle, and the concrete and brick and asphalt were slick and dark and the black kids playing games on the sidewalk or in the street, barely staying clear of the cars, were shiny laughing little specters.

Terry said to the tech, while Rose got Harry stowed in their car for the drive back to the police department, "Go over this stuff real good, okay? Real fast, expedite it. If someone makes any noise, they call me or Detective Tafoya."

"Got it," the tech promised, going to the patrol car that had brought him. He clutched the evidence bags.

Harry gazed ahead when Rose and Terry stood for a moment in the drizzle. Terry had borrowed an ill-fitting gray raincoat from McGivery, which meant he would have to put up with some bullshit diatribe about something as compensation. He offered Rose a mint.

"You got that look," Rose said, taking the mint.

"What do you think about a purse that's got a folded-up plastic trash bag, a blank CD, and a fucking big diamond in it?"

"I don't know," Rose said.

"That's why I got that look. I don't know either

and it bothers the hell out of me." He spat the mint out. "Come on. Let's get the great unwashed bedded down for the night." He jerked a finger toward the silent, pensive Harry in the backseat of their car.

Chapter Twelve

Terry and Rose worked on their reports, based on what they had gathered in the last twenty-four hours, and got Harry processed through into county jail pending his arraignment Monday morning on multiple charges of receiving stolen property and making false statements to a police officer. At the moment, the strongest of those charges sprang from the credit card purchases since the cards were definitively in the victim's name. Because it was utterly unclear who owned the diamond and the remainder of the contents of Constantina Basilaskos's purse were of negligible value, they stuck with the credit cards.

Rose passed Terry her report on Kaneesha. "Cut her loose, just like we told old Harry."

"I hate putting mothers with babies in jail. I feel creepy for days afterward." Terry shook his head in mock horror.

"What time you want to meet at the funeral tomorrow?" Rose asked.

"Do I want to meet? How about never?" Terry despised funerals. Attending the final ceremonies for both Angelo and Constantina Basilaskos at St. Demetrios Church in Stockton was not a task he looked forward to at all. But funerals were often fruitful during an investigation. Unusual people turned up. Emotions ran high. Things usually unsaid were laid bare. "I ever tell you about my Snipes case?"

"Never did." Rose shuffled papers and started tapping on her computer terminal. She was contriving to look busy and annoyed so that McGivery, roaming the office and buttonholing anybody not tied up to complain about the DA blaming him for somehow misplacing the car door evidence in Nagy, would steer clear. "Do it fast before McGivery comes over," she muttered to Terry.

Terry shuddered because his raincoat debt to McGivery looked to be coming due sooner than expected and said, "Lady is Estelle Snipes. Nice looking in her forties. Married to David. Fourteen years. Two kids. So one night, David's out on some business deal, he was in securities, I think, so he comes home about two, he goes upstairs. Boom. Estelle nails him with a shotgun they kept for protection. Practically took his head off, he goes ass over head down the stairs."

"Ouch," Rose said. "I got to remember to make sure my husband knows I'm coming home every night you keep me out late."

"Exactly. Estelle's story was that David's supposed to come back the next day, she's got the shotgun in the bedroom, she's scared some pervert's coming in, so on and so on. Good story, I might add. David's doing great business, she makes a bundle now being a widow. I'm having no luck getting much out of anybody except that at company parties for the last couple months, Estelle don't show. David's stag."

"Trouble on the homestead."

"Not much to play with. So I go to the funeral. Great big deal, minister and choir and the whole works. Got David in this casket that looks like it weighs five tons, all rolled steel or something."

"Keep it going," Rose urged, staring at the monitor. "McGivery's locked on."

Terry spotted the other detective, having forced two clericals and two detectives to run for cover by leaving the room on bogus pretexts, now making his way toward them.

"So there I am," Terry went on loudly, "at this funeral. Lots of crying relatives, because David Snipes was a nice guy, helped his family. Active in the Boy Scout troop at his church."

Rose's head cocked around the monitor. "Hey, where were the kids the night the deed was done?"

"Astute question," Terry said. "I wondered too. Seems Estelle arranged for a sleepover with some little friends. She was like making sure she was alone."

"You want to hear some real crap's been dumped on me by the DA?" McGivery drew near, about to settle in.

"No," Terry and Rose said in chorus.

McGivery looked startled at how emphatic they were. He shrugged, spotted another victim, and sauntered on. "Hey. I got some real crap been dumped on me by the DA," he said, heralding his coming.

"So what's the deal with the widow?" Rose asked.

"So there I am, not liking this funeral. They get under my skin. Then I see Estelle and she's being comforted by this guy, tall, dark hair, tan like frigging George Hamilton. 'Who's this?' I ask some old babe connected to the family. 'That's Theodore,' I get back. 'He's her cousin lives in Yakima, Washington. He's going to look out for her.'"

Rose got up and stretched. "So?"

"She ain't got no cousin Theodore. This is Theodore Mitchell, from Yakima, okay? But he flew in the day before David got creamed all over the shag carpet on the stairs. So I wait until things are real weepy, get old Theodore alone, and introduce myself. He looks at me. Swear to God, first thing this bozo says is, 'It wasn't my idea to shoot him.' Case got better from there. Which I might've missed, I didn't go to the Snipes last rites."

"That lady was pretty bold, bringing the guy to the funeral."

Terry shrugged. "Bold? I'll give her points for brass balls, sure. What she didn't figure, he's a moron."

"What time for the funeral tomorrow?" Rose repeated.

"Hell. Hour before? See who shows? Say one, meet you there?"

Rose agreed. She looked at her watch, then at the

disintegrating old clock on the wall. Six-thirty and the rain was steady outside on the streets and every puke dragged in was soaking wet and there were large water splotches along the cracked linoleum floor.

"It's kind of late, but I feel like lighting a firecracker up somebody's ass at the crime lab," Rose said. "You want to come?"

"I've done about all the damage here I can for one day." Terry stood up, the long, long day and night catching up with him swiftly so he felt as if he were made of uncooked dough, ready to slide to the floor in a sodden, limp mass.

"You do realize the crime lab isn't working OT for *us* to get something on this case?" Rose said. "Guy down there said he's going to stay however long it takes tonight because it's Bernasconi who needs it."

Terry glumly put one foot after the other, sidestepping several giggling, drunken prostitutes telling obscene jokes at the top of their voices. "Long time ago I figured out where I was on this dog team."

"Looking at the lead dog's ass?"

Terry nodded. "Get used to it, Rosie. Learn to enjoy the view."

Besides, he thought, if word had permeated through the city's law enforcement apparatus that the department's high command was critically scrutinizing Bernasconi, the astute longtime folks on the job quickly reckoned that they too were next under the magnifying glass.

Help Bernasconi, you help yourself.

Self-protection was a wonderful motivator in the service of justice.

* * *

It wasn't often that Terry had gone to the crime lab on a weekend, much less the golden hours of an early Saturday evening. The whole experience, therefore, was unsettling and disorienting, particularly in light of what came next.

Their tour guide among the charts, refrigerators, long black hard-topped lab tables, and various arcane-looking pieces of electronic equipment and scientific glassware was Lila Patterson, aged fifty, a vet with the lines and permanent cynic's squint to prove it. She had very thick black-framed glasses and a great swelling bosom that would have done a pouter pigeon proud.

"Save it, Nye," she said when Terry made an attempt at gratitude that she was working so late. "Like I told the rookie here"—she jerked a thumb at Rose, who grinned at the hyperbole—"Bernasconi's getting jammed, so I'll move your merchandise when I should be home, feet up, relaxing with a beer and watching roller derby."

"I could get behind watching TV with my daughter," Rose said. "Maybe the beer part after she went to bed."

"I doubt it, kid," she said disdainfully. "You want to see what's turned up so far?"

"Yeah, that would be nice," Terry allowed.

She walked them to a large box of carefully separated items from Constantina Basilaskos's purse. The wallet and its contents were on one side of the box, segregated by partitions; the green plastic trash bag, CD, and diamond on the other.

"What's hitting you first thing?" she demanded.

"It's a pretty odd collection. That's what we've been wondering about," Rose said, pointing at the diamond.

"If I was going to get married, which I am not, I should be so lucky to get a stone that big and that flawless." Lila picked up the diamond and held it to the fluorescent lights overhead. It gleamed, sparkled, and shot brilliantly colored rays.

"Nice rock?" Terry asked.

"Only the very best. This's been selected, cut, and polished for some very choosy brides-to-be or some very rich ladies."

"Value?" Rose took the diamond, weighed it thoughtfully in her hand.

"I'm no gemologist, but the price is going to be near a hundred grand."

"So we heard," Terry said. "Okay, what about the rest of the stuff?"

Lila waved her short, stubby hands over the wallet and its contents. "Nothing too spectacular. I had some eliminations done. Your two pukes handled everything. The victim's got her prints. No surprises."

"Are there any surprises?" Terry leered at her.

"Don't make me laugh, Nye," she said, leering back. "There are some unusual aspects to this side." She gestured at the trash bag. "What we've got is a wrapping material. Somebody used a plastic bag to wrap another trash bag, an inner package. In that inner package went your CD and your diamond."

"Like a gift?" Rose folded her arms.

"I'd say more to protect the contents. The whole

shebang was closed with strong adhesive duct tape in and out. I tried some folding." She lifted the plastic bag and demonstrated. "And it all works if you fold it this way and then the duct tape traces I found are used to secure it some place."

Terry frowned. "Secure it? What do you mean?"

Lila sighed loudly. "Tape it some place. To a wall. I don't know. Where was it found?"

"We don't know. In a diner some place."

The criminalist nodded. "Okay, so the package was secured somewhere to a surface with the duct tape. Go back and have the place checked, because you'll find adhesive residue wherever it was."

"My guess's it wouldn't be some place you'd normally tape a package," Terry said.

"Well, Nye, I don't know about you, but I don't duct-tape packages any place." She shook her head and grinned at Rose.

"I don't duct-tape period," Rose said. She compared the diamond to the sliver of a stone she wore on her ring finger. Patterson laughed.

Lila Patterson was a formidable force in the department. She lectured all over the country on criminalistics and forensic science and she had testified in nearly two hundred trials over a twenty-year career. Her only brush with mortality had come about a year earlier when a new walk-in refrigerator was installed for preserving biological evidence and clothing or other items that might contain blood or semen or saliva and would deteriorate if not frozen. It was a Friday night, she was working late, and the refrigerator door swung shut behind her. To her horror she discovered that the new refrigerator had no inner door release. She started banging on the door, shouting, frantic with fear that no one would find her until Monday. At that point the only option would be whether to thaw her out at the morgue or take her there in a dripping pan, she said later, sloshing in ice water. She said she'd look like the frozen daughter at the end of Henry Wadsworth Longfellow's "The Wreck of the Hesperus."

Fortunately, a janitor heard the commotion and let her out. Lila joked about the experience, but Terry knew she never went any place now without making certain several people knew where she was. She carried a whistle. She had known real terror.

It gets to even the thick-skinned ones, he thought. The plain stupid, vicious brutality of it, the whimsy that makes no sense and nevertheless could still kill you.

"Can you match this plastic bag to the plastic under the victim's fingernails?" he asked.

She half shook her head, pushing her glasses up. "Well, you've got some indentations on the plastic that could be consistent with someone trying to scrape it open, then getting smart and cutting the duct tape with a knife. The trash bag and the victim's plastic are consistent as to color. They're the same chemical composition. But you probably already knew it's not going to get much more definitive than that."

Terry nodded.

Lila went on, "You're disappointed. Suck it up, Nye. I do have some interesting news for you."

"Don't keep me in suspense."

He rolled his eyes at Rose, who followed the conversation more matter-of-factly.

Lila nudged the plastic bag. "I said this is really an inner and outer wrapping material. So I checked for fingerprints on the outer wrapping and got your victim and your pukes again. But it got interesting on the inner wrapping. I got a mystery right thumb and a mystery right forefinger, a good twenty points of ID on both."

Terry smiled broadly and Rose stepped closer to examine the plastic bag herself.

"You run the prints yet?"

Lila walked over to another table and they followed. She opened a file folder and took out a standard rap sheet printout. She gave it to Rose.

"Same forefinger on the CD jewel box too. That's got me stuck. I've tried it a couple of times and got our acoustical and electronic geeks to play with it. It's blank. Their opinion is that it's for burning, somebody intended to put something onto it."

"Anything special about it? You can buy blank CDs any place, you don't have to wrap them like Christmas presents," Terry said. He glanced at Rose, who studied the rap sheet. It was a short printout.

"It's just a blank CD," Lila said.

Rose held the rap sheet out to Terry. "One entry. Gerald Tate, address in Los Angeles. He got popped on July twenty-fourth for being nasty to a hooker and being an obnoxious drunk."

"We got to get the arrest report," Terry said. It was disappointing and yet exhilarating. Gerald Tate was Jerry, just like Harry had heard the driver of the getaway car call him. Jerry was a guy who had spent most of last Tuesday afternoon at the Korinthou Diner swilling iced tea until he had to take a leak, and reading Thomas a Kempis. His only interruption was when the Rutherford woman, lonely, sick, and attracted to his oddity in Sacramento, sat down and chatted briefly with him about the meaning of life and death.

And he had a gun.

And there was no one else with him in the diner.

"So he don't have a record? A guy this clean decides to shoot an old lady in the middle of the sidewalk?"

Lila tapped his arm. "Yeah? What's your point?"

"It doesn't make sense."

Lila laughed merrily. To Rose she said, "Now he wants coherence. Now he thinks there's supposed to be rationality. Look, I'm a trained scientist and you think after doing this all these years I believe there is even one orderly, rational process at work in any of the garbage we wade in?" She threw her large arms wide, her great bosom heaving. "Dig around on this guy if that makes you happy, Nye. He gets busted a couple of weeks ago because he's a drunk and he's trying to cheat a hooker. I could see that kind of guy going postal, couldn't you?"

Rose nodded. "Yeah. Might work for me."

"Okay. Thanks, Lila," Terry said sincerely. He closed the file, then opened it. "Damn. That phone number here in town looks damn familiar." The rap sheet contained not only the home address for Gerald Tate, but a local number in Sacramento as well.

"Tourist?"

"Maybe, yeah," Terry said. "Rutherford said they kind of clicked because Sacramento wasn't like the good old hometown for either of them."

Lila yawned. "Well, that's my good deed for the month, Nye. You two clowns clear out and I can lock up and maybe catch the second half of the derby."

She started herding them toward the door. Terry turned. "Let me use your phone. This number is bugging me."

"Use your own damn phone," she snapped. "Can't I go home?"

Rose interceded. "One minute. I promise."

Lila snorted angrily and led them to her office of the lab floor. A large poster of Ricky Martin hung over her desk. "Don't get any ideas," she said sourly. "The local wits stuck that up yesterday and I haven' had time to take it down."

Rose gazed up. "Now, there is one talented guy."

Terry sat down and tapped out the phone number.

Lila said to Rose, "Are you planning on staying with this ancient wreck?"

"He keeps screwing up. I probably'll have to re quest a transfer any day."

She nodded, watching Terry's face harden as he listened to the phone. "He's going to teach you a lo of bad habits if you stick around."

Terry hung up. He hurriedly got up and withou waiting for Rose and made for the door. "Thank again," he said absentmindedly over his shoulder to Lila.

Rose dashed to keep up with him.

"Any time," Lila Patterson said. She looked up a the singer's enormous smiling face and a smile creased her mouth and for a second the permanen squint softened.

* * *

"What's the big rush?" Rose said. Terry hadn't spoken at all until they got back to Homicide. He was very tense, his shoulders bunched. He frowned.

"Don't do anything, say anything," he answered. "I'm going to get that number on Tate's sheet again. Just listen, okay?"

Mystified, Rose nodded. Terry hit the buttons on Rose's phone and handed the receiver to her. Terry looked away, looked back at her, rocking a little on his heels.

There was a short silence. Then a ring. Then Rose heard a pleasant, unaccented female voice say, "You have reached the Sacramento Field Office of the Federal Bureau of Investigation. FBI Sacramento is responsible for conducting criminal and counterintelligence investigations within the five states of California, Oregon, Washington, Arizona, and Nevada. Our regional Computer Crimes Squad is responsible for investigating computer intrusions into the northwest United States. Our hours are Monday through Friday, nine A.M. to five P.M. If this is an emergency, please dial," and she slowly recited a number, "and you will be assisted. If you know the extension of the person you would like to speak with, please enter it now using the keypad on your touch-tone telephone."

Rose's eyes narrowed and Terry nodded.

"Yeah," Terry said quietly. "Use the directory."

Rose waited and the female voice went on pleasantly, "If you do not know the extension of the person you would like to speak to, please press the pound sign now to be connected to our automated directory."

Terry bit his lip and sat down while Rose tapped out the name TATE on her telephone. Terry knew what Rose was now hearing. And it made the noisy, wet, and bustling police department fade into gray nothingness.

An electronic click. Then a man's voice, gentle and strong: "Hello, you have reached voice mail for Special Agent Gerald Tate in Counterintelligence. I can't come to the phone now, but if you'll leave your name, the time you called, the nature of the call, and a phone number, I will return your call immediately. If this is an emergency and you need to speak to someone in the Sacramento Field Office immediately, please dial," and he gave the same number as the anonymous female operator.

Terry knew Rose was hearing the long dead silence on the other end of the line seep in. She hung up slowly. She steepled her fingers.

"The guy in the seersucker's an FBI agent," Rose said. "What the hell does that mean?"

Terry sat down very wearily and very nervously. "Could be Mrs. B and Angelo were on the Ten Most Wanted List. Or maybe they're superspies."

Rose moaned, "Oh, man. FBI."

Terry pulled out his dwindling bills, peeled off a ten, and held it out for Rose. "You win, Rosie. I'm throwing in the towel. From now on this one's going to be the one you wish you never heard about."

Rose took the money. "Man. First time I really don't want to win."

Terry looked around at the homicide section as the other detectives went about their usual weekend routines, the whole place always more lively, the floor show much more intense on weekends.

"This is just for us," he said quietly. "Nobody else."

Rose nodded. "Bernasconi's got to know."

"He gets call number one at home. Right now." Terry started dialing, cradling the phone. He popped two mints into his mouth, crunching them harshly. "I never had a case with the feds I didn't come away with some part of my ass missing."

"Call number two's got to go to the DA."

"Cooper. If he's around, we see him tonight."

"Soon as you hang up the fucking phone," and Rose's quiet fury gave Terry a glimpse of why she must have chosen to become a cop in the first place. To do the right thing. To be one of the good guys.

Not to be on the side of an FBI agent who shot an old woman in cold blood.

Chapter Thirteen

"This isn't exactly what I had in mind when I said I wanted to give Mr. Rogers something Monday morning," Bernasconi said sarcastically.

"It ain't my idea of a good time, Van," Terry said somberly. He kept stealing glances at Leah Fisher across the table from him.

They were grouped around Cooper's law book and file-cluttered office at nine A.M. on Sunday, August 10. Fisher wore an attractive blue and gray track suit, flushed from exercising. Rose was in jeans and a Kings cap, Bernasconi in an Arizona State sweatshirt. Cooper had on aviator glasses, which he hung in his red sport shirt and a windbreaker, as if he'd just stepped from his time-share two-seater prop plane. He had, in fact, flown to Yreka, at the north end of the state, interviewing a witness in his Nagy trial.

Cooper paced around his desk. He held the arrest report from July 24 involving Gerald Tate.

"All right, we've all had a chance to review this document." He held up the report. "We know Mr. Tate." He paused. "Agent Tate. We know he went to the Crystal Room off of Freeport Boulevard at about seven in the evening. He started drinking. He drank for two solid hours. He was approached by," Cooper flipped the report pages.

"Joanie Lathrop, a.k.a. Amber Pearl," Rose said from a chair near the open window. The morning's after-rain freshness blew softly through the tension-filled office.

"Thank you, Rose. Ms. Lathrop is a prostitute, six arrests, four convictions in the last three years. She attempts to interest Agent Tate in her services and he becomes violent and shoves her to the bar floor." Cooper grinned at Bernasconi. "Agent Tate isn't partial to hookers apparently. He curses Ms. Lathrop. He attempts to hit her but three male bar patrons restrain him and officers from the ever-alert Sacramento Police Department arrive and take him into custody."

Bernasconi finished, "He overnighted and bailed the next morning."

Cooper nodded vigorously. "He's got a court date on the disturbing the peace and simple assault case in four days. Judge Westlake's court."

Terry watched Leah taking notes, looking graceful and resilient and desirable. He wished he were younger. He wished he were younger and they were driving in the country, maybe up to Lake Tahoe for a weekend.

He sipped coffee from one of the paper cups that had been Cooper's lone concession to hospitality for this bizarre Sunday strategy meeting.

"No bagels?" Bernasconi had asked when he came in.

"No Krispy Kremes?" Terry asked right afterward.

"No yogurt?" Leah groused, taking it all off in a different direction. One thing she and Rose could agree on, healthy eating most of the time. Rose sipped from her own bottled water rather than risk Cooper's home-brewed coffee.

Now Cooper prodded. "Terry," he asked, as if trying to make him ignore Fisher, "what do we know about Tate?"

"Pretty much what it says on the report," Terry said, sitting forward on the couch. "Forty-three. Lives in Pacific Palisades, which is still L.A. County if you only look at the geography," referring to the suburb's wealth. "I checked this morning and there is a Gerald Tate and he's married with four kids, two girls, two boys. Clean record except for that bust at the bar. And the little detail he's a fed working counterintelligence."

"So why is he here in Sacramento if his family is down in Los Angeles?" Leah pointed out.

"Blank," Terry confessed. "That's still wide open."

Leah said, "Is there any question about ID at the scene, Terry?"

He shook his head, delighted to talk to her. "No question at either scene," he said in an abundance of being helpful. "I tracked down our little entrepre-

172

neur Amber Pearl this morning with Rose. She's working motels and bars around South Sac mostly. I showed her our composite, got her description, and it's Tate. Tate's ID'd at the shooting too."

"Rock solid?" Cooper demanded.

"Well," Bernasconi interjected, "one witness's critically ill and one's going down on stealing the shooting victim's purse."

"But we got this guy," Terry said. "You put our witnesses and the physical evidence together, he's dead."

Cooper looked to Leah. "This is no reflection on your assessment, Terry, but I want Leah to do an independent review of the witness identification today. If we're going forward with a case, if we're even thinking about going forward with a case in which the suspect in a homicide is an FBI agent, I want to feel a high level of confidence in the witnesses."

"No problem for me," Terry said. "I'll be glad to help out."

"Me too," Rose said and Terry frowned warningly. He didn't like the prospect of Rose glaring at him whenever he was around the new major crimes DDA.

Bernasconi put his cup on the floor. "I don't understand why an FBI agent would shoot an unarmed old woman in broad daylight and try to steal her purse."

"Or why he had a backup car along," Leah said.

Cooper shook his head. "I don't think he knew about the car. He apparently was surprised by it showing up. So let's see why he was where he was and why he killed our victim."

"Two victims," Terry said, holding up two fingers. "Angelo kicked when he found out what happened to his wife."

"What's our move?" Bernasconi asked Cooper. Leah got up and stood beside one of the bookcases loaded with official United States Supreme Court reports and the California state appellate court decisions in gold-leaf-spined rows.

"Can you take them off their other cases for a while until we get this straightened out, at least to see what we're looking at?" Cooper asked Bernasconi and gestured at Terry and Rose.

"Not really. We're behind as it is. But I don't want this one hanging over me," Bernasconi said. "Consider yourselves assigned to this case for the duration. Just don't make it a long duration."

Terry nodded and Rose nervously eyed the floor as she took a sip from the bottle of water. She was plainly unnerved by the implications of the investigation. It was not unusual for the FBI to put cops under surveillance, to mount undercover operations targeting cops for corruption or brutality. The SPD was not alone among police agencies in bitterly resenting the FBI's aristocratic attitude. But it was unprecedented in the experience of anyone in Cooper's office that morning for the SPD to be looking at an FBI agent for something as grave as murder.

It was indeed enough to make any rational police officer nervous.

"Terry, Rose," Cooper said, "I'm sorry if this messes up your Sunday, but I need answers fast. I'm in a trial tomorrow and I don't know what my schedule's going to be, so we need to find out where we stand."

Leah said, "Let me suggest we agree to meet again tonight, say seven? Here? And meet every night at seven if not sooner until we have a grasp of the case."

"Done," Cooper said, foreclosing any discussion. "I need you two to do a top-to-bottom examination of the July twenty-fourth incident. Talk to everybody, not just the hooker. Talk to the uniforms who arrested Tate. Find out what he said on the way to booking. Find out what he said to anyone in the bar. But do it quietly." Cooper put his hands down, as if lowering the volume. "We've got to stay way under the radar for now."

"You got it," Rose said sincerely.

"We're planning on going to the funerals this afternoon," Terry said. "Give us a chance to see what the family might know."

"Terrific," Cooper enthused.

"You might find out more about these trips to Canada," Leah said. "Since Tate's in counterintelligence, it might be that the victim was part of some operation he was running."

Terry hated himself immediately for the burble of laughter he gave out. "Those two old skinflints? Secret agents? If they were bringing anything besides contraband smokes into the U.S. it was goat cheese."

"Maybe so, Terry," she said condescendingly. "But you've got to admit there have been enough surprises so far. You don't want to prematurely eliminate any reasonable possibilities."

"Oh no, he doesn't want to do that," Rose quickly said.

Cooper had missed the undercurrent of the exchange entirely. He stood, hands on his lean hips, staring out at the white bulk of the Sacramento County Courthouse, the faintly exotic smells from Chinatown's restaurants a few blocks north drifting in with the breeze.

"Working hypothesis," he announced. "Something for us to hang the facts on. Gerald Tate's an FBI agent. Counterintelligence based in Sacramento. Has personal or professional problems. Starts drinking heavily. Has some kind of breakdown. Hallucinates and believes our victim's an enemy. Kills her."

"What about the driver?" Leah asked firmly. "He was not imaginary."

"So he's Tate's psychiatrist," Cooper said. "Right now we've got to get facts and make them make some sense. An FBI agent who's gone off the deep end fits our facts."

Cooper had to admit that it did. The religious angle. The sweats. The stupidity of a shooting in plain sight of a host of witnesses.

Cooper turned to them. "Rule number one, ladies and gentlemen. From this moment forward, this is our case. You do not involve any other law enforcement personnel. You do not commit anything to paper until I give you a direction to do so. We are playing hot potato with dynamite."

"I don't know how we'll do this and the Nagy trial," Leah said. She sat down beside a stack of books and accordion files.

"Neither do I, but we'll have to," Cooper said.

"The first priority is finding out all we can about Agent Tate without hitting any alarms at the Bureau or tipping anybody in our own shop about what we're doing."

Bernasconi said softly, "What do you want me to do?"

"Cover for them." He jerked his thumb at Terry and Rose. "Make everything look as normal as possible."

Terry stood up. "Okay," he said, "we've all got our marching orders, Cooper. What're you doing?"

Cooper smiled broadly, like a kid who was very good being invited to play baseball. "Before our next meeting, Terry, I'm going to ask the Bureau if they've got a missing agent."

After forty-five minutes of watching the crowd of mourners who filed into St. Demetrios Church that afternoon, Terry and Rose sought out the family of Angelo and Constantina Basilaskos just before the service began.

"My mother and father had nothing to do with the FBI. They didn't even get parking tickets," their eldest son, Nicos, replied indignantly to Rose's questions.

"They never complained about any problems with the FBI or maybe they weren't specific, they just said the government?" Terry persisted.

"Nothing. They never had any trouble."

Besides Nicos, his wife, and their silent, solemn little girls huddled beside them, the other sons of Angelo and Constantina glared at Terry and Rose. The Greek Orthodox priest, Father Paras, hovered nearby too, plainly unsympathetic to Rose's and Terry's inquiries.

"They were God's good servants," Father Paras, resplendent in his dark funeral vestments, finally burst out. "They were true friends of this faith and their friends. Look! Look around you," he demanded. "Friends. A multitude of friends. Are these people who were lawbreakers? Criminals?"

Terry said carefully, "I'm sorry. We didn't mean to imply anything, Father. We've established some connections between this case and the FBI, that's all. We're trying to make sure we cover all the bases. We want the killer, too."

Nicos snapped, "My brothers, our families, we will sell our homes and return to California and stay here until the murderer receives justice."

"No, there's no need for that," Rose said calmly. "We know where to contact you if we've got more questions. Believe me, we are working very hard to resolve this case."

None of the sons of Angelo and Constantina Basilaskos seemed persuaded. But a somber peal of organ music began, and Father Paras said they must begin.

Terry and Rose watched for a few minutes near the rear of the ornate, gilded interior of the church. There were more than a few tears and bowed heads among the largely older crowd. Two caskets, awash in a sea of brilliant flowers, lay before the altar and its stylized Christ. A mix of wax, incense, perfumes, and the flowers brought back old times to Terry, Mass on Sunday mornings.

"Karamandrachos," Rose pointed out in a whisper. "No Jerry."

"Big surprise," Terry said.

"I don't see Constantina or Angelo getting the Bureau's attention."

"Me neither. But the kids don't know everything, right? The old lady never mentioned the kickbacks, never complained about that. She and Angelo didn't tell the kids everything."

Rose shook her head, a choir's hymn swelling over her words. "Man. When I go, I hope I get this kind of send-off. I want my kid crying, I want Walt," her jealous and tightfisted husband, "on his hands and knees crawling up to my coffin."

"Jeez, Rosie. You got that a little too specific." He peered around, and grinned soberly. "Old story. Big Hollywood producer croaks, everybody hated his guts. He has this incredible funeral out there at Forest Lawn. Half of L.A. shows up. Red Skelton looks at all those people, he says, 'It just goes to show you. Give an audience what they want and they'll come out every time.'"

They slipped out of the church. Mourners' cars were parked everywhere, filling the parking lot and the streets.

"Difference is," Rose said, "the Basilaskoses have a hell of a lot of people who cared about them. Hell of a lot," she said, enviously surveying the ranks of cars.

"Check out the camera bug," Terry muttered, gesturing slightly.

Rose looked at a man in a green baseball cap at the edge of the parking lot. He had a camera with a telephoto lens. "I bet that's not for the family album," she said. "You want to go work him?"

179

"Yeah," Terry said, low. "You go get the car."

They split up and he walked at a normal pace toward the man with the camera, who made no attempt to conceal himself. Getting a little closer, Terry made out a guy in his mid-thirties, in a blue sport shirt and tan slacks. Without rushing, the man lowered the camera, pivoted, and ducked into a dark blue four-door. Terry ran forward, heard Rose coming up in the car behind him. She slowed, he jumped in.

"Bastard just took off," Terry husked heavily.

They spun toward the street. Rose craned her head, looking for the dark blue car.

"Okay, he's right here, right? So where is he?"

Terry couldn't spot the car anywhere in the traffic racing along Hammer Lane. "That was pretty neat," he allowed. "He had maybe five seconds on us and he's gone."

Rose gunned the car into the traffic. "So if he's running, why's he running? If he's taking pictures, why's he taking pictures?"

Terry nodded. "I'm getting a goofy idea somebody's been watching us since the night we rolled on this one, Rosie."

"Oh boy," she said disgustedly. "I bet I know who that might be."

"Oh yeah," Terry said. "It ain't good."

"I tremble for the Republic when Dennis Cooper calls on a Sunday afternoon and says it can't wait and we've got to meet right away," playfully said the solid, clean-shaven man strolling beside Cooper in

Ceasar Chavez Park opposite the dour old city hall, in the shadow of turquoise and emerald glass high-rise office buildings. "I want you to keep in mind I've got a family barbecue at five and I'm the designated briquettes master."

"It can't wait," Cooper said. "But thanks for coming."

Around them, in the mild August afternoon under the heavy shade trees, a few couples sat on the benches, kids threw Frisbees, a wino or two lounged against his shopping cart, and gaunt, hungry-looking people threaded among the carefree like grim reminders of mortality and the fleeting nature of happiness.

"You want to sit?" the man, whose name was Oscar, asked Cooper.

"We'll walk. I think it's safer."

"I don't like the sound of that. That sounds a little paranoid."

"Better paranoid than sorry."

"All right. We'll walk."

They slowly worked their way along the park's paths between flower beds and the bird-dropping-speckled bronze and granite statue of A.J. Stevens, dated 1889, a railroad man beloved, according to the plaque, by his friends. They were merely two strollers chatting like everyone else, equally indistinguishable.

"Oscar," Cooper said, "how good's your relationship with the FBI here in town?"

"Good. Better than good. I'm close to a fair number of the agents because I've been through white-collar crime and now computer crime at the U.S.

Attorney's office. I did a big embezzlement case involving Hewlett-Packard and the FBI came through like gangbusters for me."

Cooper thrust his hands into his pockets as he walked. "I'm going to trade on our old friendship when you were with our office and we tried cases together." He faced the other man. "I've got to ask you to keep the next information completely confidential."

"Like the recipe for a Cooper Special, with or without bourbon?"

"Oscar, I've got a homicide and the likely suspect is an FBI agent."

The other man's smile withered. He turned stonily to Cooper. "That's a hell of a thing to dump on me without warning, Denny."

"I don't have a choice. I need someone close to the Bureau and it's got to be someone I can trust." He smiled a little. "Besides, you're about the only person outside of my former wife who knows the secret ingredients in a Cooper Special. I've got to trust you."

"Jesus H. Christ."

"I'm sorry, Oscar."

"All right, what am I doing for you?"

"I need to know about an agent in Counterintelligence. Gerald Tate. He may've been transferred to the Sacramento office very recently. He's still got family in Pacific Palisades."

"Great. I get to play Deep Throat." The other man scowled. "This is a very big one, Denny. This is going to be something you'll be paying off for a very long time. I'm going to ask for a hell of a lot of things in return."

"That's only fair. But I think I helped you more

than a couple of times." Unspoken were the criminal trials in the DA's office when Oscar, a good, intelligent, and decent prosecutor, had been paralyzed by the thought of going to court. Cooper had picked up the trials. It was a debt that did not need elaboration.

"And it assumes I can get anything useful on Tate without burning myself or tipping him," the Oscar man said. "What's your homicide anyway?"

Cooper succinctly told the other man about the shooting, the identification of Tate, and the very odd contents of the victim's purse.

"We're trying to make some sense out of all of this, Oscar," Cooper said. "What's the diamond for?"

"You don't have to be clever, Denny." He chuckled without amusement. "What's a diamond? It's portable, fungible, valuable. It's currency anywhere for anything."

"So it's a payoff?" Cooper wondered. "Who was Tate paying off? Not our victims. Did our victims get in the middle of some payoff? Did they get in the middle of some covert operation? What was Tate getting that's worth a diamond that valuable?"

"I don't know." Oscar paused as two black college kids ran by, laughing and oblivious, dribbling a basketball back and forth between them. "You better be prepared that I won't be able to get deep enough into Tate's investigations to find out either."

"I understand. I don't want you to take risks, Oscar. I'm sorry to do this, but I'm stuck without inside information because the Bureau obviously won't tell me anything."

"FBI motto: We take information, we don't give it

out. But don't worry about me, Denny. I'm not taking one risk. Period. I'm not risking my family, my retirement, or my career in the U.S. Attorney's office for you."

"Accepted." Cooper nodded. "It's not for me, though. Remember the victims in murder cases we did? Their families?"

"Vividly. It's one of the reasons I very much liked white-collar crime as a fed and I genuinely adore computer crimes. No blood. No weeping and wailing."

They walked toward the city hall on the I Street side of the park. "We're still trying to see the point of including a blank CD in the package," Cooper said.

Oscar looked at him thoughtfully. "You're absolutely sure it's blank?"

"Everybody, including the guy who stole the purse, has tried playing it."

The other man stopped walking. "Okay, Denny. This starts my meter running. The CD may not be blank. I've picked up a hell of a lot of technical information since I started doing computer crimes."

"Our computer techies worked it, Oscar. They claim there's nothing on it."

"Did they try any encryption tests?"

"I assume so."

"They could've tried a whole list of standard or even exotic encryption techniques and still come up with nothing. The FBI uses a particular mode sometimes to conceal information on diskette or CD."

Cooper raised his eyebrows. "What's this magical technique called?"

"Track 40. It allows whoever's creating the CD to place information in such a way that any examination or attempt to play the CD won't work. It'll appear blank. Call it the 'invisible data' system."

"I'll have them try it."

They waited beside towering oaks as blithe weekend Sacramentans, out for a pleasant afternoon, passed by. Cooper studied his former colleague. Oscar was doing exactly the right thing, white collar cases, computer crime, family barbecues. The sharp end of prosecutions, where there were bodies and survivors and human wreckage was not his world.

But it's mine, Cooper thought. *By choice. By conscious and deliberate choice every day.*

Then Oscar said, "Do you trust your techies?"

Cooper nodded. "Far as that goes, yes. They're all good folks."

"For all of our sakes, yours especially now, Denny, you better be a lot more convinced of their loyalty than that," the other man snapped.

Cooper didn't anger or ruffle easily. "What's your point, Oscar?"

"If I'm right, if this CD's been encrypted in Track 40, you're going to see what's on it. Your techies are going to see it, too."

Cooper and Oscar walked toward their cars. "These are police technicians. They've been exposed to confidential, sensitive information before."

"You weren't so obtuse in the old days."

Cooper stopped and said coldly, "I'm not being coy, Oscar. I do realize that whatever's on that CD

185

was worth a woman's life. Tate had a diamond to go along with it."

Oscar shook his head. "If there's something on the CD hidden using a sophisticated encryption technique like Track 40, the diamond wasn't a payoff from Tate."

Cooper jiggled his car keys. "No. If we find sensitive information on the CD it means Agent Tate wasn't buying information, he was selling it."

"Selling information by someone in Counterintelligence implies a very deep covert op, Denny. It means national security. It means we've got a foreign agent on the hook. The diamond's part of the payoff."

"I've been mulling over the implications since we found out Tate's job and the way he acted when he realized Mrs. Basilaskos had his package."

Oscar nodded somberly. "Let's hope to God there isn't a damn thing on that CD. Let's leave this with the diamond as a payoff by Tate to somebody he's running. I don't even want to think that we've got some foreign country on the hook with Tate playing double agent."

"I want the truth. For my victims."

Oscar groaned. "I'll get in touch when or if I have something."

"Soon, Oscar. As soon as possible."

The other man walked away without saying anything else. Cooper frowned, and slathered the hot dog he bought from a cart with mustard, relish, and ketchup, washing it down with a root beer.

His case against an FBI agent would be difficult

enough. But if United States national security and foreign countries were also tied up in it because there was some kind of double agent operation Tate was handling, the case was going to be unbelievably hard to move off square one. Every door would close, perhaps including SPD and even his own office. He wanted to talk it over with Leah. She saw nuances and angles. She could help make sense of the irreconcilable: a valuable gem and perhaps sensitive information in the same package. They seemed to preclude each other. One signaled a payoff. One signaled a sale.

He finished the hot dog with a final savage bite. So much for dinner.

All right, he thought. *This isn't about national security or the FBI or the CIA or anybody else. It's only about murder. Two murders.*

He got into his car. He flipped on Miles Davis.

He sped back to his office a few blocks away. *Murder,* he thought, *is something I know how to deal with.*

Terry and Rose were finishing their look at the bar incident involving Tate.

"It's like I told you this morning," Amber Pearl said with exasperation, "I didn't come on to him. This guy came on to me. Then he decks me."

Terry nodded sympathetically. They sat on sofas in the lobby of a small truck stop motel off I-99 South. Big rigs rumbled into the large parking lot. Amber's trade when she wasn't taking phone-ins to the escort service that employed her.

Rose said to the attractive young woman with stiff blond hair, "How'd he come on?"

"It's kind of embarrassing," she said without blushing. "I'm kind of nonjudgmental in my business obviously, but this was over the line."

"Whisper it to me," Rose said, leaning to her.

She cupped her hand and spoke into Rose's ear. Rose's mouth curled in disgust.

"See what I mean?" Amber Pearl sat back, straightened her short purple skirt. "When I said it'd cost a lot extra, he just went nutso. Called me a whore, lots of stuff." She primped her hair. "Well, *duh*," she said with obvious self-mockery. "I tell you I'm getting my MBA this semester?"

"You told us," Terry said. "This guy saying anything else, besides trying to expand your professional range?"

Amber stood up. "First thing, he says he's very lonely. All alone. I hear that a lot."

Rose said, low to Terry, "Okay, family's in Pacific Palisades."

But Amber went on, "I go, 'Forget about your wife for tonight, baby,' and he just stares at me like I'm hurling my dinner on him. 'I'm not talking about her,' he goes, 'I mean God. God's deserted me, they've deserted me. They've left me alone in the wilderness.'" She smiled, a meltingly gorgeous smile. "We done?"

"Yeah," Terry said. Rose nodded.

"Thanks for giving me a pass tonight. Maybe I can stretch that for a couple days? I can make the semester tuition with a couple of good dates."

"The freebie card's good once only," Rose said.

She shrugged. "I'm going to court when this bastard's case comes up. Nobody treats me that way," Amber vowed. They both watched her as she walked out of the lobby and saw through the large picture window that she headed for the closest knot of big rigs and their drivers.

Rose said, "People are sick bastards. What's this guy telling her?"

"Hell if I know," Terry said, sounding as exasperated as the young professional now mingling with grinning drivers outside. "We got our meeting at seven to make. We can tell Cooper about the tails and the camera today." He hadn't wanted to risk a phone call.

But Rose didn't let it go. "Sick bastards. And the guy's got a wife and kids at home. I don't understand it, Terry."

"You think I do?"

Chapter Fourteen

"I did a thorough evaluation, Dennis," Leah said to him. "There's no question on the identification of Gerald Tate as the shooter. It's solid. Even without Rutherford or Standhope, this is a terrific ID."

"Have I told you lately what a pleasure it is to work with you?" Cooper said from the other end of the large brown conference table.

"Yesterday."

"Well, it is."

"Not just because we can swap L.A. earthquake stories? You can drop a reference to the 405 at rush hour or the old Bistro Gardens in Beverly Hills and I know gossip just like you do?" They had both, at different times, grown up in Beverly Hills and gone to Beverly High. It was a shared high-end small-town adolescence.

"In spite of that"—Cooper waved—"I didn't bring you to Major Crimes because we can cut up old touchés about how Beverly Drive's changed or how Jacopo's Pizza's stayed in business for thirty years. Or comparing prom nights at the Century Plaza, Leah."

"I'm not so sure," she said. She knew how he looked at her.

Cooper, as supervisor of the major crimes section, was in charge of six highly experienced veteran prosecutors. He had been supervisor for sixteen years, longer than anyone else. He reviewed every case that was referred to his section and then recommended whether the district attorney's office should seek the death penalty or some lesser punishment. His recommendations were invariably followed and because every death penalty case was the most visible and notorious in the county, each carried the greatest risk to the elected district attorney, Joyce Gutherie. Cooper's calls on these cases could either secure or demolish the district attorney's career. It was a singular continuing vote of confidence through the administrations of three district attorneys that he wasn't second-guessed.

So he was given great latitude in selecting assistants from any of the office's other sections, from Misdemeanors to the Felony Trial Bureau to the boutique units like Community Enforcement and Consumer Fraud. He had picked Leah from a high-rising trajectory in Felonies where she had back-to-back convictions, one in an arson case without witnesses or much physical evidence and the other a Russian car theft gang. The gang case had required special deftness since the witnesses were mostly Ukrainian or Belorussian immigrants who spoke little English and were terrified of testifying. Leah managed to coax the most damning information from them on the witness stand.

It helped he and Leah shared a common growing up too. It made working easier and he found he enjoyed being with her more and more. The life of a divorced father didn't appeal to him. He felt it even more keenly when his son Darren was away at a summer camp in the San Gorgonio Mountains until the end of August.

He was a little annoyed then when Terry and Rose arrived a moment later, breaking the developing mood. Leah became very crisp and direct. She would be worth the effort, Cooper thought, to delight and impress. They would have many cases that required long, late, after hours, he was certain.

Rose gave a clear recital of the interviews and follow-up they had worked on all day. She had to repeat what the hooker told them twice because both Cooper and Leah wanted to hear it precisely.

The two detectives glanced around the conference room's worn leather chairs and the spread-out papers Cooper had laid across the table, commandeering it all for the evening for his trial the next day and this new, perplexing case. Terry then told Cooper and Leah about the surveillance. "It's got to be the FBI keeping tabs on how much we find out about Tate," he said.

"Leah?" Cooper asked. "Assessment, please."

"Your first guess sounds good, Dennis. Tate's obviously a man in some crisis. That's my guess why the Bureau's interested in what we're doing. He's overly emotional, borderline irrational. I mean, an FBI agent picking up a prostitute is pretty far on the edge all by itself. He's a security risk."

"She's not bad looking," Rose said.

"I'm sure." Cooper got up, pen in hand, jabbing in the air when he spoke. "But my irrational hypothesis collapses when we factor in the getaway car. It doesn't work at all if Tate's engaged in a covert counterintelligence operation our victim happened to stumble into."

"The driver's his contact, perhaps," Leah said. "His agent. We know at least two people expected a meeting that afternoon. Tate and someone else. The someone else was in the car and rescued Tate."

"Why'd he shoot her like that?" Terry demanded. "That ain't intelligent."

"We'll maybe have a better idea shortly," Cooper said as he looked at his watch. "I've got Sherman, our techie, checking the CD for data in this Track 40 mode."

Bernasconi had been excused from that evening's meeting. He had a family emergency with a son who had possibly broken his ankle playing softball. He also had the meeting with Deputy Chief Mayer, the inaptly named Mr. Rogers, to brace himself for the next morning.

Leah went on, "The dichotomy is the contents of the package. It really doesn't make any sense."

Cooper stabbed his pen in the air. "Exactly. We're going to get lost in a maze if we stick with the counterintelligence angle. This is a murder. Two murders. We go after that. We've all had some practice."

They grinned, Terry a little thinly. He had had more practice at their chosen craft than anyone else in the room and it was a younger person's profession.

Cooper said, "Terry, you and Rose go down to L.A. on the shuttle first thing tomorrow. Find out about Tate. See his house, talk to a neighbor or two if you can, very quietly. Talk to the local cops. Talk to the supermarket where he shops. Find out which restaurants they go to, the church they attend. I want to hear what kind of school his kids go to, what kind of car the family drives."

They nodded and sat a little more stiffly. When the DA directed an investigation it often seemed more real and definite, possibly because it was heading for sure into a courtroom without the intermediate step of having to persuade a DA to get it moving in the first place. This investigation, of course, was more barbed than what they were used to.

Leah got up. She had changed from that morning into a simple skirt and blouse, but she still looked formidable. "I've got a bold proposition for you."

Cooper tossed his pen onto a pad of densely scribbled notes. "You're taking point. We're listening." He prayed she would suggest what had been forming in his mind since his meeting with Oscar.

"Dennis's hit the problem directly. We will be chasing ourselves forever if we try to deal with Tate as an FBI agent, and a counterintelligence agent. Too many unknowns. Too many anomalies. We should assume, very strongly after Terry and Rose's report, that the FBI will shield him, try to deal with him from their side."

Terry cocked his head. "Makes sense. That's how the bums work everything. *Mi casa es mi casa*."

"How do you suggest we compensate for the might and power of the federal government?" Cooper prompted. He enjoyed watching the boldness and verve Leah brought to her pitch.

"We do what you said at the outset. This is a murder case. The Sacramento DA should deal with it in that fashion."

Cooper smiled gratefully. She'd scored a bull's-eye.

He picked it up from her. "In practical terms, this means that Agent Tate will be in our county courthouse on Wednesday at nine-thirty to set a trial date for his assault on the hooker. I say we take advantage of that physical fact and arrest him on our murders."

"Possession is nine-tenths of the law," Leah said, sitting down beside Rose. "The feds would certainly block any normal attempt we make to arrest Tate once they know we're going after an active murder case against him. We have to arrest him now for the Basilaskos killings before the feds can stop us."

Rose grimaced at Terry and Cooper caught the unhappy prospect looming before the detectives. Play tug-of-war with the FBI for a murder suspect who was an FBI agent. That would make them run for the Maalox.

"Which means," Leah said levelly, "we've got to get an indictment drawn up and in front of the grand jury in the next day at most."

"We'll schedule a night session of the grand jury," Cooper decided quickly. "I'll call and set it up first thing before court."

"What about us?" Terry asked. Gesturing to him and Rose, he added, "I get the feeling this is coming our way."

"It is," Cooper agreed. "You'll have to wrap up whatever you can in Los Angeles and be back here in forty-eight hours. I want you both, as the investigating officers on the Basilaskos killings, to make the arrest when Tate appears in court on the hooker case."

"We'll bring backup," Rose said tightly.

"We'll bring the whole SPD if we have to," Leah said and Cooper nodded. "An overwhelming show of force in Judge Westlake's courtroom."

Cooper paced for a moment. He was electric, alert, and alive, galvanized by the prospect of an important and exciting case. He remembered one terrifying dinner when his father, who had gone deep into a fifth of gin, took out his service gun and said, "See this, Denny? The guy who holds this and a badge holds the whole world in his palm." He held out a big, red-knuckled hand. "There's no argument with this and a badge." And Cooper still felt his father wrapping his small child's fingers around the cold, heavy metal, his mother's cries of horror.

There was a loud, brain-bursting explosion when the gun went off in his hand and the large-caliber bullet smashed into the glassed cabinet of china figures in the dining room. He could still hear his father laughing, the laughter following him as he ran crying from the table. The old man, Cooper thought, was wrong. *All power doesn't come from the barrel of a gun. The law matters more. I intend to prove that again by arresting this killer on Wednesday.*

"So our logistical problem is, how the hell do we

do a special session of the grand jury and the Nagy trial?" Cooper snapped to Leah just to see if she'd jump or hesitate.

"We'll manage," Leah said coolly. She was not at all intimidated by the pressure or the sheer time it would take to do both at the same time. Cooper regarded her again with admiration.

Terry and Rose were stalwarts, unhappy about the whole thing, but good detectives anxious to catch a killer. They left to grab whatever sleep they could before the bleary journey at six A.M. to run out to the airport and the shuttle to Los Angeles International. They would drive out to Pacific Palisades, just northwest of the airport about fifteen miles.

"What about Joyce?" Leah asked as they sat down, referring to Joyce Gutherie, the still relatively new district attorney of Sacramento County who had been in office for about a year after spending ten years laboring as a DDA, the last three working with Cooper. Gutherie and Cooper had a reasonably skeptical understanding of each other's strengths and weaknesses. Cooper respected her formidable courtroom skills but disdained her ambition. He knew Joyce Gutherie wanted to bring him to heel, if possible, to give her control of Major Crimes. A misstep on a case as explosive as this one looked to be could give her exactly the weapon she needed.

Cooper reached for coffee on the conference table, ready now to deal with jury selection problems and *in limine* motions in their Nagy trial the defense was certain to make in the morning to prevent damaging evidence from being introduced.

Cooper, legs up on the table, pad in his lap, chewed

on his pen, holding his coffee in one hand. "I'll see Joyce first thing tomorrow."

"She may not agree with our battle plan," Leah said, all too aware of the politics between Cooper and the DA.

"Your plan. Damn good one too." He smiled at her. "She'll agree."

"We're dead in the water if she doesn't."

"Trust me," Cooper said. "I'll persuade her. Now. What about juror number six tomorrow? Pass or challenge?"

The phone on the conference table rang loudly, a jangle that made them both start for a second. Cooper reached for it first.

The Sacramento County District Attorney maintained a separate investigation bureau all its own. It was used to tackle cases after the police had finished their investigation, but it also took up cases that conflicted with SPD including, but not limited to, investigations in which the suspect was a police officer. SPD's Internal Affairs did handle those matters, but the DA didn't like to rely entirely on cops to check up on cops. In addition, the DA's investigation section had a small but efficient technical staff.

Cooper and Leah stood hunched over a glowing computer screen as young Sherman, son and brother of cops, worked on the keyboard. Surrounding them were wires and disconnected electronic motherboards and the hulks of VCRs, tape recorders of various vintages, and what appeared to be a very intricate stereo system.

"It's there all right," Sherman said. "I started to

pull up data right away and now"—he hit more keys, adjusted several nearby boxes connected to the computer—"it's going to pop up."

Cooper stared at the blank screen. The computer whirred, gurgled internally. Leah had a legal pad to make notes.

The text abruptly flashed onto the screen. It was a letter.

"Leah, read it out slowly, please," Cooper said quietly. "We'll follow. I don't want to lose a word."

The small technical office was bathed in bright, hard light. But it was still Sunday evening and this was a quiet place in stark contrast to the unending weekday activity around the courthouse, the jail, the police department, and the sheriff's office up the street.

They concentrated as Leah read clearly.

" 'Dear Friends,' " she began, " 'why have you been so silent? I can tolerate anything but this deafening silence from you after so many years together and so many triumphs. In the past you have congratulated me and praised my work, and this professionalism has not gone unnoticed by me. The money is meaningless. The bank accounts are only to help my family if anything should go wrong. But now, after all of our time together, why have you let two messages go unanswered?' "

Cooper held up a hand. "Stop for a moment, Leah. Sherman, there aren't any hard copies?"

"Hot off the CD, Mr. Cooper."

"Then you're going to forget this. When I take the CD with me, you won't log in that Ms. Fisher or I have been here this evening and you will keep no record anywhere that you did this work. Understood?"

Gulp. Glance at Leah, who nodded slowly and firmly. "I understand."

Cooper stood back, hands on his hips. "Good. Continue, Leah."

She started in where she had left off. " 'I have requested this crash meeting, putting aside our old signals and drop sites, because I have been transferred and I feel that my time is drawing to a close. There are disturbing signs where I work. I believe I am under suspicion. I have been promoted to a high, meaningless executive position, outside of regular access to information in the counterintelligence program. In addition, I believe I have detected repeated bursting radio signal emanations from my car. They must be listening. They must be watching. Or is it my imagination and I am losing my mind?' "

Leah made a note. Cooper's thoughts quickened. This was the tip of an iceberg. The references to other meetings, long associations. Whatever they had tapped into was established, well used, and familiar.

And still that plaintive tone in the letter, like a man adrift on the ocean without food or water or left to fend for himself. *In the wilderness*, the hooker heard him say. And he read Thomas a Kempis for spiritual solace.

But who was he entreating on this encoded CD?

" 'If I am losing my mind,' " Leah went on, " 'know why. I have come close to sacrificing myself for you. I have risked, as you know, death itself because the laws of my country punish what I have done for you with death. Why then do you leave me in silence? It is the one unbearable thing for me.' "

Leah looked at Cooper. "This next line suggests a

monumental ego. 'My analysis is that I am either insanely brave or simply insane. My coworkers would pick the latter if they knew about us and our work together. I hope others, with more enlightened and expansive perspectives, pick the former. But no matter. There is no question on one point: I am insanely loyal.'"

"Whoever wrote this is a spy," Cooper said.

Sherman sat up. "Like *The Prisoner*? Great series."

"'I am a lost and lonely soul at this moment,'" Leah read from the glowing computer screen. "'I ask you, based on our old successes, to set the signal at my new site any Monday evening. I will answer. I enclose further proofs of my continuing and undiminished loyalty and friendship. I return the diamond you provided ten years ago after our first, great success. I return it not as an insult but a proof itself that I am loyal, not because of money or rewards. I am true to you, my friends, in and of itself.'"

Cooper read softly as the letter scrolled to its end. "'Please say good-bye, if nothing else. Your farewell will have to do, if it must be so. This has been a lonely, dark time, my very dear friends. I am so lonely in your silence.' Signed, 'Thomas,'" Cooper ended.

Sherman began tapping on the keyboard. "There are files on here, Mr. Cooper. You want to see them?"

"Yeah. Pick the first one and open it."

Leah read, "It's titled 'The KGB's First Chief Directorate: Structure, Functions, and Methods,' dated 1990."

"It's got a top-secret designation," Cooper said

slowly. "And a warning notice that unauthorized disclosure is subject to criminal sanctions. National Security Information. Here we go," he read out. " 'No further distribution or reproduction is authorized without the approval of the associate deputy director for operations for Counterintelligence, CIA.' "

"He is a spy," Sherman said with amazement.

"Give me the title of the next file and then close it up," Cooper ordered.

"Top secret again. 'DCI Guidance for the National MASINT Intelligence Program FY 1991 to 2000.' "

Leah jotted down more arcane words and letters and gave the note to Cooper.

"Shut it down, Sherman," Cooper said.

He and Leah waited in silence until the technician closed the operation and handed him the CD.

Leah, in a cool and thus more cautionary tone, said, "Remember, Sherman, none of us have been here tonight. This isn't a game or a TV show."

Sherman jumped from his chair. "I got it. I'm out of here."

On the way back to the conference room and more work for the trial they detoured momentarily into his office. Cooper and Leah didn't say much. He felt the same unknowing unease that gripped Nye and Tafoya. The same sense of yawning depths and forbidden knowledge that disconcerted Oscar.

But it was Leah, a cooler player than even he had recognized, who said, "I don't think you should tell Gutherie everything."

"She's the DA. She needs to know." He locked the

CD in his office safe, alongside evidence from the
Nagy trial.

"Give her some maneuvering room, Dennis. If she
knows what we've just seen, you'll tie her hands."

"I see the point. Are you prepared to be Joyce's
credible denial if things go very wrong? Which they
can easily do?"

"If you are."

Cooper grinned. "Well. The defense always ac-
cuses prosecutors of concealing information from
them. This may be the first time prosecutors will
conceal information from the DA."

Cooper made a call from his office while Leah
worked in the conference room. The glow from the
green glass high-rise office buildings' lights and the
lights along J Street beyond his window were garish
reds, yellows, and greens against the city's darkness
and the rush of sounds not far away from streets still
busy even on a Sunday night.

"Oscar. Sorry to disturb you again. It's urgent."

"Yes."

Cooper correctly interpreted the flat, bitter response. He was not welcome. "You've got to get to a
contact with the feds, go to the Bureau if you have
to. I need to know what the following designations
mean." He read off Leah's note: MASINT. NO-
CONTRACT. NOFORN. WNINTEL. ORCON.

"When do you need it, Denny?"

"Tonight."

"I can tell you what NOCONTRACT means myself. I've come across it doing computer crime stuff.
It restricts information to government sources. It

means you can't give out the information to contractors or consultants."

"Good, Oscar. Get back to me as soon as you can I'm at the office." He gave the number of the conference room's telephone. This was not the discussion he wanted to have on a cell phone. It was not, he realized, a conversation he really wanted to have at all.

Murders were inconvenient in many ways, Cooper thought. *What they show us about ourselves. What they force us to deal with. What they shove into our faces.* The secrets thrust suddenly into the light.

Near ten, his shoulders and back aching from tension and the spirited, demanding discussions about trial details that Leah seemed to relish, the conference phone rang. He snatched it. Leah paused, typing up Points and Authorities on her laptop.

"Denny," Oscar said without preamble, "your designations are usually applied to classified information. Do you want to know what that covers?"

"Give."

"Military plans, cryptology, intelligence sources or methods, the vulnerabilities and capabilities of systems, projects, installations, or plans related to national security."

Leah gestured to ask if he could put the call on the speakerphone. Cooper shook his head. That would unsettle Oscar utterly and completely.

"Are you getting this, Denny? I mean, *getting it?* My sources are saying that those designations are stuck to top-secret data. Classification depends on the expected effect of unauthorized disclosure. So a top-secret document means one whose disclosure would be a grave, no, let me tell you what my source said, cause *exceptionally grave* damage to national security."

"What do the designations mean?" He didn't want Oscar's barely controlled panic and anger to grab him too. He was in and couldn't get out. Nor could Leah or Terry Nye and Rose Tafoya, and after tomorrow, even if he gave Joyce Gutherie some cover, she would be in too. Secrets have a way of ensnaring the unwary, like a pitcher plant drawing a doomed insect into its guts.

Which is what had happened to Constantina Basilaskos on a day like any other, when she simply went to work and made food and fed hungry Sacramentans and tourists and found something she wasn't supposed to find. And died because of it.

Oscar said carefully, "NOFORN means the data isn't releasable to a foreign national. MASINT tells you the material is sensitive, intelligence data. WN-INTEL means warning notice, intelligence sources, and materials involved. ORCON says that the dissemination and extraction of that information is controlled by whoever originated. Hands off, in plain English. You know what all of these designations come from, Denny?"

"No. Tell me."

"Sensitive compartmented information. SCI in the jargon of the spook trade. Secret secrets. The family jewels. The holy of holies. Not to be viewed by unhallowed eyes or put into unannointed hands."

"I appreciate that, Oscar."

"People go to prison for a long time if they don't have the magic passwords to handle this stuff. It's the information equivalent of highly radioactive. So I do not want to know anything else about how you got these designations or what they're being used on."

"I respect that. Now I need whatever you can find out about Agent Gerald Tate."

"I bet you do," Oscar said grimly. He hung up.

Cooper stared blindly at the bookshelves, the ordered and precise state and federal court decisions in which so many judges, over so many years, had striven to bring reason and fairness out of the brutality and chaos of so much of human affairs.

"Dennis? What was that all about? You look like you've seen a ghost."

He grinned. "Do I? I feel fine. How do you feel about jumping out of a plane, free-falling from thirteen thousand feet in the hope you may happen to catch a stray parachute on your way down?"

"It sounds exciting." She ginned back. He recalled now that she rock-climbed for mild diversion and exercise on weekends and after work, when possible, at one of the rocknasiums uptown.

"Good. I'm happy I can bring a little excitement into your life."

"Have we jumped out yet?"

"We're about to."

Chapter Fifteen

At seven-fifteen on Monday morning, August 11, District Attorney Joyce Gutherie had gotten her breakfast of plain croissant, dark-roast coffee, and a small plastic box of sliced fruit. She offered the fruit to Cooper.

"I had an apple yesterday," he said, relieving himself of any further healthful habits for the near future.

"I usually let it sit on my desk until noon and then I throw it away. I know it's healthy. I think I only buy it so the lookie loos at the G Street Café don't think I'm only having coffee and a fancy doughnut." She laughed slightly.

Cooper nodded. He stood in front of her large dark-stained oak desk. She had rearranged the office more to her liking since taking up residence after she defeated her predecessor in a nasty campaign. Cooper had worked her in the election, despite their past disagreements, and he knew Joyce was grateful.

The conference table was moved toward the back, the flags of California and the United States brought closer to the desk, and a more pleasing display of flowers and family photographs in silver frames lightened the place, Cooper admitted. He liked Joyce. He did not entirely trust her. She was elegantly dressed, as usual, with a silk scarf and a gold brooch setting off her tasteful turquoise suit.

She had much to contend with as the county's top prosecutor, which sometimes made her a very big target in the state capital. She had to run some corruption investigations on her own rather than with the U.S. Attorney's office, once targeting the misuse of state property by the governor's inner staff. That had resulted in two misdemeanor convictions and community service, very little to show for the trouble and a fair amount of ill will toward her from the governor. Sacramento County suffered when it applied two months later to the state Office of Criminal Justice Planning for a grant to help pay for the computer tech unit Cooper had just used. The grant was summarily denied by the governor's executive director at OCJP. Cooper thought Joyce would be more cautious about high-visibility cases, at least until the dust settled a little.

The effect of having a large organization to run was that the DA herself, like her predecessors, did not go to court. She was an administrator. She was a political figure, the office's champion and breadwinner in the county before the Board of Supervisors and in the state Senate and Assembly. Cooper knew he was about to add a very big worry to her list.

"Joyce, we've got a case. A double homicide really. But it's got a few unusual angles."

She drank the strong coffee gratefully. "That's why I'm here early, Dennis. Tell me all."

He did not tell her all, though. He wondered if he would have told the old DAs the whole unnerving story of Special Agent Gerald Tate. No. They would have wanted to know, but they too would have needed what he and Leah had agreed on last night. Credible denial. The DA must be preserved from the whirlwind that might sweep everyone else away.

By the time Cooper ended, Gutherie's coffee had gone cold, her croissant was unfinished, the fruit pulpy and warming. She got up and went to the window, looking down onto the crowded streets around the county courthouse.

"It's occurred to you that this FBI agent works near us, hasn't it? He's right over on Capitol Mall." She pointed north. "We could stroll over and say hello."

"It's also close to the diner where the victim worked," Cooper said. "I think that was the point. He could walk there for lunch without arousing suspicion."

"Oh my, Denny." Gutherie lapsed into an old familiar way of talking to him, turning from the window. "I don't know about arresting an FBI agent when he's in our courthouse."

"He's a murder suspect. We can make that case. I know it."

She shook her head and walked to the leather sofa, a traditional holdover from an earlier DA no one had removed. Lamps cast a soft glow on her. "Shouldn't we find out a lot more before arresting him? Shouldn't we be absolutely certain?"

Cooper nodded and sat down beside her. "We're checking on his background right now. But the critical thing is, once the FBI knows we've got him as a murder suspect, we won't be able to get at him. They'll put up firewalls in court and bureaucratically that we'll never break through."

"I see that," she said after a short breath to consider it. "All right. Get your indictment from the grand jury. I don't suppose there's really any other alternative."

"I wish there was." He got up. "My hope is that once we've got Tate he may decide to resolve a few of the mysteries in this thing. Why the shooting, obviously? Why this peculiar letter to his friends? Who's his accomplice?"

"It is a homicide and it was committed on our turf," Gutherie said, plainly trying to convince herself of the inescapability of Cooper's proposal. "My head's on the block if you drop the ball." That too was inescapable and she didn't like Cooper having so much control over her career.

He sighed and smiled. "Do you still have that contact in the Justice Department?"

She nodded, puzzled. "Saul Landowski, the assistant attorney general. We worked the Davidian bribery case together when he was an AUSA in San Francisco," she said, meaning an Assistant United States Attorney. "You remember that case? Biker trying to bribe Judge Portanova through his former law clerk? The law clerk who decided she liked being gangbanged by bikers instead of writing briefs."

"I remember the case. The first fireworks that alerted the rest of us we had a star among us."

"That's awful crap, Denny," she said, but he could tell she still enjoyed hearing it.

"You may need to reopen that connection if you haven't talked to him recently."

"May or will?"

Cooper said ruefully, "I don't see how we're going to avoid a fight with the FBI, Joyce. We'll need whatever firepower you've got at DOJ."

As he turned, she said from her desk, "Denny, keep me informed, all right? I want to know what's going on."

"Absolutely," he said without hesitation.

He disliked dissembling of any kind. He didn't do it in court to the judge, the jury, or the defense.

But there were times when the whole truth, contrary to the platitude, would not set you free. The whole truth would shackle the DA.

Cooper retained enough of his religious upbringing, sporadic and unfocused though it was, to feel guilt and resentment when he compromised principles, and suspected he had a great many more sins to answer for later than not being completely frank with Joyce.

"Nice crib," Rose allowed as she and Terry gazed from their rental car at the Tate home on Hollister Avenue in Pacific Palisades. It was a two-story colonial with brass lamp finishes and white trim and a deep green lawn and there were three cars parked in the driveway.

"I hate joints like that," Terry said. "Looks like it belongs in a theme park about the Pilgrims."

"They didn't have big houses. You're thinking of the Federal period, Jefferson, Washington."

"Thanks for the history update. Here come the kiddies."

A woman in her forties, hair up in a bun with a wooden skewer, herded four children from the side door to the sidewalk. The two girls and two boys all looked between eight and twelve. They were carefully dressed in white shirts, tartan skirts, or blue blazers.

"There's a good Catholic family," Terry said. "All in school uniforms."

"That must be Mom," Rose said, studying the woman. She was ash blond and tending toward plumpness, but her face was gentle and she had on glasses that gave her a studious appearance.

"Eight on the button," Terry said. "Here's the school buggy." And a large yellow bus with the words ST. MICHAEL'S ELEMENTARY SCHOOL rolled to a stop, took on the four children, and roared away spewing exhaust. The woman watched from the sidewalk until it was gone and then went back into the house.

"Nice neighborhood, too," Rose said a little wistfully because she lived in a small house in East Sacramento, the curbs and retaining walls decorated with gang graffiti. She was looking at the similar well-tended homes, the suburban well-being stamped on every trim lawn and the clean street and sidewalks.

"Couple cars, nice house, I guess you could manage that as an FBI agent," Terry said. "Nothing big ticket here. No boat. No RV."

"What's an agent make?"

"Hell if I know. Depends on how long you been in, what pay grade you got, just like us."

Rose nodded. Then she said abruptly, "You sleep last night?"

"I'm doing the three o'clock follies, Rosie. I haven't done that routine since I gave up drinking. You know what you do at three in the morning?"

"I watch TV," Rose confessed. "I sneak out of bed so I don't wake Walt or the kid. I been doing that regular since we got into this one."

"Wrong," Terry said, "three in the morning you sit in the best chair you got and you come up with every damn swear word you can think of, like why you're up at three in the damn morning."

It was a clear, warm day in Southern California. There were clean scrubbed kids and elderly people on the streets when he and Rose had driven in earlier. The Tate house, the whole genteel and complacent well-being of the town rankled Terry. It flew in the face of the case they were investigating, the suspect who worked for the FBI and gunned down an unarmed woman in front of witnesses.

Maybe Cooper's right, he thought, *the guy's just plain wacko.*

"You want to sit on her for a while? See if she does anything?" Rose asked.

"Naw. Let's poke around the burg a little. I like the city property records to start with."

Rose agreed. They drove downtown and spent over an hour with a chatty clerk named Lenore who helped them locate the property maps and records for the Tate home. Terry would nod every third word or so just to keep Lenore from bothering them too much. As far as she knew, he and Rose were buyers from San Diego, investors interested in the local land values. They checked on one or two other addresses just to obscure their real interest.

Rose made notes. "So Tate and his wife borrowed a hundred and fifty thousand dollars in 1990 to buy the house for three hundred and five thousand. Then he refinances up to a hundred and seventy-six thousand in 1993, and does it again for over two hundred grand a year later."

"Got a permit here for a rec room addition," Terry said, flipping through another book of records. "Permit's for fifty thousand dollars without the mechanical, plumbing, or electrical, so you can just bump that up to a hundred grand."

"You know that for a fact? Cooper wants facts."

"Listen, I got relatives in the business, and take it from me, you double the permit price when you start putting in light switches. Tell the truth, it gets doubled no matter what if my relatives work on it."

They discovered too that the Tates had taken out a fifty-thousand-dollar loan in 1993, another one for a hundred thousand in 1998, and added a forty-thousand-dollar line of credit to top it off. They also paid off the first loan.

Rose looked at the list of loans and refinancings.

"Nice clean way to launder funny money if you have to," she said.

"I hope Mom wasn't in on this deal," Terry said.

They stopped by the Pacific Trust and Loan where the Tates banked, having gotten the names of various financial institutions from the property records. Rather than introduce themselves as out-of-county cops, and raise the possibility that it would require a subpoena or court order to examine the bank's records, Terry and Rose, with their knowledge of the Tates and a cold telephone number SPD used for sting operations, told the bank's officers they were investigators doing a background on Mr. Tate for a possible sensitive government job. The bank's officers could call and verify that assertion.

The Tates had three accounts: college, checking, savings. There was not a great deal of money in any account, but a great deal of money over the last eight years had gone into and come out of the college account. "With four children, I'm not surprised they had to raid it," said the bank's vice president.

From the bank's vice president Terry and Rose got two critical insights into Gerald Tate. First, he did move his money around, innocently or not. Second, he and his family were regular, active, and devout members of St. Michael's Catholic Church.

After a quick lunch at a minimall off the freeway, turkey sandwich with mustard for Rose so she could lord it over Terry that she had forsworn mayonnaise to lose weight, and a very dry corned beef for Terry, they visited St. Michael's.

"Lot of churches in this one," Terry mused aloud as they walked to the parish hall.

"Lot of people go to church," Rose said. "We still go sometimes. Weddings at least."

Terry hadn't told his partner about his own early morning ritual, so all he said was, "You do go?"

"Now and then. You know."

"Yeah, I do," Terry said. He thought of St. Demetrios, St. Philomene, now St. Michael's, and dying Mrs. Rutherford's Good Shepherd. He was no more or less superstitious than the average person and no more than the average cop, who appearances notwithstanding could be quite prone to seeing signs and portents. But there did seem to be something especially strange about a case with connections to so many churches.

They were fortunate to catch Father Kieran Dougherty just before he departed for a scheduled golf game. "I have a lot of parishioners who walk the links on a fine afternoon," he said, unpleasantly recalling for Terry the priests of his childhood and their Irish lilts. None of them, he knew for a sure and certain fact, could have distinguished a mashie from a three iron.

"We need to keep this quite confidential, Father," Rose said after giving Father Dougherty the background check story.

"Oh, I understand. Jerry's been a solid brick about his work as an FBI agent. Truth be told, everyone's always a little awestruck when he's around." Father Dougherty was ruddy and white haired and he kept his fingers tapping as he spoke.

"He's a good family man?" Terry asked with disingenuous simplicity.

"I've got some fine, fine Catholic families at St. Mike's, but there isn't any finer than Jerry and Suzanna. Wonderful children too. Jerry's led study classes and church activities, but his main love, Suzanna's too, is Opus Dei."

"My Latin's rusty, Father," Terry said wryly. "I caught the God part, but could you translate the rest?"

"Opus Dei is the name of a personal prelature of the Catholic Church. It means 'Work of God.' You must sign an agreement to join and you work, as you always do, but you evangelize, consistent with your faith. It's a personal mission of holiness."

Rose looked blankly at Terry, then automatically to the large crucifix hanging on Father Dougherty's office wall. "Could you be a little simpler, Father? I'm not a Catholic."

"Well," Father Dougherty said, embracing in one word all of the loss and incompleteness he understood must be contained in Rose's statement. "Take Jerry, for a good example. He's an FBI agent. Suzanna teaches part-time at the community college. Their work itself takes on a spiritual significance. They are part of the world and their faith animates the way they are part of it. They make themselves, by their faith, examples for others."

"They get gold stars?" Terry asked. "For being extra good?"

Father Dougherty chuckled. "Jerry's an exemplary father, husband, and Catholic. I'm sure he's an exemplary FBI agent too."

"You don't know what he does in the FBI?" Terry asked.

"Some computer work, I believe. Jerry's a prize with these machines. Chases bank robbers, I suppose."

"We need to look a little below the surface," Rose said, still unclear Terry could see just what membership in this exotic-sounding organization meant in the case. "So is there anything you could point to that's not so exemplary about Jerry Tate?"

"We should give a complete picture," Terry said helpfully.

The priest got up and fumbled with his golf bag. "Jerry's got one flaw and he knows it and we've discussed it openly, so I'm not breaking any confidences."

"Wouldn't ask you to," Terry said.

"Jerry's a little bit *too* much, if you know what I mean. He's a federal agent and he dislikes criminals a great deal. But I've seen him get into some, well, hard arguments with people over Marxism or Leninism. Communism. Jerry's a fighter when it comes to laying into Communists or Marx. You'd expect that. If you're in Opus Dei"—the priest spoke to Terry, who at least, he recognized, had heard Latin in the past—"you're pledged to solve society's problems in a Christian way." He chuckled. "I've heard a while ago about Christian-Marxists, but I didn't believe it myself, and Jerry, well, if he wasn't such a good Catholic, he'd get himself into trouble with people who stuck up for the Soviets or the Cubans, the Chinese. Of course, there isn't any more Soviet Union to worry about."

"What kind of trouble?" Terry asked immediately.

"He'd take a swing maybe. Sure. He did once, but he was provoked by the gentleman."

"He ever get more violent than that?"

"He's not a violent man. He takes his faith seriously and fights those who would harm it. Personally, I've always thought so-called 'liberation theology' was a cancer in the church."

"Are you a member of Opus Dei?" Rose asked.

"I am. Yes. We've got a very active group in this parish. We work in hospitals and schools. Jerry's our only FBI agent. A few others work in the federal government, for the county in different departments. The mayor's office."

"Good luck on the ninth hole," Terry said. "Thanks for your time."

Father Dougherty shouldered his golf bag. "A pleasure. I'll walk out with you."

The assistant manager at Rite Shop Supermarket in downtown Pacific Palisades had a slightly different impression of Gerald Tate.

"Almost broke the guy's jaw. I had to pull this bastard off the guy, he's kicking him, swearing at him, calling him a goddamn Red, a stinking Commie, the whole nine yards. It was brutal, let me tell you."

"It started because Mr. Tate saw this man with a copy of Che Guevera's diary?"

The assistant manager rapidly nodded to Rose's question. "This bastard Tate goes up to a total stranger and starts arguing with him. Then out of the blue, *bam!* Decks the guy with a sucker punch. Worst part, Tate's wife and kids are right there." He pointed at the supermarket's parking lot.

"The cops came, right?"

The assistant manager snorted. "Cops came. The cops talked to Tate, who's much calmer all of a sudden, and the cops leave. I mean, Jesus! I'm busting, I'm telling them what this maniac did, everybody is. Shows what you can get away with when you're an FBI agent."

Terry scratched his face. "You let the FBI know?"

The assistant manager put up both hands. "I can see trouble. That guy's wired up and so I just stepped off, let it go, and made sure my customers were okay."

"The FBI's got to do something under those circumstances. You should've called," Rose said.

"You call." The assistant manager pointed at Rose. "I just told the bastard he shops some place else. Kind of too bad."

"Yeah? Why?" Terry asked.

"Every Sunday, the wife buys a premium standing rib roast. Eight fifty a pound."

"Sorry for your loss," Terry grieved.

"So this guy's thinking Ms. Basilaskos was a Communist and he caps her? Coopers's right. He's a nut."

Terry frowned. "Okay. So Tate's been flushing his meds and he's gone psycho. Who's the bozo in the getaway car?"

"Guy who's still taking his meds obviously," Rose offered.

The thorny problem of how they could handle the Nagy trial and kick-start the Tate case with an indictment all at the same time came to a resolution suddenly for Cooper and Leah Fisher when court convened on the fourth floor, Department 33 of the Sacramento County Courthouse to continue with jury selection.

The attorneys had been arguing since nine A.M. over motions to exclude evidence, outside the presence of the potential jurors. Mr. Nagy grumbled throughout and was admonished by Judge Laszlo Franchetti to remain quiet or he would be removed.

Leah argued strenuously against the public defender's motion to prevent the jury from hearing about Mr. Nagy's predilection for arson. He had started fires at every home he had ever lived in and tried to set fire to his eldest son when the boy was eight some years before, and these facts seemed, not unreasonably to Leah, to be relevant to his current charges. More grumbling and a fist slammed to the counsel table by Mr. Nagy. The judge took the matter under submission and ordered that there was to be no mention of any prior incidents until he decided what to do. More admonitions from Judge Franchetti.

Then, as Cooper began his voir dire of juror number six, the process of asking questions to determine bias or prejudice for or against the parties in the trial, he had gotten no further than, "Is there any reason you can tell us now that you could not be fair and impartial to both sides in this case?" when he was interrupted by a shriek and a loud bang.

The shriek came from Mr. Nagy as he repeated the word *"Fair!"* and the bang was the result when he leaped to the counsel table, stomping on his lawyer's hand, tearing open his own shirt, which sent the buttons spraying around the courtroom, and began screaming that someone should rip his heart out. The world was threatened by the Venus swamps.

Cooper reacted by trying to shield Leah, who reacted by trying to get a better view. Judge Franchetti banged the panic button under the bench so hard he got a blood blister and fifteen bailiffs from every courtroom came running in and subdued the bellowing defendant, carrying him bodily away through the rear of the courtroom. The potential jurors were hastily escorted to the jury room.

When he recovered enough to resume the bench, Judge Franchetti looked out on the attorneys. "Anyone have a motion?"

Cooper sprang up. "The people move that this jury pool be dismissed because the defendant has tainted it. The people also move that this trial be recessed until the defendant's competence to stand trial can be determined, Your Honor."

"*I* was thinking along the lines that a competency examination might be in order," Judge Franchetti said crossly. The public defender objected and said Mr. Nagy was merely temporarily overwrought and they could continue the trial later in the afternoon or tomorrow.

Judge Franchetti, not renowned for judicial humor, growled, "Continue this afternoon? Mr. Nagy appears to be raving. Both of the people's motions are granted," Judge Franchetti ordered, already halfway off the bench and headed, Cooper knew, for the small bar he kept in a corner of his chambers.

Not permitted in public buildings, of course, but often medicinally necessary for an overworked criminal trial department in the capital of the state with the fifth largest economy in the world.

He paused and said to the prosecutors, briskly packing their briefcases, "What was that about the Venus swamps? Did you hear that? You, Ms. Fisher?"

"We both did, Your Honor," Leah answered as if it were a question about precedent or procedure.

"Well, what does it mean, Mr. Cooper?"

"I think the court's guess is as good as mine."

"I was afraid of that. This is a lesson for us all, Mr. Cooper, and particularly you, Ms. Fisher, being the newest member of our club."

"Your Honor?" Leah asked.

"You'll come to work here some day in a case where life and death are at stake and think you've heard it all. But you haven't, have you, Mr. Cooper?"

"No, Your Honor." Cooper bobbed his head. "The day we've heard it all is the day we should quit."

Leah and Cooper trotted from the courtroom. "We've got a breather. Meet me in my office in fifteen minutes and we'll draft the indictment for the grand jury special session."

"What should I bring?"

"A focused mind. We don't have the luxury of a second shot at an indictment against Tate."

Bernasconi was admitted into Deputy Chief Mayer's spare office after waiting for nearly an hour. Mayer motioned him to a small table he used for informal meetings. A small fan whirred on it because it was a humid, warm day and the building's air conditioners were old and inadequate like the aging and over-crowded building itself.

"We've got our crime stats in general in line with the other cities our size," Bernasconi said.

Mayer blew out his sunken cheeks. "Your murder numbers are crap, Van."

"We're doing better than six months ago."

"Don't give me a snow job," he said. He grinned mirthlessly. It was one of his very few witticisms. "Open investigations, cold cases, this is going to hit you like a bulldozer." He pushed her report toward Bernasconi.

He looked at the two decorations on the flat beige walls, the formal photograph of the mayor, and a smaller picture of Mr. Rogers, with hair, graduating from the police academy. Nothing else personal, no plants, plaques, or testimonials, no family snapshots, no awards. Just a monkish police bureaucrat and his busy subordinates in their offices, everything funneling ever upward to the deities who sat in the chief's office and the City Council, all of whom held the power of life and death over cops of all ranks and dispositions.

"You have any suggestions?" Bernasconi asked sharply. "My people are working flat out."

Mayer did smile from genuine warmth and admiration for Bernasconi. He had stood by Bernasconi on several occasions in the past. But the crime stats were sacred and even he had to enforce the edict to burnish them.

"Van, you and I are going to make this happen,

all right? Look, you've got a bunch of cases that just lie here, nothing's happening." And he singled out two for Felderstein and McGivery. "What I'd really like to see is you get a jump on this one." He pointed at Constantina and Angelo Basilaskos. "Can't you close it up today?"

"We're working hard on it," Bernasconi said carefully, as Cooper had instructed.

"Just clear this one and you get two homicides off your numbers. You have a suspect?"

"We do," he said carefully again.

"Great." Mayer beamed. "Who is it?"

"It's sensitive," he said.

"Who is it? You have a name?"

"Yes," he said unhappily.

"Well, who? What's the mystery? It's a purse snatch and a shooting."

"I don't think I can tell you now, sir."

Mayer shoved his chair back and got up. "I think you can, Van. Now I'm nervous. So, this is an order, what's going on? Who's your suspect?"

Bernasconi figured this was the moment to play the only hand he had. He looked at Mayer steadily and coolly. "I think you have to talk to the DA, sir."

"I need to talk to some assistant DA? I stopped doing that ten years ago."

Bernasconi shook his head. "No, the district attorney, Ms. Gutherie. You need to talk to her. I've got a number for you to call. She's expecting it."

"Then I better goddamn call her and find out what's happening in my own department."

Bernasconi listened as Mayer irritatedly put his call in to DA Gutherie. He picked at the creased back issues of law enforcement magazines on Mayer's credenza near the door. He heard Mayer's tart questions, which had also begun diplomatically, get shorter and quieter. He folded his arms when Mayer carefully hung up.

"Oh, *goddamn*," Mayer said slowly. "I figure you knew the DA'd tell me to sit on this for forty-eight hours."

"Yes, sir."

"If I don't, I piss off the DA and the FBI won't do me any favors. If I do sit on it, Chief's pissed, Council's pissed, the FBI's pissed. That's a hell of a choice."

Bernasconi sensed an opening through his dilemma and the unnerved deputy chief's and he sat opposite Mayer, who was at his desk. "I'm with you one hundred percent. You know the kind of first-rate backup my people will give you."

Mayer chewed on his lower lip. "We have to stick together."

"I'll put Robbery-Homicide out as the division that caught this case and worked with you and the DA for the good of the department to clear it quickly."

"It is for the good of the department to keep this quiet, get it wrapped up." Mayer clearly liked the logic and sound of it. "I appreciate that loyalty, Van."

"I think we can also solve my stat problem for the good of the department by moving a few cases into the pending category. Active but not active enough for the clearance rate?"

Mayer nodded with continuing appreciation. "That sounds workable."

"Let's run the numbers again." Bernasconi took

his pen and started to rearrange numbers on the report's graph of homicides in Sacramento.

After a marathon drafting session to get the indictment in proper form, there were a few but indispensable witnesses to have ready that night. Harry Standhope was transported from the county jail, where he awaited proceedings on his case, the short distance to the courthouse to describe what he'd seen and what he had done with the victim's purse and its contents. The criminalist, who would testify he lifted the fingerprints from the materials the police seized from the apartment where Harry had taken them, reviewed his report and the results of the fingerprint identification. Cooper and Leah decided that she would make that evening's presentation to the grand jury.

At eight P.M., the long halls of the county courthouse on the fifth floor in Department 40 where the grand jury met were eerily empty and quiet, every sound loudly amplified so footsteps were booming and whispers carried long distances and the off-white fluorescent lights overhead gave the whole place a sickly appearance.

Leah rose before the twenty-three men and women of the Sacramento County Grand Jury.

They were alone in the twilight courtroom, no judge on the bench. Judge Yamatsu, the grand jury's adviser, waited in his chambers for word that the jurors had a question or that an indictment had been returned and he could officially announce it on the record.

Cooper leaned back in his chair. None of the men

and women sitting in the jury box and on a row of chairs set before it were delighted to have been summoned for a special night session. The usual grand jury term was for one year with sessions regularly scheduled on Thursday and Monday nights. The grand jurors were all middle-aged or older and the routines of dinner, maybe beer and relaxation in front of the TV counted much more than any youthful fascination with surprise and variety.

But he could see they were all curious, leaning forward to listen to Leah. More than one of the men watched her every move. It was to be expected. He counted on it, in fact.

"Ladies and gentlemen," Leah opened firmly, distinctly. "The people of Sacramento, your fellow citizens, thank you for taking the time to be here this evening to consider evidence in a serious crime that occurred on our streets in broad daylight."

Hooked them with that, Cooper gloated. Grand juror number sixteen, a retired lady seamstress worker who usually asked meandering, pointless questions, intently bobbed her head as Leah spoke.

"The people will present evidence of two murders, ladies and gentlemen. I will instruct you on the applicable law you are to follow. As to the first murder, it will involve an open murder charge, one without a degree. In the second murder, I will outline the felony-murder rule in which a killing may be a first-degree murder if it was committed during the commission of a serious crime, a felony."

Leah, dressed in a blue suit, blond hair pinned neatly, spoke without notes.

"The people will ask that you consider the evidence and return a sealed indictment for both crimes against the defendant, Gerald Tate."

Cooper sat up as she called for Harry Standhope to be brought out. Open murder. Sealed indictment. *That's got their minds pumping,* he thought. Open murder meant that the prosecution could, as proof developed, specify the degree, from first to involuntary manslaughter. And add the special circumstances that would invoke the death penalty. A sealed indictment meant that it was held by the DA to be used when she saw fit. It gave the prosecution the maximum flexibility in locating and arresting a defendant. Cooper wanted to have that kind of flexibility when it came time to face down the FBI.

It also meant, Cooper assumed, that several of the grand jurors would conclude that there was something very special about this Gerald Tate. Not FBI Agent Tate, not a man in Counterintelligence, because the grand jury wasn't going to hear anything about who Tate was. Just a mystery wrapped in an enigma, surrounded by a puzzle.

And that was the reality of the case anyway, he admitted.

Harry Standhope, in his jail-drab pants and shirt, still handcuffed, with a Sacramento County deputy sheriff to either side, took the oath.

Leah faced him. "I have a photograph marked 'People's One' for identification. Would you look at this picture and tell the grand jury if you saw the man in that picture shoot Constantina Basilaskos on August fifth at about eight in the evening?"

Harry glanced at the photograph. His handcuffs jingled melodically as he held the photograph out to Leah. "That's the man who shot the old lady. Twice."

Leah gave the picture to grand juror number one. "Please examine this picture for yourselves. It is a booking photograph from the Sacramento County Jail taken on July twenty-fourth of Gerald Tate in connection with another offense."

Cooper flushed with electric expectation. They were off.

Chapter Sixteen

Standing at the rear of Judge Albert Westlake's calendar courtroom at ten-fifteen on Wednesday, August 13, Cooper wondered what Gerald Tate would look like in person. How would he act? Would whatever demons were tearing him apart be apparent? Would he be barely contained like Bela Nagy until some innocuous word triggered a wild outburst? They were ready for whatever Tate did.

Can't see our guys sprinkled in the crowd, Cooper thought.

The preparations for arresting Tate for the Basilaskos murders when he appeared on Amber Pearl's assault case had been laid with battle planning. Loyal cops in the hall in plainclothes and uniform, plainclothes in the courtroom. Leah briefing the DDA doing calendar that there would be something different on the Tate case when it was called. Mr.

Tate, Cooper had observed when he saw the court calendar, had private counsel.

Cooper stood coolly with folded arms, surveying the crowded, noisy calendar courtroom with its one-hundred-plus cases for the morning and one hundred in the afternoon. A cross section of California babbled, wept softly, laughed, stared stonily at the judge and the court personnel attempting to move this endless stream of crime and paper efficiently from one place in the system to the next. Men and women, black, white, Hispanic, and Asian, very young or very old, victims beside criminals, a cacophony of languages and voices that irrepressibly bubbled up until Judge Westlake, half glasses way down his fleshy nose, gestured and his bailiff, a fat black woman with a stentorian voice, yelled for silence and then there was silence for a few minutes as the tension built again and the voices rose once more.

More cops, with the judge's permission, were waiting behind the courtroom in the inner corridor. Terry Nye and Rose Tafoya were seated stiffly in the front row.

Cooper wondered how Leah was doing, essentially the center of it all back in her office, ready to receive reports and send out orders depending on what happened in the next few minutes. She was unflappable during all the planning, alert to the pitfalls.

There were so many ways this could go very wrong. Cooper had briefed Joyce Gutherie personally at eight. The plain toasted bagel and cream cheese, drowned in four cups from the courthouse

232

cafeteria's home-brewed coffee, churned in his stomach. Cooper, like most prosecutors or trial lawyers generally, had learned long ago to eat lightly on court days. He had thought he was safe with the bagel.

Cooper, who didn't like cell phones, had been given one for this occasion. It throbbed almost lifelike at his waist and he answered it.

"We've got a G car coming up front," said one of the SPD uniforms observing the streets around the courthouse. "It's our guy and three others coming right up the front door."

Cooper said quietly, "Thanks." A G car meant a government car, one of the standard stolid models of Ford or Chrysler favored by United States agencies, particularly law enforcement. For an instant a thought flashed into his mind from a report or an interview, some stray fact in the case. But he couldn't catch it fast enough and other things pressed in more swiftly. He called Leah. "Tate's on his way in with three others. Probably a lawyer and somebody from his office."

"We're ready, Dennis."

"Let everybody know. I'm going to tell Nye and Tafoya."

Cooper made his way to the front of the courtroom as the bailiff shouted for silence. Judge Westlake regarded him with bored, frustrated annoyance. Cooper had only told him that there would be an arrest of a defendant on another case.

"Take it outside, Mr. Cooper," the judge had snapped just before court convened. "I've got a raft of crap to get through on my nine-thirty and I'd like, underline that please, to get some lunch before I start my one-thirty, okay?"

"We'll make every effort not to inconvenience the court, Your Honor."

"Too late for that, counsel. Just take it outside. Leave me a little bit of peace."

Cooper now bent to Terry Nye and said quietly, "We're on. He's coming in."

Terry Nye barely acknowledged him and Rose Tafoya stared ahead. "Got it."

Cooper went back to the front of the courtroom and whispered next to the DDA, "Call the Tate case out of order."

Gerald Tate as he strode into the courtroom, Cooper thought, looked like an upscale real estate salesman or a banker in his blue-black generously cut suit and cobalt-blue tie against a starched white shirt. His jowls were unusual on a relatively young man and he carried some weight. But it was the upthrust chin and the watery blue eyes sweeping around the courtroom with disdain or wariness that Cooper detected. *He thinks he's the center of the world,* Cooper realized. *He thinks everyone is watching him.*

A great many people in the courtroom were doing just that.

In front of Tate was a smaller, sharp-nosed older man in a charcoal suit, carrying a slim briefcase. Directly behind Tate were two other men, clean shaven and athletic. FBI escorts, Cooper surmised.

Judge Westlake made short work of the case.

"Counsel wants to postpone further proceedings

pending the filing of motions to dismiss?" he barked. "We've got one victim, two counts of felony assault, solicitation for an act of prostitution."

"That's correct, Your Honor," said the smaller man. "Jonathan Maksik, representing Mr. Tate. I intend to enter into further discussions with the district attorney's office about a possible plea disposition in this case. I request a three-week continuance for those purposes."

Tate stared at the judge, then around him, hands clasped in front of himself, sometimes his eyes lighting on the Great Seal of California above the bench.

"People object?" the judge demanded of the young DDA.

Cooper held his breath. Prosecutors usually did object to delays or continuances and he hadn't had time to fully tell this kid what to do. He had assumed Tate would try to work out some plea bargain this morning rather than putting everything over.

To his immense relief, the DDA barely looked up. "People have no objection."

Westlake barked at his clerk and a date in late August was selected.

Tate turned, eyes restlessly moving among the crowd, along the brown-paneled walls of the courtroom.

With efficient ease, Terry Nye and Rose Tafoya stepped in front of the trio before they could get to the courtroom doors. Three plainclothes cops fell in behind the trio, boxing them in. Cooper buttoned his coat and joined the two detectives.

"Gerald Tate?" Terry said tonelessly. "I have a

warrant for your arrest for the murders of Constantina and Angelo Basilaskos on August fifth in the city of Sacramento, county of Sacramento."

Maksik sputtered loudly, "What's going on? This is impermissible. We didn't have any notice!"

"We've got a warrant," Terry said as Rose spun Tate and began handcuffing him.

Cooper braced as the two FBI escorts reached out to Terry to restrain him.

"I wouldn't do that, Agent," Cooper said. "I'm Supervising Deputy District Attorney Dennis Cooper and this man is now in the custody of the Sacramento Police Department. If you interfere with that custody in any way, I am warning you that you will be arrested yourselves."

The FBI escorts hesitated, startled by this development, and they whispered harshly to each other. Maksik continued sputtering defiance and Cooper was uncomfortably aware that Judge Westlake had begun calling loudly too.

"Clear my courtroom right now, Mr. Cooper! I mean it! Clear out!"

"Detectives, remove this man right now," Cooper said.

"Our pleasure," Rose said with a nervous smile. She pushed aside the FBI escorts. "Excuse me, coming through." And more cops from the courtroom audience joined the procession, quickly taking Gerald Tate through a side door.

Cooper tried to concentrate on the legal invective and threats Maksik hurled at him and the angry noises the FBI escorts were making.

But he found himself fixed on Gerald Tate, solid

and fraudulent in his banker's suit and bland plumpness. Tate, as he was about to vanish through the side door, the courtroom loudly murmuring, the bailiff shouting, Westlake slapping his hand on the bench for order, the FBI agents cursing, had turned his head awkwardly, looking back at the confusion and pandemonium had caused. He turned, caught Cooper's eye, and smiled widely.

It was a smile of delight at chaos or one of gratitude that whatever role he was playing had come to an end.

Hands up, striding from the courtroom trailed by Maksik and the FBI agents, Cooper did not know what Tate had just shown him.

"We got him," Cooper gleefully told Joyce Gutherie.

"Phase one," she said dryly as they both headed for her office after stopping by to hear from Leah that Tate's booking and processing were proceeding.

"Phase two starts next," Cooper agreed. "Tate's taken to the securest cells on the eighth floor of the jail and kept in an isolation cell. No contact, no visitors, rotated guards. All visitors and requests for contact to be reported to either me or Ms. Fisher and approved before anyone goes near him."

Joyce Gutherie closed her office door. "Someone's talking already, Denny. The press office's gotten two calls from the *L.A. Times* and the *Chronicle* sniffing around. Someone's tipping them."

Cooper shrugged. "I didn't think we could keep this quiet, Joyce. Too many people have to know. We were lucky to get past the indictment. Anybody in court just now could have talked."

"I don't think the media's going to be satisfied with the statement we put together," she said, picking up the formal press statement. "Calling Tate just a murder suspect seems disingenuous."

She was having second thoughts and worrying about the political repercussions already, Cooper saw. Joyce was still gun-shy about bad moves and bad publicity. He would have to steady her every step of the way. No matter what the rough edges were between them, it was imperative, he and the DA realized, that the big decisions be made and honored. You could tack or shift as necessary, obviously, but to regret a major decision immediately was to invite disaster.

"That's the FBI's problem," Cooper said. "He's theirs. We proceed with a double murder case because that's our responsibility."

She nodded and sat down. She offered Cooper a bottle of sparkling water from the small refrigerator in the bookcase beside her desk. He shook his head. She poured a bottle into a cut crystal glass.

"I called Landowski at Main Justice yesterday afternoon. We did the 'how have you been?' exchange for a few minutes and then I said I might have to call him soon with a professional issue. He said he was suitably mystified."

"That's good. I don't know how long it will take for the FBI to react." His stomach grumbled nosily and he apologized. "Maybe I'll take that water."

He was about to point out to Joyce that he should go back to monitor developments with Leah. The DA's secretary, Annalise, an ordinarily calm and dour older woman, knocked and immediately opened the door.

"I thought I better tell you," she said breathlessly to Joyce, glancing irritatedly at Cooper, "that the FBI just showed up in force. The special agent in charge and his whole office, it looks like, are outside."

Cooper took the lead. "What does he want?"

"He wants to see whoever arranged this *goddamned fuckup*. Excuse me. His language."

She shut the door. Cooper quickly said to Joyce, "We should stick to our plan and let me be the point of contact."

The DA nodded and held her crystal glass of sparkling water. "I guess we're going to need my old friend at the Justice Department sooner than we thought."

"I guess we will." Cooper gulped down his water. "I'll go see what the Bureau is demanding."

Joyce Gutherie didn't smile at his sarcasm.

"Do you have any idea what you've done?" Special Agent in Charge Shaun Boler shouted at Cooper.

"I've arrested a suspect who shot one woman and caused the death of her husband," Cooper said. "What seems to bother you about that sequence of events?"

SAC Boler gaped in infuriated amazement at Cooper. Boler sat across the small conference table in Cooper's office with two other agents flanking him. The platoon of agents he had brought with him waited outside. Leah sat to Cooper's right. At Boler's insistence, the blinds had been pulled on the office's inner windows and the ones looking out onto the street.

"You grandstander, Cooper." Boler shook his head. "You publicity-seeking clown. You do not go around arresting members of other law enforcement agencies without first inquiring what's going on. That is law enforcement protocol. That is common sense. You don't know what Tate's doing and you just fucked it up to get yourself some headlines."

Leah tapped her silver pencil on a legal pad. "It was our impression the FBI might not produce Agent Tate if we asked first."

"Goddamn right we wouldn't have handed him over!" Boler exploded. The agents beside remained impassive. "Cooper, you don't go pulling the trigger on another law enforcement agency, because you just might be screwing up something you know nothing about."

"Enlighten us," Cooper said, hands folded.

Boler, a package of fierce energy bound in a tailored gray suit, with styled and barbered gray hair and the lean build of a runner, had come from being the regional agent in charge for the Midwest about two years earlier. He called press conferences and announced scrutiny of the state legislature for evidence of possible corruption. There was furious indignation from the insulted senators and Assembly members and political hell to pay and Boler glibly said he only meant that his Sacramento Field Office would be vigilant for signs of corruption, not that any had specifically been pointed out. The storm from outraged legislators subsided for the moment.

Boler led several very publicized raids in south

Sacramento on major methamphetamine labs and forgers turning out phony food stamp and ID cards. He personally arrested two Mexican Mafia members in neighboring Yolo County as they finished lunch at a popular tacqueria.

Cooper had told Leah, "He thinks we all work for him."

"For his glory?" she'd offered with a grin.

Now Boler stood facing them. "I can't believe I'm dealing with such unprofessional behavior."

"We're still waiting for your explanation, Agent Boler."

Boler coldly regarded them both. Leah went on tapping her metal pencil like an impatient teacher. Effective psych warfare, Cooper thought lightly.

"Is this room secure?"

"Last time I checked," Cooper said.

"I'm not joking, Cooper. I take my job seriously."

"So do I. So does Ms. Fisher."

Boler shook his head. "Jerry Tate is a longtime agent in the Bureau's counterintelligence section."

"We know that. Tell us something new."

"Okay, for the last two and a half years, Agent Tate's been the focal point of a covert operation aimed at preventing a major act of terrorism on the West Coast, probably aimed right here at the state capital. He's been able to turn several officials of another country who might supply the explosives and logistics for such an attack. Think about the World Trade Center, Cooper, Ms. Fisher. We're trying to stop an attack like that right here in our own backyard."

Cooper raised his eyebrows to Leah. She shook

her head very slightly. His take on the recitation too. What possible connection could there be to the shooting of Constantina Basilaskos?

"So what country are we talking about?" Cooper demanded. "Give me some details, Agent Boler. So far I'm just getting a lot of unverifiable generalities."

He and Leah had agreed earlier not to mention the CD or the diamond on the assumption that Tate probably hadn't told Boler about it. Knowing about the two unusual and incriminating pieces of evidence, and having them in SPD's possession, could be useful in the bitter jurisdictional combat that was certain to come.

Boler opened the button of his coat with one hand. He let them see his shoulder holster and service weapon. "I can't go into operational details, Cooper. That's highly classified, sensitive national security information. Would you give up one of your confidential informants if I asked you to?"

Leah answered curtly, "If he'd committed a brazen murder, in a heartbeat."

"Well, then that's the difference between you and me? I protect my people." He leaned toward her truculently. "Christ, I'm trying to save a couple hundred lives, maybe thousands."

"We're still looking for the driver of the car Tate used to get away. We're still got an accomplice to murder out there," Cooper said angrily.

"I can give you a little boost there," Boler answered. "The driver is a foreign national, one of the people I mentioned. Tate's in very close to them."

"What's his name and where can I find him?" Cooper demanded.

"You haven't been listening. You've already compromised a national security operation. I'm trying to convince you not to screw it up anymore."

"Then you're obstructing justice." Cooper got up, staring at Boler with equal truculence. "Your agent killed a woman last week. That's a fact. A specific, demonstrable fact."

"Is it?"

"I have witnesses."

"I'm going to suggest you keep an open mind about the incident, Cooper, Ms. Fisher. The incident isn't exactly what it appears to be."

"I'm listening."

"Have you considered that your purported victim might be involved in activities that made Agent Tate's action necessary?"

Cooper now gaped at Leah, then at Boler. "Are you saying that Constantina Basilaskos, a woman in her fifties who had worked for years at a small diner, was an international terrorist?"

Boler nodded carefully. "I'm telling you, for background only, as one law enforcement officer to another, that she was not what she appeared to be."

Leah stopped tapping her pencil. "Mr. Cooper and I aren't law enforcement officers, Agent Boler. We're officers of the court."

Boler waved a hand dismissively. His two agents stood up, blankly studying Cooper and Leah. "I don't have time for this kind of irrelevant chatter. I want you to turn over Jerry Tate right now."

"No. He's in the custody of the police and he stays there."

"Are you insane?" Boler raged. "He's in jeopardy every second he's in your goddamn jail. This man is working for the United States government, he's my employee, and I demand you turn him over to me. I can guarantee you that we will sort out any issues from the incident last week."

Cooper took a breath, his face set in a frown. "No. He stays where he is for the moment."

"Until when?"

"He goes on trial for two counts of murder."

Boler's tanned face grew darker and a vein pulsed in his forehead. Cooper estimated he would have a stroke sometime before his sixtieth birthday, exercise, diet, and good genes or not.

"I don't believe it," he finally said. "You're not that crazy."

"What's crazy," Leah said politely, "is storming in here, trying to throw dust in our eyes, and threatening us into releasing a man who killed a woman. All because you say you'll take care of any unpleasantness."

"I want to see the DA," Boler snapped.

"The district attorney has given us full authority to handle this case, Agent Boler. That's the end of it."

"I want Tate now."

Cooper got up and opened his office door.

"Cooper, you are so far wrong it's not funny. You have made the worst mistake of your pathetic little career," Boler said. He strode out with the two other agents.

"Take the Praetorian Guard with you," Cooper called out, jerking his thumb at the dozen or so FBI agents loitering outside. He watched the dark-suited procession of furious FBI agents leave the floor. The secretaries, clerks, and interns all looked back at him.

244

"It's fine, it's all right," he said brightly. "The FBI just wanted to check on an old parking ticket."

He closed the door. Leah said, "Feds don't rest, Dennis. They'll be back. They'll have some kind of federal court order compelling us to turn over Tate."

Cooper dialed Joyce Gutherie. "I know. We don't have much time to hunker down. Can you take charge of making sure Tate's not going anywhere? Put some of our cops at the jail, work it out with the sheriff if you have to."

She left at a brisk walk for her own office.

Cooper said when he got an answer on the phone, "It went fairly well, Joyce. Seriously. But this is probably a good time for us to wheel in the assistant attorney general. I think there's going to be some fireworks soon."

Cooper and Oscar met at the I Street entrance to Ceasar Chavez Park again at four o'clock that afternoon. The heat had returned and vendors wandering with cold drinks did a brisk business among the weekday tourists, schoolkids on a field trip to the legislature and other people taking advantage of the park. A fat man with a foolish grin stood near the entrance, saying nothing as coins were tossed into the hat at his feet.

"Alarms are going off all over the FBI's West Coast network, Denny," Oscar said quietly, both men walking close, speaking low. "Watch yourself. They'll be watching you."

"They've been watching my detectives. I assume that's who's been keeping tabs on our investigation."

Oscar shook his head sourly. "Crap. Let's make it quick. This"—he handed Cooper a plain manila envelope—"is my first and last delivery."

Cooper took it quickly and stuffed it into his coat. "What is it?"

"Tate's official CV. Where he's been, what he's done."

"You're taking an enormous risk after all, Oscar. Thanks."

"I told you this wasn't for free and I meant it," the other man said solemnly. "Anyway, something's bad about this one."

"How so?"

"As I was carefully digging that little document out"—he pointed to the pocket where Cooper had stowed the envelope—"I talked to a couple of secretaries. Tate's got a generally good rep around the Bureau, but one woman said she's heard from a friend at Quantico that Tate slugged a secretary a couple of years ago. Went ape shit over some remark she made and hit her."

"Why wasn't he dismissed?"

"That's the reason this feels bad," Oscar said. "I did that, you did that, and we'd be on our way back to the private sector so fast we wouldn't have time to take our nameplates off our desks. Tate got a reprimand, a reassignment, and then nothing else. Like it never happened."

"What about the secretary he hit? She must've complained."

"If she did, it didn't go anywhere." Oscar stopped

to let a man go by who was being yanked ahead by his large tawny boxer on a taut leash. "You want a theory?"

"I'd love one."

"Tate's a golden boy for some reason. He's got a guardian angel or two. He's an important fish in the pond. When he draws attention to himself, the Bureau tries to make it go away. I bet we'd find that the secretary who got hit was promoted and transferred. Same for any witnesses. That's why they'd watch your cops too."

"He must be very important."

"Missing piece of our puzzle, Denny. What makes Tate so damn worth protecting?"

"That's what we need to find out. I'll see what I can do from my end."

"You'll have to," Oscar said as they worked their way through the sweating jugglers and couples and kids toward the entrance. "I'm serious about drawing the line now. This is as far as I can go without being on someone's radar."

Cooper nodded, anxious to read what Oscar had ferreted out. They shook hands. "Be careful," Cooper said.

"Likewise."

Cooper let Oscar leave the park before him. He bought an orange soda, as he had the first meeting, and drank it on the way to his car. He stepped around large black trash bags heaped outside the restaurant built on the site of the restrooms when the park had been the favorite haunt of drug dealers, prostitutes, and assorted desperate characters. He'd prosecuted two voluntary manslaughters and assaults with grievous bodily injury from that colorful restroom. He would never eat at that restaurant, no matter how it was cleaned up. He looked up at the tall, proud buildings spearing into the hot, summer sky, felt the sweat on his chest and back. He stood still while people brushed by him, and he knew, except for a very few human beings like Leah, Nye, Tafoya, and Gutherie, he was utterly alone with a secret that could kill.

Chapter Seventeen

At the seven P.M. meeting in his office that evening, Cooper closed the windows and turned on his inefficient air conditioner along with an oscillating fan on a file cabinet. Boler's comments had at least sensitized him to security. Bernasconi waved a clutch of papers to cool himself. Nye and Tafoya looked exhausted. Only Leah, scented with verbena and holding a Palm Pilot she used to update assignments, was fresh and lively.

Cooper was in his shirtsleeves, tie loose.

"I'm sorry, Terry, but you and Rose are going to have to start running down consulates and embassies. Tate's been in touch with one of them."

"How do you suggest we get started?" Terry asked irritably.

"The car," Leah said. "We can try to correlate similar makes and models with diplomatic personnel in northern California. Probably out of San Francisco."

Bernasconi shook his head, "You're talking about a hell of a lot of people," he pointed out. "I'd need to put the whole division on it."

"No. No more personnel than what we've got in this room," Cooper said. "My source is confidential and so we've got to maintain a low profile."

"Then it ain't going to get done, Cooper," Terry said, folding his arms.

"Rose? That your position too?"

She nodded. "No way. It'd be like trying to hit the moon with a spitball."

Cooper nodded twice but said, "You've got to take a shot. We've got a car and a possible link to diplomatic personnel. We've got to make the best of it."

"I sure would like to seriously talk to Mr. Tate," Bernasconi said sarcastically. He stopped fanning himself. "Any chance?"

Leah said, "It's doubtful. His lawyer Maksik won't let anyone talk to him and unless he waives his right to have his attorney present, we're stuck on the outside."

"I doubt Agent Tate's going to be very forthcoming," Cooper said. "While Terry and Rose are doing what they can to track down the lead on the driver, Leah and I'll be setting up Tate's arraignment tomorrow. I expect Maksik will try to get an OR based on his lack of a past record, but we can block that, can't we?" An OR meant release on one's own recognizance, no bail required, only a promise to make the next and all subsequent court appearances by the defendant.

Leah opened a neat file folder. "Gerald Tate has

no ties to the community. He's still a resident of Los Angeles and he still has his family there. We've also got the prior assault on Amber Pearl to show propensity for violence and a solid case of murder one on the shooting. We're good on felony murder for the husband's death."

"I want to lock that down tight, Leah. Get back to Fabiani and make sure we can demonstrate the cause and effect between Tate's killing of Constantina and Angelo's collapse shortly afterward."

She made quick, sharp notes on the Palm Pilot and in the file. Cooper didn't think she missed much of anything. Not at work, not personally.

"What's our long-term game plan here, Cooper?" Terry asked, loosening his own tie. "Because, you want to know, I'm wondering if our case's as important as whatever this bozo's into."

Cooper searched the other faces. "Anybody else feel that way?"

Bernasconi said softly, "It's not an unreasonable position, Denny. If the FBI says Tate's undercover to stop major terrorism, maybe we should back off for now."

Cooper was about to deliver a hard-core pep talk when Rose said firmly, "No. Our victim's the one that counts. Ours. FBI can do what they need to do after that."

Leah cocked her head to Cooper. The rebellion was short and unsuccessful, she seemed to say to him.

"We're not going to prevent the feds from doing their work." Cooper paced to Terry. "It's just that Rose's right. We come first. Our dead take precedence."

251

Terry grunted. He stood up. "Okay. I let you have my two cents. We'll get on the cars first thing tomorrow."

Cooper, in a rare display, tapped the older man's shoulder. "I understand," he said. "I don't even disagree. We can have both bites at this bastard."

Cooper and Leah decamped after the meeting broke up and got provisions from the soda and chip machines. She scrounged a cup of instant risotto she'd been hoarding for an emergency. They ate and drank in the conference room.

"Are we on thin ice?" he asked her.

She paused, spoon pushed back into the carton. "I don't think so. I think the FBI will come at us aggressively, maybe as early as the arraignment, but maybe not."

"I meant Nye's beef. National security trumps one or two measly homicides."

"He'll live with it."

"Is he right?"

Leah smiled, white teeth with a very tiny bit of spinach stuck in front. "Maybe he is. But even if he is"—her smiled vanished—"we've got to go forward."

He pretended to take that in and then said offhandedly, "You've got some green in your teeth."

For a moment she was flustered, picking it out with a paper napkin. "Very funny."

"Endearing actually." He smiled and again opened the manila envelope Oscar had given him. "All right. A quick summary of the life and times of Gerald Tate. Officially."

He read it out. Tate was born in 1953, raised in

Boston. Got an AB in physics from Boston College, briefly studied zoology at George Mason University, then switched and settled on an MBA in accounting and information systems.

"That takes us up to 1977. He works as a CPA for a while back in Boston. Then he joins the Boston Police Department, works as an investigator in the financial bureau of the inspection services section."

Leah made notes again in her Palm Pilot. "Any languages?"

"Funny you should mention it. Russian while he was at BC."

"Suggestive," she said. "The Evil Empire was still a potent force. Perhaps an attractive one."

"Let's keep it in mind. Onward." And he resumed reciting from the stolen personnel records.

Tate left the Boston PD, with commendations, after three years. He entered duty as a Special Agent of the FBI, and following his training at Quantico he was assigned to a white-collar crime squad in New Orleans. He next moved onto the FBI field office in San Francisco and handled accounting problems.

"Now the fun starts," Cooper intoned. He held the papers reverently. "Agent Tate must have done such a knock-up job that he was detailed to the field office's intelligence division to help set up—get ready, Leah—the FBI's automated counterintelligence database."

"He didn't have the keys to the kingdom, he made them himself," she said admiringly. "I hope it's occurred to you, Dennis, that Tate is a very intelligent man. He's way past the usual killer or defendant we process through here."

"It has occurred to me. But he's losing it, isn't he? He shoots a woman in front of witnesses and, depending on who the getaway driver might be, doesn't seem to have thought through his escape."

"Irrational or not, we shouldn't count on his problems helping us."

"Point taken," he said. He sniffed the remains of the risotto. "That smells good."

"Bring your own."

"All right. More about Agent Tate." Cooper noted how accurate Leah was about making the keys to the kingdom. Tate had helped to create the automated database that would include a vast encyclopedia of information about foreign officials, including intelligence officers, resident in the United States. It was highly classified.

From that apparent triumph, Tate went on to the FBI headquarters itself in Washington, D.C., and was promoted to supervisory special agent in the intelligence division. He had direct access to the FBI's contribution to the United States Intelligence Community's National Foreign Intelligence Program. He had more secrets at his fingertips.

"He goes on to the Soviet Analytical Unit so he now knows all about Soviet intelligence operations and how we're investigating them. In 1996 he's moving up again, this time as an inspector's aide for the FBI's inspections staff. He gets to travel to all the FBI field offices, resident agencies, and legal attaché offices in our embassies in"—Cooper rapidly counted—"sixteen countries."

"Including Russia?"

"Russia is at the top of the list. He spent a year there."

"What happens when he comes back?"

Cooper looked down the block of double-spaced typing. "Agent Tate continues to be a factor in counterintelligence. He has two special assignments starting in 1998. He's Chief of the National Security Division at FBI headquarters so he's focused on preventing economic espionage. Then he's senior FBI representative to the Office of Foreign Missions of the State Department."

"Doing what now?"

"Another top-dog assignment." Cooper threw the papers down angrily. "This man's heading up an interagency counterintelligence group."

"Based in Washington?"

"Of course. Then he goes on to the field office in Los Angeles before he's moved here." Cooper suddenly didn't care what Tate was doing all those years. It reeked of privilege and secrecy, power wielded in the dark, perhaps for the best motives, but power in the shadows was usually, he had observed, power abused.

As a prosecutor, Cooper was outraged. He fought hard and he fought craftily, but his battles were out in the open for the entire city to see. Tate was a warrior of the shadows obviously. And a killer.

"I have no confidence we know what this man's been doing," Cooper snapped. "For all we know, he's some kind of CIA operative or some who-knows-what."

Leah threw away her risotto carton and wrapped

the spoon in a paper napkin for later cleaning. She touched the edges of her mouth. "Dennis, you didn't answer my question. Tate was based in Los Angeles for his last major assignment?"

"And I said yes."

"So he was near his family. Near his church and whatever he's been doing in this Opus Dei organization."

Cooper sat back, sighing. "Thank you. I was getting a little grumpy. It made me lose my concentration. Tate's okay as long as he's close to home. Then he's sent here to Sacramento."

"Why? What's he doing here?"

"Maybe just what Boler said. We have to face that possibility."

Leah got up and picked up papers, a volume of appellate court decisions, and her mug of cold green tea. She said. "If we could find out what he was doing in Russia that year, I think we'd find a recruitment opportunity. That's when they signed him up. Maybe they gave him flowers and dinner."

"Maybe it was just his requisite trip to Mecca," Cooper said sourly.

They returned to working on the motions in opposition to either setting a bail amount or a release on Tate's own recognizance. He was a definite flight risk.

Cooper also looked at the laconic report from the police forensic accountant. It was certain there were no untoward financial irregularities in the Basilaskos' business records. He thought it was a small but vital comfort to read that final judgment.

"I hate to interrupt," Cooper began, holding the accountant's report.

"Go ahead." She looked up.

"Do you ever wonder how the world would think of you if your whole life was suddenly exposed? Like a murder victim's always is?"

"Or Tate. We've got him laid out here."

"He's still alive. He can still defend himself. Mr. and Mrs. Basilaskos can't."

Leah shook her head, "I'm only concerned about what I do while I'm here. Afterward it's up to other people if I did the right thing or made mistakes."

Cooper put the accountant's report down. "I disagree. Reputation is all we've got that's ours, Leah. Doing the right thing because it will matter now and later."

The phone rang. A call transferred from his office line. Leah held out the phone.

He listened for a moment, his face reflecting surprise and then bemusement. He hung up, after having said little.

"That was mysterious," she said.

"Stephen Ungerman, the U.S. attorney for the Eastern District. He politely asked if I'd join him for drinks and possibly dinner at that Norwegian place, Konditori, downtown."

"The place has a good reputation," she said teasingly.

"Impeccable. Should I go?"

"He's the one asking for a dinner date, Dennis. Never turn them down."

Cooper looked at her, realizing she had introduced an entirely different topic into the conversation. Leah had the ability to focus intently and with passion on the job, and reserve some part of herself as well. He liked that talent. He wished he had it.

"Can you work on the motions? Check in with the watch commander at the jail and see if our prize guest is attracting any outside interest?"

"You bet," she said.

"I'll see you later then," he said, rolling down his shirtsleeves.

"What would strike your fancy, Denny? Plain acquavit, pepper acquavit, here's one, orange-and-lime-flavored acquavit," said Stephen Ungerman, studying the large, heavy menu.

"I'll stick with mineral water, thanks."

"This restaurant is famous for one hundred varieties of acquavit. They don't even have that anywhere in Scandinavia. Only in America."

"I've got work tonight. Water will do fine," Cooper said a little testily. He was hunched over the white-starched tablecloth, finding it a little hard to hear the U.S. Attorney just opposite him. The restaurant was in an elegant office building, set off the first floor with a separate spacious blood-red-carpeted reception room. He and Ungerman were led down broad winding stairs of polished black marble into a very large dining room that went up two stories and featured a perpetually cascading waterfall against a green-patinaed bronze backdrop. Several hundred businessmen, many from Asia, from what Cooper could see, noisily and merrily ploughed through platters and silver trays heaped with cold caviar and smoked herring, and washed it all down with large glasses of acquavit so cold the liquor steamed into the air.

It was an expense account restaurant not far from the floodlit California Capitol building and he wondered why the U.S. Attorney had chosen it.

"I picked this place because I like it and it's very crowded and nobody gives a damn who's sitting next to you or whether they're planning to rob Fort Knox," Ungerman explained without being asked aloud.

"We can't be overheard?"

"Technology's blessed us." Ungerman smirked when his steaming cold acquavit arrived and he threw it back with one practiced swallow, and chomped down heavy black bread instantly. "Nothing is forgotten. Nothing is forgiven. The microchip remembers all, perceives all. But we've got the privacy we need here." He smiled. "Best drinks in town too."

"Steve, I appreciate you reaching out," Cooper said. "We haven't been allies in the past." That, Cooper knew, was something of an understatement on the order of saying that the *Titanic* had an icy encounter. In two cases over the last three years, Cooper had wrested information from the haughty Ungerman, once about weapons the ATF had been storing in a midtown office building's basement and again over whether the U.S. Attorney or the district attorney would be first to try a bank robber who shot a teller and two customers. He recalled Ungerman's brittle, harsh contempt over the phone.

This magnanimous host was a remarkable change.

"No." Ungerman managed a laugh, waved for a second acquavit. "But we're both good prosecutors, Denny. I'm counting on that when I make my case to you."

Cooper didn't think there would much of a case to make if Ungerman had another acquavit. In his own experience, the paralysis induced by the smoking vapors dripped down from about the cerebellum and engulfed the legs and arms within five minutes.

"This is about Tate of course."

Ungerman nodded, swallowed more black bread. "Of course. Are you staying for dinner?"

"No."

"Let me do this then." He again peremptorily waved over the black-suited, white-shirted waiter and ordered salmon and dill for himself and an appetizer of graavlax for Cooper. Cooper had relished the chips and soda with Leah far more. He was also reminded, stripped of the urbanity and good fellowship, of his father at play among the bottles. It was all fraud, all for show, this hearty camaraderie.

"I can shorten this for both of us, Steve. Tate's in the county jail. He stays there until he goes on trial for murder or he pleads."

Ungerman munched on a bit of herring in sour cream when it arrived immediately on a bright china plate. "Are you offering anything?"

"We haven't decided."

"Are you going for the death penalty?"

"It's likely." Cooper and Leah hadn't made that decision and he hadn't raised it with Joyce Gutherie either, but he knew that was where the case should go ultimately.

"Not much incentive for a plea there, is there?"

"Under the circumstances, Tate can't expect much."

Ungerman nodded carefully, this time sipping his third drink. "So what are the circumstances? As you know them?"

"Boler tells me Tate's an undercover FBI agent going after terrorists."

"Shaun, Shaun," Ungerman said, the tone clearly belittling. "Did he actually tell you that?"

"In front of another assistant DA."

"Then he demanded you just hand over Tate."

"He did. I didn't."

"Of course not." Ungerman sniffed. "Shaun's a loose cannon. He wants the publicity and he doesn't care how he gets it. He wants Tate and he doesn't care how he gets him."

"Do you want him?" Cooper nibbled at his plate of different varieties of herring. He was intrigued by a culture that could find so many uses for one only mildly palatable fish.

"You bet I do. You'll give him to me, too."

"Why should I do that?"

Ungerman reached into his coat pocket and slid a stuffed plain white envelope to Cooper. "Not here. Read it back at your office. It's Tate's background at the FBI. His resume. He's been all over the Bureau and he's had his fingers in a lot of pies and when the time came, the fucker sold it all to the Russians."

The change in Ungerman's face was stark and instant. He glared at Cooper.

"I didn't really buy the undercover story," Cooper said.

"Boler's trying to save the FBI from the biggest embarrassment of its existence, Denny. Gerald Tate's been selling intelligence information, the best and brightest, first to the KGB, then when the change came, to the SVR, that's the Russian Foreign Intelligence Service." He smacked his lips and pronounced, like a student who has listened to instructional language tapes over and over, "*Sluzhba Vneshney Razvedki Rossii.* I've been practicing."

"How long has he been working for them?"

"Twelve years at least. We've been investigating him under the Foreign Intelligence Surveillance Act for the last two years. We've got the fucker on videotape, audiotape, and we've got his dead-drop sites all mapped out in Los Angeles, San Francisco, and here in Sacramento."

"Dead drop?" Cooper asked. "That's some spy term?"

"An agent and his controllers set up a place to leave and pick up messages and information. The agent and his controller don't have to be at the same place at the same time. Tate's been about the most clever anybody's seen. He *never* met any of his controllers, insisted on that, and only cleared his dead drops when he was certain no one was around. So there's no pictures of him meeting with some Soviet cultural attaché who's really a colonel in the KGB." He chewed. "His Sacramento dead drop was across the river in Discovery Park, under the bridge. Perfect place to leave or retrieve packages after hours when the park's closed."

Cooper sat back. At least this story made more sense than Boler's yarn. Discovery Park was fairly large, with bike trails and miles of foliage and a busy dock into the Sacramento River. Still, with Tate's background either story could be true. Perhaps both were.

"I'm not persuaded to change course," he said to Ungerman.

"Let me persuade you."

"Be my guest."

"Hand Tate over. I promise a multicount federal indictment. I promise you that we will seek the death penalty on our side."

Cooper frowned. "Who else has he killed?"

"Tate burned five Russians who were working for the CIA when he first offered his services to the KGB. We've got dead-solid information that the Russians executed all of them within three months of Tate's exposing them." He again glared angrily at Cooper.

"What happens to my case?"

"It becomes part of our prosecution of Tate."

"You deal it out," Cooper said flatly.

"Denny, the laws of physics apply. We can only give Tate a hot shot once. He's not a cat with nine lives."

Cooper pushed his plate of appetizer to one side. A young man and woman, sitting alongside each other at a table of six others, both elegantly dressed, both flushed, were laughing loudly and she began to rub his back vigorously. He wiggled as if his skin were afire. More laughter.

Ungerman was commenting on the tenderness, the succulence of his salmon, which had just been presented to him, and he enthusiastically wielded knife and fork. The deal, Cooper saw, was simple. Tate would face a federal indictment, federal capital punishment, for his crimes as a spy. The deaths he caused were distant, indirect assassinations. The murder of Constantina Basilaskos, which he had committed himself, would be sacrificed to that higher prosecution.

It came down to the same thing, Cooper thought. *Our victims aren't as important.* The lives of two innocent people mowed down by Tate in Oak Park mattered less than his disclosure of American agents abroad.

Amid the gaudy, expensive gaiety of the restaurant, smoothly cajoled and entreated by Ungerman, Cooper knew his father, the cop who had direct and simple solutions for most things in life, would dismiss everything but the essence of what Ungerman proposed. One side gives in this deal, the other takes. *Where's the percentage?* his father would have asked. *What's my cut?*

"What do we get out of giving Tate up?" Cooper said.

Mouth partly full, dabbing at it with his cloth napkin, Ungerman said huskily, "Your killer is off the streets. He can't do any more damage to the United States."

"He pleads to my case," Cooper said, "I'm immovable."

"Offer him life without possibility. He'll eat the sheet on ours, lethal injection."

Cooper didn't see why Tate would even entertain such a deal.

Unless the federal death penalty was bargained away too.

And California's state charges were already off the table.

That was a deal a man facing multiple murder counts, state and federal, would look on with desperate delight. Cooper glanced at Ungerman, still eating and appearing earnest. *They want information from him,* Cooper thought. *They want Tate telling everything so they'll threaten him with the death penalty, one they control completely and then give it away if he cooperates.*

My victims lose. Period.

"I'll give it some thought," Cooper said, with inwardly acknowledged disingenuousness.

"All right, Denny. This is a major decision, go ahead. But the clock's ticking. Tate's been exposed." He pushed his plate away sadly. "So we'll have to move quickly to keep as much of his misbehavior nonpublic as we can."

Cooper stood up. "I'll let you know after the arraignment tomorrow."

"No dessert?"

"No. Thanks."

"Can I trust you, Denny?" Ungerman leaned forward, red hectic spots on his cheeks from the food and liquor. "It could hurt this country a hell of a lot if Tate's espionage gets out tomorrow in your state proceeding."

"We're dealing strictly with his murders last week," Cooper said, tossing his napkin down.

"Then I'll trust you. I think I'll stay for some

265

dessert." He craned his neck toward a nearby table. "I see that poached pear in brandy looks inviting."

Ungerman and his wife had a son away at a boarding school in New Mexico. They lived separate lives, rarely going to parties or social functions together. Cooper assumed Ungerman ate a great many dinners like this, by himself, alone with the poached pear of the evening and the specialty liquor.

"My case has some gaps." Cooper paused, towering over Ungerman. "I don't know who the driver of the car that snatched Tate away was. Do you?"

Ungerman nodded. "Oleg Maslenikov. Tate's newest controller. Assigned to him when he was transferred to Sacramento in mid-July."

"Where can I find him?"

"Moscow, I guess. He was sent home over the weekend."

The vanishing accomplice, Cooper thought. "I assume I wouldn't have much luck tracking him down in Moscow or getting any help from the Russian cops?"

"I don't think you'd have any."

"Can you tie him to the car? If I'm going to go along with a deal, I've got to give Gutherie a solid case, Steve. We'll deal because it's a good policy call, not because our evidence or facts are weak."

Ungerman nodded agreeably. "Understood. DA has to run again. She wants to be able to say she gave way to a federal prosecution because it was in the best interests of the country." He waved for a waiter. "We'll make sure the car rental information and Maslenikov connection get to you in time for your arraignment."

266

Cooper turned. He was being conned and Unger-man had to believe the con was succeeding. Unger-man then said, loudly enough for anyone at the tables close to his to hear, "The Nepalese have a saying, Denny. They hunt tigers. Hunted them for centuries. Tigers are dangerous, they can turn on you before you know it. The Nepalese say you don't see a tiger until he wants to be seen."

Cooper nodded again. "I'll call you tomorrow."

"Looking forward to it. Best to Jerry, please. You'll see him before I do. Tell him I'm getting the spare room all spruced up just for him."

Cooper passed more excited diners on his way back up the shiny black marble stairs. He grabbed some peppermints from a large ornate crystal bowl, discovering that they were wafer thin, sharply spiced breaths that melted the moment he put them in his mouth.

He very much needed to walk for a minute. He strode with long steps up toward Capital Mall, the broad six-lane grass centered boulevard that led in a majestic line of sight to the white buttery state capitol building itself. Dark cars glided by. A lone Hispanic trumpeter stood on the plaza of the Department of Education sending out sharp, wailing notes. A few people on foot headed for the lights and activity along K Street.

Tate was the tiger, invisible and deadly all those years when he was selling his country's most valuable secrets and pointing the finger at men who were then killed because he spotlighted them to their enemies.

Cooper stepped around a knot of young men and

women, hooting to each other, fashionably and brightly disheveled. So after so many years in the shadows, Tate emerged like the tiger who now desired to be seen in all of his awful glory.

But why now? Why so madly, shooting an old woman?

Why the sweaty, uncomfortable wait at the Korinthou Diner, reading Thomas a Kempis until the time came to stalk Constantina Basilaskos?

Cooper stopped and stared up at the capitol's white scrollwork and columns rising high against a black seemingly starless night sky.

Illusion. All is appearance and illusion and deception. Tate's reading of Thomas a Kempis. *Turn from outward appearance and the fleshly eye's false images of things seen and heard. Look to the secret place of your heart for relieving of perils and for the mischief of men.* That's what Terry's report had conveyed from the dying witness. Tate's favorite passages.

Cooper walked back to his car, hands in his pockets, head down, a myriad of impressions welling up in his mind. Flying his time-shared Cessna on weekends in brilliant blue sky, tacking into the wind, holding on in clear air turbulence. Tate's expression in court as he was led out, relief and exultation mingled improbably.

He sold out everybody and everything. Cooper fumed at the illogic. Then he basically threw himself off a cliff. Did he know his controller was close by? Did he care?

Why now? Always that question. Why the bleating, lonely voice in the encrypted letter on the CD, the diamond handed back as if from a child who doesn't want to play anymore?

I've got to talk to Tate, he realized. He looked at his watch, chagrined he'd left Leah so much of the next day's work to do herself.

I've got to talk to his wife.

He had learned, and continued to learn, many things as a prosecutor. Like his first murder trial, a beer party in Galt, the victim shot five times by the host. To his horror, Cooper discovered midway through his trial that the victim had crashed the party, threatened guests, waved a bowie knife, and tried to rush a bedroom door behind which two women cowered. That's when he got shot.

It took the trial to make clear what the muddled, drunken statements witnesses had given really meant. His dead victim was the aggressor. It was self-defense.

He leaned on his car roof, cars passing and honking sometimes. He didn't believe that Constantina Basilaskos or Angelo were anything other than bystanders who got fatally in the way.

But that was the grand-prize question.

He got into his car.

What had they gotten in the middle of anyway?

Leah stretched and dialed the watch commandeer at the county jail.

"How is Tate doing?" she asked after they had settled the identifications of each other.

"Lights out early. Got a report a couple minutes ago and he's sound asleep."

"Any comments to anyone?"

"Asked a CO for a Bible." CO was a correctional officer, a guard.

"You didn't give him one, did you?" she asked, alarmed. No one knew what kind of signals Tate and his outside contacts, whoever they were, had set up. A Bible or a passage from it might mean anything, some emergency escape plan possibly.

"He's got his underwear, his slippers, his shirt, and his pants."

"And he's on a twenty-four-hour suicide watch?"

"He's got eyeballs on him all the time."

She relaxed a little. Her eyes ached and she touched them lightly. "Has anyone shown any interest in him?"

"Well, we've got two FBI cars outside the main entrance. Four agents passing the time."

"Since when?"

"About two hours ago. They rolled up. Identified themselves and said they were going to wait."

"For what?"

"Didn't say."

"Have they asked to come in or see Tate?"

"No to both," the watch commander said. She heard a bell faintly, a voice booming over a loudspeaker. The county jail's nightly routine invariably rolling on, moving inmates into their cells, closing the doors, lights out in an hour.

"What are the FBI agents doing right now?"

"Right now? Let me see the monitors. I can see both cars. They're in their cars. One's sleeping, it looks like."

270

"I want you to call me immediately if anyone tries to enter the facility or the FBI agents do anything at all." Her voice was steel and sharp.

"Count on it."

As soon as she hung up, Leah dialed a number Dennis had left on his legal pad at the top. "Lieutenant Bernasconi? Vance? This is Leah Fisher. I know you're off duty now, but I need your help."

She smiled. "Thanks. The nights are getting longer for all of us."

She reached awkwardly for her cup, intending to get some hot water and make more green tea. "We need to put some of our own uniforms at the county jail entrance. As soon as possible. The FBI is camped out, waiting for something."

Leah shook her head. "I don't know what we'll do if the FBI tries anything. But we've got to get our people there now."

Cooper got back shortly afterward and rode up the elevator to the bright hallways, buffed every night by the cleaning crews that worked around any late-toiling DDAs.

He threw his coat onto the back of one of the conference table chairs.

"It's a good cop, bad cop drill," he said to Leah sourly. "Boler comes on like Bull Connors and Ungerman sugarcoats the same garbage."

"We don't have to go along, Dennis."

"No, we do not. But we've got to make sure Joyce's all right with doing that. Ungerman's right. Her head's on the block."

271

He relayed the whole conversation and Leah told him about the FBI agents standing guard at the county jail downtown.

"What do they think we're going to do? Smuggle Tate out tonight?" Cooper demanded.

"We've got a standoff now anyway. We're there. They're there."

He grinned in spite of his anger. "They're *there*? For a product of one of the finest educations available in America, that is a singularly infelicitous statement, Ms. Fisher. Not very impressive for a courtroom advocate either."

"I stand rebuked."

He sat down, pulling the draft motions she had done to him. "Piecing this all together, I think we can see what happened. At least the outward facts."

She nodded and jotted with her pen as she spoke. "Tate's transferred and undergoes some personal breakdown. He comes into possession of terrific information he wants to give to his Russian handlers right away."

"He sets up a crash meeting, Ungerman calls it a dead drop. He uses the diner because it's handy. For some reason he couldn't use the usual dead drop over in Discovery Park apparently."

"But something went wrong," Leah said, looking at Cooper intently. "Angelo Basilaskos is sick, his wife is doing everything, including the cleaning and general chores."

"Constantina Basilaskos stumbles on Tate's package," Cooper said. She tries to open it with her fingers, hence the green plastic residue under her fingernails. Then she loses patience and just cuts the package open and finds the diamond. She must've shown something for people to see, somehow Tate realized she'd gotten the package meant for his handlers. He follows her, confronts her, shoots her, and then his controller, this Masilenikov, saves him from being caught."

"A lot of suppositions and inferences," Leah observed. "Tate can fill in the blanks."

"I would love to know what happened before we go any farther down this yellow brick road," Cooper said. "I forgot," he said abruptly and retrieved the envelope Ungerman had given him from his coat pocket. He opened it. There were seven pages. "Well. A second copy of the life and times of Gerald Tate, courtesy of the U.S. Attorney. He is trying to woo me with favors."

Cooper tossed the pages to the table and Leah idly picked them up and began leafing through them.

"Leah, I'm thinking we need to up the stakes for tomorrow. We've got to put more pressure on Tate and the feds too."

She didn't answer, then looked at him coolly. "I hate to say this, but your new best friend just tried to pull a fast one."

"What do you mean?"

She handed him pages four and five of the official Tate background. "Take a look. Do you notice anything missing?"

Cooper read down the pages and smirked at her. "Well, well. Ungerman doesn't know we've got an authentic copy of Tate's bio. There's nothing in Ungerman's version about Tate setting up the automated counterintelligence database, his time in the

Soviet Analytical Unit, or the work he did with the State Department."

"Now we know what kind of secrets he gave away."

"We also know what the feds are going to try to cover up."

He started writing quickly. He said sharply, "Okay, then that's how we'll play it. I want to file a motion to amend the indictment tomorrow, Leah. In addition to blocking any bail or release for Agent Tate." He peered at her. "Can we make contact with his wife? She might be able to give us something useful. I'm assuming she might not have known what her husband, the suburban poster boy and Opus Dei member, was up to when everyone was asleep."

"I tried the number in Pacific Palisades earlier," she said. "No answer."

"Disconnected?"

"No, just no answer. I don't think anyone's home. I tried several times."

"Interesting. I wonder if we can anticipate a family reunion in court."

Leah said, "Probably. Which means it'll be fairly uncomfortable if Mrs. Tate and the children are hearing all of this for the first time. Tell me how you want to amend the indictment."

"Let's make the feds very worried. While we're at it, let's increase the heat on Agent Tate. We'll move to amend by adding the death penalty." He grinned at her, enjoying the exhilaration of it all. "Do we have time to get all of that together by court tomorrow morning?"

She pulled her laptop closer. "If we don't sightsee along the way."

"Pedal to the metal it is, Ms. Fisher."

The cameras mounted all along the main entrance to the county jail facility on L Street downtown immediately relayed to the COs inside the jail's security center when three SPD patrol cars drove up and parked across the street at ten o'clock that evening.

The Sacramento police vehicles came to slow stops about twenty feet parallel and across the street from two plain G cars containing four agents of the FBI. One agent had been out of his car smoking a cigarette. He hastily got back inside. The jail cameras detected what appeared to be radio communication.

No one got out of the SPD vehicles. Their lights switched off and except for the high-security beams on the jail exterior illuminating the faces of uniformed men and women inside the cars, they could have been empty.

The news that the FBI and SPD were outside and in their vehicles was conveyed instantly to the watch commander, who grunted and went back to his work.

Meanwhile, in the warm August night, as occasional yowls and cries from inside the large and modern new jail drifted out like the calls of exotic and dangerous nocturnal animals, the five cars remained motionless and silent, regarding each other balefully across the twenty feet of asphalt paving like adversaries separated by the Berlin Wall.

Chapter Eighteen

On Thursday, August 14, Cooper parked in the tree-shaded jurors' parking lot across the street from the courthouse, walked up the broad stone stairs to the wide plaza and its peculiarly stark angular fountain and into the white and glass sprawling building. Once upon a time he had had a parking space behind the district attorney's building on the opposite corner, but he relinquished it in favor of a young DDA who was pregnant. He was now on a waiting list for another space, and even his seniority in the office only helped make everyone painfully aware of the need to get him one. It did not actually free up a space.

He had slept soundly. It was seven-thirty and a little early to be coming to work, but this promised to be a special day. He and Leah had finally finished the papers for this morning around midnight, gotten them printed up, copied, and ready for service by hand in court.

The early birds were already in the courthouse, people with court dates as soon as the judges in their cases took the bench. They sat outside the building on the steps or around the fountain or lounged against the stone walls and smoked nervous cigarettes. They flowed through the first floor. Cooper took the elevator to the sixth floor and got in line at the cafeteria. It was full and noisy and he had to shout to order toast, coffee, and scrambled eggs to go. His breakfast was dumped into a plastic carton by a black man in a plastic hairnet and plastic gloves. At least the plastic lent the illusion of hygiene.

Juggling his briefcase, the carton, and a Styrofoam cup of hot coffee, Cooper went through the intricate elevator game. Even at that early hour, elevators would ring open and people would rush in and overcrowd. The trick, he had learned over the years, was figuring which elevator would return first or come up from the basement and place yourself right in front of its doors.

The ride to the fourth floor was slow, people stopping to get on or off at every floor. He wondered when he had become indifferent to the smell or the odd sights so many people presented. The Guatemalan mother in front of him, balancing three small children, the stale milk on her wrinkled blouse's shoulder. The dwarf Asian man with a goatee and a pungent reek.

Cooper was still very hungry. He decided that he no longer noticed the people or the coarse, cruel world that ebbed and flowed from the building the day he had done his first jail rape trial. The cops had brought over the defendant's remarkably stained underwear, still in an evidence bag, of course, and he had had to rush to get to the court in time. You could not be especially fastidious about the human condition when you were constantly surrounded by so many people or had to trot to a courtroom, presided over by a judicial martinet, toting a paper bag stuffed with stinking underwear.

He got out on the fourth floor and went to the clerk's office for Department 33. He grinned engagingly at the very-long-necked middle-aged woman who let him in. "I brought you the best the county of Sacramento has to offer." He opened the plastic carton, letting her select a piece of wheat toast.

"This is the best, don't show me the second best," Claire, Judge Buckman's clerk, said in a nasally, gravelly voice. "What's the bribe for, Dennis?"

"Bribe? Claire. I am shocked, shocked you'd accuse of me of trying to buy your official responsibilities with a single not very well buttered piece of wheat toast."

"Yeah, yeah, yeah." She chewed loudly and visibly. "What do you want?"

Cooper set his briefcase down, and put the carton of scrambled eggs on the edge of Claire's cluttered desk. "When's the judge coming in?"

"He called about fifteen minutes ago. Traffic on I-5. So he's on his way now."

Cooper munched on his toast with as much pleasure as Claire. "I need to see him first thing."

"I'll think about it."

* * *

At eight, he met Leah outside the courtroom.

"I gave Buckman a little briefing," he said wryly. "We'll be first up on the calendar. Any sign of Maksik or a contingent from the Bureau?"

"No. No calls either. Did you tell the judge we intend to move to amend the indictment?"

"Buckman's a stickler about ex parte communications. Since Maksik wasn't there, all I could do was inform him Tate's a high-security case."

Leah led him to a steel bench, the marks of countless transient tragedies scratched on it. The blacks and sullen whites milling nearby edged away.

"All's quiet at the jail," she said confidentially to him. "Tate's been transported here by himself, which was a little bit of a miracle. He's in the building now, in a holding tank alone."

"I put a call in to Joyce first thing," Cooper said. "She's not entirely happy with adding the death penalty, but I laid out our reasoning. She'll be fine once she digests it."

Cooper nodded. "I left messages for Nye and Tafoya to be here too."

Cooper stood up, jiggling his briefcase a little nervously and looking at his watch. "Then I think we're all set." He smiled. "You look remarkably well rested for someone who spent a somewhat longish night."

"I slept like a log."

"Me too," he said. He saw a group of somber, dark-suited men striding almost in formation toward the courtroom. "Here comes the esteemed Mr. Maksik and his entourage," Cooper said without irony. "It's showtime."

The bailiff bawled the case number, the holding tank opened, and Gerald Tate in his loose-fitting numbered jail-orange coveralls, slippers without socks, shuffled into the enclosure to the judge's right. He hadn't shaved. His thinning brown hair was clumped and his fleshy face lined. He stared ahead, then swung his watery blue-eyed gaze to Judge Leonard Buckman, who was still moving files and papers anxiously on the bench as his clerk handed him more papers from Cooper.

Cooper stood at the counsel table, Leah sat to his left. It was a typically overburdened morning calendar of arraignments, bail motions, discovery requests, and various other procedural matters. He looked quizzically at Leah after they both tried to determine who now stood with Maksik on the defendant's side of the counsel table. A large man, with a widow's peak, in a charcoal pinstripe and some kind of gold pin in his lapel. Two assistants were sliding files to him.

"Your Honor," Cooper said firmly, "the people will move to amend the indictment this morning against the defendant Gerald Tate to allege special circumstances."

That was the legal formulation for the death penalty. Enough of the court veterans knew the ominous words to make the crowd mutter loudly and the judge to call for silence.

Buckman fanned the pages of the motion Cooper and Leah had prepared. "Mr. Maksik? You wish to be heard?"

Maksik cleared his throat. "Yes, Your Honor. I

have a motion to file on Mr. Tate's behalf to dismiss the second count of the indictment alleging felony murder in the death of Angelo Basilaskos."

More papers circulated to the clerk, judge, back to Cooper. He felt no concern. They had anticipated this from Tate's lawyer. Tate himself stiffened and then lowered his head. Cooper quickly looked to the back of the courtroom. A blond woman, dressed simply in light blue, was being helped to a packed row of seats by one of the bailiffs. She had two older children with her, all of them sleepless, grim, and sad.

Mrs. Tate. Leah urgently pushed her legal pad in front of Cooper. She had scratched in block letters JEREMY FABER.

He read the name at the same moment he suddenly recalled where he had seen the large man before and Faber intoned, "Your Honor, my name is Jeremy Faber. I have been retained by the Tates to represent the defendant. I am requesting that the court permit me to substitute in as counsel."

Cooper thought quickly. Faber appeared on behalf of soldiers and government officials involved in misdeeds overseas, usually with young women, and often entailing the alleged transfer of American technical or intelligence information to people who normally would not be permitted to have it.

The transfers were alleged because, as Cooper now recalled with a sinking sensation, Faber's clients were never convicted.

And the financially strapped Tates probably could not pay Faber for his expensive services. There were things going on behind the scenes that Cooper didn't like at all.

"Mr. Tate," Judge Buckman said, "is it your desire that Mr. Maksik turn over representation of you in this case to Mr. Faber?"

"Why not?" Tate said, looking back at his wife and children.

"You'll have to be more definite," the judge said.

"Then, yes. I wish Mr. Faber to be my lawyer. *My* lawyer," Tate said sarcastically.

Leah whispered, "Dennis, we've got to do something to keep Faber out."

"Tate's entitled to the lawyer he wants. He's paying."

"No, he's not," she whispered sharply.

But he knew what worried her. And it came fast.

"Your Honor," said Faber, stepping from the counsel table to stand closer to Tate, "I have a hearing tomorrow morning before Judge Sarah Kincaid Lonsdale in federal district court. I am requesting that Judge Lonsdale assume jurisdiction and that this case be removed immediately to federal court."

Cooper called out, "Judge, the people have had no notice of this hearing and we've certainly seen no moving papers. It is unthinkable to snatch a case from state court to federal court without a full and complete hearing."

Faber smiled toothily, one of his aides shoving a thick stack of appears at Leah. "I'd like the record to reflect that I am serving the DA with a motion requesting that the federal court assert jurisdiction over this case for all purposes."

Cooper shook the thick sheaf in the air. "This is unacceptable, Your Honor! We can't possibly be ready to respond to this motion on such short notice."

Now the judge looked irritated, frustrated, and a trifle bewildered. He bit his lip and flipped the papers as if something noteworthy would fly from them and show him how he ought to rule.

Cooper and Faber spoke simultaneously. It was, Cooper discovered, very hard to outshout Mr. Faber. He had a bass voice and he deployed it like a general mounting an assault with overwhelming force.

Judge Buckman put up both hands in annoyance. "Quiet. Quiet. Both of you."

Tate spoke up. "Your Honor, I would like to be heard. I would like to say something to the prosecutor."

Cooper cocked his head in surprise and Leah was on her feet, as if that would encourage the judge. But Buckman waved Tate to be silent. "This is not the time or the place, sir. Talk to your new attorney, Mr. Faber. He will advise you if you should speak to the district attorney. I can tell you, as a former defense lawyer in this city for a number of years, if Mr. Faber does let you speak to Mr. Cooper he needs a brain as much as the Scarecrow in *The Wizard of Oz*."

Tate nodded glumly; he shot Cooper the same exultant, despairing glance as he had yesterday. *He wants to confess something,* Cooper realized with elation. But that was tempered instantly when the judge spoke.

"I want this courtroom to be quiet!" And he pointed at the extra bailiffs present because of Tate. "Now, I can't get in the way of a federal judge, Mr. Cooper, so you'll have to have your hearing tomorrow and see what happens. What I can do is schedule a hearing in this court late tomorrow to rule on your motion and Mr. Maksik's motion. How's that?"

"I still think it's unacceptable, Your Honor. The people also have a right to a fair trial and this is not it. Besides, I haven't heard that Mr. Faber is even bothering to be admitted to practice in front of this court."

The judge raised his thick eyebrows. "Good point. Mr. Maksik, are we going to get a *pro hac vice* on file for Mr. Faber, because I assume he's not a member of the California bar, is he?"

Maksik uncomfortably looked down for an instant. "He isn't, Your Honor." And then Faber boomed over him. "Your Honor, I meant no disrespect to this court, but I am utterly confident that my motion to remove this case to federal court will be granted immediately. I have filed a *pro hac vice* in Judge Lonsdale's court."

"That's demonstrates a certain arrogance," Cooper said sharply.

"Counsel. Please," Judge Buckman warned. "Mr. Maksik, Mr. Faber, do whatever you wish in front of Judge Lonsdale, but get a *pro hac vice* on file for this case in this court today so Mr. Faber can be admitted to practice in this case. That is an order. And we'll set a hearing on the motions for . . ." He looked at his clerk. Claire rasped out, "Four-thirty. Department 36."

"Thank you, Your Honor," Cooper said automatically, gathering his papers and shoving them angrily into his briefcase. Tate was taken back through the tank door, his head swiveling to catch a look again as his wife and two of their children came forward to Cooper.

Leah said, "I know there are federal abstention grounds here, Dennis. We can keep the case in state court."

"You heard Faber." He jerked his finger toward Faber and Maksik and their assistants, who seemed to be trying to prevent Mrs. Tate from coming any nearer. "The fix is in. They've greased this with Judge Lonsdale. I bet the order has already been signed. National security. Need for secrecy, need to keep the case as tightly controlled as possible." He spat the words out. "The hearing's for show. It's a fraud."

Leah was about to argue when she said softly, "It looks like Mrs. Tate isn't getting along with her husband's legal team."

In fact, three of the extra bailiffs had moved in to guide the squabbling tangle of people away from the counsel table because the judge was impatiently calling for his next case on the calendar. Mrs. Tate broke from Faber's hand on her arm.

"I need to talk to you," she said fiercely, shaking Faber away, holding on to both of her children, a boy and girl about six and seven. "You've got to listen."

"Mrs. Tate." Faber tried to get between her and Cooper. "Please, come back to Mr. Maksik's office with me. You're tired. We can discuss the situation quietly and completely."

Cooper and Leah and the bailiffs were now embroiled in the tense tangle just as Terry and Rose strolled up. "Trouble, counselor?" Terry asked Cooper.

"Detective Nye, would you and Detective Tafoya escort Mrs. Tate and her children to my office? I'll be there in a minute."

Terry grinned like a shark. "I would be happy to do so. Would you come with me, Mrs. Tate?"

Rose covered their walk to the courtroom, Faber following and trying to get closer. Rose put her hand on the bigger man's chest. "Far enough. You're harassing this lady. We've got stalking laws in California."

"Very amusing, Detective," Faber said sharply. But he let them go on.

Leah walked beside Mrs. Tate and her children, the whole agitated group fortunate to vanish into an elevator that magically opened before them.

Jeremy Faber, Maksik, and their assistants paused as they passed Cooper. "Call me, Mr. Cooper. There doesn't have to be bad feeling about this, believe me. This case is just way beyond you. It's nothing personal."

"So everyone seems to tell me," Cooper answered. "I'll see you tomorrow, Mr. Faber."

Cooper walked briskly to a grimy tall window, plucking out the office cell phone he carried when he was in trial.

He dialed from memory. "Joyce? They lowered the boom on us just now."

"How bad is the damage, Denny?" she asked calmly.

"It's critical. We need to see your friend Landowski today. It's urgent."

"I'll set up an appointment and put you and me on the earliest flight to Washington I can." She hung up.

His father had once imparted the unassailable truth about prearranged official or private decisions. *The only way to unfix a fix is with another fix.*

Terry intercepted him as he came through his outer office, picking up a stack of messages.

"Cooper," Terry said, "we got the missus in with Rose and Fisher. Look, we started trying to line up Oleg Maslenikov and the Russian embassy's cars. We got nothing. Doesn't mean if we spend all of our time for the next couple months we won't come up with something, but right now we can account for the embassy cars, personal and official. Nothing like our suspect vehicle."

"What about rentals?"

"Too soon. Could be under another name too."

"Which means we could look forever unless we had another lead." Cooper cursed under his breath. Terry studied him, waiting for guidance. Again, something from the reports about the car flashed into his mind, but it refused to linger long enough for him to make sense of it.

"I'm sorry, Terry," he said apologetically. "You've got to stay with this. We need to show some connection between the car and a Russian official."

"You're killing me," Terry said.

"Here's the bright side, if the case is ordered into

federal court tomorrow, it won't make any difference. We're shut down."

Suzanna Tate clasped her red-knuckled hands tightly. Her children were outside Cooper's office chatting with two female DDAs and solemnly sipping canned sodas. Arrayed around the room were Nye and Tafoya. Leah and Cooper faced Mrs. Tate. She had a Styrofoam cup of untouched cooling coffee in front of her.

"You have very nice children," Leah said, trying to prompt the woman into saying something relevant. The conversation for fifteen minutes had been about getting to Sacramento on short notice, finding a couple from church who would watch the two youngest children for a few days.

"All of our children are special," Suzanna Tate said, looking up. "Jerry and I thank God for them. Even on the days . . ." She smiled slightly. "Well, there are those days sometimes even with good kids."

"Of course," Cooper said. "What did you want to tell us, Mrs. Tate? You understand that anything you do tell us is not privileged. We're not your husband's lawyers. We represent the people of California."

"That's why I wanted to talk to you, to talk to someone who'd listen. Faber's no more Jerry's attorney than you are, I know that."

"How did he get into the case then?" Leah asked.

"He showed up yesterday. With Jerry's supervisor, former supervisor, at headquarters. Jerry was in serious trouble, they said. He needed specialized legal assistance. Faber could give it. In return . . ." She faltered.

"Yes? What was the other side of the bargain?" Cooper gently prodded.

"Jerry would agree to cooperate with the Bureau."

Cooper shot Leah a hard glance. Faber had an irreconcilable conflict and had known it going in. He was being hired by the FBI to represent the FBI's interests, not Tate's, and that was a breach of the most basic canon of ethics attorneys must abide by. It was also something that could get Faber thrown right off the case in federal court tomorrow.

"I have to ask this," Cooper said carefully. "I assume from your last comment that you have some idea why Jerry's been arrested here in Sacramento."

She nodded. She was smooth-faced, eyes red-rimmed.

"I'm also assuming you know about your husband's clandestine activities, don't you?"

She sat back and studied Cooper, Leah, and the two detectives for a moment. They all heard her daughter giggle, then swiftly suppress it.

"I have to make you understand," Suzanna Tate said. "Jerry is a very good man. He loves his family and his country. But he's a very complicated man too. He's one of the smartest people I've ever met." She smiled sadly. "I think that's what first attracted me to him. The sense of humor, the quick intelligence. Then I discovered his faith. He believes absolutely and utterly in God's grace, Mr. Cooper. He believes, we all do, that God has a design. Jerry tries to live his faith too."

289

"We know you both belong to Opus Dei," Leah said.

"Then I have to admit . . ." She faltered again.

"Would you like a glass of water, Mrs. Tate?" Cooper asked. He was exhilarated at being in proximity to answers about this strange man and his inexplicable crimes.

She shook her head. Terry said, "I'll get some anyway." He left the room.

"Please go on," Leah said. She was sympathetic and reassuring.

Suzanna Tate's hands twisted and she said, "Ten years ago, three years before Theresa was born." She pointed out to her daughter sitting on a chair much too big for her. "Jerry told me he had been selling information to the Soviet Union for five years. He swore he would stop now that the Soviet Union had collapsed."

Cooper nodded, feeling a little sickened at the depths of this betrayal. "Did he tell you why he had spied for the Russians?"

"He thought it would hasten the end of the Soviet Union, knowing what they faced from our side. He thought they would despair. Like a man who loses his faith despairs because he no longer sees God. Their secular faith would fall apart."

"He justified it as part of his own beliefs?" Leah asked.

"Completely. He was so sincere, so lucid. I remember him telling me how the inspiration had come to him, the pains he took to carry it out. He knew the risks he was taking because this was certainly not officially approved. He could go to prison."

Cooper leaned forward. "Mrs. Tate, did you believe your husband when he said he would no longer spy for the Soviet Union?"

"Yes, I did." She pulled herself straighter. "He confessed to Father Dougherty. He took a solemn, binding oath to me and his children."

Leah put a hand to her mouth for an instant. Cooper knew the feeling. It was a visceral, completely unintellectual reaction to evil. He had encountered it in courtrooms when he was close to defendants who had strangled their own children or committed brutal rapes. He had seen jurors faint or spontaneously break into tears when they viewed crime scene photographs. The reactions sprang from the sudden and inescapable recognition that there were other human beings on earth, in your city, perhaps your neighborhood, who were capable of anything. It was the sight and reality of evil.

Gerald Tate was an evil man. Cooper knew this. Now Leah grasped it fully too. But Tate's wife did not, could not in fact. His children were also unaware of his nature. Cooper, who had little but vestiges of religious upbringing left, did not know how to encompass that paradox.

He said quietly as Terry came back, putting water in front of Suzanna Tate, "But today, Mrs. Tate, you do know that your husband continued spying for the Russians right up until last week, don't you? He shot and killed a woman because she mistakenly picked up a package at a dead drop meant for his Russian

associates. He was apparently helped to escape by a
Russian working at the embassy here in Sacramento.
That's why the FBI is willing to hire an attorney for
him."

She didn't say anything. She sipped the water. She
let the silence increase in Cooper's office.

"I knew," she said finally. "I'm guilty too."

Leah interrupted, an unusual thing to do during an
interview. "We'll look into everything, Mrs. Tate, but
it's too early for the district attorney's office to say
what, if any, your degree of involvement might be."

Before Cooper could continue, Suzanna Tate finished her water and thanked Terry. Then she said in
a clear voice, "I found some things yesterday, Mr.
Cooper. In Jerry's workroom, where he has his computers. I found sixteen guns and ammunition for
them. I found an AK-47. In a drawer I found passports in several names, bank records for accounts I
hadn't known about in Switzerland and Russia, and
four diamonds. Two are quite large."

Cooper nodded to Terry and Rose. They would
have to get a search warrant immediately and that
meant working through the police in Los Angeles.
Even though Suzanna Tate could give them permission to search the house, her husband also resided
there and the room was apparently largely under his
control. A search warrant was essential in a case
where every move could result in a legal catastrophe.

"That changes things," Cooper admitted.

"How did you find these items?" Leah asked.

Suzanna Tate's voice shook. "Jerry called yesterday. It must have been right after you arrested him.
He told me where they were. He told me it was evi-

292

dence. He said that all of it would be misinterpreted by the police and used against him. He told me to destroy all of it." She shook her head. "I don't have the slightest idea how to destroy a weapon like an AK-47. I was stunned to know all of that had been in my house, where my children might have found it."

Terry broke in. "You know what we have to do, don't you?"

Cooper was startled at first by her reaction, but then it made perfect sense.

Suzanna Tate said, "I want you to have all of it. Jerry and I believe firmly . . ." She paused. "Maybe I don't know everything he believes, but we both think that there is no salvation without admission of sin. Jerry has sinned. So have I. It must end."

Cooper wondered if she knew about the Russians her husband had exposed and who were then executed. He didn't think so. And he didn't, at that moment, have the courage to tell her. "We'll take care of what has to be done now," he said. "We appreciate how difficult this must be for you."

"What will happen, Mr. Cooper?"

"It depends entirely on your husband." There is no absolution without confession, and thus far, Jerry Tate had not admitted the extent of his crimes to anyone.

On the hastily arranged flight to Washington at eleven that morning, Cooper and Joyce Gutherie tried to determine exactly what to say to her old friend. He left Leah at the office to work with Terry and Rose on the search warrant and to prepare the opposition to removing the case to federal court.

"I'm putting too much of this on her," he said to Joyce Gutherie.

"I wouldn't have let you have her in Major Crimes if she couldn't take the pressure, Dennis."

"Leah's doing fine. I guess I feel uneasy about delegating to this extent."

"Welcome to higher executive responsibilities," Gutherie said. She glanced out her window at the flat expanse of white clouds below. "What's your assessment of our case if Tate's transferred to federal court tomorrow?"

"I told Terry Nye we're finished. Ungerman and the FBI will work some kind of deal and that's the last we'll see of Agent Tate. He'll be stashed in a federal facility somewhere for the rest of his life."

"I thought the U.S. Attorney promised they'd go for the death penalty in their case."

Cooper shook his head. The plane was filled with tourists and commuters, half of the latter tapping away on laptops, the rest chatting and reading. Tate's crimes seemed very remote indeed up here with these self-involved travelers. "That was to sweeten my decision. They can't execute Tate and they know it. He knows it. He's got fifteen years' worth of stolen secrets to tell them about and that's his bargaining chip."

"We'd better be very persuasive with Landowski."

Cooper said, as the seat belt sign binged on again and the flight attendant announced they were starting their gradual descent into Dulles International Airport, "I've been trying to put this all into some kind of context. Why our victims are important.

294

Why they matter against national security, the fate of the world, or whatever the government's going to say tomorrow in federal court."

"What did you come up with?" Gutherie asked. She sat back, eyes wide open, looking ahead. "I'd like some context myself."

"I finally remembered something Stalin was quoted saying. I don't recall the circumstances. He said that a million deaths were a statistic. One death was a tragedy. Stalin knew a lot about statistics."

Gutherie nodded. "Thank you. That is the perspective. I don't know this traitor's other victims. I don't know the hundreds who die in clashes all over the world every day. But this old Greek couple lived in my city and read the same newspapers, complained about the same Caltrans delays on the freeways and our endless street construction detours. Who knows? Maybe they might've voted for me in the next election."

"That's why they matter. They were part of us."

The landing gears whined, the plane descended over the nation's capital. Cooper stared down at the monuments and monumental buildings and the rows of poorhouses radiating out all around the city.

He hoped the fix hadn't reached Joyce Gutherie's friend in the Department of Justice.

Chapter Nineteen

They entered the Department of Justice or Main Justice, on the Constitution Avenue side of the building, passing through security checkpoints, going up the elevators to broad marble-floored corridors.

"Joyce," Assistant Attorney General Landowksi said warmly when they were shown to his inner office, "I was just recalling the Shelburne case. Remember the fifty boxes of documents we had to index? And this was using Kaypro computers." He laughed. "We spent two weeks with that damn hand-cranked machine. Practically the horse and buggy."

"I remember, Michael," she said. She introduced Cooper.

"Please, sit. Make yourselves comfortable," Landowksi said.

Cooper took a reproduction of a Federal period chair near the large oak desk. The office had sconces with soft light, schooner models on the marble fireplace, and oil portraits of Edmund Randolph, and more recent attorneys general. Scattered among the ancient legal ghosts were photographs of Landowksi with John Mitchell, Ed Meese, and Griffin Bell.

"It's a matter of great urgency, Mr. Landowksi," Cooper said.

The assistant attorney general looked to Gutherie. She said, "I think Mr. Cooper can best tell you what we're facing."

"Then you better continue, Mr. Cooper."

In short, vivid sentences, he framed the problem. He told Landowksi who Gerald Tate was, what he had done, and why the FBI and the U.S. Attorney were working so desperately to get the case transferred to federal court immediately.

"We're very concerned," Cooper said, sitting forward, speaking earnestly to the assistant attorney general, "that the murder of Constantina Basilaskos and the death of her husband will be bargained away in return for some disposition of Tate's federal case."

"So you object to the prospect that there won't be any consultation?"

Gutherie broke in. "Michael, as district attorney, I'm going to see that murderers in my city are punished."

"It sounds to me," Landowksi said, steepling his fingers, a gesture Cooper didn't think anyone did anymore, "that we all may be worried prematurely. I mean, there's been no status conference, no discussion with the judge in your federal district. I really think you ought to wait and see what the judge decides."

Cooper shook his head. "With all due respect, it will be too late. If our state case is transferred tomorrow to federal court, we lose all control. We have no jurisdiction. We can't influence any decision about the case's disposition."

Landowksi stood up. He was a white-haired man and it irritated Cooper that he wore wire-rimmed glasses so that he looked as though he'd stepped from a 1930s picture of the National Recovery Administration. "Joyce, I'm not sure what you want me to do."

"We've got to keep this case in Sacramento, in a California state court," she said firmly.

Cooper sat back. "The people of California will be delighted to hand over Agent Tate to the federal government when our case is complete and he's been sentenced."

The assistant attorney general sucked in a deep breath. He frowned and appeared unhappy. "Well, Joyce, both you and Mr. Cooper know that the Department of Justice has no authority over a federal judge. I can't pick up the phone and tell Judge—" He looked at Cooper.

"Sarah Lonsdale."

"I can't tell Judge Lonsdale to do anything at all. In fact, it would be highly improper for me to call her about a pending matter anyway. You see that."

"We don't want you to intercede with the federal judge, sir," Cooper said, standing up. He was facing the assistant attorney general across the large neat desk.

"Then I don't know what you're asking me."

"You should contact Jeremy Faber, Tate's lawyer,
nd tell him to withdraw the motion tomorrow.
Cancel the hearing."

Joyce nodded and her old law enforcement col-
eague blinked and Cooper thought the wire rims
vere about to pop off and end up on the carpet.

"You can't be serious," Landowksi said incredu-
ously. "You want an official of the Department of
ustice to direct a defense attorney to drop a motion
e's got every right to make?"

"Yes," Gutherie said calmly. "That's exactly what
want."

"I'm dumbfounded."

"If it helps you to understand the full implications
ere," Cooper said, "Mr. Faber is being paid by the
'BI or some entity within the federal government.
'he Tate family is not paying his legal fees. He is not
eally representing Gerald Tate."

"That is a serious accusation."

"It's easily demonstrated. Mrs. Tate confirmed it
o me and another DDA this morning. Mr. Faber
ould be ordered to disclose any conflict."

"I'm sure you realize there's only a conflict here if
he defendant objects to someone else paying Faber's
ee," the assistant attorney general said.

Cooper shook his head. "Not so. Tate's in no po-
ition to make a free and voluntary waiver. Having
im waive it doesn't absolve the court of responsibil-
ty to inquire whether a conflict will deny him a fair
rial."

He decided at that moment that Gutherie's old
riend was either a self-protective coward or part of

the fix. Faber's incredible tangle of conflicting loyal
ties would make any plea negotiation or sentence
Tate received instantly suspect.

Unless there wouldn't be a review. Tate had to be
playing his part too.

No higher court would ever inquire into defects in
representation because there would be no appeal
Ever. That had to be the starting point of any bar
gaining between Tate and the U.S. Attorney.

Cooper had no doubt that the bargaining had al
ready started. He was in a race against Tate, the FBI
Faber, Ungerman, and apparently the Department o
Justice.

The assistant attorney general spread his hands
"Joyce, I'm very sorry. You're asking me to step very
much over my authority and insinuate the depart
ment in a sensitive criminal matter with national se
curity implications."

Cooper's sometimes impetuous anger erupted. "Ex
cuse me, sir. The criminal case is no more sensitive
than any other brutal shooting I prosecute every day."

Landowksi adjusted his glasses and owlishly
stared at Cooper. "Well, then you're a naïve and
dangerous man, Mr. Cooper. You don't know the
first responsibility of a prosecutor."

"I think I know very well what a prosecutor's re
sponsibilities are," Cooper snapped.

"To do justice. That is our job in three words."

Joyce Gutherie stood up carefully and smoothed
her dress. "Justice is what we came for, Michael."
She put out her hand and shook his. "I guess we're
not going to get it."

"Don't be so sure," he said, guiding them to the door.

Cooper swung to face the assistant attorney general. "I am sure that we're on our own against the executive branch and you won't do anything."

"Mr. Cooper," Landowksi said, "you need to see the forest for the trees."

"I've got two victims."

Then Landowksi said something that astonished Cooper, and that he noted, Joyce as well, for its candor. The assistant attorney general opened the door to his office so they could leave. "Two isn't enough, Mr. Cooper," he said almost sadly.

On the flight back to Sacramento that seemed so much longer than the flight out, after painful silences punctuated by bitter reappraisals and plotting, Cooper sipped scotch in a plastic cup filled mostly with ice. He said to Gutherie, "That went well."

She smiled thinly. "I don't agree with him, but I can see his point of view."

Cooper chewed loudly and roughly on a piece of ice. "From his point of view Tate should've mowed down a whole block of people. Even that wouldn't beat national security. We'd be right where we are now."

"Where are we, Dennis?"

"Fighting like hell in federal court tomorrow morning."

She looked away from him. He wondered, and was sorry he wondered, what calculations she was making about him and the case.

* * *

Leah gave him a list of items as he filled his coffee cup with water from the cooler. It was nearly midnight and he was jet-lagged and very angry. "The search produced exactly what Mrs. Tate told us she found," Leah said. "The cash alone amounted to nearly sixty thousand dollars. The AK was locked and loaded."

"Tate was expecting trouble."

They walked back to his office. Leah was still sharp and kept prodding him. She went on.

"Nye and Tafoya are still coming up empty on checking the Maslenikov connection and a car."

"That rounds out a nearly perfect day." He sat at his desk and saw the neat piles of notices and motions Leah had put together so expeditiously. "You've been busy."

"I think I found good cases and some good arguments. There really is a strong line of cases for the federal court to stay out of a state case before it concludes. We've got even more compelling grounds to keep Tate because we're prosecuting him criminally."

"My compliments," Cooper said sincerely. "Let's serve the defense forthwith."

"Tonight? They'll scream bloody murder in court tomorrow."

Cooper grinned at the tease. "Forthwith in court in the morning, you and I better go over the federal abstention arguments very closely. How are we on rebutting Maksik's motion to dismiss the murder count involving Angelo Basilaskos?"

Leah smiled too. "Well, assuming we stay in state court to litigate it, pretty good. I've spent a lot of time with Fabiani and he can testify about Mr. Basilaskos's physical ailments and how fragile his health was. Tate's murder of Constantina was a direct cause of Angelo's sudden death."

"Good, good," Cooper said. He told her about the meeting with the assistant attorney general.

"So you're not optimistic we'll get a fair hearing tomorrow before Judge Lonsdale?" she asked bluntly.

"The hearing will be scrupulously fair," Cooper answered, brooding. "The decision's already been made, however."

Leah sat down, deflated and tired herself, he saw now. She looked very beautiful and vulnerable. He couldn't let her stay down. "Did I tell you about my North Highlands Five trial?"

"No, you have not."

"The North Highlands Five were five defendants, as you'd expect." She smiled at that and he continued more confidently. "All Mexican nationals who went on a crime spree one weekend. Committed half the crimes in the penal code. My witnesses were Vietnamese immigrants, Guatemalan immigrants, and Russian immigrants. I had eight translators going through the whole trial. We all got a headache from the constant buzzing of the translators. Long trial. My witnesses started falling apart the minute they hit the stand. Didn't remember. Didn't understand questions. Didn't recognize any of the defendants."

"How depressing."

"Yes." He grinned. "Then on the fourth day of the eighth week, the girlfriend of one of the Five walked into my office and told me everything. She was a magnificent witness."

"And the result?"

"Jury was out three days"—he held up a hand—"just to figure out the 122 verdict forms. They convicted the Five on everything."

Leah sighed and nodded. "That's a happy ending. Where had this magnificent witness been while you were sweating it out?"

"Oh, in rehab in a halfway house in Stockton. My point is a simple one, Ms. Fisher."

"They're the best," she said, her mood lightened.

"Expect the unexpected in every trial."

Cooper recalled that flippant but accurate declaration when, a few minutes later, as he and Leah tried to find the weak points in her briefing on federal abstention, Jeremy Faber called. Cooper immediately put him on the speakerphone. He sounded like a furious merchant confronting a petty thief. "Mr. Cooper. Ms. Fisher," he said with exaggerated courtesy.

"Mr. Faber. What can we do for you at this late hour?" Cooper asked levelly.

"My client, very much against my repeated warnings, insists on talking to you. On matters of mutual interest, he tells me."

Cooper looked at Leah, and she raised her eyebrows and frowned in surprise. "When?" Cooper asked, his fatigue and anger dissolving.

"Now. If you're available. You'll need to call the jail and set it up."

"I think we can arrange it," Cooper said casually.

Chapter Twenty

They drove through the heavily secured Fourth-Street entrance to the county jail and down into the basement garage. Two off-white sheriff's department buses were lined up for the early morning run to the courthouse or to bring inmates housed at the Rio Consumnes Correctional Center downtown for court appearances. The garage was partly filled with cars and vans belonging to the jail's twenty-four-hour on-duty staff.

They passed through security and to the first floor initially, Leah's eyes straying to the rubber-floored booking room where everyone from drunk drivers, to new felons and others, first got their glimpse of the county's penal system. Some had to be hosed off before they could be processed further.

"You just missed the old jail," Cooper said as they hurried to the elevators. "The seats in the public waiting room came from a movie theater that had been torn down."

"Quaint but not efficient."

"I'd say it had character." He looked at the gray antiseptic walls and floors around them when they got off on the first floor. "This is mass-production justice. No character."

"Whatever gets the job done quickly, Dennis."

"There's that unexpected callous streak again."

"I'm just not sentimental."

He frowned. "That is a disappointment." He did not like to think of Leah as a green-eyeshade prosecutor. It seemed too coldblooded and he imagined her as warm and passionate. *Imagination so far,* he thought. *Reality ahead. After this is over.*

The Sacramento County Jail had a large first-floor lobby on the street level and courtrooms dedicated to security or in-custody cases. Rising above that floor were the blocks for inmates, each block clustered in a pod around a central observation area. Experience in penology had shown the virtue of solid construction using stainless steel and sturdy plastics, tables and most chairs and any devices like televisions mounted to the building or placed high up. The cells were controlled from a guard station in the center of the pod and there was a pervasive surveillance capability supplied by the multitude of cameras everywhere. Cooper saw a few faces of the trusties as they moved into the jail but didn't immediately recognize anyone.

"Tate's got to be in shock," he said. "First arrest a couple weeks ago, now this. For a civilian it's always a shock to be shown what a jail looks like. He's law enforcement. There's shame and shock."

"Maybe no shame," Leah said. "He's a spy."

Faber joined them as they headed for the most secure cells on the eighth floor. He was strained and obviously angry that he couldn't control his client. It amused both Cooper and Leah that Faber was even asked to remove his shoes when he continually set off the metal detectors. His expensive watch and belt buckle were triggers apparently.

"Jails were described best by Tolstoy," Cooper said to Leah as they hurried ahead to the steel visiting room on the eighth floor where Tate would be. "Remember the opening to *Anna Karenina?* All happy families are the same. Unhappy families are unhappy each in their own way."

"The worst of the worst have to be locked up some place, Dennis. I can't feel much sympathy."

"Not sympathy. I'm only being descriptive. All jails are unhappy because they all share three things. Noise. Smell. Light."

Noise because so many men locked up naturally made a lot of random, angry, or exultant noise or just screamed, Cooper knew. Smell likewise derived from the many bodies locked up. And light because all jails banished shadows where plots could be made or prisoners concealed even for a short time from the watchful, wary gaze of the COs.

"This must be a happy jail," she said, as Faber panted up behind them. "It's so quiet."

"Twenty-three hours in their cells. Time to reflect on their crimes," Cooper said. "A true penitentiary."

"I want to be clear on the ground rules," Faber said, his dignity only partly restored. "My client is talking to you against my advice. I will not permit him to answer any questions or say anything that I believe will compromise his right against self-incrimination or to a fair trial."

Cooper didn't pause, waving ahead to a CO who would open more steel doors. "There are no ground rules, Mr. Faber."

In truth, Cooper was apprehensive and excited about talking to Tate face-to-face. Defendants occasionally wanted to talk to the prosecutor. But the conversations, even in most murder cases, were banal and self-serving, generally tedious.

Tate would certainly be self-serving, but as Leah had pointed out, he was probably the most intelligent defendant they had prosecuted.

The watch commander and his deputy greeted them, explained the precautions to ensure that Tate didn't communicate with anyone, including the COs, without at least one witness present. No visitors. No telephone calls. No books. No radio or television. The last were standard on the eighth floor anyway.

"I'm warning you, Cooper," Faber said, "if you think you can manipulate an obviously disturbed individual like my client, then I'll terminate the interview instantly."

"Are you claiming Tate's mentally incompetent?" Cooper demanded. "Because if you are, you're committing malpractice by letting Ms. Fisher and me see him at all."

308

"I am foreclosing nothing," Faber said.

"Noted. We'll make our own assessment of his mental state."

They were shown into the steel room, without windows. Waiting for them was Gerald Tate, shackled to a steel chair bolted to the floor. He sat with his hands clasped prayerfully on the steel-topped table. He was waxen and still. For a moment, Cooper even imagined he was dead.

Then the watery blue eyes turned to him and Leah, ignoring Faber.

"Hi, gang," Tate said hoarsely, as if he'd been shouting recently. "Thanks for stopping by."

"The ball's in your court, Mr. Tate," Cooper began brusquely. "We're listening."

Gerald Tate took a deep breath and let it out slowly, like a mystic's breathing exercise. "Can I see Suzanna or my children?"

"No," Cooper said. "We're concerned, just like the U.S. Attorney, about messages being passed to you or for you."

"My wife doesn't know anything about my activities."

Leah said, "She knows all about them. She told us this morning."

Faber tightened his lips. He hadn't known about her visit.

Cooper waited. He had perfected stillness when necessary. It was necessary now. Tate had the answers and he had to give them up without reservation. So Cooper waited. Leah sat back. Only Faber looked anxious.

Finally Gerald Tate unclasped his praying hands. "Suzanna has got to be left out of whatever happens to me, all right? She had nothing to do with what I did."

"We're still listening, Mr. Tate. You haven't told us why you wanted to talk to us," Cooper said.

Faber broke in. "Apparently my client made a mistake. I think we should end this meeting now."

Gerald Tate's quiet shattered. "No" he said sharply.

Faber, sitting beside him, leaned in. "Jerry, there are wheels in motion. There are arrangements. Suzanna will be looked after. The children will be taken care of. It all depends on you right now."

Cooper's mouth hardened. "I agree with your attorney on that one point, sir. Everything depends on you. Now, for the last time, tell us what you want to talk about or we're leaving."

Gerald Tate smiled. He had large, yellowish teeth stained from wine and coffee and maybe from smoking sometime in the past. "I asked Faber about you. I asked Ungerman. They were right, Mr. Cooper. You are the enemy. You are implacable. You are incorruptible."

"I'm growing impatient."

"I want to apologize."

For a moment, Cooper didn't believe what he had heard. It was so trivial sounding. It was the self-serving remark of many criminals when caught. Leah said, "What does that mean?"

"I never meant to cause harm or to cause pain. Believe me. It's not in my nature. Everything that's happened is so"—he looked beseechingly at her—"inexplicable, like a bad dream."

310

Faber visibly relaxed. His client was merely pleading for a pat on the hand. Many did. Cooper didn't like to see Faber's smugness surging back, nor did he want to waste time listening to Gerald Tate's maudlin chatter.

"Mr. Tate," he said sharply, "we know about your fights. We know about the prostitute you assaulted. This pretense is a waste of everyone's time. I need to hear something substantive."

Gerald Tate lowered his head, the fleshy face drawn. "I hope you'll believe me when I tell you those events were very out of character for me. I was losing control, I was separated from my family, who mean the whole world to me. If you've talked to any of my friends or neighbors, my priest . . ." He paused. "You know that I'm not a violent or irredeemable man. Mr. Cooper, believe me when I say that my nature is to array myself always with the underdog in any struggle. If you understand that, you'll understand everything about me and what I did."

Cooper stood up, solid and irate. "Mr. Tate, you spied for the enemies of your country for fifteen years. You murdered an old woman violently and viciously. I can't take your explanation seriously. Frankly, I can't even believe you want me to."

Faber put a hand up. "That's enough, Cooper. This isn't an inquisition. No assaults on my client."

Leah leaned toward Gerald Tate. "Your wife said you told her years ago you spied because you thought it would help the United States."

"Yes, exactly," he said eagerly. "Exactly."

"Jerry," Faber warned. "This is dangerous."

"Let your client make his own decisions, Mr. Faber," Cooper said. "Well, Mr. Tate?"

"I am on the side of the underdog, the weaker, the oppressed in any struggle. There was no more titanic struggle going on during my lifetime than the one between us and the Soviets, between Marx and Christ."

"So you chose Marx?" Leah asked.

"I chose to help the losers to see how defeated they were, to hasten the end to their futile struggle. Did I give them information from our intelligence services?"

Faber rose, towering over Tate. "Jerry. Enough. Stop *now!*"

"I have to make these people understand. No good will come of what's happened unless they do. I gave the Soviets our intelligence information. Then I gave it to the Russians when the Soviet Union dissolved. It appeared plain to me that my purpose was being accomplished."

"Without any official sanction? You told no one, just took it upon yourself?"

And Cooper realized that was precisely what Gerald Tate wanted him to see. It was a cross he had shouldered and martyrdom he had borne. It was the ultimate act of selflessness, the complete faithful service of a man who found Opus Dei his door to salvation.

Leah folded her arms, revealing her skepticism. "Then why the guns and phony passports? Why the bank accounts? Why the diamonds?"

"They meant nothing." Gerald Tate's shackles rattled as he swept his hands to one side. "I needed o convince the Russians that I was a genuine agent. They knew I was a professional because of the infornation I had access to. They'd never believe me if I didn't go through all the motions."

Cooper gazed at him. "Why didn't you just use your usual dead drop at Discovery Park? Why the liner this one time?"

"Something happened. The county was repairing he Garden Highway entrance to the park. I couldn't get to the bridge. Neither could my contact. I had to use the backup near my office downtown."

Leah said softly, "So I suppose you realize none of this would have happened if you hadn't been so impatient. You'd still be free. Mrs. Basilaskos and her husband would still be alive."

"I believe there are designs in our lives we aren't aware of," Tate said innocently to her.

Faber took out a very white, monogrammed handkerchief and dabbed at his eyes. He shook his head. No client control at all, Cooper thought.

This stench of holiness was getting to Cooper. It was so convenient and so ennobling. It was, he knew, so selective as to the facts. "Mr. Tate. You shot Constantina Basilaskos, and her husband died almost immediately from the shock of that crime. Are you prepared to take responsibility for those murders?"

Faber shook his head. "Do not answer, Jerry. You do not have to answer any question like that."

But Gerald Tate looked quizzically at Cooper. It was a reflective, searching glance. "I don't know, Mr. Cooper. I know I must take responsibility for

313

the awful events that have happened, but I just do
not know if that's the best course. I'm thinking of
my family. Not myself."

Cooper's anger surged. "You are undoubtedly an
intelligent and clever man, sir. Don't think you're so
clever you can fool either me or Ms. Fisher or you
can avoid punishment for those two deaths. And
deaths you caused in Russia."

Gerald Tate snapped instantly at Faber, "How
does he know about that? Are you working with him
against me too?"

"Your attorney hasn't given us anything," Cooper
said angrily. He had his hands on his hips and he
glared at Tate. "We have your CD. We've read your
letter. I know what you are."

Tate lunged from his chair. He didn't get far because the shackles were very short. Cooper simply
stepped back. But for a moment the fleshy face was
suffused with rage. "That wasn't for you!" Gerald
Tate shouted. "That was for people who've helped
me, worked with me, understood me!"

Cooper and Leah simultaneously reached the
same conclusion. They were looking at a killer.

Faber tried to quiet Tate, but the other man shook
his hand off and said furiously to Cooper, "Do you
have any conception what it's like to go to work
every day with people who are so stupid they
shouldn't even be on the same planet as you? Do
you? Do you know what it's like to spend years with
people who don't think, can't talk, have no purpose
in life at all? *It's soul-killing, Mr. Cooper.* Every day
in every way, your soul is stabbed and lacerated and

mutilated and you feel every single injury. It is unacceptable," he spat, "to be the mercy of people like that. They decide your assignments, your promotion, your status. *They presume to decide your worth*." Gerald Tate breathed heavily, quickly, his shackles rattling constantly, like an enraged child trapped in a confining high chair. His fleshy face, white with rage, even looked like that of a furious baby. "When any *intelligent* person stops to realize that these same pygmies and half-wits hold our country's national security in their hands, then any *intelligent* person must do something. For his country's sake. For his own sake so he doesn't go crazy."

"So you turned to espionage," Cooper said.

"Nothing's that simple!" Gerald Tate swore. "You're still a cop's son. Simple answers for everything. I was never a cop, even when I was wearing a uniform, Mr. Cooper. It requires a development of your mind and your temperament to rise above the simple and the obvious, and you are clearly, *clearly* incapable of doing so."

Abruptly, Gerald Tate's face froze and his eyes locked into the distance just above Faber's head, on an invisible spot on the featureless gray wall. His hands clasped again in front of him.

"This interview is over," Faber announced. "My client's obviously very upset by your badgering. I intend to report this to Judge Lonsdale in the morning."

Cooper turned wordlessly, Leah beside him. They buzzed to be let out. He didn't bother looking back at Gerald Tate, who was transported to whatever place he went to when the burden of being surrounded by so many petty tyrannies became unbearable. Looking inside again, Cooper thought, *Because that's where he hears the voice of God.*

Or that's his act. And he can play it to perfection.

Faber blocked them as they started down the corridor. The watch commander and his deputy were approaching.

"You have government property, Cooper. That CD contains highly classified information and you shouldn't have it. Turn it over to me immediately and I'll give it to the FBI."

"It's evidence in my murder case. The FBI can have it when the case's concluded."

Faber snorted and strode from them. "Your case just ended. I'll make it formal in the morning."

Cooper and Leah let him go. They spent a few minutes thanking the jail officials for their cooperation in handling a very unusual inmate like Gerald Tate. They made sure the extraordinary security around him was going to be maintained.

"No one talks to him, no one gives him anything unless you personally have cleared them with me and you've checked whatever he gets."

"No, sir," the watch commander said. "The sheriff got the word from Ms. Gutherie personally and we got it personally from him." There was an unmistakable apprehensive edge in his voice. The case of Gerald Tate was pulling everyone to the edge.

When they were outside driving away, the early morning's slight breeze coming off the river, rich with the delta's brine and age and the city, Leah said, "Except for that last outburst, I don't think there was a word of truth in anything he told us."

Cooper let her drive through the quiet city streets, under the shadowing lights. He was somewhere else.

"Dennis?" she asked finally. "You're quiet."

"He knew my father was a cop. They must've briefed him very thoroughly about me. You too, I assume."

"Don't let it get under your skin."

He glanced at her, the shadows and streetlights alternating across her beautiful face as they drove. "It doesn't bother me that an intellectual thug like Tate takes a shot at me. That's his style. Lies. Then beating you with whatever fact or piece of information happens to be handy."

"Or his fists when argument doesn't work."

"Yeah." He scrunched down in the seat. "But what does bother me is that everything we know about him is a collision of contradictions. Patriot. Traitor. Religious. Utterly self-centered. Family man. Picks up hookers. FBI agent. Secret passports and bank accounts."

"So what's real? Where's the real Gerald Tate?"

"I think in that letter. When he was sitting alone in the diner, waiting for his contact to show up. Mrs. Rutherford spoke to the real Tate."

"And who is that?"

"The Apostle Paul in Acts 17:23." Cooper stared ahead and quoted, " 'For as I passed by, and beheld your devotions, I found an altar with this inscription, TO THE UNKNOWN GOD. Whom therefore ye ignorantly worship.' " He turned to her. "Don't look at me that way," he said lightly.

"Biblical quotations? I'm wondering about the real Dennis Cooper."

He chuckled. "Shakespeare, the King James Bible, and bits of Eliot and Yeats sometimes if the occasion's right. That's the result of my misspent liberal arts education. I am a sentimentalist and a romantic."

"Wonders never cease. What's your point anyway?"

He sat up as they turned toward the office and the only lights on in the surrounding buildings were the bail bondsmen. "Paul was writing to the Greeks, who had so many gods they'd set up altars to nameless gods just in case they forgot to bow to one who could help or harm them."

She turned left again and headed for the parking lot. She did have a spot. "Tate's never met his controllers, isn't that right? He labors alone for years and years. He sends offerings, he gets money, jewels, and praise from the great beyond."

"Then there's a silence that stretches on," Cooper said. He glanced out as she expertly fitted into the parking space. "So Tate makes up his final offering, puts his best diamond in it, and waits for the servant of his god to appear."

"Instead Constantina Basilaskos finds the package and he's enraged."

"Nye's report a couple of days ago said the techs located duct tape residue in the men's room under the sink. Agent Tate went over the edge when he realized Constantina Basilaskos had his package. She was going to sever his last link to his controller."

"So he killed her."

"It's a terrible thing to believe you're about to be lost in darkness forever. That letter he wrote was a cry for some sign, one word."

They got out. It was humid again and the weekend promised to be even more so, with a return of the thunderstorms that had plagued the previous weekend.

"Maybe it's the weather," she said as they walked through the lobby and passed through the guards at the security station, showing their ID badges. "But I feel like I need a shower."

He smiled. "An occupational necessity in Major Crimes, Leah. I keep putting in requests for hoses in the parking lot. At least you could clean up before you got your car." He gave her a mock frown. "But it could just be the weather. Let's see if we can't raise Joyce and give her the benefit of our session with Agent Tate."

"We need to spend some time making sure we're bulletproof for tomorrow's hearing, Dennis. So we don't get blindsided."

They got onto an empty elevator. "Rule one for a prosecutor," Cooper said, stabbing the button for the fourth floor. "You will be blindsided. Your job is to make sure it isn't fatal."

"That's the trick?" Leah asked.

"The trick is not minding that it always hurts like hell," Cooper said.

The district attorney was still in her office working. She often worked into the early morning. Cooper had loosened his tie.

Joyce Gutherie said, "The word's out that Tate's an FBI agent, Denny. The press office's got"—she fingered a stack of messages—"interview requests for me from everybody. *L.A. Times, New York Times,* everyone in between, the networks. The thinking at the moment is that I'd better do a formal statement in the conference room."

Cooper nodded solemnly. Leah said, "Why not here in your office? It will look more like you're taking a personal interest in the case."

Gutherie sat back, glasses in one hand. "I am taking a personal interest. But you might be right about the office. Denny?"

"I have no expertise in media relations," he protested.

"Well," Gutherie said slowly, "at least it will be so crowded if I do it in here, none of them will want to prolong things."

He told her about the meeting with Tate and his fury. "So this is the last chance, Joyce. We can concede the motion in federal court tomorrow, let the U.S. Attorney and the FBI have the case, and wash our hands of it."

"I appreciate the gesture, Denny," she said. "We both know the answer."

"You're the one most exposed now."

"We all are," she corrected him. "The police, you, Leah. It's the right thing to do for all the right reasons."

He now knew the calculations she had been making mentally on the flight back.

He nodded. "Then we've got more prep to do tonight," he said, pointing to Leah.

"Aren't you exhausted?" Gutherie asked, shaking her head wearily. "I'm dead on my feet."

"Satan never sleeps," Leah said, grinning at Cooper. Joyce Gutherie looked at both of them thoughtfully. "Just don't lose tomorrow. There will be hell to pay if you do."

Chapter Twenty-one

On Friday, August 15, the temperature just before ten in the morning was eighty-five and rising and a thick cover of spotlessly white clouds hung motionless over the city.

Cooper and Leah, heavily laden with bulging briefcases and accordion files, pushed their way up the wide stone steps of the soaring green glass and gray stone federal courthouse directly across the street downtown from the sprawling Southern Pacific Railroad Station and its yards. They had to struggle past a shouting, moving mass of reporters and cameras, microphones shoved out at them. The name Tate rang and echoed against the great courthouse again and again. Cooper, grim, with Leah equally grim at his side, said he had no comment time after time. Their hearing before Judge Sarah Kincaid Londsale was at ten sharp.

Just when Cooper figured they had successfully

beaten back the horde of reporters by sheer forward movement, he found his path blocked by U.S. Attorney Steve Ungerman, flanked by Shaun Boler and two other FBI agents.

"I don't have time, Mr. Ungerman," Cooper said, the reporters now ringing them, completely hemming in him and Leah.

"Mr. Cooper, I'm Stephen Ungerman, United States Attorney for the Eastern District of California. I have an order signed early this morning by a judge of the Foreign Intelligence Surveillance Court directing you to immediately produce items illegally in your custody." Ungerman raised the court order above his head like a sword. "Specifically, I'm ordering you to produce a CD and various items seized in connection with the arrest of Gerald Tate."

Cooper swore under his breath. He lowered his briefcase and one-handedly glanced at the order. He had never heard of the Foreign Intelligence Surveillance Court. But there were, as Oscar had hinted and he had learned, a host of obscure and arcane entities lurking in the dim world of intelligence and counter-intelligence. All he knew for certain was that this document bore a judge's signature.

"All right. I'll make sure they're turned over to you this morning."

"*Immediately,* Mr. Cooper. This is a matter of national security," Ungerman said, speaking more to the microphones and cameras. "Special Agent in Charge Boler will accompany you to your office now and secure these illegally held items."

Boler grinned wolfishly.

Cooper looked at his watch. Court order or not,

federal judges never accepted excuses for tardiness. He said to Leah, "Will you go and take care of this?"

"What about the hearing?"

"I'll solo," he said tightly. "Ms. Fisher, a deputy district attorney, will accompany Agent Boler and make certain the property is handed to him personally."

"Special Agent in Charge Boler, please carry out your duty," Ungerman pronounced, pointing back in the direction of the district attorney's office.

"Now excuse me," Cooper said, lowering his shoulder, hefting his briefcase. "I have a court date."

He muscled past Ungerman and the reporters who clung to the U.S. Attorney for more comments, a few darting around him, following him into the elevators. He remained tight-lipped and impassive. He hoped Leah had taken his life lesson last evening to heart. One word recurred in his mind as he raced to Judge Lonsdale's courtroom.

Blindsided.

Federal courtrooms, Cooper thought, were very nice. If your taste ran to the gargantuan and overwhelming.

Judge Westlake's court, in fact, any courtroom at the county courthouse, could be fitted into Judge Lonsdale's federal courtroom with space to spare. The ceiling soared up, the walls were paneled, the lights soft but bright, the bench high and broad, the seats longer and roomier. Even when the bailiff softly announced that any cell phone or pager going off while court was in session would result in an instant five-hundred-dollar fine, the reaction among the packed spectators and lawyers was to quietly, guiltily fumble at belts and purses. No chatter or raucous noises here. It was like being in a library. With a very stern librarian.

The Tate case was called first. Cooper took his lonely place at the counsel table. At the other counsel table Faber, Ungerman, and then Tate came and sat. Tate wore a coal gray suit and blue-black tie. He murmured to Faber, who nodded. He glanced icily at Cooper.

"All rise," the bailiff softly commanded and the whole huge courtroom rose as Judge Sarah Kincaid Lonsdale, a black woman who had been on the federal bench for just two years, came in and sat down.

Cooper felt the familiar flutter whenever a court opened, a case really started. This was the first battle in the case of the *People of California vs. Gerald Tate.* He opened his files and briefcase and took a breath. He did not intend to lose.

Faber, who had the burden of convincing the judge because he had filed the motion to remove the case from California state court to federal court, began first. He was organized and persuasive. At a table to the judge's right sat her three very young law clerks, all busily writing. Cooper didn't like their earnest, scrubbed intelligence.

Faber spoke from the lectern immediately in front of the bench between the two counsel tables. "Your Honor, this case is about the most serious it is possible to imagine. Nothing less than the safety and the security of the United States hangs on the trial of this defendant, Gerald Tate. You may have noticed that the U.S. Attorney for this district has joined me at the counsel table." He bowed to Ungerman slightly. "Which in itself is highly unusual."

"I've never seen the prosecution and defense at the same table before," Judge Lonsdale said. She was about fifty and had streaks of gray hair and a long doleful face.

"The federal authorities and the defense are agreed completely, Your Honor, that this case *must* be tried in federal court. It is utterly inappropriate and . . ." He hesitated dramatically. "Dangerous for it to be left in the muddle and confusion of lower state courts."

"Dangerous?" the judge asked.

"There is information of such a sensitive nature that very special federal statutes and procedures are in place to protect even their description, much less their content, from being exposed in court. The state court has no facilities, no training, and no incentive to treat this secret information about our country's most sensitive intelligence information and methods with the safeguards that are required."

Judge Lonsdale put her chin on one hand. "So what, in your view, Mr. Faber, is the federal question I need to find in order to take this case from my very capable colleagues on the bench a few blocks from here?"

Faber gingerly handled a paper. "The case against Gerald Tate is one that will be governed by the Constitution and the operative laws of the United States prohibiting treason, espionage, and the unlawful possession of and release of highly classified material. If I could refer you to 18 U.S.C. section 794(a) and (c) particularly, Your Honor. But my brief contains references to all of the relevant code sections."

Cooper thought of his two victims. In this magisterial courtroom, stacked up against the whole fate of the nation, didn't they seem diminished in importance even to him?

No, he thought coldly, *they don't. Individual lives matter. Individual victims matter.* He turned. Behind him in the audience he saw Suzanna Tate and two of her children. To their left, in another section, like wedding guests separated by bride and groom, the sons of Angelo and Constantina Basilaskos and their children, all watching with quiet intensity.

Tate himself was deeply absorbed in Faber's argument.

No different, Cooper finally realized, *from any defendant I've ever taken to trial. Tate figures the world pivots around him. To hell with what happens to anybody else, even including his own wife and children.*

Faber said, almost sorrowfully, "But if the court is even entertaining the idea of letting the district attorney prosecute Gerald Tate, I must point the court to a disgraceful episode just this morning. On the steps of this courthouse, Your Honor, the U.S. Attorney had to order Mr. Cooper to turn over the most secret, sensitive documents of the United States government he had come into possession of. Now, where were the safeguards? Where was the vigilance?"

Cooper rose instantly. "Your Honor, that is preposterous. Evidence in state courts is guarded with great care. It doesn't matter if it's a gun in a murder or the recipe for the atomic bomb."

Judge Lonsdale waved a hand. "Not just yet, Mr. Cooper. You'll have your chance."

He sat down, boiling at the cheap shot. Ungerman shook his head. Tate sat back pensively. *All right,* Cooper thought coldly, *all bets are off.*

Faber finished a few minutes later and sat down. He turned to wink at Suzanna Tate, who ignored him, but her daughter winked back.

Judge Lonsdale said, "Now I'd like to hear from the district attorney."

Cooper buttoned his coat and went to the lectern. His mind was very clear. It often happened, he thanked God, that the confusions and disordered facts of a moment before would fuse coherently as he rose to question a witness or to address the jury.

"Your Honor, as our briefing makes plain, this is about the most clear-cut case possible for federal abstention. The leading case is *Younger vs. Harris* in which the United States Supreme Court specifically held against federal courts interfering in already pending state court proceedings. Mr. Tate has been indicted by the Sacramento County Grand Jury on two counts of murder. And, as you know, *Younger* stands for the proposition that a state court may also adjudicate any federal claims presented."

"Sacramento wants to put this man on trial for espionage?" the judge asked in surprise.

He shook his head. "No, of course not, Your Honor. But the issue remains the same. A federal court must abstain from interfering in an ongoing state proceeding where important state interests are implicated and where there is an opportunity to raise any federal questions. Any violations of federal law can be addressed in state court if need be . . . "He paused and looked at Ungerman and Faber. "But the better course is to let the people of California prosecute this defendant for murder and then handle any federal case at that time in federal court."

He paused. "That is the strictly legal argument, Your Honor. The argument in equity is that two murder victims deserve to have their deaths heard by a jury before any other case. Even one involving national security."

Faber rose, heading for the lectern. "Your Honor, that's ridiculous. The comparison is totally ludicrous."

But Judge Lonsdale motioned him down and made a note. "Is the matter submitted?"

Faber opened his mouth, plainly expecting to say something more. Cooper had been in front of enough federal judges to know that their patience was generally even more attenuated than state court judges when it came to hearing things they didn't want to hear. He hoped he had struck a nerve with Judge Lonsdale if she was wavering about the legal reasons to keep Tate in state court.

Even so, he sat down, hearing the faint whispering behind him like the distant rustling of leaves. Maybe the spectators sensed which way the judge was leaning.

Judge Lonsdale said carefully, "Thank you both. This is a difficult case. Time is of the essence for exactly the reasons Mr. Faber so ably articulated. The nation's security may be at risk."

Cooper flushed with disappointment.

The judge went on, "Yet there are good reasons why a federal court should let the processes of state courts work their way to completion. Mr. Cooper noted them. He also noted a very persuasive reason for this court to abstain when he mentioned the alleged victims of this defendant." She looked down at Tate, who listened as if to a lecturer on plant physiology.

Cooper leaned forward. It was starting to sound interesting.

Judge Lonsdale said, "Bearing in mind all of these factors, I will—" and Faber cut her off.

"Your Honor." He stood up, quivering with emotion. "Before you rule, you must carefully consider—"

She in turn cut him off. "Mr. Faber, do not interrupt the court. But while you're on your feet, I want to know if this defendant has been indicted for any offense by a federal grand jury."

Faber looked to Ungerman, who shook his head. "No, Your Honor."

"So there is no pending federal court proceeding against Mr. Tate?"

"That is correct, Your Honor, but in the very—"

She again silenced him. "I will deny the motion to remove this case from California State Court to federal court. Mr. Cooper, will you prepare the order for my signature?"

He said with great relief, "Within the hour, Your Honor."

He pushed his papers and files together, elated at the unexpected ruling. The fix wasn't everywhere, nor did it embrace everyone. That was a saving grace.

As he moved away from the counsel table, making way for another set of lawyers on the next matter, he saw Tate in animated conversation with Faber and Ungerman, and Boler, face again reddened and flushed with anger, shaking his head. Cooper had to get back to the office and let Joyce know what had happened. It would certainly change the tone of her press conference to have this victory under her belt.

He paused at the courtroom doors. Judge Lonsdale was immersed in a major corporate fraud case. She didn't even notice him. But he knew she had heard him.

At the elevators, he felt a touch on his arm. Suzanna Tate and her children were standing beside him.

"Mr. Cooper, I'm pleading for my husband's life."

"This isn't the time or place," he said uneasily, noting how the two children clung to her. "I'll be available any time up to the hearing this afternoon, Mrs. Tate."

But she said in an anguished voice, "Don't kill him, Mr. Cooper. I beg you. You can show mercy. You asked the judge just now to be merciful and she was."

He guiltily got into the elevator, hoping she wouldn't follow him. A racing tangle of cameras and reporters headed for him. The elevator doors closed as she began crying.

Victories in his world were always ambivalent.

He was not so lucky outside as he attempted to drive away from the federal courthouse. Reporters surrounded his car and he gamely tried moving forward, repeating that if they had any questions the district attorney would answer them all at her press conference shortly.

But the picture that flashed across California and the rest of the country, as he saw again and again when it was rebroadcast, was that of the eldest son of Angelo and Constantina Basilaskos, who slipped among the closed ranks of the reporters. Before Cooper knew what was happening, Nicos Basilaskos reached through his car's window and clutched him in a fierce and smothering embrace. The other sons and their children were suddenly all around Cooper's car.

Nicos Basilaskos whispered hoarsely, "Now the murderer will die. Now you will kill him for my mother and my father."

Cooper angrily pulled away. "Mr. Basilaskos, I'm after justice, not revenge."

"He will die," Nicos Basilaskos shouted triumphantly to the cameras and into the eyes of Americans watching television. "There is justice! The killer will pay!"

Several uniforms saw the commotion and belatedly ran into the crush of reporters and the Basilaskos kin and extricated Cooper, shielding him and forming a lane as he sped around the corner and turned onto H Street. Another set of uniforms escorted him through the similar crush outside the district attorney's building. He hurried inside.

He wheezed and sat down at his desk. Leah came in. "Congratulations. I wish I'd been there."

Cooper shrugged off his coat. "I've lost two buttons. My tie was grabbed. I don't think you would've enjoyed it at all."

"Don't pretend you don't have an adrenaline rush, Dennis."

He smoothed his hair. "I have a distinct impression of being pawed."

She stopped smiling. "Boler took custody of most of our physical evidence. We've still got Standhope's shirt, but we don't have the CD or the diamond, and without them the shooting doesn't make any sense."

Cooper leaned back, a look of delight spreading across his face. "Don't bet on it. Boler got the physical evidence? Okay. We've got Boler. We'll put him on the stand to say he took custody of the diamond and the CD. We don't have to get into what's on the CD. The jury just needs to hear about it and the diamond."

"Standhope can describe the CD and the diamond."

Cooper said happily, "Sure he can. But I relish the prospect of putting Agent Shaun Boler on the witness stand. He won't expect it. Ungerman won't either. It comes under the heading of . . ." Leah nodded, appreciating the turnabout.

"Blindsiding," she said.

"Exactly put, Ms. Fisher. So. We go brief Joyce now and then we do battle in Department 33 this afternoon on our motion to add the death penalty."

"Nye and Tafoya are running down Tate's movements for the last four weeks, and I've got Dr. Fabiani on call on the other side's motion to dismiss Angelo Basilaskos's murder count."

Cooper got up. "If we win, I'll let Nicos Basilaskos hug *you*."

Chapter Twenty-two

Bernasconi came out of his office and said to Terry and Rose, "I just called the DA and told him he could dump the Basilaskos case this afternoon."

"You did what?" Terry asked in confusion.

"My deal with Mr. Rogers looks a lot better if I've got two less homicides." Bernasconi chuckled. "Shit. I wished Cooper good luck."

"You had me going for a split second," Rose admitted.

"I try." Bernasconi grinned, clearly upbeat after hearing the news on CNN and the radio about the hearing in federal court. "I do try." He went back to his office.

Terry blew out a ragged breath. "Watch out, Rosie. Here comes McGivery."

Before she could move aside, McGivery clumsily thudded against her desk. "Oops," McGivery said. "That's going to bruise. I can feel it."

"Why don't you stay at your damn desk?" Terry pointed angrily. "You go have laser eye surgery from some fly-by-night and you can't see anything now."

McGivery grinned and bobbed his head. "Crap, Nye. I can see a hundred times better now than I could day before yesterday. I was still in that crappy Nagy trial, I'd be squinting like always." He straightened up. "Guy did me a huge favor, going nuts in court."

"Look, spare us. We got work," Rose said.

"I can see that," McGivery said archly. "Okay, screw you guys. Felderstein's got a gang together after work, have a little fun. But you guys can go." And he walked away, taking short, careful steps.

Terry didn't look up when there was a loud crash, McGivery cursed, and a woman began squealing. "When he could see, he was a pain. Blind he's unbearable," Terry said crossly.

But Rose got up. "Hey, we are going down blind alleys, sorry about the pun. Nothing on a Russian and that car that picked up Tate."

Terry nodded and rubbed his puffy right eyelid. Felt as if there were sand under there. "No kidding. We tell Cooper now, he's not going to mind so much. He's got to be high off that deal in federal court."

Rose got a cup of coffee, spiking it with a generous dollop of the immortal nondairy creamer that sat in a carton beside the coffeemaker. Terry was on the phone. He suddenly motioned sharply and Rose carefully punched up the same line, listening in.

Terry made notes. The man on the phone said, "I watched the whole thing on TV just now. Jerry Tate gets away with murder."

"Not at all," Terry said calmly. "Now, did you just say something about information for us? We'd appreciate it."

"Yeah, well, it bothers me you guys are so dumb that a guy like Tate can do handstands around you."

"Help us out," Terry said. "Your name'd be a big help for starters."

"Not from where I sit. Okay," the man said. It was a peevish, young-sounding voice. "You guys missed the car, right? Tate's car? Where do you think it's been and who do you think's been driving it?"

Terry's eyebrows went up several feet and Rose nodded. "Tate's car is at his house, isn't it?"

The man laughed. "No wonder he got away with spying for so long. Dumb and Dumb-Dumb. Listen, Tate's car's been around since he got to Sacramento. You want some insight into this whole deal?"

"Please," Terry said.

"Here's the deal. He gets busted over a 'ho that won't put out,'" the man said with an exaggerated drawl. "Now, what happens to his car, you ask? How about it gets towed? How about—" There was a muffled noise, then, "Hey, guys, got to go."

"No, just a second," Terry said quickly. "What about his car getting towed?"

"Check out A-1 Towing. Check out the county impound lot off Sixty-fifth." The line went dead.

Terry hung up and Rose said, "Yeah, okay, well, I guess we find out if there's an A-1 Towing."

Terry grabbed a telephone book. "Yeah. County impound, I know. Assholes got my Chevy Cavalier a couple of years ago. So that much's righteous."

"Got A-1 Towing," Rose said, looking through her telephone book.

"I'd like to shake those bastards at county impound just for the hell of it," Terry said, jotting down the address.

He was certain only that he would upset the gentle souls at the purgatory the county ran where cars were towed for all reasons from overdue parking violations to involvement in murders to abandonment on city streets, and from which many only departed during a yearly auction for pennies on the dollar or coverage of the storage fee. He was also reckoning the two dozens tips and many more false leads he and Rose had run down in the last few days.

The odds favored adding this latest and very vague one to the list.

"I'm sorry, Dennis. That's the way it has to be," Joyce Gutherie said, arms folded.

"I'm speechless," he said bitterly.

"I've thought about our conversation yesterday a great deal. Now we will have a chance to pin the responsibility for these deaths on Tate. That's exactly the way it should be."

"But you're crippling me, Joyce," he said. "Take the death penalty off the table unilaterally and we are going against this man with one hand tied behind us."

Joyce Gutherie, he suspected, was taking the opportunity to trim him down to size and limit her own exposure if the Tate prosecution in Sacramento Superior Court fell apart. The summons to her office twenty minutes earlier, after he had thoroughly briefed her, should have been a rehearsal of what she might be asked at the press conference. Instead, an explosion went off beneath him when he walked in.

"I agree with you that Tate deserves the death penalty," she said, hand up when he was about to break in. "Not just for the Basilaskoses but the Russians he betrayed."

"Yes!" he said vehemently. "For all of them!"

She walked past her desk to the conference table, its surface so polished the beautifully shaped lamp hanging over it was reflected in glimmering detail. "But I can't allow this office to go in front of a jury with less than we can prove. Tate's behavior from every witness is going to show heat of passion when he committed murder, not premeditation."

"He stalked her, for God's sake. He sat and drank iced tea and thought it all out."

But Joyce was immovable. "No, Dennis. You're not looking at this with any detachment. We can't prove he was a spy. To prove he was a spy a judge would have to allow in evidence of what he gave away, and you and I both know no judge on our bench is going to do that."

"Even if you're right," Cooper said tenaciously, "we can still show he had a motive. We can show the distance between the diner and Constantina Basilaskos's home. He had ample time to formulate the requisite mental state for murder one with specials if he was planning to rob her and she wouldn't give him her purse."

Joyce Gutherie shook her head. "My decision is final. We can prove murder one. Maybe. But the jury's going to hear all about his spotless record, his family, his churchgoing. It will be a major victory if we get a verdict of murder one without special circumstances and don't"—she paused and took the plunge—"go all the way down to voluntary manslaughter."

"You're wrong," Cooper said, frustrated that he could persuade a judge a few hours earlier and found himself stonewalled by his own district attorney.

"Then it's my responsibility. You said I'm the one who's exposed."

"Don't compromise this case if you're working out something with me, Joyce."

She regarded him icily. "It isn't about you all the time. I'm insulted you think I'd do that."

"We're handing this man an undeserved break."

"So be it," she said and Cooper, long fancying himself an expert in recognizing when witnesses or jurors had drawn lines in the sand they would not cross, saw that Joyce Gutherie, for whatever personal or professional reason, had done just that.

Cooper and Leah sat in Ungerman's seventeenth-floor office overlooking Capitol Mall, the rest of the city as far as Arco Arena to the north and the American River to the west spread around them. Cooper thought the next few minutes would truly prove whether his evaluation that Leah was ready for Major Crimes was correct.

He crossed his long legs and adopted a semibored expression. He still burned from his meeting with Gutherie.

Ungerman and Faber stood beside Ungerman's glass and steel tubing desk.

"Listen, Denny," Ungerman said, "that pantomime at the federal courthouse was necessary this morning. Not to demean you, to show how important Tate is. Publicly. The world knows about him and we had to show how seriously we're taking what he did." Faber beside him gave the impression they were brothers, heavyset and in dark suits, avaricious for power of one sort or another.

Leah said, "Maybe so, Mr. Ungerman. The effect was to hold our office up to ridicule."

"Denny, you do understand?" Ungerman argued.

Cooper allowed a small nod. Barely. "Which leaves us where at"—he glanced theatrically at his watch—"a two P.M.? With our hearing set for four-thirty?"

"We've been authorized—" Faber stopped himself. "I've been authorized by my client to open discussions about a possible plea."

Cooper looked at Leah as if they had both heard a joke. "Fine. You know the charges."

"But you've got a motion to add the death penalty, Denny," Ungerman said. "That makes a plea impossible."

Cooper uncrossed his legs. Ungerman's office was spare and metallic, plaques with badges adorning the walls. Lean efficiency and cold intelligence were the impressions it was designed to leave. But Cooper and Leah had talked over Gutherie's decision at length before a call came unexpectedly from the U.S. Attorney. Now they had a lever. And a little window in which to use it. Gutherie's press conference had been moved back to three P.M. That gave them an hour lead.

"You know he deserves the death penalty," Cooper

said to Ungerman. "You told me you'd go after it yourself."

"Right on both counts," Ungerman said, lumbering around the desk. "Let us nail the bastard."

Leah was troubled. He, however, was inwardly delighted with the performance. "What do the people of Sacramento County get in return if we withdraw our motion to amend?"

Faber said firmly, "A guilty plea this afternoon. No uncertainties about evidence or witnesses. No delays. A quick, clean plea that makes the district attorney look quite good."

Cooper feigned disagreement and he and Leah appeared to consider the idea. A clock chimed softly in the carefully filled bookcase that took up one wall. "Mr. Tate would have to lay it all out on the record in open court, Steve. Does he understand that?"

Faber answered, "No question. He will specifically articulate what happened on August fifth."

"But," Ungerman said warningly, "for the purposes of your state plea, Tate can't discuss any espionage-related activity."

"The crime hardly makes sense without it," Leah interjected.

"Make it a robbery gone very bad. That's true and it limits exposure in state court of national security information."

Cooper stood up, frowning. "Ms. Fisher, what do you think?"

"I'd like to go all the way down the line with Tate," she said, "but a quick plea is always good."

He again pretended to think the matter over. He thought he and Leah made a fine team, apparently pondering these suggestions carefully. "All right. Withdrawal of his not guilty plea, full admission of factual guilt on the record, plea to both counts straight up. Maximum sentence recommendation."

Faber nodded and patted his stomach as if he had indigestion. "I think I can persuade him to take that."

But Ungerman said, "Jeremy, aren't you forgetting something?"

Cooper waited.

"Mr. Tate still wants to litigate the motion to dismiss count two involving the death of Angelo Basilaskos. He truly does not feel morally responsible for that death."

Leah was on her feet. "A guilty plea to one count, life without possibility of parole? When he deserves the death penalty for two killings?"

Cooper didn't like the exchange either, but he saw the virtue in a quick, unassailable guilty plea. He believed that count two would always be susceptible to a successful appeal down the line and thus delay Tate's execution unnecessarily.

Joyce bargains. We all bargain, he thought.

"If the judge denies your motion to dismiss count two, Tate won't plead?"

"Probably not."

"I think he's bluffing," Cooper said. "We stand a good chance of prevailing in state court just like we did this morning in federal." He motioned for Leah and they walked toward the office door. The constant ringing and murmuring of secretaries answering phones floated in.

Two steps, three. Come on, come on, he thought. *We'll be out the door and the moment will be lost.*

"Wait," Faber said, muttering to Ungerman, hands gesturing, then he turned to them. "All right. As long as the death penalty's off the table, Tate will plead guilty even if we lose the motion to dismiss count two."

"See you at four-thirty," Cooper said.

On their way down in the elevator, he looked again at his watch. "That was too close."

She said, "We've got just enough time to get back to the office and it'll look as though Joyce agreed with our plea bargain."

"Sometimes in this unruly profession," Cooper said, stepping out with her into the noisy lobby on the first floor, "you have to make lemonade without a lemon in sight."

At three-ten P.M., Joyce Gutherie, wearing her glasses even though her brief statement was printed in her reading type-size of twenty point, stepped behind a lectern bedecked with microphones set up to the left of her office desk. She faced a phalanx of ten cameras, reporters squatting or seated in every space, many with pads, many with tape recorders. The state flag of California was to her right. The flag of the United States to her left. It was an imposing setting.

Cooper and Leah stood back in the doorway, just able to peer over the shoulders and between the heads and cameras. It was, he admitted, a nice feeling that Joyce was about to play a part in a script he had devised and she didn't even know about. Ungerman and Faber would see this announcement as the fulfillment of his part of the deal.

"Go, Joyce," Leah whispered under her breath.

In a clear, firm voice Gutherie read her press office's statement about the prosecution of Gerald Tate for the murders of Constantina and Angelo Basilaskos. She described how her staff had fought hard and quickly to keep the case in Sacramento, where it belonged.

Then she said, "We have concluded, after a lengthy legal review of all of the physical and testimonial evidence, that the death penalty is inappropriate in this case."

She took off her glasses and, with a subdued press secretary beside her, called for questions.

"Is Gerald Tate a spy?" asked the *New York Times* reporter who had rushed down from San Francisco and managed to outshout his colleagues.

Gutherie paused, just for an instant, and she recalled a conversation about life and death held at thirty thousand feet. She caught Cooper's eye for a moment.

"Mr. Tate is a murderer. Nothing else matters," she said. "Next?"

Terry grimly held on to the edge of the golf cart seat as the fat, chattering driver skidded around turns between row after row of cars. Rose in the backseat seemed to be having a fine time, calling out a vintage model or ogling a particularly fine flake paint job, hair blowing as they sped on.

The breeze from the wild ride at least dried the humid sweat on Terry's face. He would be glad when this miserably humid summer ended and the cold, crisp autumn settled in. He particularly liked clear, cold days in Sacramento when the ducks and geese flew in great arcs overhead on their way south for the winter. Everything looked clean and invigorating. Something to look forward to on days like this.

"How long to your office, Mr. Candela?" he asked, gripping the cart again as it swung sharply left.

"We got five *hunnert* cars here, any day. Five *hunnert*."

"Hate to think of washing them." Rose whistled. She seemed to like the ride so much Terry was afraid she'd squeal out like a little girl on a merry-go-round.

Candela, all three hundred pounds in mechanic's overalls and an unlit cigar, grunted with amusement. Terry longed for autumn.

The official Sacramento County Impound Center's office was small, even hotter inside, and decorated with old pictures of the Raiders and *Playboy* centerfolds. Two other men, fiddling with calculators, barely looked up when they came in.

"Can you check if this car came in?" And Terry read off Tate's Camry's license number. "And how it got out?"

"Yeah, sure. Crank it up." Candela lowered his bulk behind a computer on a filthy desk and typed in the numbers. He shook the cigar at the flickering numbers.

Rose squinted. She shook her head at the mess.

"See, we got a call for the car about four A.M. on July twenty-fifth. Impounded the car, deal with the city." He gurgled phlegm. "Meaning you guys hauled it out here, row seventy-eight, slot twenty-three."

"How long'd you keep the car?" Rose asked.

"Let's see. Until July twenty-eighth. Guy shows up, identifies himself as the rightful owner, and his pals pay the tow charges and storage for three days."

Terry took out the booking photo of Gerald Tate. "This the guy who said he was the owner?"

Candela pointed the cigar at the picture, then nodded. "Yeah, that's the chump. Cost him five *hunnert* plus. Like I said, his pals paid. But I figured he wasn't going to need a car, that's why they paid for him."

Terry stowed the picture in his coat. He felt the gaze of Miss November 1986 on his neck. "So why wasn't he going to need his car?"

"He was going away." Candela smirked. "Away. That's what you guys do, right? You send guys like that away."

Rose said, "What guys like us?"

"Cops. FBI. This guy's got three FBI guys on his butt and they haul him in here, pay for his fucking car, haul him out, one of them drives the car away. The guy's in a car with these FBI agents. So what'd he do anyway?"

Terry glanced at Rose with nervous puzzlement, and scratched the back of his neck where Miss November's piercing eyes locked on him. "Good question, bud. You sure they were FBI agents?"

Candela called out to one of the studious calculators, "Lorenzo. Remember the FBI come out here couple weeks ago?"

The man nodded. "Sure, sure. FBI. Elliot Ness. J. Edgar Hoover."

"He's studying for his citizenship exam," Candela confided with a wink.

But Terry didn't like the answer. Rose didn't either as they careened back to their own car at the entrance to the County Impound Center.

It meant the Sacramento FBI Field Office was willing to help Tate out of a jam.

Which they hadn't bothered to mention to anyone.

Which in turn suggested there might be more they hadn't gotten around to mentioning. He and Rose had to get this to Cooper right away.

Terry said quietly to Rose, "I make Lorenzo's buddy there for our caller," meaning the other young man at the calculators.

"What's he get out of it?" Rose nodded. Candela screeched to a stop at the entrance.

"End of the line," he called in a phlegmy shout.

"You wouldn't be bored out of your mind here? You'd get an itch to have a little fun, some excitement," Terry said to Rose as they awkwardly got out of the cart. "Even with Eliot Ness, J. Edgar Hoover, and Miss November?"

Chapter Twenty-three

Every reporter and satellite-dish-topped camera truck in northern California appeared to be camped in the barricaded streets circling the county courthouse so that traffic stopped and then crawled throughout all of downtown Sacramento. The city police and the sheriff's department provided crowd control around the courthouse, but the swelling crowd and the noise, the car horns and obscenities that filled the air, made Cooper think of a sporting event more than a major criminal case.

He and Leah hurried to Department 33 in the county courthouse on the fourth floor, grateful it only required the elevator, which in turn required five county sheriff's deputies to be their escorts through the reporters and spectators.

A little breathlessly, Leah said, "Remember Tate's answer about why he used the Korinthou Diner instead of his normal dead drop at Discovery Park?"

"Unanticipated construction," Cooper replied. "I checked. The county was refurbishing the park entrance like he said."

She kept up with him as they hurried down the corridor, fending off reporters and spectators. "I've got one for you. It scares me just like this case. It was my first murder case when I was in Felonies," she said.

"Before you joined the few, the proud, and the brave in Major Crimes."

"The Ramos brothers, eighteen and twenty. The older one goes to see his girlfriend at an apartment complex in the middle of a foggy December night. They get lost coming out, miss their bus home. They decide to steal a car."

"Speed it up," Cooper said. "We're charging into court."

"Some white boys had been celebrating. One of them was joining the marines the next day. They see the Ramos brothers and start chasing them with bats and tire irons. Everybody gets lost in the fog for an hour. But then the white guys run into the brothers. The white guys break a couple of the older brother's ribs with a bat. There's a knife fight, the kid who was joining the marines gets stabbed by the younger Ramos and dies. I take the brothers to trial and get two lifes with possibility on them. So both of these brothers, who had no records, will be in jail until they're forty."

They trotted into the courtroom, the deputies securing the doors behind them, more deputies roaming the aisle among the seated crowd. Cooper stopped. "Yes? Point?"

"Denny," she said, using his nickname for the first time, "it scared me because if anyone had done anything the *slightest* bit different, a kid would be in the marines, the Ramos brothers would be helping their sick mother, getting married, having kids. Everyone lives happily ever after. It took everything happening *just exactly one way,* like it was a timetable, it was that precise, for it to be a violent messed-up tragedy. That sounds like God or fate to me."

"Which means Agent Tate's nothing more than a chess piece? I don't buy it," Cooper said flatly. "He planned. He thought about what he did. His choice."

"Things don't always happen for our reasons."

"They have to, Leah. For our world to make any sense," he retorted. "This case is our call. You just have to accept the exigencies we live with."

"I hope I can."

"I hope so too."

He assumed Leah would sort out the afternoon's activities with Ungerman and Faber. She certainly seemed to have the intellectual aptitude for Major Crimes. But there were mental adjustments, even moral shifts that were required. It was rarely possible to do justice and not make a compromise or two. The breaking point, he had never met but knew existed, was when to make the most radical compromise, to maintain the semblance of order in the chaotic universe. Leah, on the other hand, had said she was willing to do anything for justice. She would have to accept that there were lines to be respected or move on.

Judge Sidney Bell took the bench. He was the oldest judge still practicing in the building and he had no hair, and scrunched low on the bench like a retiree driving a large car. Leah pointed Cooper across to the counsel table. Tate sat stiffly upright. He dabbed at his eyes every so often. Faber busied himself with papers.

"Tears should be saved for a jury," Cooper said, low and cold.

"He just had a visit with his wife," Leah said.

"I'm not moved. If Tate was serious, he'd drop this motion to dismiss count two."

Leah glanced back at Suzanna Tate and her children near the front of the courtroom. Suzanna Tate had both arms around the children. "Maybe it's finally sinking in to Tate," she said.

Judge Bell called the case, the reporters began writing, and Cooper had Dr. Fabiani take the witness stand. Where were Nye and Tafoya? he wondered. Terry Nye certainly had wanted to see Fabiani squirming under questioning.

Cooper deftly led the pathologist through his conclusions about Angelo Basilaskos's medical condition. Through Fabiani he also made the judge aware of Angelo's medical history, which his primary care physician had provided.

Fabiani closed his file folder. "In summary, Mr. Cooper, my answer to your questions is that Angelo Basilaskos died as a result of a coronary thrombosis caused by a severe emotional event. In this instance, the news of the death of his wife shortly before."

"There is no doubt in your mind, based on a reasonable degree of medical certainty, Dr. Fabiani, that his death was caused by the very upsetting news of the death of his wife?"

"None," Fabiani said. Cooper was sorry Nye missed seeing Fabiani's clinical certainty on display. Terry Nye knew the pathologist had been wrong at least once before.

"Mr. Faber?" Judge Bell asked in a croak.

"Thank you, Your Honor." Faber rose and without asking the judge's permission, approached Dr. Fabiani. It was arrogant and a breach of courtroom etiquette. But Judge Bell only shook his head slightly. Cooper thought the judge had decided it would waste too much energy to call Faber on it. Besides, famous and blustery defense attorneys seldom realized their arrogance.

Leah whispered, "Nye and Tafoya," to Cooper. He turned and saw the two detectives come in, standing at the back of the courtroom.

"Terry looks worked up. Can you go see what he wants?"

She nodded and quietly slipped from the counsel table.

He had to concentrate on Faber's cross-examination. He noted that Tate was sniffling too. It was always an incongruous sight, a middle-aged man like Tate, in a dark suit, carefully dressed, crying from fear or shame or embarrassment or sometimes all three.

And sometimes, Cooper had discovered, merely for show.

"Dr. Fabiani, as a forensic pathologist who's testified at many trials, you are familiar with the legal doctrine of an intervening cause, aren't you?" Faber exuded condescension.

"Yes, I am."

352

"That very basic doctrine says," Faber elaborated, apparently for the benefit of the reporters and the wider audience rather than the judge, "that an intervening cause cuts off a particular individual's responsibility for a crime, doesn't it?"

"Yes," Fabiani said a little irritatedly.

"The most famous illustration is the one in which someone throws you off the roof of this building. As you fall, I lean out from a ninth-floor window and shoot you dead. You hit the pavement. The man who threw you off the roof is not responsible for your death, is he?"

"No, he isn't."

"So, in the instance of an older man with severe arterial disease, weakened by blood loss already, it isn't the shock of his wife's demise that causes his death, but the news of her death. You just testified to that fact."

"I said Angelo Basilaskos suffered a major heart attack when he learned his wife had been shot. Yes."

"Dr. Fabiani, haven't you simply identified for us the doctrine of intervening cause? Mr. Basilaskos did not die because he witnessed his wife's death or because he was present when she died, but only because he was told of her death, isn't that so?"

Cooper saw the color rise in Fabiani's face. It was a perverse but perhaps accurate statement of facts.

Fabiani said, "You are correct that it was being informed of her death—"

Faber cut him off. "Informed by the Sacramento Police Department. Informed by half a dozen police officers and detectives. Not known for their gentleness in breaking bad news."

Cooper stood. "Your Honor, I object. Counsel has interrupted the witness and made statements, not asked questions."

"Sustained," Judge Bell said in a throaty burst. "For your information, Mr. Faber, I've known a great number of police officers in this city and they are very careful with people who've had losses."

Faber bowed slightly. "I apologize, Your Honor. I simply wanted the court to be aware of the circumstances under which this man, who was already in a very precarious physical state, learned of the tragedy that had just occurred."

Cooper sat down too. Fabiani leaned over to one side, annoyed obviously at the direction of the cross-examination.

"So, Dr. Fabiani, it is true, isn't it, that Angelo Basilaskos, plummeting to earth, died because someone leaned out and shot him?" Faber realized how tasteless that was and went on hastily. "So that when he metaphorically hit the pavement, he was already dead. He died from the intervening cause, in this instance the Sacramento Police Department."

Cooper was on his feet as Leah returned to her chair, shoving a note in front of him, and Judge Bell flapped a fleshless hand. "I've gotten the substance of the doctor's opinions, thank you. Any redirect, Mr. Cooper?"

It was, Cooper knew, folly to jump back to questioning a witness when the judge was clearly signaling his desire to close the testimony. But he had to put one final point on the record. "Dr. Fabiani, setting aside defense counsel's picturesque law school example, didn't Angelo Basilaskos suffer his fatal heart attack precisely because this defendant"—and Cooper pointed over to Tate—"killed his wife brutally, viciously, within sight of the home the two of them had shared for years? Isn't that what killed this man?"

"I believe that is so," Fabiani said tartly.

"Thank you," Cooper said.

Tate wadded up a tissue after loudly blowing his nose. He was growing leakier by the moment. Leah pointed emphatically at the note. Cooper tried to read and listen. *FBI is helping Tate,* the note read.

But he didn't have time to ask what it meant. He and Faber argued to the judge for another thirty minutes, Judge Bell sinking lower, then pulling himself upright.

"What's going on?" Cooper managed to whisper to Leah.

"Terry says the FBI helped Tate get his car out of impound in late July."

"Did they?" Cooper said. He very much needed to contact Oscar. But Judge Bell, without leaving the bench, had decided to rule. It was growing late and the court staff, even though it was a sensational case, was restless.

"I've heard and considered the arguments, read and considered the documents filed by both sides in this matter. The death of a human being is not something to treat lightly. One death is a human tragedy of great proportions." The judge himself coughed hoarsely. "But in this instance, the death of Angelo Basilaskos appears sufficiently attenuated from any action by the defendant. Motion to dismiss is granted."

He started to stand, a slow and inelegant process.

Cooper was up, angry at the decision, but determined to salvage the rest of the bargain immediately before Tate had a chance to reconsider.

"Your Honor," Cooper said, "pursuant to discussions with defense counsel, the people are prepared to accept an immediate plea to the remaining count of the indictment, with a recommendation of a maximum sentence, in this case life without possibility of parole."

The courtroom stirred with anticipation. The judge sank down and said, "Mr. Faber, is that your understanding?"

Faber said, "Yes, Your Honor. Mr. Tate will enter a guilty plea."

Before the judge could continue, Cooper said sharply, "The people will require that Mr. Tate fully state the details of his crime for the record before we accept his guilty plea."

"Mr. Tate? Is that what you want to do at this time?"

Shakily, as if ill, Tate stood up, hands clasped penitently in front of him. "Yes, Your Honor. Mr. Cooper is correct. I will tell you what happened and enter a guilty plea."

Leah gestured excitedly and Cooper bent so she could whisper, "Boler and Ungerman just came in. Everybody wants to watch Tate's performance."

Cooper frowned, nodding, bothered about the news Nye and Tafoya brought. But the important event to keep in sight was the plea. Do it now so that Tate couldn't somehow twist away, perhaps with help from Ungerman and Boler. What the hell were they here for? To gloat? To make sure he didn't withdraw his offer on some pretext? He'd never do that. *I keep my word,* Cooper thought sourly.

The courtroom fell silent very quickly as everyone watched Tate come forward, standing before the old judge. The late afternoon was racing into evening, and the change heralded the drama about to begin.

"Mr. Tate," Cooper began levelly, "did you shoot and kill Constantina Basilaskos on Tuesday, August fifth, in the Oak Park, within the city and county of Sacramento?"

"I did," Tate said. He sniffled and dabbed again at his eyes. His face was puffy and reddening.

"Describe to the court the circumstances of that crime."

Tate looked up, then back at his wife and children, then over the faces of the several hundred reporters and spectators, catching Nye and Tafoya standing at the back of the courtroom. He cocked his head, raising his hands so he could use them expressively.

He spoke about loneliness and his life in general. His work was secretive, he said, his colleagues distant or foolish. His bedrock was his family and his children, his church, and his community.

The sobbing was obvious in the stillness. Leah said softly, "Mrs. Tate. She and the kids are the only ones I feel sorry for."

Cooper nodded. He was thinking again as he listened intently to Tate, but bothered again by some detail connected to the getaway car. He had to call Oscar as soon as court recessed and Tate was safely taken away to start his life sentence.

Tate talked on, his voice losing its tremor, growing stronger, more like the hard contempt he had sounded at the county jail. He had *friends,* he said, who helped him stay sane in the darkness of stupidity around him, who helped preserve his family against the rising tide of moral decadence everywhere in America.

"Friends?" Judge Bell said. "Can you be more specific?"

Faber said, "Your Honor, the district attorney and Mrs. Tate have agreed that certain aspects of his admission of guilt today will be limited to the elements and details of the crime itself."

"That's correct, Your Honor," Cooper said. Ungerman and Boler certainly weren't about to let Tate shout his true criminal history to an open courtroom.

"I had a gift for my friends," Tate went on, now turning to survey the courtroom, "and I taped it underneath the sink at a small diner near my office. My primary place of contact had become unavailable and I couldn't wait to use it. I had to make contact with *my associates* immediately. I had just been transferred to Sacramento and I had a gift *my friends* would like to have. But it turned out that the woman who ran the diner was cleaning that day, cleaning the men's room too. She found my gift and she took it, and she brought it out, and I saw her scraping away at it and I couldn't do anything about it." His voice grated.

"Did you see Mrs. Basilaskos open the package?"

"No, no, but I could tell she had. She took it some place, an office, and when she came out she was so excited it was sickening," he rasped. "She had no right. That wasn't meant for her. It was for *friends,* truly decent human beings who had helped me." And Tate rambled until Cooper brought him back roughly.

"You followed Mrs. Basilaskos on the bus after waiting for several hours in the diner?"

"I followed her, just as I had been *taught . . .*" He paused, a slight smile, a knowing, childlike delight thinking about mischief. "Excuse me. I can't say anything else."

He followed her, growing more angry, more enraged in fact, thinking of this fat old woman, rapaciously clinging to his property, causing him so much anguish because his friends would never know what he intended to give them.

"And then, when she stopped for a moment, just after we'd gotten off the bus, I decided to make her give me the gift she'd stolen."

"But you didn't give her a chance, sir. You simply shot her twice."

"She was a *thief,*" he said harshly. "You know that, Mr. Cooper."

"Your Honor," Cooper said, "the people are satisfied the defendant has committed the crime with which he has been charged and ask the court to accept a plea."

"Mr. Tate, Gerald Tate," said Judge Bell, "what is your plea to the single remaining count of this indictment, namely murder in the first degree committed on August fifth in which you are charged with the unlawful killing of a human being, Constantina Basilaskos?"

Tate's watery blue eyes roamed across the bench, then to Cooper and Leah. *He's teasing us,* Cooper realized. *This is a grotesque performance.*

But Tate said, "I plead guilty. I am guilty."

The judge began the prescribed litany of accepting the guilty plea, remanding Tate into the custody of the Department of Corrections, and Cooper let out a breath he didn't realize he'd been holding. The sobbing was louder. Leah nervously let out a breath too. "I hope they're all not that exciting," she said.

As Cooper was about to reply, Tate turned from Faber, who had been talking to him, and said in a clear, firm voice audible throughout the courtroom, "As a senior FBI agent in Counterintelligence I know the names and locations of agents of this country posted abroad."

Already Faber had started to motion Tate to stop talking and the agitated rustling from the spectators, Cooper saw, came from Ungerman and Boler pushing to get toward the front of the courtroom.

Tate shook Faber off, his face shining with exultation. "American agents in Russia are Tatiana Rutkowski, Gregori Adamovichh—" And the other names he started to spew out more rapidly were drowned in Ungerman's shouts. Echoed by Boler.

"Your Honor! Stop the proceedings! Clear the courtroom!" Which in turn prompted bailiffs to swarm over Tate, Ungerman, Boler, and set the entire crowd into confusion and uproar. Judge Bell leaned forward, calling futilely for order.

Tate was yanked backward, pulled by bailiffs and Boler, who shoved him viciously. But it was the beatific grin on Tate's face that burned instantly into Cooper's mind, amid the noise and shouting and the chaos.

Nye and Tafoya managed to push forward to the counsel table. Bailiffs were forcibly clearing the courtroom, the judge hustled from the bench. A woman screamed behind them. Leah looked at the pandemonium with astonishment.

"Bright boy pulled a number on us," Terry said or rather shouted.

"But we got our guilty plea," Cooper shouted back. "I don't care if he screwed Boler or Ungerman."

They jostled together as the bailiffs unceremoniously herded everyone quickly toward the doors. Rose called out, "So he double-crossed the FBI after they helped him out with his car."

"It's his nature," Leah said. "Like a scorpion. He stings."

Cooper smiled. It was a nice image of Gerald Tate. It had the virtue of directness too, very different from his twists and turns.

"You missed Fabulous," Cooper said to Terry. "He didn't distinguish himself."

"I could've told you that," Terry said, barking at an energetically pushing bailiff, "Hey, don't shove. I'm in the same union as you."

"Very neat, Denny," Leah called out to him as they were pushed out the doors with the crowd.

"It was." He grinned at her. "It was indeed."

Chapter Twenty-four

They took refuge back at Cooper's office and he generously poured a round for everyone, except Terry, who declined and accepted sparkling water instead.

"To guilty pleas, however you get them," Cooper said, everyone's glass raised.

Rose looked up. "I just gave Lieutenant Bernasconi the news. He's loving clearing this one. He says have a couple for him."

Cooper smiled at Leah. "I'll deputize you to undertake that task, Ms. Fisher."

Joyce Gutherie had gone home, but Cooper talked to her by cell phone. "You can do another statement in the morning," he promised. "This is a pretty clean victory."

Joyce's voice crackled and broke up. "I'm sorry we lost the husband, Dennis."

"It's the victory that counts, Joyce. Not the casualties." He sometimes almost believed that.

He stepped into the next door office while the others traded stories of how they were treated by the bailiffs, the pleasure of winning without a trial. Cooper dialed Oscar.

"Oscar, I have to call in a last favor."

"You're old tab hasn't been paid."

"I need this one," he said, rolling his glass in one hand. "The Bureau's up to something with Tate and I need to know what it is."

"He pleaded."

"Call it insurance. Call it my conscience. I need to make sure the plea sticks and I didn't give away the store." He told Oscar about County Impound and Tate's car. "Can you give me something, anything, about why the Bureau was helping him get his car?"

"All right, Denny." Oscar sighed. "To clear up the last loose ends. All right. Don't expect anything right away. Tomorrow at the earliest."

"Tomorrow's Saturday."

"Monday."

"Thanks."

Nye and Tafoya left first. Cooper and Leah were alone and he felt very satisfied, if not completely happy with the outcome.

"Tate wanted to make sure Ungerman and the FBI knew he's ready, willing, and able to wreck our entire intelligence network," Leah said. "The ultimate bargaining chip."

"With a suitable flair for drama, very much in keeping from a man like him, he shouts his secrets into an open microphone just long enough to make the threat stick."

She pushed her long blond hair back. She had her legs up on the sofa, completely at ease. The city's light had come on, the night ablaze beyond Cooper's windows with glittering, alluring colors and invitations. It was the capital of the biggest state in the country and this was the biggest case, at that moment, in the nation.

"His threat means he'll never face a federal death penalty, will he, Denny?"

"It was never on the table. We knew that."

"That's why we made our compromises? The play-acting about bargaining away our death penalty?"

"I told you, Leah, this is who we are."

She didn't say anything or make any sign she agreed. She sipped her drink and let her head fall back. He let the moment linger. He took a drink. Then his phone rang. She sat up.

He grabbed it, annoyed. "Cooper."

"Denny. We have to talk right now. Right now. My office. Your office. On the sidewalk. Right now, Denny."

"What's wrong, Oscar?"

"I've got someone you've got to meet."

Cooper put his glass down. "Okay. Where are you?"

"In my office on Capitol Mall. We can meet you in about five minutes if you start driving. Upper level of the Downtown Mall parking lot."

"Why not your office?"

"People are listening. They're watching." There was a tense, frightened note in Oscar's voice. "I don't know anything about losing surveillance, we've just got to be some place nearby where there are people."

"All right. I'm walking to my car," Cooper said. "I'm bringing another deputy DA in Major Crimes."

Oscar's laugh was mirthless, revolting in its disgust. "Bring the DA if you want. It won't do you any good." He hung up.

Cooper got his jacket on. "Let's go for a little drive," he said to Leah.

"Problem?"

"Undoubtedly. I'm only hoping we haven't been hit below the waterline."

Cooper and Leah met Oscar and a third man on the sixth level of the parking lot. It was almost filled with cars, and the stores and restaurants below, the nineteen-story Howard Johnson's hotel across from it, were still busy. The leaf-heavy trees along the streets were starting to sway in a breeze that had sprung up, the rumble from approaching thunder growing louder.

Oscar shivered, even though the breeze was warm. The introductions, except for the third man, were perfunctory. The man was in his late thirties, slim and alert, with a ruddy face. He kept breathing in short gasps, as if he'd been running or was upset, and he shook his head as if arguing with an unseen opponent.

"Denny, this is Agent Lewis Hamilton. Sacramento Field Office."

Cooper didn't shake hands. Leah folded her arms.

"Agent Hamilton, what do you have to tell us?" Cooper asked.

"I watched the coverage of the hearing," Hamilton said. "We've all been talking about it. It's pretty much all I think about. Tate."

"I started making some calls," Oscar said. "Right after you and I talked, Denny."

"I heard about the questions he was asking right away," Hamilton said, hands shoved into his pockets, breathing in gasps, trying not to look at Leah because her level gaze discomfited him. "Someone's got questions, that's what I heard."

The thunder was closer and the sound thick, deadly, and relentless.

Cooper knew he was not going to like whatever this upset FBI agent had to say.

"We can go back to my office," Cooper said. "We can talk there. But what's on your mind?" he asked again.

Hamilton said, "I picked Jerry up right after he shot that woman. I drove the car."

In retrospect, after questioning Agent Hamilton for hours and taping his statement and having him do it again just to make certain it was the same, Cooper saw how much sense it made. He still felt as if a silent, terrible explosion had gone off under his feet.

Leah took charge of the statement and securing it in her office. Oscar on his way out said, "I thought I was worried whether the bastards found out I was helping you, Denny. I don't care. I really don't now."

"Oscar, this is between us. Just the four of us."

"Jesus, Denny. I assumed you'd want to tear someone's head off, shout this outrage from the rooftops. My God, this is a crime that stinks to high heaven and they're all in on it. Ungerman, maybe not all, but Boler absolutely. Tate's other associates."

"Trust me, Oscar. You've given me an incredible gift. I'll use it the right way."

Oscar looked confused and startled. "Okay. It's your play. Maybe it won't involve your DA?"

"Maybe not," Cooper admitted. Oscar, for the risks he'd taken and his damaged faith in his life's work, was owed that much. "Good night. Thanks again."

Hamilton left next. He looked very young and betrayed. He said to Cooper and Leah, "That's my confession. My career's over."

"It's up to you. I think your superiors can make a fair case for national security. I think your best course is to move on. The Bureau probably isn't your best bet."

He looked as surprised as Oscar, and appreciative. "Yeah. Probably. I did what I needed to do tonight anyway."

When they were gone, and he and Leah were alone, she shook her head. "I don't believe it."

"After all the things we've come through as a nation in the last thirty years? This isn't so horrific or even so wicked." He poured himself another drink, a very stiff one, and his hand shook slightly.

"I don't understand your nonchalance," she said. "Not after what we just heard."

"I'm only saying that in their shoes, I might have done exactly what Boler or Ungerman did."

"I don't understand that kind of relativism," she snapped. "I apparently don't understand how you do your job at all."

He drank, sad he was going to do what he felt necessary, and sadder that he might have to lose Leah if she didn't very soon make the effort of will to comprehend what had to be done. He was going to do nothing more than what she already said was required for justice to be done. The discovery of how alike they thought and yet perhaps how differently they would act when confronted with the choice of actions perplexed him.

"Good night, Ms. Fisher."

He turned so he wouldn't see her leave and drank steadily and emptied the glass.

The thunder was directly over the city, rainless and ominous, crashing and bellowing across the night.

On Saturday, August 16, Cooper went to the office. After Leah left him to go work out, he opened her filing cabinet. He took Hamilton's audiotapes and written statement from the night before and put them in his own safe. He then sat at his desk for a long time. Finally, he called U.S. Attorney Steve Ungerman's home. Ungerman answered.

"You only have to listen, Steve," Cooper said, dumping three strong aspirin tablets from the bottle on his desk onto his blotter as he talked. "I have credible and irrefutable proof that the FBI had Tate under surveillance for the last year. You said as much yourself. Video and audio. He was also being followed wherever he went. I should've thought of that when we got the reports of the car that helped him get away. It was a standard-issue G car. But it was so obvious and so impossible to be that obvious because of what it meant that none of us made the connection." He popped the aspirins and realized he had no water and felt the acid, bitter tablets go down his throat.

Ungerman breathed on the other end of the line.

"An FBI agent was tailing Tate when he shot Mrs. Basilaskos. An agent transferred in from Kansas so he wouldn't be known here in case anyone got a description. Tate was rescued by that agent and the Sacramento Field Office, and perhaps higher, has known about his crime and aided and abetted him in its commission."

Cooper leaned to the desk. He heard the breathing at the other end.

"I can understand the quandary, Steve. A major case of espionage would have been compromised if Tate was arrested on the scene. All that work, all those foreign agents he knows, all the secrets he sold, you would lose it all. The hard choice you made, or someone made, was to keep Tate close, handle him yourselves."

He rubbed his eyes. The trees around the building snapped and twisted in the wind. The storm was very near after a night of dry thunder. It would be a long, hard rain.

"But that doesn't excuse the crime, Steve. So my proposition is simple. I will keep my credible and irrefutable evidence. I won't use it. You can be fairly certain it won't become public from my side. In return, you will make certain that no one, at any time, attempts to bargain away or appeal the guilty plea

Tate entered yesterday. It is never, I underscore that, *never* to be a bargaining chip in any future deal the federal government makes with Mr. Tate. If my guilty plea is threatened, I will make public the very shocking evidence I have. If that's clear, Steve, if you understand perfectly, then hang up."

Cooper heard the breathing and thought he heard a woman's voice querulously asking who was on the phone.

Then the line went dead.

He hung up. He hoped his gut-churning headache would go away soon. He stood and looked out the window. A few cars lazily drove by; a few stray newspapers rolled by in the wind. An old Chinese couple, the woman clutching a prematurely unfurled umbrella, passed by, heading to Chinatown four blocks away.

This is who I am, he thought.

This is what I must do.

So be it. Nora's words.

He made another call.

Leah settled into the booth at the noisy, bright, and trendy downtown restaurant. She smiled and motioned to his glass.

"You got started first."

"Endurance is a great virtue, Leah."

"Then I've got to play catch-up." She signaled a waiter. "So. I didn't know you liked this place."

"I don't. I mean, I don't know if I do. Someone told me you liked it."

She studied him. "This isn't about Tate or another case? You implied it was when you called."

Cooper drank again, unaccountably nervous and feeling adolescently awkward. "It's about dinner. A good dinner. Pleasant conversation."

"All right," she said, sitting back comfortably. He noticed she had dressed for a night out with the rain poised to fall, in a loose and attractive pale yellow blouse, her hair pinned loosely. She hadn't quite believed it was a summons to a legal conference after all. "Relationships in the office can be risky," Leah said as her drink arrived.

"I'll take that risk," he said, clinking his glass to hers. "You?"

"Let's see," she said with a small smile.

Monday near noon, Terry and Rose scraped their chopsticks and waited for their orders. The lunch crowd was starting to fill the small Chinese-Vietnamese restaurant quickly and very loudly.

"Okay," Rose said, setting her perfectly prepared chopsticks on the table, as if they would hasten the food's appearance, "give up the deal about the leg at the Greyhound bus station downtown."

Terry took a slug of lukewarm water. "Hey, it's a story of pure police work and observation, Rosie."

"Yeah?"

"I catch the call. Funny smell from locker number fifty-six. The Greyhound station's head janitor opens it, finds this leg, a man's right leg, cut off just below the knee. Had a sock on it, I swear to God. Little boats."

The waitress set their steaming plates of chicken and pork in bright sauces down, and left a plate of fried egg rolls. Terry ate and talked. He felt very

371

good. He had gone to Blessed Sacrament that morning and it was quiet and he felt, for the first time he could remember, a genuine sense of peace. It lasted only for a split second, but it was the real thing and he wanted it again and he wanted it to last.

He heard himself talking. He decided he would soon feel comfortable enough with Rose to tell her about it. Not quite yet. This last case had made him feel very good about having her as a partner.

Rose grinned and ate. "ID the leg?"

"Christ, I didn't want to go near the thing. It was hard enough keeping people away."

"So what'd you do? What's the pure police work?"

Terry artfully twirled rice and pea pods and chicken and spattered his tie with sauce. He swore. "What? Oh. I hung around the locker while we're figuring out what to do. This guy comes out of the crowd in the bus station lobby, he's on these really cheap metal crutches, he's wobbling, he obviously don't know how to use them very well."

"Don't." Rose sat back, mouth half open.

Terry nodded. "One leg. Other one's gone at the knee and he's got these tattered shorts on so you can still see the bandage he's got on the stump."

"Don't, Ter." Rose raised her chopstick warningly. "I mean it."

Terry said, "So I go to him, I say, 'Excuse me, *did you lose something?*'"

"Damn," Rose said. "I told you."

"I don't make this stuff up."

"You're not telling me how his leg got in the locker, right?

"Right."

"Guess I'm going to have to stay stuck to you, old man, until you do." She went on eating.

"Don't do me any favors," Terry said, inwardly intensely pleased.

FOR THE DEFENDANT
E. G. SCHRADER

Janna Scott is a former Assistant State's Attorney with a brand new private practice. She's eager for cases, but perhaps her latest client is one she should have refused. He's a prominent and respected doctor accused of criminal sexual assault against one of his patients. It's a messy, sensational case, only made worse when the doctor vehemently refuses to take a plea and insists on fighting the ugly charges in court.

Meanwhile, a vicious serial killer who calls himself the Soldier of Death is terrorizing Chicago, and it falls to Janna's former colleague, Detective Jack Stone, to stop him. Body after body is found, each bearing the killer's gruesome trademark, yet evidence is scarce—until a potential victim escapes alive. . . .

THE MOON POOL
MAX McCOY

Time is running out for Jolene. She's trapped by a madman, held captive, naked, waiting only for her worst nightmares to become reality. Her captor will keep her alive for twenty-eight days, hidden in an underwater city 400 feet below the surface. Then she will die horribly—like the others....

Jolene's only hope is Richard Dahlgren, a private underwater crime scene investigator. He has until the next full moon before Jolene becomes just another hideous trophy in the killer's surreal underwater lair. But Dahlgren has never handled a case where the victim is still alive. And the killer has never allowed a victim to escape.

JOEL ROSS
EYE FOR AN EYE

Suzanne "Scorch" Amerce was an honor student before her sister was murdered by a female street gang. Scorch hit the streets on a rampage that almost annihilated the gang, but it got her arrested and sent away. That was eight years ago. Now Scorch has escaped. The leader of the gang is still alive and Scorch wants to change that.

The one man who might be able to find Scorch and stop her bloodthirsty hunt is Eric, her prison therapist. Will he be able to stand by and let Scorch exact her deadly vengeance? Or will he risk his life to side with the detective who needs so badly to bring Scorch back in? Either way, lives hang in the balance. And Eric knows he has to decide soon. . . .
